SAM HAWKEN lives near Washington, DC, with his wife and son. This is his third novel set on the US/Mexican border. *Tequila Sunset* and *The Dead Women of Juárez* were nominated for CWA Dagger awards.

Praise for *Tequila Sunset*

...wken trades in gritty realism' *Irish Times*

'This brilliantly written, dramatic but vicious novel will keep you on tenterhooks all the way to the end ... *Tequila Sunset* is realistically composed, deftly put together and drenched with violence and aggression that would make any sane person run for their life ... Hopefully a book that will become a classic and will be read for years to come. Well worth losing sleep over' Ayo Onatade, *Shots*

'... novel is a thrilling ride, but it also makes you appreciate the seriousness behind it' David Hebblethwaite, *We Love This Book*

'Raw and gritty' *Shortlist*

'Interesting, refreshing and engrossing' Francesca Peak, *Latino Life*

'A gri...   ...ott, *Hera...*

'A fast moving and well plotted story … Hawken continues to deliver' Robin Leggett, *Bookbag*

'Haunting … recalls the best of James M. Cain' Christopher Fowler, *FT*

'A fascinating, tense and engaging read that draws you into the lives of the characters with consummate ease until you reluctantly turn that final page' *Crimesquad*

Praise for *The Dead Women of Juárez*

'A heartfelt book' *Guardian*

'A tense, gripping read and a plea for justice' *Sunday Times*

'His debut novel is a hard-boiled plunge into damaged lives that grippingly evokes the dust, decay and pervading sense of death in Juárez, leaving you with a lingering sense of sweaty unease' *Metro*

'A powerful and shocking novel' Dreda Say Mitchell

'A beautifully written and deeply affecting crime novel dealing with the wasted life of an American boxer in the city of Juárez, Mexico, the missing women of that city and ultimately a small amount of justice that is awarded them. Hawken writes with a maturity that is rare for a first novel, and achieves both a great crime novel and a work that transcends the genre. This is the real deal: tragic, dark, heartfelt. *The Dead Women of Juárez* deserves to be massive' Dave Zeltserman

'Sam Hawken's novel, *The Dead Women of Juárez* is the most stunning piece of work I've read in a long time. Based on the horrific true murders of those women, it is an instant classic. The main character, Kelly, is one of the most utterly compelling characters I've ever read. A beautiful compassionate gruelling novel, as ferocious to read as it is soul wrenching. Think *The Wrestler* meets *Under the Volcano* with the awful truth of the main events being true. The depiction of the underbelly of Mexico is Dante's vision of hell, fuelled on drugs. A wondrous love affair between the washed-up ex-boxer and the Mexican lady Paloma is epic and beautiful in its terrible foreboding. This book will haunt you for a long long time and the dignity given to the mothers of the lost women is writing of a whole other dimension' Ken Bruen

'The book roars into gear as a bluntly forceful hard-boiled thriller that also manages to address, movingly and respectfully, its troubling subject matter' *Publishers Weekly*

SAM HAWKEN

Missing

First published in 2014 by Serpent's Tail,
an imprint of Profile Books Ltd
3A Exmouth House
Pine Street
London EC1R 0JH
www.serpentstail.com

ISBN 978 1 84668 942 0
eISBN 978 1 84765 961 3

Designed and typeset by sue@lambledesign.demon.co.uk

Printed and bound in Great Britain by
CPI Group (UK) Ltd, Croydon CR0 4YY

10 9 8 7 6 5 4 3 2 1

For the missing of Los Dos Laredos

PART ONE

JACK

ONE

J ACK SEARLE ROSE JUST AS THE FIRST
pink shades of morning colored the sky
over Laredo, Texas. He did not shower, but brushed his teeth
and checked his stubble. He wore a goatee that was starting
to grow a little shaggy and there were gray hairs in it that
sometimes he dyed. Tonight he would shave things back into
shape.

Breakfast was cornflakes and milk, buttered toast and
orange juice. A few strips of bacon would have been welcome,
or a couple links of sausage, but the doctor said beware of
nitrites. The cholesterol was no good, either. Jack was fifty-
seven years old.

He took a moment to check in on the girls in their rooms.
They were both asleep and would probably stay that way until
ten. Even on days when he wasn't working, Jack woke early and
could not sleep in even if he wanted to. Maybe once when he
was a teenager he might have slept an extra hour or two, but he
could not remember anymore.

It was still cool outside when he closed and locked the front
door. Jack took a moment to pull up a few sprouting dandeli-
ons on the lawn and tossed them onto the driveway. Like his
goatee, the grass was looking unkempt. That was something to
look into on the weekend.

Jack went to his truck. It was a Ford F-250 that started out white but had picked up dirt and scrapes and dings over time so that it was shabbier than anything else. It dwarfed the little Galant that shared the driveway. Jack noticed that the Marine Corps sticker on the cab's back window was starting to peel.

He was out early enough that the neighborhood had barely begun to stir. Jack put down the window and let the breeze play in the cab, the radio tuned in to something soulful and homey.

Twenty minutes later he saw the big orange sign of the Home Depot. The sun was rising to his back but the street-lights were still on. Even so, he knew he would find men there; they got up earlier than he did and sometimes they would stay all day.

They were scattered all around the big parking lot of the Home Depot, some close to the roadside and others nearer to the doors. In groups or alone they waited, attentive to every vehicle that passed: whether it slowed down, whether it was the cops in unmarked cars. Jack could see the stir pass through them when he right-handed into the parking lot and there was the sudden sensation of everyone moving in at once, closing a gauntlet around the truck.

Jack had no particular men in mind for the day. He did not come to a stop because then he would be swamped; instead he slowly cruised along the assembled line of men watching for a face that held a certain something. Not hunger or despera-tion, but assurance that a good day's pay followed a good day of work.

It took a minute or two to find that face. He pulled up in front of two men together. One of them had a cup of coffee from Dunkin' Donuts that he rolled between his hands as if he were trying to keep them warm. Jack put down the passenger-side window. '*¿Busca trabajo?*' he asked. He caught sight out of the corner of his eye other men closing in behind the truck.

Soon they would be packed in so closely he wouldn't be able to move.

'We can work,' said the man with the coffee cup. He was razor thin, as they all were, his face lined so much that he could have been weathered or old. His dirty cap had the Texaco logo on it. 'Both of us together?'

'I just need one. We're going to tear down a bathroom. I'll pay eight dollars an hour and you get lunch from McDonald's. *¿Suena bien?*'

'That's good,' said the man.

'Get in.'

Another man appeared at Jack's window. 'I can work,' he said.

'I've got what I need.'

'I can work cheap,' the man insisted.

'*No, gracias.* I have what I need.'

The man reached out as if he wanted to put his hand on Jack's arm, but he pulled back when he saw Jack's face. Others pushed their way up behind him and the murmurs of I *can work* surged louder.

'No more,' Jack told the assembly. 'I just needed one.'

The man with the coffee cup opened the back door of the king cab and climbed in. Jack put up the windows to cut off any more talk and revved the engine to tell the others to step back. They fell away all at once and Jack pulled out.

'Thank you,' the man with the coffee cup told Jack.

'No need. You want work, I got work. Everybody's happy.'

'I am Eugenio,' the man said.

'Nice to meet you.'

He left the parking lot behind and merged with the thin morning traffic. There was a good song playing on the radio so he put it up a notch. If the man in the back seat minded, he didn't say so.

TWO

THE NEIGHBORHOOD THEY DROVE TO was made up of newly built houses stomped down on too-small lots that were etched with near-identical walks and broad driveways to two-car garages. Despite the summer the lawns were all green and perfectly kept, unlike Jack's. He was willing to bet that not a single one of these homeowners looked after their own grass.

He parked the truck by the curb in front of a sandy-bricked house with a big window in the front. A small sitting porch had a swing on it, but this was the kind of neighborhood that had no sidewalks. Porches were for watching people passing by on foot. There was none of that here.

A junk hauler was stationed in the driveway: a big, blue steel box about fifteen feet long. Right now it was empty.

Jack got out and told Eugenio to wait by the truck. He went up to the front door and rang the bell. A Latina woman in a short-sleeved blue shirt answered. The housekeeper. Jack introduced himself to her and she left the door open for him.

Jack went to the truck and opened the tool bin behind the cab. He passed a heavy toolbox to Eugenio and took a long metal pry bar for himself. He pointed Eugenio to a bunch of rolled plastic in the bed. When they had it all, they went back to the house.

The house had a big foyer with a chandelier and a curved

staircase leading to the second floor. The carpet underfoot was white and easily stained. The bathroom was up the stairs and down a hall all the way.

'I want you to put plastic down behind me,' Jack told Eugenio. 'Understand?'

'I understand.'

'Okay, follow me.'

They went up the stairs, Eugenio spooling out the plastic behind them. At the top Jack took out his folding knife and cut the sheet to start a new one in the hall. They had a good thirty feet rolled into the master bedroom and then into the bathroom itself, where Jack cut the plastic again.

'I put this back in the truck,' Eugenio said.

'Good idea. There's a tarp. Bring that, but put that toolbox down over there.'

Jack surveyed the bathroom. Like the rest of the house it was too large, with a shower stall and a deep tub. Half of it still looked sparkling and new and the other half was torn down to the drywall. Tile was missing from the floor. A thin film of dust sprinkled the broad mirror above double sinks.

Mr Leek, the client, was a lawyer. Jack didn't know why the man had ripped up the bathroom when it looked perfectly fine, but the lawyer had started a job he was not prepared to finish. Everything still worked—the toilets flushed and the faucets ran—but it looked as though a bomb had blasted the room. It would look worse before it would look better.

Leek wanted a *new* tub and a *new* shower stall and *new* sinks and a *new* toilet. Just about the only thing that would remain the same was that dusty mirror. Jack spent two days with the lawyer looking through catalogues, picking out the fixtures, the tile for the walls, the new lights. Leek had very specific ideas and Jack did not argue with them. His job was to make it happen, not offer opinions.

'What we do first?' Eugenio asked when he returned. His light jacket was off, his cap in his back pocket and his eyes alert. Yes, he had been the right one to pick.

'We'll start by chipping all the rest of the tile off the walls,' Jack said. 'When we're done with that, we'll get the tub out.'

The canvas tarp went down and Jack passed out the tools. Jack started by the window, Eugenio near the sinks.

'Don't worry about the drywall. We're gonna tear all that out and put in cement board,' Jack told him. 'Just toss everything in the tub.'

They returned to what they were doing and except for the crack and clank of the work the men made no noise. Clean, white tile fractured and came away in chunks, exposing flat gray underneath. Jack threw the pieces into the tub, where they shattered again. Tearing down a bathroom was easy, mechanical. Destroying things was always simpler. They'd be finished with this part by lunch.

The smell of dust rose to their nostrils. They breathed it in and went on.

THREE

REMOVING THE TILE WENT MORE QUICKLY than Jack expected and so they took an early lunch. Jack found the housekeeper in the kitchen scrubbing down counters and told her they'd be gone for a while. In the truck the two of them smelled like work.

Jack took Eugenio to McDonald's and each man got a Big Mac meal with fries and a Coke. He parked in the corner of the lot under the eye of the sun, put the windows down and ate. It was good to beat the rush and Jack watched cars stack up in the drive-through. If the rest of the day went so smoothly, he might cut out a little bit early, though he'd pay Eugenio for eight hours of work. This was a long job and it didn't make any sense to kill himself on the first day.

He saw Eugenio looking out the window at a lonesome tree planted in a narrow strip of grass at the edge of the parking lot. The tree looked pathetic, hemmed in, and wilted from the heat. Somehow it survived. 'Eugenio,' Jack said, 'where you from?'

'Me?'

'Yeah. If you don't mind my asking.'

'Anáhuac,' Eugenio said.

Jack nodded. 'I know it. West of Nuevo Laredo, right?'

'Sí.'

'That's not far. You ever get back there?'

'Not too much, *señor*.'

'No need to call me "*señor*." Just Jack will do.'

'Okay.'

Jack thought about inquiring further, but he could feel the tension coming off Eugenio now. He sat stiffly in the back seat. Jack put his empty Big Mac box in the bag and balled everything up. The trash went into a little plastic bag dangling from a hook on the driver's-side door. He worked his truck hard, but he kept it clean inside. 'I'm not asking for any reason,' he told the man. 'We're just talkin'.'

'*Está bien*,' Eugenio said.

Jack checked his watch. Time.

They worked the rest of the day and then he drove Eugenio back to the Home Depot. All the men from the morning were gone, replaced with customers' cars. A man rolled a steel cart with about a hundred pounds of lumber on it out to his truck.

Jack parked by the entrance. He dug into his pocket and came up with a roll of bills. 'All right,' he said. 'That's eight hours at eight bucks an hour. I'm going to bump you up to seventy bucks because you did good work. Here you go.'

'Thank you,' said Eugenio.

'If you're back here tomorrow, we'll do some more work, okay?'

'Tomorrow,' Eugenio said.

He climbed out of the cab and Jack left him behind. When he glanced up into the mirror, he saw Eugenio was already headed away.

FOUR

THE LITTLE GALANT WAS MISSING FROM the driveway when Jack reached home. He parked to leave plenty of space for the car and clambered out of the truck. Down the street a bunch of kids were playing basketball around a portable hoop set up on the curb. The noise of their shouting carried to him.

He wasn't sore now, but he might be tomorrow. Jack could feel the stiffness threatening in his back and arms from all that chipping and bending and lifting. Once he would have been able to do days like that end to end for a week without feeling a thing.

His keys went in a glass bowl by the front door when he came in. The television was on in the family room, playing some game show. Jack stopped in and saw Lidia stretched out on the couch with her phone in her ear, half-watching while she talked to someone on the other end. She was thirteen years old and talking on the phone and texting were all she wanted to do with her free time.

'Hey,' Jack said to her.

'Hi, Jack.' Lidia put her hand over the phone. 'You're home early.'

'No, I'm right on time. Where's your sister?'

'At Ginny's. She said she'd be back in time for dinner.'

'All right. I'm gonna take a shower.'

He walked away and heard Lidia say, 'It's okay. Just my stepdad.'

In his bedroom he stripped off his clothes and put them in the hamper, then went to the small attached bathroom to wash. He did not have all the room the Leeks had. He had no tub, just a frosted-glass shower stall with metal fittings that had begun to corrode. Maybe he should have replaced the whole thing a year or two ago, but he never got around to it. At least it didn't leak.

Jack stayed in a little longer than usual just to enjoy the heat. When he got out he put a towel around his waist and went to the sink. He put shaving cream on his face and took care of his stray whiskers. A small pair of scissors did for trimming his goatee into something neat. Aftershave stung his skin.

He put on shorts and a T-shirt with a few holes in it and went to the kitchen. It was a little too soon to start making dinner, so he dipped into the refrigerator and got out a beer. Jack sat at the table looking out through the sliding glass into the back yard, at the chain-link fence, the plain square of a concrete patio. Once years ago he thought about putting a swing set out there for Lidia, but she was already too old for that kind of thing when he met her and Marina was older still. He would have liked to have known them both when they were younger.

No one came through the front door and hustled into the kitchen. Right about now Vilma would have arrived home after twelve hours at the hospital. She would have come found Jack and given him a hug and a kiss and asked him about his day. Even now Jack waited for the sound of Vilma's Mitsubishi Galant pulling up into the driveway, but this time it would be Marina and not her mother.

Jack finished his beer. He put the bottle in a paper bag set aside for recycling. At the stove he put a big skillet on to heat and when it was ready he took two pounds of ground beef out of the fridge and crumbled it in. There was sizzling and the smell of searing meat.

A while later the Hamburger Helper was simmering when he heard Marina come home in her mother's Galant. Jack heard the jingle of her keys joining his in the bowl. 'Hey, Marina,' he called out.

'Hey, Jack,' he heard back.

'Another ten minutes, all right?'

'Ten minutes.'

Lidia appeared in the kitchen, her phone still attached to her head. She rooted around in the refrigerator. 'Do we have any more of that strawberry soda?' she asked.

'It's all gone. Look, who are you talking to? Get off the phone and set the table.'

Lidia rolled her eyes and vanished. Jack thought she wasn't coming back, but she reappeared after a minute, the phone in her pocket. 'I was right in the middle of something,' she said.

'You can call back after dinner. Besides, you're burning up all our minutes.'

'Minutes are cheap.'

'You're not paying for them.'

'What kind of Helper did you get this time?'

'Beef Pasta.'

'Oh, yuck.'

'You'll survive.'

Lidia set the table for three and put a two-liter bottle of Sprite in the middle for everyone to share. Jack kept one eye on the skillet so that it wouldn't boil over and the other on Lidia. He wanted to say Lidia was like Vilma, but the truth was that they did not look much the same at all. Vilma said Lidia took after her father. Jack had only seen pictures of him once or twice and he couldn't be sure.

Marina was ready when the food was ready. She was a tall girl, slender and dark-haired and brown like her sister, but very much like Vilma in the face and sometimes in the way she moved. When she entered she touched Jack on the arm. It was the same as a hug. 'What smells good?' she said.

'The usual.'

'I *love* the usual!'

Jack took the skillet off the heat. 'Now you're just poking fun.'

'Yeah, maybe a little bit.'

'Well, sit down and let's eat.'

He doled the food out straight out the skillet onto the plate. Lidia wrinkled her nose at it, but she was already picking away with her fork by the time Jack came to sit down. They did not say grace anymore. That had been Vilma's habit and for five years they had not done it.

At first they ate in silence. Jack was surprised at his hunger. 'How's Ginny?' he asked finally.

'She's good,' Marina said. 'She's going away next week to Padre Island.'

'Going with her folks?'

'Yeah, I think so. She wanted to know if we were going anywhere.'

Jack frowned. 'I've got work.'

'That's what I told her.'

'Her dad works in an office, doesn't he?'

'In a bank.'

'Close enough. Paid time off. I got nobody to pay me to take a vacation.'

'It's no big deal,' Marina said, and she looked down at her plate.

'Maybe we can go when you're done with this job,' Lidia said.

Jack chewed, but the food was losing flavor. He washed it down with Sprite. 'It's going to run a few weeks,' he said. 'By the time I'm finished school will be back. But I tell you what: next spring we'll all go together. Take the weekend. Or maybe a few days.'

'Okay,' Lidia said, and Jack knew it was not.

They were quiet a while. 'I remember once when we went to Tampico. Remember that?' Jack asked.

Lidia nodded. She was picking at her food again.

'That was a good trip,' Jack said, and he thought about the drive, the beach, and the nice hotel with the twin swimming pools. Vilma looked so healthy then. There was no way to know.

'It was good,' Lidia agreed.

'Yeah, it was.'

'I'm all done,' Lidia said.

'How can you be all done? You got half a plate to finish.'

'I'm really all done, Jack.'

Jack sighed. 'Okay. Just scrape your plate into the pan, all right? No sense wasting it.'

Lidia did it and put her plate in the sink. She vanished into the front of the house and after a minute Jack heard her on the phone again.

Marina looked at him. 'I'm sorry I brought it up,' she said.

'What? No, you can talk about whatever. It's good that Ginny's family gets to go to the coast. You know it's hard to get away in the summer. Everybody wants their work done when it's warm.'

'I know,' Marina said, and she put her hand on Jack's. 'I said it's no big deal.'

Jack had food on his plate, but he wasn't interested in eating it anymore. He got up from the table and scraped off his leftovers. 'I take you girls where I can, when I can,' Jack said. 'I don't want to say no all the time.'

'Jack—'

'Yeah, I know: it's no big deal. It's just I have to make hay while the sun shines. Winter comes, there's nothing but little jobs, and we'll need what I can save up now.'

'You want me to help clean up?'

'Yeah, sure.'

He watched Marina deal with the food, portioning it off into plastic containers and stowing it in the refrigerator. Now was one of the times when he could see her mother in her, getting things done, not making a fuss. Jack put hot water and dishwashing soap in the sink. He washed and Marina dried.

'I was thinking maybe I could find a job,' Marina said.

'Doing what?'

'I don't know. Part-time somewhere.'

'It's hard to find anything right now.'

'I could still look. And then I wouldn't have to ask for spending money.'

The plates and the glasses and the skillet were clean. Jack let out the water. 'I don't want you to think you *have* to work. We're not starving.'

'I know. Ginny got a job at the mall at the earring place and I might be able to get a few hours there every week after school. It's something.'

Jack nodded. 'That's okay with me. But school comes first.'

'Always.'

She stood on her toes and gave him a kiss on the cheek. He smelled the clean fragrance of her, completely different from the antiseptic scent Vilma carried with her after a shift. Jack could see her in nurse's whites.

'I'm serious now,' Jack said. 'Grades.'

'You don't have to worry about it. Thanks, Jack.'

Marina turned to go. 'What are you going to do now?' Jack asked.

'I'm going to my room. I'll leave the door open if you need me.'

'At least you're not going to use up all our minutes on the phone.'

'Minutes are cheap.'

He watched her leave and then he went to the fridge for another beer. He would not have a third. Two was the hard limit. He sat back down at the table and watched the sun lower over the roofs of houses on the next street. It would be a long time going down and he would go to bed when there was still light.

Lidia exclaimed something in the other room. Jack had his beer. Down the long hallway that split the house, at the very end, Marina's door stood open and Jack could see her at her desk in front of the computer, typing. Everyone was doing something.

FIVE

JACK DID AS HE ALWAYS DID IN THE morning and got out the door earlier than he expected. As a treat for himself he stopped off on the way to the Home Depot to buy a sausage biscuit and a large coffee. He thought of Eugenio and his cup and considered buying a second, but the moment came and passed and Jack did not.

The coffee was too hot to drink so Jack ate the greasy sausage biscuit in the parking lot before driving away. The Home Depot wasn't far, close enough to see the sign from the sidewalk, and even though he was ahead of schedule Jack could see clustered men.

Today he knew who he was looking for and he spotted Eugenio quickly. He pulled up and put down the window. 'Jump in the front here.'

He waited until Eugenio was buckled in before he moved away, ignoring the slowly coalescing crowd of eager workers.

Eugenio did not have a coffee cup with him this morning. Jack lifted his out of the cup-holder and held it out. 'Here,' he said. 'Coffee.'

'I don't need it.'

'Go on, take it.'

Eugenio hesitated and then he took it from Jack's hand. '*Gracias*,' he said.

'*De nada*. It's got creamer and sugar in it if that's okay.'

'It's fine.'

Jack watched out of the corner of his eye as Eugenio drank. He wondered whether Eugenio had eaten any breakfast this morning or whether he was taking caffeine on an empty stomach. Buying a coffee took half an hour's wages. It was a luxury for mornings when nothing else would do. Jack could live without it today.

They went to the lawyer's house, and spent the morning taking up floor tile until the detritus was piled up in twin cairns. Dust lingered in the air and Eugenio's hands were chalky. 'Get cleaned up,' Jack told him. 'Let's go get something to eat.'

They ate in a booth at McDonald's, the sun slanting through the big window at their right hand, the golden arches painting a shadow over the table and the floor beyond. Jack noticed that Eugenio was always careful not to meet his eyes; he was always looking off to the left or the right, but never straight on. It was quiet a while. The restaurant got busy.

'You do good work,' Jack said at last.

'Thank you,' Eugenio said without looking at him.

'I mean, I don't have to show you anything. You just do it.'

This time Eugenio said nothing. He studiously unscrewed the cap of his water bottle and took a long swig. Again his eyes never strayed toward Jack's.

Jack considered. 'You know, yesterday I was just making conversation, asking about where you come from. Like I said. I didn't mean anything by it.'

'I have a green card,' Eugenio replied. He said it simply.

'I wasn't going to ask.'

Eugenio nodded and for just an instant he glanced toward Jack's face. Jack wanted to come right out and tell him, *Damn it, just look me in the eye*, but he did not. 'I have a green card,' Eugenio repeated.

'I believe you.'

A new silence fell between them until Jack asked, 'Got any family here?'

For a long time Jack thought Eugenio would not answer. Jack could see struggle on his face. He couldn't be sure why he was asking at all.

'No. There is only me,' Eugenio said finally.

'You got family on the other side?'

More quickly this time. 'I have a wife. Two daughters.'

'No kidding? I have two daughters. Well, they're my wife's daughters. I'm their stepdad.' Jack went for his wallet and unfolded it on the table. 'Here they are. The younger one's Lidia and the older one's Marina. This picture's a couple of years old.'

Eugenio looked at the picture and nodded slightly. 'My daughters are younger,' he said.

'How old?'

'Eight and nine.'

'You got pictures?'

Again the nod. Eugenio brought out his wallet, a battered leather envelope with a pattern stitched onto it. There were two pictures tucked inside and Eugenio laid them on the table like playing cards. These pictures, too, were out of date, but the girls were healthy and round cheeked and happy.

'What are their names?'

'Evangelina,' Eugenio said, and pointed to the older girl. Then he put his finger on the other picture. 'Antonia.'

'Pretty names. *Usted tiene hijas bonitas.*'

'*Gracias,*' Eugenio said, and this time he raised his gaze from the table. They looked directly at each other for the first time, but only for a moment. Eugenio swept the pictures from the table and put them back in his wallet.

'How long has it been since you've seen them?' Jack asked.

'A year.'

'Long time.'

'Yes.'

'My wife was Mexican,' Jack said. 'Got herself married to an American, came to Texas, had her girls. And then her husband died. We got together a while later, hitched up. She got sick. Been gone five years now.'

'You raise your wife's daughters on your own?' Eugenio asked.

'Yeah, it's just me. I keep 'em in school; keep 'em in clothes and food. They got Mexican family and we keep in touch, but they're Americans. I don't think they'd know what to do with themselves if they had to live across the border. They've got… what is it? Marina calls it "first-world problems." Like their cell phone doesn't work or they don't have enough money for the mall.'

Eugenio nodded again and now Jack sensed he was losing him. He wasn't even sure what prompted him to talk except that Eugenio was another man who might get it, but Eugenio would not understand 'first-world problems.' Eugenio thought in terms of one day at a time, one dollar at a time, one job at a time.

'Let's get going,' Jack said.

They got on the road.

There was roadwork along the way and three lanes were blocked down to one. Traffic inched ahead, blinkers on, everyone trying to merge on top of everyone else. Jack turned on the radio and waved a hand at it. 'You got a station you like? Go ahead.'

Eugenio hesitated, as if the knob might burn him, but then he twisted through the channels. He came to a Mexican station at the end of the dial, broadcasting from across the border in

Nuevo Laredo. Jack didn't recognize the names or the voices of the crew, but the format was no different from anything played on the Texas side. He had some trouble keeping up with the rapid patter of the DJs making jokes between songs.

'Funny,' Eugenio remarked after a few minutes.

'It is that.'

It took nearly half an hour to drive a single mile, but finally they were beyond the orange barrels and heavy equipment and on the road to the lawyer's house. The urge to put the pedal down and make up for lost time was strong, but Jack resisted. Vilma always told him to be careful behind the wheel. He did not forget.

'Gonna finish scraping down that floor,' Jack told Eugenio after a while.

'Okay.'

'I figure that'll take a while. If we have time, we'll—'

Lights flashed in his rear-view mirror and Jack shut his mouth. A black truck eased up behind them, red and blue blinkers hidden behind the grille and flickering just inside the windshield.

Eugenio saw the lights, too, and Jack did not have to look at him to know his body went tense. Jack slowed until he found a clear stretch of curb in front of a supermarket and stopped. He put the truck in PARK and killed the engine.

He leaned over and opened the glove box. A little black booklet held his registration and his insurance card. When Jack straightened up again he saw two men out of the truck and coming closer. Neither of them wore a uniform.

One approached on the left, the other on the right. The first man rapped on Jack's window and showed a badge Jack didn't recognize. Jack put the window down. 'I don't think I was speeding,' he said.

'No, you weren't speeding,' said the man. 'My name is Jesse Dreier, I'm an agent with Immigration and Customs Enforcement. The other gentleman there is my partner. Would you mind telling me where you're headed?'

Jack wanted to look right and see Eugenio, but he did not look away. He held the black booklet in his hands uselessly. 'I'm a contractor. I'm headed out to a work site.'

'This man with you is your employee?'

'That's right.'

'Would you mind stepping out of the vehicle, please, sir?'

He did as he was told, vaguely aware that the other man was opening Eugenio's door and telling him in Spanish to get out of the truck. Jack saw that Dreier had a gun holstered at his hip and what Jack first took to be a stocky build he realized was due to the man's body armor.

'Let's go over here,' Dreier said, and he pointed toward his truck. The lights were still flashing. They stopped by the front bumper. Jack's back was to Eugenio now and he could not hear what they were saying.

Dreier looked at Jack. 'How long has that man been your employee?'

'A couple days.'

'You're hiring him as a day laborer?'

'That's right.'

'Have you requested any legal paperwork from him? A work permit? Anything like that?'

'He says he has a green card.'

'Have you seen it?'

'Well, no. I didn't ask to see it.'

'So he's not an American citizen,' Dreier said.

'No. He says he's from Anáhuac.'

'Okay. Can I have a look at your ID, please, sir?'

Jack brought out his wallet and showed the man his driver's license. Dreier slipped it out of its plastic sheath and handed the wallet back. He went to the truck and got inside. Jack saw him dial a cell phone.

He glanced back toward Eugenio, half-expecting to see Eugenio on the ground, the ICE agent on his back with cuffs, but the two were only talking. Dreier's partner turned a small card over and over in his hands.

Dreier emerged from his truck and returned Jack's license. 'Thanks, Mr Searle, I appreciate it.'

'Is there going to be trouble here?' Jack asked.

The man looked at Jack without expression. 'No trouble. We're just trying to sort some things out.'

'I'm just asking.'

Dreier's partner made a signal with his hand and caught Jack's eye. Dreier signed back. 'Mr Searle,' he said, 'I'm going to have to ask you to follow us back to the local police station. Your employee will have to ride with us.'

'I don't even know where the police station is.'

'We'll show you the way.'

SIX

THEY MADE HIM SIT IN ONE OF A LONG LINE of plastic chairs all bolted together. Jack's Coke went flat, but he nursed it because that was the only thing he could think of to do. Cops came and went without looking his way and Jack didn't see Dreier or his partner for well over an hour. Jack wondered whether the Leeks' housekeeper was waiting on him, whether he should call.

Of Eugenio he saw nothing at all. They handcuffed him before they put him in their truck and Eugenio would not look at Jack when they unloaded him. Jack could think of nothing comforting to say, so he kept quiet and let them take Eugenio away.

He spotted Dreier a few minutes before the man came out to get him. Two uniformed cops and Dreier's partner clustered together, talking, on the far side of a glass wall. Once Dreier's partner looked directly at Jack and Jack dipped his eyes reflexively. They had not cuffed him, but he felt as though they had.

Finally an electric lock buzzed and Dreier emerged with a few pages of printout in his hand. 'You want to come with me, Mr Searle?'

At the end of a seemingly endless hallway they made a left and passed along a row of identical closed doors marked with numbers. Dreier used a key to open one and held it for Jack.

Inside was a small table and three chairs in a space barely big enough for them. A camera with a red light on it perched high in one corner, staring down at the room.

'Have a seat.'

Jack sat.

'Before you ask,' Dreier said, 'you're not under arrest. You're not being charged with anything. In fact, you can go any time you want. You don't even have to talk to me.'

'That's fine,' Jack said.

'Okay.' Dreier sat down. He put the papers face down on the table. 'Just so long as you know where we stand.'

'What can I do for you?' Jack asked.

'By what name do you know the man you hired?'

'Eugenio.'

'No last name?'

'No, I never asked.'

'And he said he was from Anáhuac in Mexico.'

'That's right.'

'You hire men out of that Home Depot parking lot often?'

'From time to time. I take all kinds of jobs and I can't afford to keep people on the payroll when I can't use them. It's easier to pick them up.'

'How much do you pay?'

'Eight dollars an hour, plus lunch.'

Dreier raised his eyebrows. 'Not a whole lot of contractors paying minimum wage for day labor out there these days.'

'I pay what I think is fair.'

'Sure, I understand. And you don't worry about things like taxes or anything.'

'Look, I don't—'

Dreier held up a hand. 'I'm just saying, Mr Searle. No need to get defensive. You're not the first guy to cut corners on paperwork and you're not going to be the last. We're just talking here.'

'All I ask for is an honest day's work for an honest day's pay,' Jack said.

'I get you. How many men do you think you've hired out of that lot over the last, say, year?'

'Five or six.'

'Can you remember any names?'

'Not really.'

'Could you pick out faces from a photograph?'

'Maybe. Is that what you want me to do?'

'Not right now,' Dreier said. He steepled his fingers. 'You know, we figure nine out of ten men in that parking lot are here illegally. We could sweep it every day. That's what we did this morning. And you know what? That lot will be filled tomorrow morning with all new faces.'

'If you want me to stop hiring day labor, I will,' Jack said.

'I'm not saying that. It's just that you have to know what you're doing is against the law. There are plenty of legal workers you could hire. Plenty of guys from Mexico if that's what you prefer.'

'Look, he said he had a green card.'

'He did have a green card. It's fake.'

'I wouldn't know,' Jack said.

'To be honest, if I didn't know what to look for I wouldn't have been able to tell either,' Dreier said. 'But it was a fake and "Eugenio" is here illegally. You were lucky: some of these guys have criminal records and they'll rob their employers of cash, tools, whatever. Your boy was clean. Hell, he might really be named Eugenio.'

Jack took a deep breath. 'So what happens to him?'

'In a day or two he'll be deported.'

'What happens to me?'

'Nothing.'

'Nothing?'

'That's right. I'm going to be straight with you: I don't really have time to bust every contractor who's looking for some cheap hires. And in this case you were employing someone who claimed to have a green card and even had the document on him. It's not worth the effort.'

'So what's that?' Jack asked. He pointed at the papers.

'Oh, these? It's your driving record. No tickets.'

Jack's shoulders fell. He hadn't noticed the tension until it was gone. He sat up straighter in his chair. 'I guess this is where you tell me to watch myself.'

'I don't think I have to. You get it.'

'Can I go, then?'

'You can go.'

Jack rose from the table and so did Dreier. The man offered Jack his hand. They shook. 'I can find my own way out,' Jack said.

'You mind if I walk you anyway?'

'Could I stop you?'

They retraced their steps down the long hallway and out into the station's lobby. People bustled back and forth, hurried by the business of policing. Cops and criminals. Victims. Light cast in brilliant squares across the tile and Jack was caught in the center of one.

'Take care, Mr Searle,' Dreier said. 'Hopefully we won't cross paths again.'

'I hope so, too.'

Jack left the station and went back to his truck. It was nearly three.

SEVEN

THE STATION IN DOWNTOWN NUEVO Laredo was not large, just one of a few scattered across the city. Once there might have been some reason for putting the buildings where they were, but now they seemed almost randomly set out, their spheres of influence roughly overlapping and the Army and Federal Police filling in the rest. The entrance to the building was reinforced with barriers made of concrete and spirals of barbed wire. Some of the windows had sandbags stacked on their sills.

Gonzalo Soler was not the first person to notice the thin man in work clothes when he entered the police station. A spill of reports arranged themselves in rows on Gonzalo's desk, each one crying out for his immediate attention, and it was his job to determine which would be pushed back and which brought to the fore. A policeman was like a doctor judging the severity of wounds among a crowd of the injured. He could not give everything his full scrutiny, though he would do his best to see to it all.

It was Pepito Barriga who saw him first. 'Oh, shit,' he said at his desk.

Gonzalo glanced up. 'What's the problem?' he asked.

'It's that guy again,' Pepito said. 'He was in here yesterday and the day before that. I told him to go home and stay home, but he doesn't know how to take a hint.'

Gonzalo looked and it was then that he saw the man. He was thin to the point of starving and he wore battered tan work clothes that blended into his sun-darkened skin and gave the impression of some weathered, dirty scarecrow in a dying field. He stood in the open space beyond the duty officer's desk, wringing a baseball cap in his hands, looking with pleading eyes toward busy cops who paid him no mind at all.

'What does he want?' Gonzalo asked.

'It's his kid. Believe me, it's nothing to bother with.'

From here it looked as though the man might cry on the spot. The desperation was etched into his face, palpable even at a distance. Gonzalo closed the folder in front of him and got up. He put on his jacket.

Pepito saw him rise. 'I'm telling you, don't waste your time.'

'I'll only talk to the man.'

'Whatever. Just don't ask me to help out.'

'I won't.'

Gonzalo passed among the desks, some empty and some occupied, until he reached the reception area. He put out his hand when he came near. 'Hello,' he said, 'I'm Inspector Gonzalo Soler. My colleague tells me that you have a problem.'

'Yes,' the man said. 'Him, over there. I've talked to him before.'

'If you don't mind, I'd like to hear your story. What's your name?'

'Tomás Contreras.'

'You live in the city?'

'No, sir. I work on a farm near Sabinas Hidalgo.'

'That's an hour or so, isn't it? Not far.'

'No, sir, not far.'

'Why don't you come back to my desk and tell me your problem?'

Gonzalo led Tomás to his desk and found a chair for the man. He ignored the looks of Pepito. From a drawer he brought out a notepad and pen and he turned to a fresh page before writing Tomás's name at the top.

'It is my daughter,' Tomás said when Gonzalo was ready. 'Her name is Iris.'

'How old is she?'

'Twenty.'

'Do you have other children?'

'Yes,' Tomás said. 'Two others. A boy and another girl. They are younger.'

It occurred to Gonzalo that it was difficult to tell Tomás's age from the look of the man. Long days and weeks and months in the sun had weathered his face; it seemed dust had settled in every line. Gonzalo's own father had looked much that way before he died. 'Where is your daughter now?' Gonzalo asked.

'Here. In Nuevo Laredo.'

'She lives here?'

'Yes. For three months.'

'What does she do?'

It was then that a look of such reflexive, intense pain passed over Tomás's expression that Gonzalo thought the man was injured somehow. The man clearly struggled with the sensation and his face twisted before his eyes began to shine deeply with tears. 'Forgive me, sir,' Tomás said.

'It's all right. Take your time and tell me when you're ready.'

Tomás nodded and breathed deeply and put knuckles to his eyes to crush away the wetness. His chest hitched. 'I've told all of this to the other policeman,' he said finally.

'I understand, but I'm hearing this for the first time now.'

The man looked at Gonzalo and every crevice in his face was drawn. 'My daughter… Iris… she works in Boy's Town, sir. In Boy's Town.'

EIGHT

H E WAS EARLY GETTING HOME AND neither of the girls had come back from their day trips to friends or to the mall or wherever they kept busy on lazy late-summer afternoons. Jack put on the radio in his bedroom and turned the volume up so he could hear it in the shower with the bathroom door open. With no one around to hear him, he sang along under the spray. He discovered a cut on his hand that he hadn't noticed before and washed it clean. A contractor's hands were always getting filthy and he didn't need an infection.

When he was washed and dressed again he went out in the back yard and plucked weeds for half an hour. He cast the plants into an old, rusty wheelbarrow that had once been bright orange. After that he brought the wheelbarrow out front and did the same all over again. It would do until the weekend when he would drag out the lawn mower and do the grass up properly.

The wheelbarrow seemed heavier somehow when he ran it back to the side of the house, but it was just his sudden mood and not the dying weeds. He emptied the wheelbarrow by the handful into a garbage can, and then put it in the garage.

The house was very quiet again. Jack tried to imagine it this way all the time, Marina and Lidia both gone, but that sent a dark cloud skittering across his thoughts.

When the day came for Marina to go to school, she'd take classes at the community college or somewhere else local. She would live in this house and sleep in her bed and Jack would take care of her as he always had. The same went for Lidia. He had never told them, but they had to know that as long as he was alive they had a place under his roof. That was the promise he gave to Vilma, the one he would not break.

'Beer,' Jack said aloud. He found a bottle and let it start to sweat before he twisted off the top. In the family room he took a spot on the old La-Z-Boy and stared at the blank screen of the television. He could smell the traces of the perfume Lidia had taken to wearing all the time. The couch was like her command post, feet always up and cell phone always working.

He heard Marina's car in the driveway and waited. There was the jingle of keys but the front door was unlocked. Jack didn't call out when she entered. She saw him right away.

'Drinking alone?' she asked.

'Just one,' Jack said.

'I counted all the bottles in the fridge, so I'll know if you're lying,' Marina said. She hung her purse from a hook by the door.

'You did not,' he said.

'Maybe I did and maybe I didn't. You won't know.'

'This is the only one I had,' Jack reiterated.

'I believe you.'

Marina came into the family room and sat on the couch. Jack saw that she was in a new blouse and good jeans. She wore pumps instead of sneakers. 'You look nice,' Jack said.

'Oh, this? I went by the earring place like I told you. Talked to the manager. I wanted to look professional, you know?'

'Sure, I know.'

'Anyway, the manager said I could come by next Tuesday

for an interview. She said it was just a formality. Got to follow the rules.'

Jack nodded. There was only a little beer left and he tilted it into his mouth.

'It's not a lot of hours. Maybe ten a week? But that's good to start, right?'

'Right.'

'Ginny says they have a girl there who might quit and then I could get her hours, too. That'll add up.'

'Mm-hmm,' Jack agreed. 'You know where your sister is?'

'With Saundra, I think. They were going to go to the movies.'

'So long as she's back for dinner.'

'Nobody misses dinner, Jack,' Marina said. She got up. 'You want me to bring you another beer?'

'If you trust me with it.'

'I told you: I counted them all.'

'Okay, I'll have another beer.'

'Coming up.'

NINE

SOME PEOPLE CALLED IT 'BOY'S TOWN,' but in the city it was known simply as La Zona. It was three blocks sealed off by a wall, the interior built up like a small city. The place even had a little police station staffed by pairs of officers in shifts, though it was primarily just a place for drunks to be held until a wagon could be sent to ferry them to larger accommodations downtown.

The police station was just inside the entrance, a metal sign advertising its presence, but the officers assigned there did not patrol. La Zona was a place of tolerance where prostitution and sex shows abounded, but it was also a community, with rooms to rent and small stores for tourists and locals alike. There were many bars and restaurants on its streets, interspersed with brothels and strip clubs and even a place where one could see the notorious donkey show. A policeman's first instinct was to dismiss La Zona as a nest of criminals and those who trucked with them, but couples came here for dancing and working-men stopped for cheap beer. But in the daytime it was a place for hangovers and ghosts.

Gonzalo parked outside the gates and walked the rest of the way. He thought briefly of checking with the police on duty, but there was nothing they could do to help him with his task today and he would only waste their time. He had his badge and his gun, for what good they would do him, and that would have to be enough. Even those would probably be no use for what he would have to do.

He followed the Circunvalación Casanova, which formed a sort of loop around the whole of La Zona's interior. From what Tomás Contreras had told him, Gonzalo knew he could find the way. La Zona was like a warren, but like all warrens it was not infinite and there were only so many places to hide. Fewer still if being visible was important for business.

A long stretch of street was lined on one side by shabby whitewashed buildings. The apartments opened directly onto the unpaved street and there were other, narrow doors squeezed between the tiny units that led to upper floors. No building was more than two stories. Only some of the apartments were numbered. The one he wanted was marked with a few splashes of paint that marked out the numeral nine.

Iris Contreras's crib was on the second floor. The walls of the stairwell closed in so snugly on either side that Gonzalo's shoulders rubbed them. At the very top was a single door with no landing. He stood awkwardly on the steps and knocked twice.

When there was no answer, he knocked again and waited. It was possible that she was gone, or perhaps too exhausted from the night to even hear his rapping. Gonzalo waited longer.

After a while he heard a thump of feet on floor and the pacing of steps. He sensed the presence of another human being on the far side of the door and then her voice came through the wood. 'Who is it?'

'Iris Contreras?'

'Who wants to know?'

'My name is Gonzalo Soler. I am a policeman.'

'What do the police want with me?'

'Open the door, please.'

There was a long pause as Iris Contreras considered, but

then a chain rattled and the door came open. It was dark inside. The girl appeared.

She was not a beautiful young woman, though darkness and makeup would make all the difference. She was slender like her father and did not have large breasts or rolling hips. Instead of a pretty dress, she wore a simple white shift for sleeping. She was barefoot. 'What do you want?' she asked.

'May I come in?'

'I'm not working right now.'

'May I come in anyway?'

'Let me see your identification.'

Gonzalo showed her and only then did she step back and hold the door wider for him to enter. He stepped into the gloom.

It was a tiny room without so much as a bathroom or a kitchen, though it had a small sink. A yellowing scroll of paper taped in place shaded a single, undersized window. The largest single thing in the room was the bed, and even that was small. There was the strong smell of cigarettes and sweat. A bucket beside the bed held a layer of butts.

Iris closed the door. 'I haven't done anything wrong,' she said.

'I'm not here to arrest you, if that's what you think,' Gonzalo said.

'Then why are you here?'

'Why don't you sit?'

The girl looked at him sourly, and then lowered herself to the bed. Her hair was mussed. It was noontime, but she looked as though she had only been asleep a few hours. That was probably true.

'Yesterday your father came to see me,' Gonzalo said.

'*Mierda.*'

'He's very worried about you. Your mother and your sister

and brother, too. He asked me to come speak to you.'

'Why?'

'I think you know why,' Gonzalo said.

'I'm not going home.'

Gonzalo looked at her. She seemed younger than twenty. 'Is it so bad there?'

'It's worse. No money, no food. Slaving away all day with my mother and my sister to keep a house with nothing. And there is no work for anyone.'

'Your father works.'

'For now. But if the drought goes on, the farm will lay off all of its hands and we will have no chance. I'm doing them a favor by coming here.'

'There is other work in the city. The *maquiladoras*—'

'Are all full of other country girls who came to city for work. This isn't Juárez, where there's always something. I found what I can do and I make good money.'

It was true that in Ciudad Juárez there were jobs despite the danger. It was bigger there, busier there. Nuevo Laredo would not ever be such, though it strained toward something greater. Gonzalo feared it would be a forever passing through, where the progress of cross-border commerce would serve to keep the city alive, but never thriving.

Gonzalo scanned the shabby room. The walls were water-stained and peeling and had last seen paint so long ago that it might have been before Iris was born. 'What is good money for you?' he asked.

'Six hundred pesos.'

'Per man?'

'Of course.'

'How many men do you see in a night?'

'I don't count,' Iris said, and she glanced away.

Gonzalo pressed. 'How many?'

'I don't know. Ten. Fifteen.'

'In this hole,' Gonzalo said. 'How much are you paying to rent this crib for the night? Three thousand pesos? Four thousand pesos? Which leaves you how much?'

'You can get out!' Iris exclaimed. 'I don't need to explain myself to you!'

'Has someone come to "watch out" for you yet?' Gonzalo asked. 'Because it's only a matter of time. No girl works here on her own for very long. Some man comes calling and says he'll look out for the bad customers if you just cut him in for fifty percent. And if you say no, then it will be more, plus he'll beat you. Are you looking forward to that?'

She did not look at him at all now and Gonzalo knew the answer without being told. 'It's none of your business,' she said without fire.

'So it's happened already,' Gonzalo said. 'And it won't stop. Every night it will be the same until you're no longer young enough, no longer healthy enough… whatever it means to get you out of here and sent back to where you came from. Broke, addicted or whatever else happens along the way.'

'Please go away,' Iris said.

'I'll go away when you've packed your things and we can leave this place together.'

'This isn't illegal!'

'No, it's not. That doesn't mean it isn't wrong.'

Iris raised damp eyes. She wiped her nose with the back of her hand. 'Are you going to go save all the other girls now?'

'No.'

'Would you?'

'No. I am here because you have a family that loves you. And because it's not too late to put things right. There are too many things that can never be put right.'

They stared at each other. A tear tracked down Iris's cheek, followed by more, until she could hold Gonzalo's gaze no longer and she dissolved into violent sobs. Gonzalo bit his lip for silence.

When she was finished crying, she said, 'I don't have much to bring.'

'Whatever you have is enough. I'm sure your father won't mind.'

'Will you wait for me outside?' Iris asked.

'Of course,' Gonzalo said, and he left the stinking room by the stairs without looking back.

TEN

ON SATURDAY MORNING JACK DID NOT get dressed right away and made coffee in the kitchen in his sleeping shorts and a T-shirt. He drank alone in his recliner looking at some celebrity magazine Lidia liked to read. He recognized none of the faces and fewer of the names, but there was a human-interest story about a family who saved their home from foreclosure by taking up a neighborhood collection and that held his interest for a while.

This house wasn't paid for, but the mortgage was reasonable and he kept up with the payments. When something needed fixing, he did it himself. Sometimes he got the girls' help. Someday they'd need to take care of a problem and he didn't want them to have to rely on anyone else to get it done. His girls would handle themselves.

Once he heard them stirring he went to the kitchen and started breakfast. On Saturdays he allowed himself all the indulgences and there were pancakes and scrambled eggs and bacon to go with milk and orange juice. Lidia and Marina came to the table in their pajamas like little children.

'Uncle Bernardo today,' Jack told them.

'Is that today?' Marina asked. 'I thought I was taking Lidia to the pool.'

'Nope, it's today, so get yourselves all cleaned up and we'll leave here in an hour. Look good for your cousins, okay?'

Jack put on his best pair of jeans and a work shirt without any holes in it. He wore his good boots and not the battered old steel-toed pair he wore on jobs. When the girls came out of their rooms they were clean and brushed and in bright colors. They didn't dress up like it was Easter Sunday anymore, but in the back of his mind Jack could still see them that way: in dresses with bows and buckled shoes.

'Okay, let's hit the road.'

The morning was already turning into a hot day and Jack put on the air conditioning in the truck. It used to be that both girls sat in the back seat as if they were being chauffeured, but now Marina sat up front beside him. Reflected light flashed off her wraparound sunglasses as they drove, dancing at the edge of Jack's vision.

They went downtown to Laredo International Bridge and joined the thin line of traffic headed south across the border. On the other side, where Mexicans passed into the United States, it was four solid lanes as far as the eye could see, but there were not many who made the trip this way anymore.

Nuevo Laredo had been the destination for generations looking for deals or distractions or a little fun. Jack remembered carnivals and music played in open plazas. The first time he ever sat on a horse was at a Cinco de Mayo fiesta. For a few centavos an old man let him sit in the saddle of a swaybacked animal and led the horse in a wide circle inside a rough corral. Jack thought he was a cowboy and the nag a stallion.

Things were different now. Once on a Saturday like this the pedestrian crossing was bustling with tourists, but today there were only a few and they did not look happy to be going. The license plates on the cars ahead of Jack in line were almost all from Mexico and the state of Tamaulipas. That was the way it always was.

Vehicles were stopped first on the US side. Uniformed men and women circulated among the cars and trucks, checking papers, walking trained dogs between the lanes, stopping to talk with drivers. A dark-skinned Latino man waved Jack forward and then signaled for him to pull up. Jack put down the window. Warm air rushed in.

'Good morning, sir,' the officer said. His nametag read GALLEGO. 'Going into Mexico?'

'I am.'

'What kind of business do you have there?'

'We're visiting relatives.'

'Who are these people with you?'

'My stepdaughters.'

'Does everyone have passport or other form of ID?'

'Yes, we all have passports.'

'May I see them, please?'

Jack handed them over. In the side mirror he saw a woman officer leading a German shepherd up to the tailgate of the truck and then along the bed. The dog sniffed, but did not hit.

The officer named Gallego examined the passports and then passed them back to Jack. 'Are you carrying anything in your vehicle that we need to know about? Guns, illegal drugs?'

'Nope.'

'Do you have more than ten thousand dollars cash with you?'

'No, sir.'

Jack looked the officer in the face. The lenses of the man's sunglasses were impenetrably black and Jack saw himself reflected darkly. The officer nodded. 'Okay, then. You have a nice day now.'

He raised the window and drove on. A gap had formed ahead of them and they cruised out over the river until they passed a broad yellow line painted on the bridge that marked the border. On the far side were the Mexican customs officials in their little booths. They collected the toll of three dollars. Jack would pay again on the way back.

Just beyond the booths, where the bridge widened out into a broad intersection, Jack saw a black Humvee waiting with one wheel up on the sidewalk. A soldier with a machine gun stood up in an open turret in the back while two others watched the incoming bridge traffic from behind the flat windshield.

The Mexican asked the same questions and Jack gave the same answers. He paid the toll. They waved him on. He thought he saw the soldiers in the Humvee tracking him as he pulled away from the booths, but he did not want to stare.

Anyone who expected a sudden change across the bridge would be disappointed. The streets looked the same, though the storefronts were festooned with Spanish signs and there were no white faces among the brown. Jack piloted carefully along these blocks, careful not to speed because the police were everywhere and where there were not cops there were more soldiers.

He was not afraid. The soldiers were there for a reason and a person would have to be deaf and blind not to know why. When he watched the news, Jack saw the reports of fresh killings, of shootouts in the streets, but he had never seen them with his own eyes. To him Nuevo Laredo looked the same, felt the same, though he knew it was different. The people he met were friendly and the stores happy to have his business. Maybe he was just lucky, or maybe it was not as bad as they said.

ELEVEN

THEY DROVE INTO THE HEART OF THE city and then turned toward the neighborhoods where the buildings did not crowd so close and the streets weren't so narrow. Houses appeared, some with courtyards and others with lawns. The truck navigated ruts in the asphalt and deep holes that threatened to swallow up the wheels. Jack saw a car that had no wheels, propped up on bricks in front of a house whose tiny front yard was festooned with hanging laundry.

The house of Bernardo Sigala did not have a stretch of grass in front of it, but was fronted by a six-foot wall along the edge of the street. An iron gate allowed access to a little car park where a blue Toyota squatted. Part of the gate could be opened separately for people and two locks secured this entrance.

Jack parked on the side of the road and got out under the sun. Lidia went to the gate and jangled a string of bells. The noise was like a collision of cows.

Bernardo came out of the house and into the shade of the car park. He wore a bright yellow shirt with a collar and pants with a sharp crease. They dressed up for these occasions, too. '¡Hola a todos! ¡Bienvenidos!'

He unlocked the gate with two separate keys and held it open for Lidia and Marina to enter. Jack came last. They shook hands. 'Bernardo,' Jack said. 'Are we late?'

'Late? No, not at all! I was just watching some *fútbol*. Reina is in the kitchen. The kids are around. Come in.'

Bernardo brought them inside where it was cooler. A ceiling fan stirred the air and all the windows were open. The house smelled of cooking. In the front room there was Bernardo's television and a battered couch. Little Bernardo sat there wearing a Bravos team shirt. The Bravos de Nuevo Laredo was a Second Division team without much in the way of prospects, but the boy was a fan. Jack checked the TV. He could not tell who was playing.

'Marina, Lidia,' Bernardo said, 'you'll find the girls in their rooms, I think. You look very pretty today, Lidia.'

'Thank you, *Tío*.'

'Jack, do you want a beer? Sit down and be comfortable. Bernardino, make some room for Jack. Sit over there.'

Little Bernardo left the couch reluctantly and took a seat in a straight-backed chair near the wall. He was not a talker and mostly he looked at Jack with wary eyes. The boy was a baby when Jack first saw him. Now he was seven. They would never be close.

Bernardo vanished into the kitchen and returned with a bottle of Corona and a wedge of lime. 'Here you go,' he said. 'Come on, sit. You look like you have the nerves today, Jack.'

'It's been an interesting week,' Jack said. He took over the spot Little Bernardo left behind.

'Whatever happened, I bet I can top it,' Bernardo said.

'You probably can. How's it been?'

Bernardo took the far end of the couch. He was a round-faced man with a mustache that made him look jolly, but he frowned now. 'Lots of shootings this week. Very bad. One happened two blocks from here.'

'Everybody all right?'

'Sure, we are all fine. It's *narcos* killing *narcos* mostly, but sometimes someone gets caught in the middle and...' Bernardo made a gun gesture with his thumb and forefinger.

'But you're careful,' Jack said.

'Always.'

The beer was clean and crisp, the lime tangy. Jack looked at the TV again and saw the score was two to one. He still couldn't tell who was playing. 'Seemed quiet when we came in.'

'They say there will be more soldiers soon,' Bernardo said.

'How many are here already?'

'I don't know. A thousand? It seems like they are everywhere already. But Los Zetas and the Golfos, they still manage to get around.'

Jack thought. Bernardo and Reina had three children. Little Bernardo was the middle child and Patricia was nineteen now. Leandra was only four. Both parents worked and after school the little ones came home on their own, where Patricia watched over them. They made do.

Bernardo clapped Jack on the knee and put a note of joviality into his voice. 'I'm glad you came today. It's always good to see you and the girls.'

'We're glad to come. I just wish things were going better for you.'

'We are all alive and healthy. We have family. It's good. Tell me more about you.'

'Well, there's not much to say. I'm working steady, the girls are growing up. It's kind of hard for me to believe Marina's almost a grown woman. By this time next year she's going to be looking for her own place.'

Bernardo nodded. 'Maybe she won't be so quick to leave. You're her father now, just as much as Arturo ever was. Those kinds of ties are hard to break.'

'Maybe you're right. Patricia still talking about moving out?'

'Every week it's something new. She has a job now, but she's not saving any of it. I would be putting it away for tomorrow, you know, but she spends it as soon as she earns it. Her mother hates it, her staying out late, but she's an adult. She has to have her space. I can't ground her like I used to.'

'That's exactly what I'm afraid of,' Jack said.

'Don't be. It's a phase every young one has to go through. Remember when we were that age? No one could tell us any different.'

'I just want to make sure she's on the right path.'

'She is, my friend. You show her the way by how you raise her. I can tell.'

Jack swilled the last of the Corona and stuck the remains of the lime wedge into the bottle's neck. 'As long as you're convinced.'

'You have nothing to worry about. Now sit, watch some television. I'm going to see if Reina needs anything. We have a big meal for today. You're going to eat until you burst!'

Bernardo slipped out of the room and Jack caught the sound of spoken Spanish drifting from the kitchen. He turned around in his seat. Little Bernardo was still in the chair, watching the TV intently. They looked at each other without words.

'You want to sit up here with me?' Jack asked.

Little Bernardo nodded.

'Then come on up. Maybe you can tell me who's playing.'

TWELVE

THE LUNCH WAS A WHIRLWIND OF FOOD
—beans, rice, enchiladas, tortillas, salad
and more—served around the long harvest table in the
oversized kitchen. Bernardo sat at one end while Jack sat at the
other. Reina fluttered around them, making sure every plate
was full and stayed full and that every glass had something
in it. She barely sat until Jack insisted she take a chair and eat
with them.

Bernardo was Vilma's brother and though he did not look
much like his sister, Jack saw the family resemblance in his
children. Patricia was alike enough to Vilma that she and
Marina could have been sisters. Lidia and Little Bernardo had
the same eyes. Leandra was round cheeked and babyish. She
was shy and looked away whenever Jack tried to catch her
eye.

They ate until they could eat no more and still Reina forced
more food on them. Finally Marina begged for mercy and
offered to help clear away the meal. Lidia and Leandra retreated
to Leandra's room and Little Bernardo gravitated toward the
television once more. The sun had moved and the courtyard
out front was mostly in shadow. Bernardo collected more beer
and took Jack to sit.

There were four bottles. Jack took one. 'This is my last,' he
told Bernardo.

'*Está bien*. I will have the rest.'

Jack drank and Bernardo drank and a silence deepened between them. A truck ground past beyond the wall, jouncing in the potholes and making the shocks protest.

It was Bernardo who spoke first: 'I hear construction is not so good in Texas right now.'

'Not really,' Jack said. 'I've been doing renovation work, mostly. Keeps the lights on.'

'It's the same here. No one wants to buy bricks because no one's building anymore. Some days I make no sales at all. I had to let one of my men go.'

'I'm sorry.'

'It happens. He understood.'

Jack rolled the cold bottle between his hands, considering. 'I had a good guy working for me a couple of days last week. His name was Eugenio. Came up from Anáhuac, crossed over looking for work.'

'What happened to him?'

'*La migra*,' Jack said. 'Came by and plucked him right out of my truck. Tried to put the fear of God into me, too. But they know how it is: when I need help, I have to go where I can find it.'

'They'll deport him,' Bernardo said.

'Probably.'

'You know, the buses with *los deportados* come right into the city. They drop them off at the plaza and leave them there with whatever they had with them when they were caught. Some of them have nothing at all: no money, no nothing. Where do they go? I wonder that when I see them.'

'Back to the border,' Jack said.

'Back to the border,' Bernardo agreed. 'In twenty-four hours they are back. Or less. No one is going to stop them because they have nothing to lose. But they have to look out: Los Zetas are always watching. If one of the Zetas catches them, they have to pay and if they can't pay, their family must pay. And if the family cannot pay… it does not go well for them. Bad enough that they have their money taken on the way north, but to be squeezed again…'

'Someday it'll get put right,' said Jack.

'I like to think so. It can't go on forever like this.'

Jack heard the scuff of a shoe and looked over his shoulder. Marina was there. 'Everything's cleaned up. You guys doing all right out here?'

'Fine,' Jack said.

'I was going to go out shopping with Patricia. Is that all right?'

Jack turned to Bernardo. 'What do you think?' he asked.

Bernardo shrugged. 'The shopping district is patrolled. Lots of police and army. They should be fine.'

'Okay,' Jack said. 'But stick to places Patricia knows. Don't go wandering off somewhere.'

'We won't,' Marina said, and she kissed Jack on the cheek before vanishing.

Jack sighed. 'You sure it's safe?'

'As safe as anything is these days.'

Bernardo finished his second beer and took up the third bottle. The golden liquid caught the light and Jack found himself thirsty. 'I'm going to grab something to wet my whistle,' he told Bernardo.

'Of course. I'll keep your seat, don't worry.'

In the front room he bumped into Marina and Patricia as they headed for the door. 'Heading out,' Marina said.

'How long will you be?'

'A couple of hours.'

'All right. Remember what I said.'

'She is safe with me,' Patricia told Jack.

'I'll hold you to that. Have fun.'

Reina was in the kitchen, seated at the big table with a book open in front of her. She still had her apron on. She looked up. They spoke in Spanish. Bernardo and Patricia could converse in English as well as anyone and the little ones had some command, but Reina had never learned. 'Hello, Jack. Is everything all right?'

'I just wondered if you had a little *limonada* or something. It's dry out there.'

'Of course.'

Their refrigerator was short and looked old. Reina brought out a plastic pitcher and poured a measure of lemonade into a jar that served as a glass. Jack was not afraid of what was in it. To him, Mexican water was the same as from his own tap. 'Thank you,' he said.

'Is Bernardo getting drunk yet?' Reina asked.

'Maybe a little,' Jack said.

'I tell him he should be more like you and watch what he drinks. But he never listens.'

'It's different for him than it was for me,' Jack said.

'Jack, anyone who suffered as you did could take the same path.'

'Maybe.'

'You were strong and you got better.' Reina came to Jack and put a hand on his arm. She was a small woman and he towered over her, but she had an unbending air about her that made her seem larger, stronger. 'You would never let the girls down. I never told you, but I believed it. I thank God every time I see you and the girls that He sent you to Vilma. You are always in my prayers.'

He felt his face flush, but he did not pull away from her. 'I'm glad someone's praying for me,' he said finally. 'I need all the help I can get.'

Perhaps she saw it in his face, or sensed it from her touch. Reina lifted her hand from his arm and stepped away. 'It's always good when you come, Jack,' she said.

There were echoes of Vilma here, in word and touch, and Jack found he missed Vilma in that moment more than he had in a long while. He pushed it away, and said, 'I like it, too.'

'Tell my husband *no más cervezas* when he's finished with those.'

'I will.'

Bernardo's bottles were empty when Jack returned. He watched a moth fluttering around on the border between light and shadow, confusedly weaving back and forth. The courtyard seemed very small just then and Jack wondered what it would have been like if Marina and Lidia had come to live here instead of with him. How different would they be? It was impossible to know. They were American girls raised the American way, but they always had one foot in Mexico. That much Jack promised Vilma and days like today were his payment.

'Reina thinks you're out here getting drunk,' Jack said when he sat down.

'Nonsense. It would take much more than that to get me drunk. She doesn't know me at all.'

Somewhere far away a police siren suddenly piped up and was almost immediately silenced. Automatically Jack thought of Marina. He considered calling her on her phone just to make sure everything was okay, but she would only laugh and poke fun at him for worrying.

As if he had read Jack's mind, Bernardo said, 'It's nothing. If there was real trouble there would be many sirens. The police gather like locusts.'

'Force of habit,' Jack said, and he tried to smile.

'In this city we learn all the sounds by heart. That was probably someone being pulled over for a ticket. That's one thing *la policía* like to do: hand out tickets. If they were half as good at catching *narcos* as they are about giving parking fines, we would be out of this mess tomorrow.'

'It's the same all over,' Jack said, though it wasn't true.

THIRTEEN

THE LANES HEADED NORTH WERE NO less packed at the end of the day than they had been hours earlier. Jack could not ever recall a time when the port of entry wasn't packed with vehicles leaving Mexico: trucks hauling goods, Mexicans traveling and Americans caught in the mix. They were behind a tall truck with a fruit logo painted across the back doors. It blocked out all view of the road ahead.

Jack put the radio on quietly just to have something playing. The girls were quiet. The air conditioner occasionally spat tiny droplets of condensation from the vents.

'Jack,' Marina said.

'Yeah?'

'I want to ask you something.'

'Sure, what?'

'I was talking with Patricia today and she said there's going to be a concert in a couple of weeks. She can get tickets for us if I want to go. It's supposed to be a good band.'

'A concert? You mean across the bridge?'

'Yeah. It's not too far from Tío Bernardo's house. Patricia says she has some friends going and I'm invited, too.'

Jack glanced toward Marina and saw her watching him intently. Already his mind was grinding through what to say. 'I don't know,' he offered. 'I don't know.'

'There's no problem,' Marina said. 'It'll be me and Patricia and three or four other girls. It's just that it's at night on a Friday.'

'A *nighttime* concert?' Jack asked. 'No way. Maybe if it was during the day we could talk about it, but you're not going across the bridge at night.'

'Seriously, Jack, it's no big deal. We'll be in a big group. And it's not *late*. The sun will probably still be up half the time.'

'It's not the sun I'm worried about. You know what's going on over there.'

'Tío Bernardo's doing fine.'

Jack drummed the steering wheel. 'Bernardo's careful and everybody in the family is careful. They don't go around taking big risks. That's how you stay out of trouble. I'm not letting you go to some concert at night. It's too dangerous.'

Marina sat back heavily in her seat. 'I knew you'd say no. I told her you would.'

'It's not like I want to say no. I just have to be smart about things. You're seventeen and you shouldn't be out on your own in the city.'

'But I wouldn't be on my own, that's the whole *point*. Patricia would be with me the whole time. And she's an adult.'

'Barely.'

'But she is still an adult.'

Jack caught sight of Lidia in the back seat pretending not to listen. He found himself willing the truck in front of him to move so they could be across the bridge and to the customs booths before he had to say anything else. The feeling of irritation emanating from Marina was like radiant heat.

Marina went on. 'I'm just saying it's not like I'd be out partying. I'd go to Tío Bernardo's, pick up Patricia and go to the concert. Afterwards we'd grab something to eat and then

I'm right back at Tío Bernardo's for the night. I wouldn't even try to come back until morning.'

'Marina—'

'There'll be plenty of cops around! You should have seen all of them today. Cops. Army guys. If we have any problems, we'll go right to the police.'

'I don't know about this,' Jack said.

'Come on, Jack, it's just one concert. As soon as I go back to school there won't be time for *anything*. I never ask you for stuff!'

'You can't even cross the border without a notarized permission slip from me,' Jack said.

'Then we'll get that. They notarize stuff at the shipping place by the mall.'

'It's just that easy, huh?' Jack asked.

'It doesn't *have* to be hard.'

'Don't you understand that they've got a war going on over there? There's a reason they have all those police and army guys around. What you're asking… it's not just about a concert.'

'You trust me, don't you?'

'It's not about trust, either. I know you won't put a foot wrong.'

'Then what's the problem?'

Jack tried hard not to glare, but he felt his face screwing up despite himself. The truck in front of them inched forward barely. 'Goddamn it,' he said out loud.

'I swear I won't ask you for anything else this year,' Marina said. 'Honest, I won't. You can ground me for a month if I do.'

'You promise me you'll do exactly what you told me?' Jack asked. 'No detours, no "oops, I forgot," but exactly what you said you would do?'

'I promise. Cross my heart.'

'I must be out of my mind,' Jack said. 'You know, your mother wouldn't have let you do something like this. I can hear her right now telling me it's crazy to even think about it.'

'Mom would be totally cool with it,' Marina said.

'That's what you think, huh?'

'Jack, I just really want to go. It'll be fun and I get to have a little adventure on my own.'

'No,' Jack said. 'No adventure. This is the opposite of an adventure. You're going out, you're coming back. And if I find out you went out someplace drinking or something like that you can forget about ever having an adventure.'

'I completely understand.'

Jack eyed her in her seat. She bit her lip the way Vilma did. They were so much the same. 'I'm saying *maybe*. I'm not saying yes. You got how long? A couple of weeks, you said?'

'Two weeks.'

'I'll think it over and I'll talk to Bernardo and if we figure you'll be safe to go then I'll make my decision. But if I say no then that's it. We won't argue about it anymore.'

'Okay. Thanks, Jack.'

'Don't thank me yet.'

FOURTEEN

JACK WORKED BY HIMSELF FOR MOST OF a week in the lawyer's house. He avoided the Home Depot studiously. Every time he drove past he redirected his gaze away from the long sidewalk that fronted the lot lest he spot Eugenio among the men gathered there for work.

On another afternoon he went to the shipping place by the mall and got the guy on duty to notarize a typewritten note that gave Marina permission to cross the border into Mexico on the specified date. Marina gave Jack a hug and a kiss after that. Jack tried not to worry about what he'd done.

New calls were coming in from people wanting renovation work done. Jack had jobs scheduled out for three months, which was good. Steady work meant steady money. One day the jobs would come less and less often and then he'd have to lean on whatever savings he'd managed to put together over the years since Vilma's death. He was still paying on some of her medical bills.

He enjoyed his evening beers and went to bed and woke up according to schedule. The calendar checked off days toward the start of school. Already they'd gotten a supply list in the mail and Jack spent a couple of hours at Walmart gathering all the little things Marina and Lidia needed for their year. Once upon a time the school had paid for all these things itself, but those times were long past. Now they scrambled for every dollar, like all those anxious men gathered in the parking lot of Home Depot.

Marina bought a new dress with money she earned from her job. Jack thought it showed off too much shoulder and too much leg, but Marina laughed at Jack's concerns. Maybe he was getting to be like an old man, after all, worrying about things that didn't matter. When she told him she was going to wear it to the concert, his only suggestion was that she wear a light sweater just to cover up a little bit. Of course she wouldn't. Even if he put the sweater on her himself.

FIFTEEN

THE PHONE ON GONZALO'S DESK RANG twice. He answered. 'Soler,' he said.

'Is this Inspector Gonzalo Soler?' asked a man whose voice Gonzalo did not recognize.

'Yes. Who is this?'

'Valdez. I work La Zona.'

'What can I do for you, Officer Valdez?'

'I think you had better come here.'

'Now?'

'Yes, now.'

'What's this about?'

'It's better if you see for yourself.'

Only Pepito was near when Gonzalo left his desk. 'I'll be right back,' Gonzalo told him. 'I have to go to La Zona.'

'What's going on?'

'I'm not sure.'

'Good luck.'

It did not take long to drive there and this time Gonzalo drove through the gates of Boy's Town itself to park near the police station. A pair of uniformed officers waited outside and they waved to him as if expecting his arrival. When he climbed out, one came to him and offered his hand. 'Herminio Valdez.'

'Gonzalo Soler. What's going on?'

'Do you know a man named Tomás Contreras?'

'Yes, I do.'

'Come with me, then.'

Valdez led Gonzalo up the Circunvalación Casanova to a place Gonzalo recognized immediately, only now there was an ambulance in the street and two more policemen, accompanied by a pair of medics in bright yellow jackets. Gonzalo knew what he would see before he saw it: the body of Tomás Contreras lying in a pool of blood with one hand clawed in front of him as if to catch the bullets.

A police unit was there and Gonzalo saw there was someone in the back. By the open door of unit number nine, Iris Contreras stood with a blanket around her shoulders. Both of her eyes were beaten black and they were thick with tears. A policeman interviewed her.

'What the hell happened?' Gonzalo demanded of Valdez.

'From what the girl says, her father was shot down by the killer we have in custody,' Valdez replied. 'She says that her father came to her crib to bring her home and met up with Enrique Guerrero. He's the girl's pimp. The men fought and Guerrero threw Contreras out on the street. When Contreras wouldn't leave, Guerrero came out and shot him.'

'Witnesses?'

'The Contreras girl herself. She says she'll offer a full statement to the prosecution.'

One of the medics brought out a black, rubberized canvas body bag and laid it on the ground beside Tomás Contreras's body. With the help of the other, the corpse was handled into the bag and the yawning mouth of the thing zipped up.

'May I speak to the girl?'

'Of course. We're going to throw this whole case to you once we have the scene wrapped up. The Contreras girl gave us your name.'

'Thank you,' Gonzalo said, and he left Valdez behind.

When he reached Iris, he asked for privacy and the policeman went away. Now there were only the two of them. Iris looked markedly thinner than she had when they last met, though it had not been long. The bruises on her face were appalling and dark.

Gonzalo could ask no other question. 'Why did you come back?'

'There's no place for me at home.'

'Your father—'

'Called me a whore and beat me. I was better off here. I came as soon as I could.'

'And now your father is dead.'

'Yes.'

She was watching the body bag. The medics picked it up by its ends and carried it to the ambulance, where they muscled it through the back doors. Gonzalo only glanced that way. 'Is this what you wanted?' Gonzalo asked.

'No, of course not.'

'Do you think you're free just because your father is gone and your pimp is headed to jail?'

'I don't know.'

'There will be another one, Iris,' Gonzalo said. 'And another and another. It doesn't end here.'

'I don't care,' Iris said.

'Listen to me, Iris,' Gonzalo said.

The doors of the ambulance closed. Iris blinked and looked away. When she turned to Gonzalo, he saw she was a thousand miles from him, in a completely different world. He thought to ask what drugs she was on, but it didn't matter. She would only lie and he would become angry and they would get nowhere.

'This is where I want to be,' Iris said finally.

'No, it isn't.'

'Yes, it is.'

Gonzalo dropped his hands to his sides. There was no argument to be made. 'Then I suppose you have your wish. Good luck, Iris. I will be in touch when it's time for more testimony.'

'Goodbye,' Iris said.

She turned back into the open doorway and vanished into shadow. Gonzalo watched her go.

SIXTEEN

JACK HAD A BOOK, A DETECTIVE NOVEL that he'd been trying to finish for over a year. There was nothing wrong with the book. It was only because Jack had never been much of a reader that the process took so long. He read a few pages here and there, tried to remember what had come before and then put it down again. The spine was battered from the book being laid open on its face.

The lawyer's bathroom was finished. Jack had done most of the work alone and hired day labor only when he absolutely had to have it. He did not learn those men's names and did not make small talk with them. Always he was on the lookout for the black SUV and the cops, but no one came to get him. He paid the men their wages and sent them on their way unknown. It was better like that.

Now Jack had time to himself. It seemed a good moment for reading, and so he made a pitcher of Kool-Aid to take out on the back patio. He had a small, round table made of iron that was the perfect height to lay a drink on and put a folding lounge chair by. A square of red-and-white striped awning kept the sun off but not the heat. The pitcher and his glass began to sweat immediately.

He read for two hours straight, which was more than he'd managed in three months of trying. The hero had just discovered the head of the man he was supposed to be looking for.

Things were picking up. Jack barely heard the back door slide open on its track.

'Jack.'

'Hmm?'

Lidia wore cool white and pastels. She had the faint smell of the house about her, gathered up from her favorite space on the couch. When she stood in front of Jack she folded her arms and stared down at him. 'We need to talk,' she said.

Jack put the book down on the table. The pages brushed up against the pitcher of Kool-Aid and a spot darkened with moisture. 'What about?' he asked.

'Marina's concert is tonight.'

'Yeah, right. I know.'

'What about me?'

'What about you?'

'I mean, what am I supposed to do tonight? Don't I get anything special?'

Lidia was a teenager, but at times like these Jack could still see the little child in her. Standing with her arms crossed made them look chubby like they were when she was small. Her face was pouty.

Jack put up his hands. 'I don't know, what do you want?'

'You never asked me if I might to want to spend the night at a friend's house.'

'Was I supposed to?'

'You could have *asked*.'

'All right. Okay. I'm sorry I didn't ask. Did you have somebody you wanted to do a sleepover with?'

'It's too *late* for that now, Jack. Nobody's going to want to have me over when I can only give them a couple hours' notice.'

'Why didn't you say something earlier, then?'

'I thought you would *ask*.'

Jack covered his eyes and rubbed them with his thumb and forefinger until he saw colors. He took a breath and then another and then he said, 'I'm sorry I didn't ask. What should I do now?'

'I don't know. Something special.'

'We could order pizza.'

'I'd rather eat out.'

'Okay, we can eat out. You got somewhere in mind?'

'How about Italian food?'

'Sure. Italian food sounds nice.'

'And I want to rent a movie.'

'We can rent a movie, too, if you want. They've got one of those vending machine things at the grocery store now. You can pick the movie. Whatever you want.'

Lidia looked at him, her arms still crossed. She let them down. 'Okay.'

Jack tried a smile. 'Okay?' he asked.

'It's just that I never get to do anything cool.'

'That's because you're thirteen. When you're older, you get to do better stuff. Your time will come,' Jack said.

'I don't mean to be bitchy.'

'I know you don't.'

'Can we go before Marina leaves so she knows she's missing out?'

'That I can do,' Jack said. 'I'll even put on a nice shirt. Want some of this Kool-Aid?'

'No thanks. They say the dye in that stuff can make you sick.'

Jack poured himself another glass. The pitcher was half empty. 'Never made me sick,' he said.

'Nothing can stop you, Jack,' Lidia said, and then she went inside.

He considered the glass of red liquid, half-melted ice cubes floating. Food dye making you sick. What were they going to come up with next? Already it was elbow pads and crash helmets for kids on tricycles and now every day there was some new scare about what you shouldn't eat. Vilma knew better than that. She never wanted to shelter their children.

Their children.

At the start they figured Vilma was just having trouble getting pregnant because she was getting older, or because she was working too hard or something else they hadn't known to watch out for yet. For a while they thought it might be Jack who was the problem. They didn't know that fate was just setting the stage for them, that they were denied this because there were further denials to be had.

Maybe they would have been better prepared for it when it happened if they had taken heed of those early-warning signs. The doctors told them no, it wouldn't have made a difference, but Jack could not help but think he had made some terrible mistake. If he had only insisted on one more checkup, one more test. But that took responsibility out of Vilma's hands and put it in his alone. It didn't work that way.

He drained the glass and the ice clicked against his teeth. He opened wide and swallowed the ice cubes too: two spots of cold traveling deep down inside where they would vanish like bad feelings and doubts. Their children.

There would be no more reading today. The urge had left him and now the book just sat there, waiting for him to come back to it in a day or a week. Someday he'd find out more about the head of the dead man, but not now.

Jack got up from the lounge chair and gathered up his things. He had laundry to do.

SEVENTEEN

MARINA WORE THE DRESS SHE BOUGHT and Jack was no happier about it now than when she first brought it home. She wore it with heels and Jack asked her how she was supposed to dance wearing those things. 'I've got it, Jack,' she said.

'How about that sweater?' Jack pressed.

'It's, like, ninety degrees,' Marina replied.

'It'll cool down overnight. You'll be glad you brought it.'

'Okay, okay, I'll take the blue one you got me for Christmas.'

He fussed over her though he knew she hated it. Was her bag packed? Did she make sure she had her toothbrush? Was her cell phone fully charged? Were all her documents in order for the crossing? She answered yes to all of these things, but Jack knew she would; she was responsible and she thought ahead. Jack had taught her those things, and before him there was Vilma, too.

They stood on the front lawn. Marina had her bag over her shoulder. 'Let me have one more look at you,' Jack said.

'I'm going away for one night,' Marina said. 'I'm not moving out.'

'You know I just want to make sure you're all right,' Jack said.

'I know. But, really, the sweater? I'm just going to leave it in the car.'

'Leave it in the car, then.'

'I will.'

'All right.'

He saw her off in her little Galant and he waved at her until the car was out of sight. As he walked back to the house, he thought in the back of his mind that maybe they would turn her away at the border and send her home and then he would have nothing to worry about. Maybe that would be the best thing all around.

Lidia caught him just inside the front door. She was dressed up in a shirt and a nice blouse. 'Hey, I thought we were going to leave before her,' she said.

'She went a little early. Don't worry, she knows she's missing out.'

'Good.'

Jack changed into a white shirt and jeans and even considered putting on a bolo tie but reconsidered. The restaurant wasn't that nice and he wasn't trying to impress anyone. He'd never started dating again after Vilma. He doubted he had the stuff to draw eyes anymore.

They drove to the place in Jack's truck. It was a family restaurant where they had gone a hundred times before. The owners were not Italian, but Mexican. The food tasted authentic anyway and the music they played was always Frank Sinatra or some other Italian crooner.

Lidia ordered an appetizer and Jack did the same. The waiter offered him a wine list. 'No, thanks,' Jack said. 'I'll stick to water.'

After the waiter was gone, Lidia asked, 'Why don't you drink wine, anyway? Is it because of—?'

'No, it's not that. I figure there are two kinds of people: ones who drink wine and ones who drink beer. It just so happens that I'm a beer drinker. Wine's just grape juice that went bad.'

Lidia smiled. 'That's a good one. I'm going to remember that.'

The food came and then it was time to eat. They had gone out early and most of the restaurant was empty, but there were a few other families scattered around the big dining room. A child in a high chair made a demolition job out of a little plate of spaghetti. There was more on the outside of the kid than on the inside. It made Jack smile.

'What do you think Marina's doing right now?' Lidia asked.

Jack checked his watch. 'I don't know. Getting dolled up some more. Girl-talking with your cousin. You're not missing anything.'

'How old do I have to be before I can go out to a concert?'

'We'll see how tonight goes. Your sister sets a foot wrong, it'll be a cold day in hell before I let either of you out of my sight.'

'You're just saying that.'

'Believe it.'

Dean Martin sang 'Ain't That a Kick in the Head.' The food was good and there was plenty of it. Jack knew he should watch it, but it was a special night and special nights had special rules. He even sprang for a dessert both of them could share and followed all of it with a cup of coffee.

'You given any mind to what you want to watch tonight?' Jack asked Lidia.

'I'm thinking a comedy. Something with romance. What?'

'Nothing. Romance is good.'

'You were making a face!'

'I wasn't,' Jack said. 'Come on, let's pay the bill and get out of here.'

They were on their way out the door when the dinner-hour diners were coming in, the foyer full of people. Jack cleared the path for Lidia and held the door for her. Out in the parking lot the temperature had already dropped from the afternoon to something not quite so stifling, though heat still radiated from the asphalt.

The grocery store was on the way home. Jack stood by while Lidia used the machine to slowly flick through the selections. When someone looked impatient, Jack turned his frown on them and they glanced away. She finally picked out something frothy and girly that would probably be horrible and Jack paid.

The rest of the evening was spent with popcorn and the movie, the two of them on the couch. Jack found he hated the thing less than he thought he would and afterward Lidia said she thought it was kind of dumb, but fun anyway. They both ended up going to bed later than usual.

Afterward Jack lay awake in his bed, listening to the whisper of the air conditioning. The clock at the bedside said it was nearly eleven o'clock. The concert would be finishing up soon and Marina would be back at Bernardo's by midnight. He hoped she had a good time and he hoped she put on that sweater.

PART TWO

MISSING

ONE

ORNING CAME AND JACK ROSE QUIETLY. He showered and shaved and went to the kitchen in shorts and a T-shirt. Today he would go nowhere and do nothing and that suited him just fine. The smells of a cooking breakfast lured Lidia out of her bedroom and they enjoyed the meal together.

'What time do you think Marina will be home?' Lidia asked.

'I don't know. Why?'

'I was thinking we could go to the pool. You could come, too.'

'Nah, you know I don't like swimming.'

'You don't have to swim. You could just, like, put your feet in the water.'

'Maybe.'

They cleaned up the dishes and Lidia slipped away to get dressed. Jack almost didn't hear his cell phone ringing in his bedroom until it had nearly gone to voice mail. He hurried to it.

'Hello?'

'Jack, it's Bernardo.'

'Hey, Bernardo. I was going to call you later.'

'Jack, is Patricia with you?'

Bernardo's voice was sharp with tension and the question hung in space for a long moment before Jack realized what he was asking. He immediately headed for Marina's room. The door was half-open. Jack pushed it wide and inside was the bed, still made, Marina's things neatly put away.

'Jack? Are you there?'

'I'm here. No, Patricia isn't with me. Marina didn't come home last night. She was supposed to stay over with you.'

'I know, Jack. I had a call on my phone last night, late, but I didn't answer. It was from Patricia. There was no message. I thought maybe they changed their minds and went home to your house.'

Jack steadied himself against the wall. Lidia emerged from her room, a question on her face, but Jack's expression silenced her. 'I don't know anything about that,' Jack told Bernardo. 'I didn't have any messages.'

'This is no good,' Bernardo said, and Jack caught the first notes of burgeoning desperation in his tone. 'I'm going to call the police. I'm going to hang up and call the police now.'

'Okay, okay. Call the police. I'm on my way just as soon as I can.'

'All right, Jack. I will see you soon.'

They broke the connection.

'Jack, what's wrong?' Lidia asked.

'It's your sister,' Jack said. He saw a wave of raw panic rise in her and he put a hand out to quash it. 'She's not hurt. It's not like that. Uncle Bernardo says she didn't come home with Patricia last night.'

'Then how do you know she's not hurt?'

'I don't want to think about that right now. Get your shoes on, we're gonna go. Let me change. We're gonna go.'

First he dialed Marina's number. It rang five times before it switched over to voice mail. He left a message and then immediately dialed her number again. More rings. Voice mail. Again.

Jack changed out of his lazy clothes and found Lidia waiting by the door, bouncing on the balls of her feet. His hand shook when he put the key in the lock, but it was steady by the time they reached the truck.

It was early enough that the traffic into Nuevo Laredo was not thick. The tremors had started up again by the time he reached the US customs cordon and he gripped the steering wheel to stop them.

He refused to think what he knew he had to think: that Marina should never have gone, and that he should not have let her. 'Not now,' he said out loud.

The man from Customs and Border Protection waved for Jack to put down his window. Jack already had his passport in his lap and Lidia handed hers over to the man, who examined them.

'Nice to see you again,' the officer said.

Jack looked at him sharply. 'What?'

'Nice to see you again. You passed through here not too long ago.'

Jack forced himself to look at the man's name. Gallego. He didn't recognize it, but he nodded and tried to smile. 'That's right,' he said. 'We come through here a lot.'

'Is everything all right?'

Gallego's eyes were impossible to read behind his sunglasses. It was not too bright yet, but still he wore them. Jack picked a spot on the man's forehead and looked at that instead of the lenses.

'We got some bad news this morning,' Jack said. 'Family news.'

'I hope it's not serious.'

'I hope not, too.'

Gallego held on to the passports for a long beat and Jack

thought he was going to ask them both to get out of the truck. The man handed them back. 'Be careful across the bridge,' he said. 'I heard there was a big shootout around dawn. You don't want to get in the middle of that kind of thing.'

'We won't.'

'All right, then. Move along.'

Jack's mind was working before he put up the window, imagining things he did not want to put into words. A shootout before dawn, but where? Who was there? Who was hurt? Marina would not be out so late, he told himself, even if she decided against going home to Bernardo's. If an American had been hurt, they would know already, wouldn't they?

A military roadblock cut off the direct route to Bernardo's house so they were forced to go the long way around. There were still more army vehicles buzzing around downtown like angry hornets whose nest had been disturbed. Seeing them made Jack feel better. So many soldiers and one of them must have seen something. Maybe Marina had been turned away by another roadblock and gotten lost. It could happen that way.

With one hand on the steering wheel, Jack called Marina again. The same. He stopped himself from throwing the phone. 'Do me a favor,' he told Lidia, 'start calling your sister. Just keep calling even if she doesn't answer.'

'Okay, Jack,' Lidia said, and Jack could hear the threatening break of panic in her voice. Not now. Not yet.

TWO

REINA MET JACK AT THE DOOR WITH A strong embrace. She looked as though she had been on the verge of tears for a long time, but had not succumbed. Jack heard Bernardo talking on the phone in the front room and when Jack came in Bernardo paused for only a moment to wave.

'Yes, I understand that it is very busy,' Bernardo said into the phone. 'That is why I've waited so long to talk to an officer in charge. I realize it is difficult. Yes, I will hold.'

'What's happening?' Jack asked Reina.

'The police are all crazy because of the shootings this morning,' Bernardo cut in. 'Everyone's out of the station, they say. But someone has to come back soon and then they can hear my report.'

'Can't someone visit the house?' Jack asked.

'I already asked. They don't have anyone to spare for that.'

'There's got to be *somebody*!'

'I'm *trying*, Jack. We have to give it some time.' Bernardo straightened up. 'Yes, I'm still holding.'

Jack turned back to Reina. 'What time did you realize they hadn't come home?' he asked.

'This morning. We didn't expect them before midnight, so we went to bed. I thought about staying up, but I didn't think we had to worry. There are always so many police at these things. I'm so very sorry, Jack.'

'I could have called. I could have had Marina call.'

Reina's face wrinkled up and Jack saw the tears pushed back again. 'Let me get you something to drink,' she said. 'Lidia, come help me.'

They left. Jack spotted Little Bernardo and Leandra watching from the back hallway. Leandra clutched a naked baby doll to her side. Jack smiled at them, but they shrank back. He looked away.

Lidia brought Jack a hot cup of coffee he didn't want. Reina urged one on Bernardo. 'Come and sit down,' Reina told Jack. He thought to say no, but did as she asked. She settled in beside him. 'We called some of Patricia's friends to see if she went to stay with them. They all told us no.'

There was a piece of notebook paper held to Jack's refrigerator by magnets. The paper held the names and numbers of a half-dozen friends Marina knew well. Jack chided himself for failing to grab it. He could be calling now, too, instead of waiting for Bernardo.

'They probably went with friends we don't know,' Reina added. 'They're probably there now.'

Believing that would be good. Jack could imagine Marina taking a drink she wasn't allowed to have, partying hard, drinking more and then hiding away somewhere to ride out the inevitable hangover where no one could judge. Reina and Bernardo could not know all of Patricia's friends. Jack didn't know all of Marina's friends. Soon someone would call.

Lidia stood by, looking lost. 'Are you still calling your sister?' Jack asked.

'No, I stopped.'

'Well, keep on calling. Call ten more times.'

'There's no one answering, Jack!'

'I don't care! She can't answer the phone if it's not ringing!'

He didn't want to yell at Lidia. She retreated to the kitchen, dialing her phone. Jack wanted to bring her back and apologize. Maybe he would in a minute.

The coffee tasted like ashes. Bernardo paced the floor without taking a sip from his cup, pausing only to look out the front window as if his daughter and niece were coming through the gate. Now and then he would tell the faceless person on the other end that he was still waiting. Jack wanted to get up and pace with him.

Lidia emerged from the kitchen. 'I tried ten times, Jack.'

'Just—' Jack said. *Try ten times more*, he thought. Try a hundred times more. Try until your ear hurts from pressing it up against the phone, listening for the sound of someone picking up the line. 'Okay. Come in and sit down.'

'I think I'll go see Leandra.'

'You do that. I'll be here.'

Reina was wringing her hands so forcefully that Jack thought it must give her pain. Again she looked at him, the lines of her face drawn. 'She has her ringer turned off,' she said. 'That's all. She doesn't hear.'

'Right,' Jack agreed. 'That's it.'

Bernardo spoke up: 'Yes, I haven't gone away. Who do I see? Soler? And where can he be found? When? Yes, I will be there. Thank you. Thank you very much.'

'What is it?' Jack asked.

Bernardo put his phone in his pocket. His face was flushed and he was sweating. He set his coffee on a side-table untouched. 'They say there's an investigator I can speak to if I come to the station. He just started his shift. Gonzalo Soler. I have to go.'

'Wait,' Jack said, 'I'm going with you.'

Reina rose from the couch and Bernardo embraced her. She clung to him so tightly that he had to push away. 'Everything's going to be all right,' she said.

'Of course it is,' Bernardo replied. 'Come on, Jack.'

'Let me tell Lidia first.'

The house was rectangular and long and Leandra's room was the second-to-last door before the exit to the rear. Jack found Lidia there. Leandra had set up a small table and chairs and a tea party was assembled. The naked baby doll seemed to be the queen of the proceedings.

Lidia looked at him. 'Did they find her?'

'No. I'm going to the police station now. Stay with your cousins. If you need anything, ask your aunt. And try Marina's phone again. Please.'

'I will.'

Jack went.

THREE

GONZALO WAS CALLED IN FOUR HOURS early to deal with a *narco* shootout that broke before dawn. The *narcos* killed other *narcos* until the army arrived and killed everyone. After that the photographs were taken, the bodies were collected, the shell casings swept into bags and all that remained was the blood. He stayed at the scene until finally he was relieved, but there was no break for coffee and a breakfast of eggs and sausage; he was expected back at the station, where long reports had to be drawn up about what he had seen, what he had done and what was still left to do.

From his desk he could see people coming in and going out. The computer he used was years out of date but there was no money for a new one. The Federal Police had all the new things.

Gonzalo saw them enter, the American and the Mexican. It was hard to miss the American because he was so tall compared to his companion and broadly built. They stopped at the front desk and Gonzalo could just hear the Mexican speaking quickly. Gonzalo's name stood out clearly.

He went to them. The shorter man, the Mexican, had a look of panic. The American was calmer, but Gonzalo could see echoes of that panic in his eyes. Gonzalo offered his hand for both of them to shake. 'I'm Gonzalo Soler,' he said. 'Who are you gentlemen?'

'I am Bernardo Sigala,' the Mexican said. 'This is my *cuñado*, Sr Jack Searle. We were told to speak with you.'

'I'm here,' Gonzalo said. 'Speak to me. But come back to my desk so we can sit.'

Gonzalo found a second chair so the American could be seated and the two settled in before his desk. 'Thank you for seeing us,' Bernardo said.

'Does your brother-in-law speak Spanish?' Gonzalo asked.

'I speak it,' Jack said.

'Oh, good. I speak English, but it is faster if we go in Spanish, okay?'

'It's all right.'

'Tell me, Sr Sigala, what brings you here today.'

Bernardo Sigala told the entire story completely, breathlessly, as if he could not be rid of it fast enough. He told Gonzalo of the concert, of his daughter and his niece, of the night they left and when they did not come home. Through all of it the American, Jack Searle, was stone-faced, his fingers interlaced in his lap. Only the muscles of his forearms working betrayed him now.

Gonzalo took notes. When Bernardo was finished, Gonzalo asked, 'You say you've called your daughter's friends? Are these the same friends she went to the concert with last night?'

'Yes.'

'And they said that after the concert they all split up to go home, is that correct?' Gonzalo asked.

'Yes.'

He looked to Jack. 'Sr Searle, have you talked with any of your daughter's friends?'

'Not yet. But she didn't cross the bridge with any of them.'

'But she might have gone back to the Texas side last night anyway.'

'I don't know why she would do that.'

'I have to consider everything. Sr Sigala, you say your daughter called you late last night, but left no message. What time was that?'

'After midnight.'

'Do you always ignore calls after midnight?'

'No.'

Bernardo's eyes reddened and Gonzalo thought the man might start to cry right then and there. He kept his expression neutral. 'If only you had taken the call. We might have some idea where they went after leaving their friends.'

'I know,' Bernardo managed to say. Jack put his hand on Bernardo's shoulder.

'You don't have to worry, *señor*,' Gonzalo said. 'We will do everything we can to find your daughter. But it's possible that she went somewhere else to sleep last night and tried to call you to let you know.'

'Then where is she *now*?'

'I don't know. But we will find out.'

Jack leaned forward. 'Is it a question of money? Because if it is...'

Gonzalo stiffened and he felt his face go sour despite himself. He put his pen down too hard. 'Not everyone is looking for the *mordida*, Sr Searle. I said that I would help you find your daughter and I will. There are simply questions that must be asked before we proceed any farther. Do you understand?'

Jack blushed and sat back in his chair. 'I understand. I'm sorry.'

'Have you been to the American consulate, *señor*?'

'No. No, I haven't.'

'When you have finished here, the best thing to do is to speak with your consulate.'

'What will that do?'

'Your daughter is an American citizen?'

'Of course.'

'Then the consulate should know. It's the best thing.'

Bernardo sniffed heavily and covered his mouth. His eyes were shining now.

'It's important that you stay calm, Sr Sigala,' Gonzalo said. 'Not every story in Nuevo Laredo has an unhappy ending. Most people who are missing even a few hours turn out to be fine. Your daughter is somewhere safe and when this is all over with you will laugh at how worried you were.'

'As long as she is not dead,' Bernardo managed, and then the tears came. His body shook with them and he put his hands over his face. Jack drew him closer, put his arm around him and said something too low for Gonzalo to hear.

Gonzalo spoke up to be heard. 'Sr Searle, I think it would be best if you called all of your daughter's friends just to be certain she is not with them. I know it seems like a waste of time, but you could be surprised.'

Jack nodded. 'I'll do it.'

'In the meanwhile there are forms to fill out. Do you think Sr Sigala would be able to do that?'

'Let me take care of it,' Jack said.

'I'll get them for you. Wait here.'

Gonzalo left them at the desk and went away for a while. He dawdled at the copying machine, giving Bernardo Sigala a chance to compose himself. By the time he returned the man was almost under control, his breathing ragged, his lips still trembling. Gonzalo gave the paperwork to Jack. He waited while it was filled out, line by line. When he got the forms back, Gonzalo saw that Jack Searle had a simple man's handwriting, printing large.

'How long until… until you know something?' Jack asked.

'I will put these through to our officers immediately,' Gonzalo said. 'It would be helpful if you could produce some photographs of the girls. Something recent if you have it. You'll need it for the consulate, as well.'

'Marina took her passport with her,' Jack said.

'The United States keeps those kinds of pictures on file. Anything will help.'

'*Gracias*,' Bernardo forced out. 'Thank you for all your help.'

'You need to remember what I said: most disappearances resolve themselves. By this time tomorrow… well, I don't want to make predictions. I will make copies of these forms for you to take with you.'

He let the two men have their space again and saw them speaking to each other, their faces close together. Gonzalo wondered whether Bernardo was going to be able to make it home in his condition or if the American brother-in-law would have to drive. Jack was no less concerned, but he steadied himself better. Of the two of them, Gonzalo predicted Jack would withstand the process intact.

Armed with copies, Gonzalo turned them over to Bernardo and Jack. He tried putting on a smile for them, but neither seemed prepared to accept it. 'And that is all for now,' he said. 'Be sure to get those pictures to me just as soon as you can. I will be on duty until eight o'clock tonight. Here is my card. You may call me any time if you have questions and I will do my best to answer them.'

'I'll have those pictures for you soon,' Jack said. He helped Bernardo to stand. 'You'll make sure they get out to the people who need them?'

'Of course. You have my word.'

'It's just that you have everything else to handle.'

Gonzalo gave Jack his most serious look. 'I take my work very seriously, Sr Searle. If I tell you that you have my word, then you can know it's true. This is at the top of my list.'

'Okay. Thank you.'

'*De nada*. Now, please, take your brother-in-law home and let him get some rest. I will contact you the second I learn anything.'

He walked them to the station entrance and waited there until they had reached the corner and vanished around it. An army Humvee roared down the street in the opposite direction, dragging a cloud of dust and diesel fumes behind it. When he was sure the men were not coming back, Gonzalo returned to his desk.

Gonzalo studied the paperwork. The girls were nineteen and seventeen and out for fun with friends. It was not a wonder that they'd gone astray. He could have named half a dozen cases of missing persons just like it. He was not worried.

Amando Armas was the second inspector on duty. Gonzalo waved him down. 'Put these in the fax to all stations, would you?' he asked. 'And write a note saying photographs are coming.'

'What is it?' Armas asked.

'Nothing exciting. Two girls who didn't come home last night. It will be cleared by the end of shift.'

Armas riffled the papers. 'Then why bother putting it out?'

'The fathers are upset. Even if it does no good, at least I can say we did our best.'

'You're too much of a soft touch, Gonzalo.'

'Don't tell anyone.'

'I won't. Let me take care of this.'

'Thanks, Amando.'

Armas left and Gonzalo turned back to his computer. He thought briefly then of Iris Contreras. Gonzalo had not known her father, but surely he must have felt as these men felt now that their daughters were not at home. So long as the end result was not the same.

He would think about it no more. There were still reports to be written on the morning shootings. If he was lucky, he would be finished with it before the next emergency was called in.

FOUR

THEY WERE BACK AT THE TRUCK AND Bernardo looked as if he was about to be sick. Jack stood with him on the street as cars passed randomly by, his hand on Bernardo's shoulder, aware of people watching them, wondering about them, but not caring what they thought. Bernardo wilted further, as if the hot sun were diminishing him. Jack hung on more tightly.

'It's gonna be all right,' Jack said. It felt like lying, but he could think of nothing else to fill the space between them. 'You heard the man. This isn't Juárez. They'll turn up. They might be at home right now.'

'I'll call,' Bernardo said, and he straightened a little to bring out his phone. Jack listened while Bernardo talked. He looked at his own phone. The policeman said to call all of Marina's friends. He needed that sheet of paper. He had never needed to know these things because Marina was always responsible and never stayed out too long, never strayed with strangers.

Bernardo was finished with his call. 'Well?' Jack asked him.

'They aren't there,' Bernardo said, and his voice was hollow.

'We need pictures,' Jack said. 'Do you have something decent on your phone?'

'I think so. Yes. I took it last week.'

'I don't have anything. I need to call Lidia.'

Lidia picked up on the second ring. 'I've been trying to get her, Jack,' she said. 'It just keeps going to voicemail over and over.'

'You can stop for now,' Jack said. 'I need to know if you have any pictures of Marina on your phone. Something recent.'

'Yeah, sure, I have something.'

'I need you to email it to me. Can you do that? Can you email it me?'

'I can. As soon as we hang up.'

'Thanks.'

'What's happening, Jack?'

Jack looked at Bernardo. The man was starting to melt again, his face tinged with gray. If they didn't do something soon, he would break down and weep in the street. Jack knew that if that happened, he could not bring Bernardo back. 'I'll have to tell you later,' he told Lidia. 'We're doing everything we can here. Just send me the picture.'

'Okay, I will.'

Lidia broke the connection and Jack stepped closer to Bernardo. 'Hey,' he said. 'Hey, hey, look at me. Email me that picture of Patricia. Then we have to find a printing place. Somewhere with computers. Do you know where we can find somewhere like that?'

Bernardo nodded. 'I do.'

'Show me.'

They got in the truck and Bernardo directed him listlessly from his seat. Jack wanted to shake him, tell him to listen to the police and keep himself together, but they were driving. Eventually they came to a little storefront sandwiched between a small grocery and a shoe shop. Jack parked the truck in front of a fire hydrant.

Inside there were a trio of elderly looking computers at desks and a narrow counter beyond which were copying machines and printers arranged on metal racks. A sign said the computers were for rent, 30 pesos for 15 minutes. The man behind the counter put down a magazine and took Jack's payment in dollars.

The computers were old, but they still accessed the internet. Jack navigated to his online mail and found the pictures waiting for him there. 'Can I print from here?' he asked the man behind the counter.

'One peso per page.'

'I need to print in color.'

'Two pesos, then.'

The man told him which printer to send the pictures to and when they were finished Jack closed his email and paid for the papers. He looked at them. Lidia's image was candid, with Marina partly turned from the camera seeming thoughtful. Patricia's picture was full of smiles and life. '*Gracias*,' Jack told the man behind the counter, and then he went outside.

'What do we do now?' Bernardo asked.

'I'm going to take you home. I'll go to the US consulate first and then back to the police. We'll get the pictures out there.'

'I'm afraid, Jack.'

'I know. But we're doing the right thing. As soon as they get these pictures, they can spread them around. Somebody has to have seen something. It's like the man said: by this time tomorrow—'

Bernardo gripped Jack's arm with sudden strength. His face was tight. 'We have to *find* them!'

'We're going to find them. Get in the truck.'

Bernardo was quiet on the drive back and Jack did not look at him. Once he thought he might have heard the shudder of a hidden cry, barely audible above the blast of the air conditioning, but he could not be sure. By the time they reached Bernardo's house, the man's eyes were more red-rimmed than before. Jack could not be near him anymore. He pulled up to the gate and let the truck idle there, willing Bernardo out.

'Jack, I'm sorry,' Bernardo said, and this time his voice was calm.

'I'll call you when I'm done,' Jack replied. 'Until then just do what the cop said: call Patricia's friends. Try her phone. If you hear anything before I'm finished, you have my number.'

'*Buena suerte.*'

'It's going to be all right,' Jack told Bernardo. 'Go be with your family.'

Bernardo climbed down from the truck and slammed the door lightly. Jack waited until he had gone through the gate before he pulled away, checking only once in the rear-view mirror to see if Bernardo reappeared. He did not.

He had put his phone in the cup holder and now he picked it up. He dialed Marina. The phone rang five times and then it went to voicemail. Jack listened to her voice. 'Marina, it's me,' he said after the tone. 'I'm coming to find you, honey. Wherever you are, just stay safe and I'll be there.'

Jack killed the connection and put the phone back in the cup holder where he could see it. No one called back.

FIVE

JACK DID NOT KNOW WHAT TO EXPECT from the United States consulate, but he nearly missed it the first time he passed by. It was a plain white building with windows and a ceramic-tiled red roof over the sidewalk. An enclosed parking lot to one side had walls topped with barbed wire, but he saw no guards at the gate or at the entrance to the structure. All the curbside along the front of the building was marked red for no parking. As Jack found a space half a block away, he saw a Mexican army vehicle trundle slowly down the road, the man behind the turreted machine gun watching from behind a black mask.

He had the police report and the pictures in hand when he came to the main doors. A camera watched from above and the glass was heavily reinforced on the inside by strips of steel. An intercom was set into the wall to one side, with a sign in Spanish and English that read PRESS BUTTON TO ENTER. Jack pressed the button.

The intercom came alive. '¿*Puedo ayudarle?*' said a woman's voice.

'I'm an American. My stepdaughter is missing. I just came from the police. They told me to come here.'

'One moment,' the woman said in English.

An electric lock buzzed and then Jack was able to open the door. He stepped inside into cool air. The lobby of the consulate was not large, with most of the light coming through the metal-lined windows. A woman in a red blouse sat behind a semicircular desk with a computer and a phone. Double doors led farther into the building, but a man in a black shirt and pants wearing body armor and carrying an M4 carbine guarded these. The man watched Jack closely, his body half-turned. The carbine could be brought up in an instant.

'Welcome,' the woman said. 'You said you just came from the police?'

Jack went to the desk. 'Yes. My name is Jack Scarle. My step-daughter's name is Marina Cobos. She was in Nuevo Laredo last night and didn't come home.'

'I'm sure I can find someone to help you. Do you have ID?'

'Sure. Here.'

The woman looked at Jack's passport. 'You live in Laredo?'

'Yes.'

'Have you called the Laredo police yet?'

'No, I didn't think I needed to. Like I said, she was in the city last night.'

'You really should file a report with your local police, too, just in case.'

'Can I see someone here first?'

'Of course. Just sit down over there. It won't be long.'

Fifteen minutes passed. The man with the gun was still watching him. Jack started to feel cold and his arms prickled. The woman had been on the phone for a little while, but now she spoke to no one. She clicked at her computer's mouse. He could not see what she was doing.

He caught movement in the hallway beyond the armed guard. A man in shirtsleeves and a tie reached the doors and swiped the magnetic card hanging from around his neck to open another electric lock. He passed the armed man without glancing in his direction and came to Jack. 'Mr Seal? I'm Ted DiMatteo.'

Jack got up. They shook hands. 'It's Searle,' he said. 'Jack Searle.'

'I'm sorry, Mr Searle. Like you don't have enough problems today. Do you want to come with me? My office is in the back of the building.'

The guard stepped aside. DiMatteo had to swipe his card again to reenter the hallway and he held the door for Jack. Together they followed the main corridor back into the heart of the building and then made a series of turns down smaller, shorter halls, all lined with offices. The consulate was like a warren, with many places to hide.

DiMatteo's office was small. His workspace was crowded with papers and multicolored folders. A framed degree hung on the wall, along with some pictures of DiMatteo with a woman who must be his wife and a pair of young children. He had a corkboard festooned with notices.

'Try to make yourself comfortable if you can.'

Jack sat. His knees pressed against the front of DiMatteo's desk. He tried shifting around in the little chair until he found a way to free one leg. 'I have a police report,' he said. 'And a picture of my stepdaughter.'

DiMatteo got behind his desk. 'Right, right. We'll get to that. Let me just call up the right screen. There we go. They said at the front that your daughter went missing last night?'

'My stepdaughter. Yes, she was in the city to see a concert.'

'Is that something she does often?'

'No, this was the first time.'

'And you're sure she's not just off somewhere you can't reach her?'

'Pretty sure, yeah.'

'Let me get some basic information from you and we'll go from there.'

DiMatteo asked questions and Jack answered them. They were not much different from the ones the police asked, only DiMatteo was able to pull up Marina's records on his own. Jack saw Marina staring out of the monitor in the corner of DiMatteo's screen as he worked. He found himself uncomfortable again, but no amount of changing positions could help.

'It says here that Marina is a minor,' DiMatteo said.

'Yes. She's seventeen.'

'She had permission from you to cross the border? What about her mother?'

'Her mother is passed. I'm all she has. Just her and her sister.'

'Do you know there's a traveler's advisory warning Americans against cross-border travel. Especially at night. There's a serious safety problem in Nuevo Laredo at night.'

Jack felt his face get hot. 'We come into the city a lot. My girls have family here. We've never had a problem before.'

'Well, you have a problem now.'

'I know that.'

'You said you've been to the police. May I see the report they filed?'

Jack turned it over. 'They said they'd get right on it.'

'They would say that. Chances are good they put it on a pile and forgot about it the minute you walked out the door.'

'What do you mean?'

'I mean they're overloaded with cases related to drug crimes. Something like this hardly rates at all. It's a good thing you came to us because we can file a direct petition with law enforcement for priority status. If they know someone's watching, they work a little harder. Listen: how well do you know this girl your stepdaughter was with?'

'She's her cousin,' Jack said. 'They do all kinds of stuff together.'

'Including going out for a night on the town?'

'No, that's new. But they've gone on shopping trips, day trips, and things like that. I'm telling you, there's never been a problem.'

'Mr Searle, Nuevo Laredo is like every other border town in Mexico: there's nowhere truly safe.'

'She was going to a *concert*, for Christ's sake. There were going to be cops around and plenty of people.'

DiMatteo was silent a moment before he said, 'I understand what you're going through. I don't want to make this any worse than it already is. I'm just trying to explain what we're dealing with here.'

'What are you saying exactly?'

'I'm saying that something may have happened and it could have happened despite there being police around and despite there being people everywhere. I'm going to go make copies of this report and then I'll be back.'

'I have her picture here, and a picture of her cousin.'

'I'll make copies of those, too. Just wait here.'

DiMatteo left him. Jack listened to the hum of work coming from other offices, the faint snatches of a radio tuned to an American station, the sudden upraised voice of someone calling to someone else. He felt exposed in his little chair. He wanted to get up and walk around, but there was nowhere to go.

Finally DiMatteo returned. He gave Jack the pictures and the police report. The copies went on top of a stack beside the man's computer. 'Okay,' he said.

'What are you going to do?' Jack asked.

'The first thing we're going to do is send this information

to the State Department so that action can be taken. In the meanwhile, you're going to go home and wait for your stepdaughter to either call you on the phone or show up.'

'You said you could contact the police and tell them to give this higher priority,' Jack said.

'That'll happen in about a day. I can't do anything without permission from higher up. But rest assured that we *are* going to get on it and we *will* pressure the Mexican authorities for results. That's assuming the problem doesn't just resolve itself.'

'I know my stepdaughter,' Jack said. 'She wouldn't just go off on her own.'

'She's a teenager, Mr Searle. Sometimes teenagers do things we can't even begin to understand. I have a teenaged niece and she gets away with things I never could at her age.'

'Marina knows better.'

'Look, I'm not telling you not to worry. I'm a parent myself and if this were one of my kids I would be going out my mind. You're doing the right things, though. I wish I could move faster, but everything takes time. Here's my card. If you have questions that you forgot to ask, call me. Even if you just want to get an update, call me. I want to find Marina as much as you do.'

Jack looked at the card DiMatteo held out to him. It had the State Department seal on it, glossy and embossed. He took it. 'I am going to call,' he said. 'Every day if I have to.'

'I'll show you out.'

DiMatteo led him away from the office and out through the maze of hallways to the lobby, where the armed guard still stood watch. Jack thought that US Marines were supposed to guard American diplomats, but the man had no uniform. His face was stone, but the woman at the desk looked sorrowful and tried to smile for Jack when he looked at her.

'You'll call the police tomorrow?' Jack asked DiMatteo.

'Tomorrow,' DiMatteo said.

'I'll be on the phone with you first thing in the morning.'

'Whenever you want to talk to me is fine. Just… try to keep your chin up.'

'Keep my chin up,' Jack repeated.

'Yeah.'

'Goodbye, Mr DiMatteo.'

'Goodbye.'

SIX

GONZALO WAS JUST FINISHING A SANDWICH he bought from the little vendor on the corner when he saw Jack again. The man filled the doorway at the front of the station, momentarily blocking out the sun from outside, his features blotted out in shadow, and then he was in the common area with papers in his hands, concern written deeply on his face. Gonzalo went to him. 'Sr Searle. Welcome back. Come to my desk.'

They took only a few steps before Jack Searle shoved two color printouts at Gonzalo. 'I got the pictures you wanted,' he said. 'Here.'

'This is good. Excellent. Please come and sit down. If you're thirsty there's a soft drink machine in the back you can use. Or there's water.'

'I don't need anything.'

Jack sat down in front of Gonzalo's desk and Gonzalo took his seat. He looked at the pictures. The girls were young and pretty. He could see them turning heads. 'Which one is which, please?' he asked.

'That's my stepdaughter. The other is her cousin.'

'I take it Sr Sigala is at home now?'

'Yes. He's calling all his daughter's friends, just like you said he should.'

'That's good. And you? Have you tried calling your

daughter's friends?'

He saw Jack hesitate and a haze of darkness pass over his expression. 'I don't know them,' Jack said. 'There's a list, but...'

Gonzalo spoke quickly: 'It's all right. Soon they will call you, won't they? All it takes is one looking for your stepdaughter and you can contact them all.'

'Maybe.'

'Did you go to the consulate?'

'I did.'

'What did they say?'

'They said you have better things to do than tracking down missing girls,' Jack said, and he looked squarely at Gonzalo then.

Now it was Gonzalo's turn to hesitate. He was not angry, but he knew it would sound that way to Jack's ears. Gonzalo took a breath and let it go. 'I am not surprised that they would say this,' he said at last.

'Is it true?'

'No, it's not true. And even if it might be true of some officers, it is not true of me.'

'Have you looked for missing people before?'

'I have. It doesn't make me proud to say this, but kidnapping is not unknown in our city, though most of the time it isn't something so serious.'

Jack nodded. 'The man at the consulate told me Nuevo Laredo isn't safe for Americans. I guess that means it's not safe for anybody.'

'There's some truth to that. But we are not just a city of violence, Sr Searle. If we were, would you have allowed your stepdaughter to come here alone? Would you cross the border yourself?'

'No.'

'They want to make you feel guilty for what's happened,' Gonzalo said, 'but it's not your fault. Our city is a beautiful one full of wonderful people. Yes, there is crime, but that is why we are here.'

'What will you do now?' Jack asked.

'I will make copies of these photographs and distribute them to all of our officers on patrol. While you were gone I distributed a description of your stepdaughter's vehicle and her license plate number to both municipal and federal police officers in the city. Everyone is on the lookout for her now. These pictures will help.'

'If you don't mind, I'd like to wait while you do that,' Jack said.

'Whatever you like.'

Gonzalo left Jack and went back to the copying machines. He ran off thirty duplicates and left a pair on Amando Armas' desk. The rest he took to the duty officer with instructions to issue them to all policemen headed out of the building. Twice he looked back to see Jack Searle waiting in his seat, one knee bobbing quickly in time with his thoughts.

When he was done he came back to the desk. 'It's done,' he said. 'Here are your originals in case you need them again.'

'How long will it take everyone to get their pictures?'

'Officers are in and out of the station throughout the shift. By tomorrow morning we should have full coverage. You don't have to worry.'

'I just want to know someone's doing something.'

'I understand. Do *you* understand that this is all we can do for now?'

Jack dropped his eyes and nodded. His knee was still bouncing.

'Let me buy you a cola. It's no bother.'

Jack said nothing and Gonzalo went to the machine to buy two small bottles of soda. They were already sweating by the time Gonzalo returned. He offered one to Jack and the man took it without enthusiasm.

'What else did the consulate tell you?' Gonzalo asked.

'That I should go home and wait.'

'That's good advice. You've done everything you can for now.'

'I'm not real good at sitting on my hands.'

'No, I don't expect you are. May I ask what you do for a living, Sr Searle?'

'I'm a contractor. Remodeling. Building.'

'And before that?'

'I was in the service. United States Marines.'

Gonzalo took a long drag from his cola, let it wash down cold and fizzy. 'We have a great deal of experience with the military in this city. You may not have noticed, but they are everywhere. Like you, they don't like to be kept on the sidelines.'

'One of my girls is missing.'

'And we'll find her. The question is whether you will worry yourself to death before then. Go home, *señor*. You are in good hands with me.'

Jack slowly unfolded himself from his chair. Gonzalo stood with him and offered his hand to shake. Jack Searle's grip was firm, but Gonzalo could also feel his reluctance. 'I'm counting on you,' Jack said.

'I will not let you down.'

'Okay.'

Jack turned away. Gonzalo watched him go.

SEVEN

ON THE DRIVE TO BERNARDO'S, JACK willed his phone to ring and Marina to be on the other end. It was all a huge mistake, she would say. She went to a friend's house, someone Bernardo didn't know, and she accidentally left her phone in the car where she couldn't hear it ring. Apologies would come and Marina would turn up at her Uncle Bernardo's house embarrassed and chastened. There would be tears of relief and Jack would be so thankful that the thought of punishing Marina would never even come to mind.

But his phone did not ring and Marina's car was not parked on the street in front of her uncle's. Jack discovered the front door slightly ajar and came into the front room to find the television silent and Bernardo sitting on the couch alone, simply staring at the blank screen. He looked up at Jack and the bleakness had not gone from his eyes. 'We called everyone,' he said. 'She is not there.'

'I talked with the consulate and I talked with the police,' Jack said. 'We've done everything we can do. Now we have to wait for them to do their jobs.'

Lidia emerged from the back hallway with Leandra in tow. The little girl held her naked baby doll close to her body, as if protecting it. Her expression was not as bleak as her father's; what Jack saw there was confusion infused with sadness. He imagined this was what she saw in him.

'How are you?' Jack asked Lidia. He could think of nothing else to say.

'I kept calling,' Lidia said, 'but now my battery's dead. What if she tries to call me back?'

'We'll charge you in the truck. Where's your aunt?'

'In the kitchen.'

'Bernardo, I'll be right back. Reina needs to know what's going on.'

'I told her already.'

'Then I'll tell her again.'

Bernardo made a vague gesture with his hands, as if giving Jack dispensation, then looked again to the darkened television.

'Are we going soon?' Lidia asked Jack.

'In a little bit.'

'I'm going to sit in the truck with my phone.'

'You'll need the keys. Here. Don't drive off.'

The joke went flat. Lidia did not smile. She touched Leandra on the head briefly and headed for the front door without her cousin. The child gave Jack that look again. He could scarcely bear to look at her.

Reina sat at the kitchen table where they had so recently eaten. Little Bernardo was with her, drinking chocolate milk with a straw and keeping vigil by his mother. For her part, Reina looked deflated, more worn than she had been at the start of the day. Jack imagined her husband telling her the news and with every word pressing her down a little farther. He did not want to do that.

'Do you want something to drink?' Reina asked him.

'What? No, I'm fine.'

'Sit down. You have to be tired.'

Jack did not feel tired, but he sat anyway, close enough that Reina was able to take his hand and hold it more tightly than her thin, work-worn fingers seemed capable of. She was the kind of woman who would hold on for the sake of the little ones and only let go when she was completely alone. Bernardo was near to broken already. If both of them went, there would be nothing left.

He told her where he had been and what he had done there. Reina nodded slowly, her expression no lighter. 'Bernardo thinks...' She glanced at Bernardino before she went on. 'Bernardo thinks something terrible has happened to them. He doesn't say so, but I know he's thinking it because I am thinking it.'

'You both have to stop.'

'Why?'

'Because it does no good. I would rather believe that it's something we don't understand yet. They got lost or they got distracted or something stupid that teenagers do. I want them to laugh at all of us when they get back. When they get back.'

Reina squeezed Jack's hand again. She did not have soft fingers. They were toughened by work like Jack's. Marina's aunt was tough on the inside, too, because it was not enough in Mexico to persevere without inner strength. This was how the family was held together, how it was happy, how it prospered. 'If you believe it, then I will believe it, too,' she said. 'When I make dinner tonight, I set aside Patricia's portion. She has to be hungry and I will make her favorite.'

'That's good,' Jack said. 'That's real good.'

'What will you do? Will you stay with us?'

'I'm going to go home. It makes sense for us to cover both places just in case. Wherever they might go, we should be there.'

'Can I make you something to take with you? It won't take long.'

'No, that's all right. Lidia and I will get something on the way.' Jack slipped his hand from Reina's and stood up from the table. She seemed tiny when he looked down on her.

Bernardo hadn't moved from where he sat before. Jack stood between him and the television and only then was the spell broken. Bernardo lifted his eyes slowly. 'Everything is done?' he asked.

'You call me the second you hear anything,' Jack said. 'I'll do the same on my end.'

'I will call you,' Bernardo agreed without energy.

Leandra still waited in the back hallway, her doll clutched to her in an unbreakable embrace. '*Adiós, Tío Jack*,' she said suddenly.

'I'll see you soon,' Jack told her, and then he left.

EIGHT

THEY RETURNED HOME WITHOUT speaking to each other and Jack did not even turn on the radio to breach the silence. Lidia held her phone in her lap, a black wire curling from it to the dashboard lighter, and Jack's, too. She only gave his back when they were in their driveway. Wordlessly they parted. Lidia let herself in the front door with her own key and vanished into her room.

Jack took the list of Marina's friends from the refrigerator and sat down to call them. With each call he had to tell the story again and by the sixth repetition he was tired of hearing his own voice. No one had anything to tell him.

He thought about beer. The call was strong and the moment was right. He lingered in the front room for a few long minutes before going to the kitchen.

The first beer he polished off standing in front of the open refrigerator. The second followed quickly on that. He paused before he brought out the cardboard bottle-holder, four beers still nestled in its pockets, but finally carried it out through the back door onto the tiny patio with the folding lounge chair.

It was evening, but the sun was still high enough that somewhere near by someone was mowing their lawn. Jack cracked open his third beer and wasted no time finishing that one, too. The next three he would pace, he decided, while in a little place in the back of his mind a voice said they should go back into the refrigerator and be left for another day.

'It's not going to kill me,' Jack said to the voice.

He brought out his phone and dialed Marina's number. It rang and rang and then he heard her voice saying, 'This is Marina. Leave me a message. Bye.'

'It's me again,' Jack said. 'Me and Lidia are home now, so if you want to meet us there, you can. I know you have a lot of messages, but I hope you're getting this one. Listen, you probably... you probably think everybody's mad at you, but we're not. We just want to make sure you're somewhere safe with people you can trust. So just call from wherever you are. It doesn't matter if it's late, all right? Just call and let somebody know you're all right. Can you do that for me? Okay, I'm gonna go now. Call back.'

Jack closed the phone and it did not ring. He stared at it a long time, just sitting in his palm with the hour on its postage-stamp-sized display, until the phone went to sleep and the miniature window went dark.

Another beer. This one he took his time with, sipping instead of gulping, savoring the coolness in his hand and the chill of the liquid on his tongue and in his throat. These were the sensations that made drinking so agreeable, so easy. Being drunk was something teenagers and barely grown adults strove for, but not Jack. He believed in the journey, the steps toward the chasm. On the way he could forget the things he wanted to forget, long before they could be blotted out. He was a master of the craft and he had practiced it when Vilma was sick. When Vilma was gone.

He put the empty bottle on the concrete by the lounge chair and it painted a dark circle around itself. There was a pleasant warmth in his belly that asked for more fuel, but he held off.

Better now to concentrate on something else, like the sound of the lawnmower going round and round on some stranger's lawn, a faraway sputter that was absorbing, distracting, all-encompassing. Jack was thinking about nothing now. This was where he wanted to be.

NINE

GONZALO HEARD NOTHING ABOUT the missing girls from the patrol units during the rest of his shift and he left after midnight for home. Streetlights glowed here and there where they were not broken or burned out, and the roads were deserted. His only driving companions were the army vehicles that crisscrossed his path, slowly trundling down empty streets. Once he saw a truck from the Policía Federal doing a long circuit through a cheerless neighborhood, but that was all. He never saw a municipal policeman.

His apartment was a small one in an L-shaped building, the front doors facing a courtyard taken up primarily by a swimming pool that was not maintained. The basin of the pool was half-full, the water a deep shade of green. Time and the elements had loosened tiles on the sides and many had fallen to the bottom out of sight. The manager of the building sometimes claimed the landlord was going to pay for renovations but it had been four years since Gonzalo moved in and there was no change. He did not know how long things had been like this before he came.

He came inside and did not turn on a light, as enough filtered through the blinds to see by. A short couch and a chair bisected the main room of the apartment with holes in the upholstery. Gonzalo owned an old television that he watched only for *fútbol* games and it stood like an inkblot against the front window. The back half of the room was a kitchen with vinyl flooring, a little refrigerator and a stove with just two burners. A tiny cabinet opened up over the single-basin sink where a few unwashed dishes lay waiting.

The apartment door had three locks and a chain. Gonzalo set them all. Anyone who really wanted in could probably kick the door loose, but it was a comforting ritual to turn the bolts. Iron bars protected the windows in front and back.

In the bedroom Gonzalo left his weapon on the bed stand. In the darkness he took off his clothes and put his jacket up on a hanger on the closet door. He went to the bathroom where there was only a sink, a toilet and a shower stall crammed against each other and brushed his teeth. By now his eyes were used to the dark.

Wearing only his undershorts and a white T-shirt, he crawled into his unmade bed. He set his alarm for late in the morning and, without thinking another thought about his day, went to sleep.

Sunday-morning light tickled his face before his alarm could wake him. The room was bright despite the closed blinds, exposing four white walls with nothing on them. Once he had a framed picture of Jesus hanging over the bed, but the wire had broken and the whole thing fell on his head while he was sleeping. The picture was behind the door now, waiting for him to take it to a framing shop, but he had never remembered to do it.

He dressed. Putting his weapon in its holster made him feel ready for anything, though he knew it was being careful and not his pistol that kept him safe. It was for the Federal Police and the army to carry the big guns, and they were the ones who carried the water in battles with the cartels. The Municipal Police existed to clean up the messes, to work around the edges, to be the low men on the totem pole. Gonzalo knew he and his fellow officers were considered little more than ticket-takers and traffic guides, but when he stood in front of a mirror with his gun he still felt the tingling reminder of being a freshly graduated policeman ready for his first assignment. Nothing could change that for him.

He still had an hour before he was due at the station, but he left the apartment and got on the road anyway. He ticked over the things he must do when he reached the station, the leftover tasks from the last shift that still needed his attention. He thought about Jack and his stepdaughter. Maybe there would be good news for him to share.

A traffic snarl caught him up along the way, a fender-bender that blocked an intersection. By the time he was clear all his extra time was gone and he had to hurry just to make it to the station to check in. Armas was already at his desk sorting through the last shift's reports. He raised a hand in greeting.

There was nothing in his basket about the girls. Gonzalo tried not to be disappointed. After a while he would call the uncle and see whether either girl had reappeared. He was willing to bet that they had. Most of these cases cleared themselves. It was much worry and gnashing of teeth over some little thing.

Gonzalo engrossed himself in paperwork and before he thought to check the time over an hour had passed. He found his copy of the missing-persons report, rose from his desk and went to the duty sergeant in his office. Sergeant Ahumada was a veteran officer, almost completely gray, and his belly strained at his uniform shirt. He was mostly found sitting or eating and here he was doing both, consuming a sandwich while thumbing through the thin white pages of a faxed report. 'Gonzalo,' he said.

'*Sargento*, I wanted to ask if there was any word on those girls. You remember them? Two girls who went missing? I put their pictures out and we're supposed to be watching for a car with Texas license plates.'

The sergeant grunted. 'Sure, sure. I put the vehicle report on your desk.'

'What? When?'

'A couple of hours ago when I came on. You didn't see it?'

'There's nothing on my desk about that.'

'Goddamn it, I know I put it there for you.' Sergeant Ahumada left his office and pointed toward a desk that belonged to Pepito Barriga. 'It's right over there.'

'Pepito doesn't even work on the weekends!' Gonzalo exclaimed.

'What can I do?'

'You could have *said* something!'

Gonzalo found the paper on Pepito's desk, a short note in Sergeant Ahumada's scrawl. *Vehicle found: white Mitsubishi Galant, Texas plates YRM-273. Impounded.*

He came back to the sergeant. 'It says the car was impounded. Where was it?'

'I don't know. You'll have to ask the officer who called it in.'

'It doesn't say who called it in.'

'Do I have to do everything for you? They'll have all the details at the impound yard.'

Gonzalo hurried back to his desk and searched out the number for the impound yard. The line was busy. He called three times more and each time it stayed busy. '¡*Mierda!*' he said.

'Trouble?' Armas called from his chair.

'I can't get through. Listen: will you cover for me? There's something I have to check out.'

'How long will you be gone?'

'I don't know. A couple of hours maybe? It's important.'

'You'll owe me.'

'Thanks, Amando.'

Official vehicles were for policemen on patrol or assigned to traffic duty. Gonzalo took his car instead and made the drive across town with the midday sun baking down. His air conditioner didn't work and even with all the windows open he sweated freely. The impound lot was a large square of long grass and bare dirt enclosed by a tall chain-link fence casually draped with barbed wire. The vehicles inside were arranged more or less in rows, though they meandered. Some had been there long enough to start rusting and probably as many didn't run as did.

Gonzalo stopped at the open gate where a cubical guardhouse splashed with white paint stood sentinel. A gaping window with shutters pointed outward, the inside of the building in shadows. After a moment one black shape moved against another and then a man appeared at the window. He wore a blue work shirt stained with perspiration and a badge was pinned to his breast, but he was not a policeman. The man was a *segurata*, a rent-a-cop.

'Inspector Gonzalo Soler, Municipal Police,' Gonzalo told the man. 'I tried to call, but the phone is busy.'

'The phone is broken,' the man said.

'How does anyone contact the yard?'

'They don't.'

'It doesn't matter. I'm here to see a vehicle that was brought in this morning.'

'Come in and we'll find it for you.'

The man's truck was parked in an empty space beside the guardhouse and Gonzalo slotted in beside him. When he got out he saw the man had fetched a cap with his security company's logo on it and come out into the glare. He had a clipboard thick with papers, a pen attached to it by a piece of string.

'It's a white Mitsubishi Galant,' Gonzalo told the man. 'Texas plates.'

'Oh, yes, I remember that one. They had to put it way in the back.'

They walked together along the rows, kicking through the grass and stirring up grasshoppers. The impound yard could have been a junk pile, with all the cars destined for the crusher. Some would end up that way for sure, while others would be auctioned off. Gonzalo's car was an impounded vehicle whose owner never claimed it. He paid less than 7,000 pesos for it.

'Down here.'

Gonzalo saw the trunk of the car first, peeking out from behind the bed of a truck on a high suspension. His pace quickened and he left the man behind.

If he had expected something dramatic, he was disappointed. The windows were not broken, which might have told him it was a theft. A quick once around the vehicle revealed no bullet scars and no evidence of a crash. Both front doors were unlocked. Gonzalo opened the passenger side and was hit with a fresh wave of stifling heat. He stepped back to let the worst of it fade.

'Do you want the paperwork for this car?' the man asked Gonzalo.

'Yes.'

Gonzalo took a yellow sheet from the rent-a-cop and looked it over. He recognized the name of the street where the car was found, but could think of no landmarks near it. The officer who discovered the vehicle was named Suazo, and he had first seen it parked illegally on Saturday and then again that morning, the citation still under its windshield wiper. Suazo called for a tow and impounded the car.

The invisible fire from inside the Galant had faded and now Gonzalo stooped to look in. There was no visible blood, no sign of a struggle. A CD dangled from the rear-view mirror, reflecting a rainbow onto the dash. The car smelled vaguely of cinnamon air freshener.

'What do you see?' the rent-a-cop asked Gonzalo.

'Nothing,' Gonzalo said. 'Excuse me.'

He used his cell phone to call Armas and arranged for a forensic unit to visit the impound yard to take prints from the car. 'Is it a crime scene?' Armas asked.

'I don't know.'

'The commander won't like you wasting the time for nothing.'

'Then don't tell him. I just want to be sure of some things.'

'Like what?'

'I can't say, but it's very strange. Can you go to my desk? There's a file open there. I wrote down the name and address of the venue where the girls saw their concert. Give it to me.'

He waited while Armas searched and wrote the information down in a little notebook that fit in his pocket. 'I'm going to be covering for you a while longer, I guess,' Armas said.

'Not too long. Do you mind?'

'No, it's all right. Take all the time in the world.'

'Don't be an asshole, it doesn't suit you.'

'Hurry back, all right?'

'As soon as I can, I promise.'

Gonzalo put his phone away and turned to the rent-a-cop. He scribbled his number in the notebook and tore off the page. 'Soon a team of officers will be here to examine this vehicle. You will show them where to find it and tell them how to contact me?'

'Where are you going?'

'To continue my investigation.'

'Oh, okay. There has been a crime?'

'When I find out you will be the first to know.'

TEN

THE PLACE WHERE THE CONCERT WAS held was an old dance hall with indoor and outdoor stages. It looked run-down in the daylight, but at night it was probably much more impressive, with neon lights framing the façade and illuminating the name of the place: the Town & Country.

Only one vehicle was parked in the big front lot, a pick-up truck glossy with wax and painted jet-black. Gonzalo pulled up beside it. He checked his watch. The place wouldn't open for hours.

All the glass in the building's windows had been painted black on the inside and the front door was solid metal. Gonzalo pounded on the door for a while, but no one came. Back at the car he brought out a map of the city from the glove box and spread it on the hot trunk. He searched for the street on the impound report and found it only a few blocks away.

The door of the dance hall swung open and a woman emerged. 'Why are you banging? What do you want?'

'Police,' Gonzalo said. He held up his identification for her to see as he crossed the lot. 'I'm conducting an investigation.'

The woman waited until Gonzalo was close and examined his credentials carefully. She was young, maybe twenty-five, but she carried extra weight and she had an unpleasant face that made her seem older. 'What investigation?' she asked.

'A missing-persons case.'

'How do I know you're really a policeman?'

'I just showed you my identification, didn't I?'

'You could have bought them.'

'If you think that, then there's nothing else for us to talk about, is there?'

The woman hesitated. 'Come in,' she said.

The interior of the place was shockingly dark after the brightness of the parking lot. Gonzalo blinked away the light until he could see tables and booths and the bar. A large dance floor spread out from a central stage at the far wall. A mirror ball hung from the ceiling over the wooden space. He was led toward the bar.

'Are you the owner here?'

'Me? Oh, no. I'm just one of the managers.'

The woman came around the end of the bar and faced Gonzalo. He took a seat on a leather stool. His notebook went on the bar-top, which was protected by a layer of clear plastic that had smudges and scratches that could not be wiped away. 'Were you here Friday night?' he asked.

'I was.'

'Was it busy?'

'Very. Friday nights are always busy.'

'I want to show you some pictures. Just tell me if you recognize either of these girls.' Gonzalo brought out the pictures of Marina and Patricia. He put them in front of the woman. 'Take your time.'

She shook her head. 'I don't know them.'

'They were here to see live music.'

'Lots of people were here, I told you. Maybe one of the bartenders would know. Or you could ask the people we have working security.'

'How many are they?'

'Three. Do you want their names?'

'Please.'

'Armando Cosme, Víctor Almazán and Fernando Simón. They all come from the same security company. They work the live shows.'

Gonzalo wrote quickly. He looked at the woman. 'Do you have the number of the security company?'

'I can get it.'

'Please do.'

He waited while the woman vanished into an office at the far end of the bar. Gonzalo wondered whether the forensic team had reached the impounded car yet, but he wouldn't know until someone contacted him. The damned phone at the yard. Who was in charge that let things like that happen? It was useless to spend even a second thinking about such things; there was nothing to be done.

Eventually the woman returned with the number written on a yellow Post-it note. She gave it to Gonzalo and the sticky strip clung to his fingertips. 'I don't know if there will be anyone there today. It's Sunday.'

'It's still useful. Thank you for your help.'

'What happened to those girls? Were they murdered?'

'No, they weren't murdered,' Gonzalo said. 'We don't know what happened.'

'So you don't know they weren't murdered.'

Gonzalo put the pictures away and palmed his notebook. 'It's nothing for you to worry about,' he said. 'I'll see myself out.'

Sun stabbed his eyes as he left the dance hall and he wished for shade. His map was still unfolded on the trunk of his car and after checking it once more he gathered it up and put it away. Behind the wheel he called the number the woman had given him. The phone at the other end rang a few times and a machine answered. Gonzalo left his name and his number.

He left the lot and navigated his way to the street where the girl's car had been found. There were few numbers on the buildings here and Gonzalo drove up and down the blocks searching for the right spot. He discovered it almost by accident: a stretch of road faced by the long wall of a machine shop of some kind. There was plenty of space to legally park, but a short section of the curb was painted in chipped yellow before a rusted fire hydrant.

The block was quiet except for the scattered laughter of little children. Gonzalo got out of the car. The neighborhood seemed to be mostly businesses—an auto mechanic here, a paint company there—but there were apartments, as well, and the children played in the courtyard in front of one building. Gonzalo brought out the map again and looked at it three ways, plotting the courses that would take them back to Sector Centro and, beyond, to the Sigala household.

'What were you doing here?' Gonzalo said aloud.

His phone rang. The number was unrecognized. When he answered, a man's rough voice came down the line. 'My name is Víctor Almazán. This is Inspector Soler? You called my office.'

'Yes, Sr Almazán. Thank you for calling me back so quickly.'

'I check my messages every couple of hours. What do the police need with me?'

'You work private security at a place called the Town & Country?'

'Sometimes. Did they say something about me?'

'No, it's nothing like that. Listen: I'm looking for two girls that may have been at the concert Friday night. I have pictures I'd like to show you and the other men who worked then.

When can I see you?'

'I can meet you at my office in an hour. I'll try to get my crew together to be there.'

Gonzalo took down the address and they finished their call. Driving to Almazán's office took twenty minutes and brought him to a small building with a parking lot the size of a postcard. He called Armas at the station.

'Where are you now?' Armas asked.

'Meeting with some hired muscle that worked the concert. Have you heard from the forensic team? Are they at the car?'

'They checked in. You didn't say what you wanted exactly so they're going over the whole car. It's going to take some time. If something comes up, they'll have to leave the job unfinished.'

'They'll do it. I'm feeling lucky.'

'Where do you think those girls are?'

'I don't know. But I will.'

'Commander Peláez called looking for you. I told him you had a hot lead on an important case. I hope I wasn't lying.'

'You don't have to worry about it.'

'Keep in touch, all right?'

'Talk to you soon, Amando.'

He put his phone away and sat, slowly baking in the rising heat. The roof of his car was like a hot plate. The wall of the office building, a frosty light green, reflected the sun directly into Gonzalo's face, striking off the dash and blinding him. Finally he had to take off his jacket or be roasted.

Almazán arrived almost exactly on the hour, driving an SUV painted a glittering silver. When he got out, Gonzalo saw that he was an immense man, heavy through the neck and chest, and his two companions were much the same. One of them had extensive tattoos up both arms, starting at the wrist and crawling into the sleeves of his T-shirt. All of them had the same close-cut, nearly shaved heads.

'Let's go up to my office,' Almazán told Gonzalo.

The office itself turned out to be tiny: just a single room with a desk and a chair and a telephone. Almazán looked like a giant behind the desk and the other two crowded Gonzalo in. The one with the tattoos was Armando Cosme, the other Fernando Simón. They had flat, unaffected faces.

'You want to know about Friday night?' Almazán asked Gonzalo.

'Yes. I want all three of you to look at these pictures and tell me if you recognize either of these girls. We know they were at the concert, but I'd like more information.'

Each man took a turn inspecting the pictures, passing them around the small office. Almazán turned on an oscillating fan in the corner behind the desk and it stirred the warm air around just a little. Gonzalo was acutely aware of the space, the way the big men blocked the door and that he had told no one he was headed here.

'I don't know them,' Almazán said.

'I do,' said Simón.

Gonzalo took out his notebook. 'Which one did you see?' he asked.

'Both of them. I remember they were up close near the stage, yelling at the musicians. They were drinking a lot. I thought about moving them out, but the band didn't seem to mind. Cute girls. You know how it is.'

'Were they talking to anyone besides the band?'

'I think they were with some friends.'

'Did you see the girls leave? Were they with anyone? A member of the band, maybe?'

'No, I remember they went out together and their friends stayed a little while.'

'About what time was that?'

'I don't know. Midnight, maybe? It's hard to remember.'

'It's all right. This is very good. Thank you.'

Almazán spoke up. 'If something bad happened to those girls, my crew wasn't involved. We were there until three o'clock. All of us.'

'You're not suspected of anything.'

'I just wanted you to know. We don't break the law.'

'I appreciate that,' Gonzalo said.

'Are we done?'

'We're done.'

Gonzalo let them lead him outside again and he waited until they drove away before he got in his car and left. He checked his watch. He could make it back to the impound yard before the forensic team was done with the car.

ELEVEN

THAT MONDAY JACK TRIED MARINA'S number again, but now the phone did not even ring before it went to voicemail. Either the battery was dead or it had been switched off. Jack felt it like a blow.

It was past noon when Bernardo called. 'I heard from the police,' he said. 'They found Marina's car. How soon can you get here? We can see it right away.'

'I'm already gone,' Jack said.

Lidia was in her room in front of her computer. Jack hurried her into her shoes and out the door for the trip across the border. Everything seemed to take too long, every delay was forever. He was practically out of his truck before it stopped rolling in front of Bernardo's house.

'I have the address of the place where they're keeping the car,' Bernardo told him. 'The inspector will meet us there.'

They went out together. Jack paused long enough to see the rest of the family arranged together in front of the house, expectant and watching. He waved to Lidia and drove away.

He followed Bernardo's directions, driving to a part of the city he had never visited before. They parked outside the gates and Jack saw the policeman, Gonzalo Soler, waiting for them with a man who looked like a nightwatchman. Hands were shaken. Jack was led.

The car was so deeply buried in the yard that Jack began to

entertain the thought that they had the wrong vehicle or that it would not be there when they arrived, whisked away magically back to Laredo where he would find it in his driveway and Marina at home with it. When he saw it he felt something shrivel in his chest.

'This is your stepdaughter's car?' Gonzalo asked.

'Yes.'

'It was brought here yesterday. I wanted to wait until our technicians were finished with it before I called. You can take it if you want. The impound fee has been waived.'

'Was there... was there violence?' Bernardo asked.

'Not that we can tell from the car itself. The car is unlocked. Look inside and see if you can find anything out of place.'

Jack opened the driver's side door. There was black dust on the frame and all over the surfaces inside the car, fingerprints looking like dirty smudges. He looked in the front seat and the back seat and under the seats themselves for any sign of Marina, but there was nothing. 'I'm sorry,' Jack said.

'I had hoped for a purse or some personal item that would indicate your stepdaughter left the car against her will,' Gonzalo said. 'You can see for yourself that there isn't anything to find.'

'Do you have something?' Jack asked.

'We know a few things: that your stepdaughter and her cousin were at the concert just as they said they would be, that they left around midnight... and that they had been drinking.'

'Marina is only seventeen,' Jack said.

'If she didn't buy the drinks for herself, her cousin could have bought them for her. A witness says they were loud and drunk and they went out alone.'

'Patricia called me that night,' Bernardo said. 'If it was midnight, she might have been calling for a ride home. She was a responsible girl and wouldn't let Marina drive drunk.'

'That's a possibility,' Gonzalo said.

Bernardo covered his face with his hands. 'I didn't take the call!'

Jack looked away before Bernardo cried. He heard Gonzalo trying to placate Bernardo, but his attention was back on the car. After he put the seat back, he got in and put his hands on the steering wheel. Black dust coated the palms of his hands and the rubber burned him. Despite the heat, he didn't get out.

It was a brilliant afternoon, but Jack tried to imagine it was dark. He did not know where the car was found, but he tried to visualize the street. Where was she going? Why had she stopped? Her hands had been where his hands were now. If he concentrated, he could feel her in his place.

A shadow fell over Jack. It was Gonzalo. 'Do you know of any friends your stepdaughter may have had in Mexico? Besides her cousin, I mean.'

'No, she didn't know anyone. We didn't spend a lot of time here. Just visits to family once a month.'

Jack levered himself out of the car. Bernardo stood near the trunk, his face dark. Gonzalo went back to him. 'Did you know that your daughter had been arrested, Sr Sigala?' he asked.

'What? Arrested? When?'

'A year ago she was arrested for shoplifting at a store in El Centro. She was released after booking, but her fingerprints are in the system. We're going to use them to compare with the fingerprints in the vehicle to confirm that she was in the car.'

'What about Marina's fingerprints?' Jack asked.

'We don't have a record of those. And it will take a few days for my request to go through. As you can imagine, our forensic teams are quite busy. Do you have your stepdaughter's prints somewhere? I understand that in America parents sometimes have their children fingerprinted in case they are lost or need to be identified.'

'That's for little kids,' Jack said. 'Marina's grown.'

'I only ask because it would assist my investigation.'

'I'm sorry I can't help you.'

'*Está bien*. You've been a help already, Sr Searle.'

Jack looked to Bernardo. 'I've got a spare key for the car. Can you bring it back to your place? I won't leave it there for too long. I just want to get it out of here.'

Bernardo nodded without speaking. Jack peeled the right key off his ring and handed it over.

'May I speak with you a moment alone, *señor*?' Gonzalo asked Jack.

'Of course.'

They walked a short way into a stand of tall grass. Jack saw Bernardo get into the car and start the engine. The air conditioner would be blowing hard. Marina always liked the air conditioner on full blast.

'I know you must be disappointed,' Gonzalo said.

'I won't lie and say I'm not.'

'I want you to know, and I hope you can explain this to your *cuñado*, that considering how little time has passed, we are making excellent progress. I can trace your stepdaughter's movements up to a certain time and a certain place and it won't be long before I know more. We have local patrols that pass through the area and I haven't yet spoken to the Federal Police about their agents. Someone will have seen them. Nuevo Laredo is not so big a city.'

'How long until we know more?' Jack asked.

'That's impossible to say. It could be tomorrow, it could be a week from now.'

'The longer they're missing, the more likely something bad has happened to them,' Jack said.

'Not necessarily. I haven't given up hope that there is a reasonable explanation for this.'

'Oh, come on! You found the car abandoned! Why would they leave the car somewhere in the middle of the night? The engine's working, there's gas in the tank.'

Gonzalo looked solemn. 'I understand your frustration.'

'Do you?'

'Perhaps I can help you to understand. This is a city at war with itself. The Municipal Police, the Federal Police, the army… we are all just players in the larger scheme of things. We have the Zetas and the Golfos to contend with and things happen in this city that are terrible beyond description. But that does not mean there is no chance of success. It means only that we must address our problems with patience and determination. But mostly patience.'

'But—'

'Please, Sr Searle, let me finish. In just two days we have learned a great deal. When the fingerprint report comes back from our forensic technicians we will know still more.'

'Just promise me you'll keep me in the loop.'

'I will promise you,' Gonzalo said. 'Everything is on the table with regard to this investigation. If I have to, I will pull in one of my colleagues to help chase down leads. You can trust me.'

Gonzalo offered Jack his hand and Jack shook it, though his palms were sweating and dirty. He spared a glance toward Bernardo and the car. Bernardo was hunched over the wheel, but at least he was not weeping.

'If there's anything more I can do,' Jack said, 'you just ask. Anything at all. There's nothing more important to me than this.'

'Take your stepdaughter's car. Console your brother-in-law. Stay by the phone.'

'All right.'

TWELVE

IN THE END IT TOOK MOST OF A WEEK FOR the forensics team to render up results. Gonzalo found them in a folder on his desk when he arrived for his shift, a sticky note affixed to the front saying FOR YOU, as if it were a box of chocolates.

He did not look into the folder right away, but cleared his desk of other pending items before turning to it. There was little to expect: a confirmation that Patricia Sigala was in the car, but not much else. The case would not hinge on the finger-prints lifted from the car.

Gonzalo would have rather gotten some lead elsewhere. A telephone call would have helped, or a new witness, but these things had dried up quickly. He spent time tracking down both bands that had played on the night in question, quizzing them about the girls, but the best he had been able to come up with was what he already knew: they were drunk and noisy and trying their best to come on to the performers, but in the end they left of their own accord. It occurred to Gonzalo that one or more of them might be covering up having sexual relations with a minor, but their story dovetailed neatly with that of the security crew. There was nothing to it.

Though it gave him no pleasure to do it, Gonzalo called Bernardo Sigala every day. He hoped for some news that would make the search moot, but it did not come. Four days into the investigation Gonzalo was drawn into a double homicide at a fast-food restaurant and he was derailed completely. It forced him to put a positive light on the stone wall that faced him. Still, he could not tell Bernardo that there was no movement on the case. The man sounded fragile on the phone and Gonzalo knew the wrong word would break him.

The fingerprints would give him some good news to report. Gonzalo opened the folder and perused the first page. Patricia Sigala's prints matched those found on the passenger side of the car, the dashboard and the armrest. On the second page were a variety of unidentifiable fingerprints, but these were pulled from the steering wheel and other places the driver would touch. These were Marina Cobos's.

There was a third page. Gonzalo turned to it. More sets of identifiable prints, including those of a municipal tow-truck driver and other impound personnel. These last were lifted from the roof and the doorframe on the driver's side. Gonzalo scanned down to the name: Eliseo Guadalupe. The report even provided a photograph. It showed a man in a police uniform.

Gonzalo dropped the folder on the desk and reached for the phone. He misdialed the first time, but got it right on the second try. Eduardo Telles answered the call. 'It's Gonzalo,' Gonzalo told him. 'I have your fingerprint report on my desk.'

'Which one?'

'The missing girls.'

'Oh, okay. Is there something wrong?'

'You pulled a set of prints from the car matching a local policeman. How did you identify them?'

'We have one of those new computers from the States. The whole system's being computerized now, thanks to those American grants. Government employees were the first ones input for testing purposes. You say it was a cop? I don't remember.'

'Eliseo Guadalupe. I don't know him.'

'His name doesn't ring any bells for me, either.'

'Listen, can you run the prints again, just to be sure?'

'I can, but if the computer made a match then you can be sure it was accurate. These new machines are terrific.'

'Pull his print card and double-check them by hand,' Gonzalo said.

'That will take a while.'

'How long?'

'Tomorrow?'

'How about this afternoon? We have two girls who've been gone for a week. The longer we wait, the more trouble they could be in. Put a rush on it for me.'

Telles paused. 'I have a lot of work here, Gonzalo.'

'For me. Please. A favor.'

'All right. For you. I'll call you by five. Or is that not soon enough for you?'

'It will do. Don't forget, Lalo!'

'I won't.'

Gonzalo hung up the phone and examined the report again. A generic diagram of a four-door car was used to illustrate the vehicle and the exact spot Guadalupe's fingerprints were taken from was circled in red pen. Clearly on the outside of the car and right on the doorframe. A perfect thumb and forefinger. Even a machine could not mistake them for anyone else's prints, Gonzalo knew, but he wanted to be certain.

Gonzalo keyed up Eliseo Guadalupe's records. Guadalupe was thirty-seven years old, a fifteen-year veteran of the Municipal Police. He had been decorated once for distinguished service, but his career rise had stalled out long ago and he remained exactly where he was: behind the wheel of a patrol vehicle. When Gonzalo searched for disciplinary actions or other black marks, he found three, all for suspicion of receiving bribes. There was no indication of what had followed from the accusations, but he was still on the force, so assumptions could be made. Guadalupe had once shown promise, but after the charges he had settled into a life without exceptionalism.

His partner's name was Darío Fregoso. This Fregoso had no distinctions on his record, but he had only five years to his service. Gonzalo printed off color pictures of Guadalupe and Fregoso so he would recognize them when he saw them. He pinned them together with a paperclip.

Armas was at his desk. 'Amando,' Gonzalo told him, 'have you ever heard of a uniformed officer named Guadalupe?'

'Guadalupe? Maybe.'

Gonzalo showed him the picture.

'Oh, yeah, sure, I know him. He works out of a substation, but I've run into him a couple of times.'

'What's he like?'

'I don't know. Likable enough. Seems to know his job. Why do you ask?'

'I can't say. His name came up in connection to one of my cases. Do you think Ahumada might know him?'

'It's worth asking. Sergeant Ahumada knows everybody.'

Gonzalo sought out Ahumada in his office. The man was reading a newspaper, a stack of unattended reports waiting for his attention. He barely glanced up when Gonzalo came in. 'What do you want?' he asked.

'Eliseo Guadalupe. He's a uniform who works out of—'

'I know where he works out of. He's not my problem.'

'What do you mean?'

'I mean if he's done something wrong I don't want to hear

about it. Take it up with his boss.'

Gonzalo came closer. Ahumada glared at him over the top of his newspaper, then folded it with a frustrated sound. 'Does Guadalupe get in trouble a lot?' Gonzalo asked.

'Are you asking if he is as sparkling white as you are? Because the answer is no. He's like every other uniform in this city: he gets by.'

'He's taking?'

'I didn't say that. Why would I say something like that?'

'You just said—'

'I said he gets by. You don't remember what it was like to wear the uniform, so you can pass judgment all you want. It's hard out there for a cop. Caught between the PF and the army. You can't even breathe without someone jerking your leash.'

'I work with the PF all the time.'

'But it's different for you. You wear a jacket and a tie.'

'Look, if this is some kind of complaint about inspectors and uniform cops not getting along, I'll tell you about a dozen uniformed officers who are glad to work with me.'

Ahumada unfolded his paper and made a show of shaking it out. 'In that case, I guess I don't know what I'm talking about.'

'Damn it, I came here to find out something about one of our officers and you're twisting it up!'

'If you want to find out about Eliseo Guadalupe, I'm not the person to ask.'

'Then I'll ask the *right* person.'

'You do that.'

Gonzalo turned sharply and left the office. He felt a pain in his ear and realized he was gritting his back teeth. The fingerprint report was clutched in his hands.

THIRTEEN

HE WATCHED DARÍO FREGOSO DIRECTING traffic from the curb where he had parked for half an hour. It was a busy intersection and Fregoso was good at keeping the cars flowing. Gonzalo could not remember the last time he'd blown a police whistle, let alone signaled cars and trucks on their way.

From time to time Gonzalo let his eye flick over toward Guadalupe's vehicle, a white pick-up truck with POLICÍA MUNICIPAL emblazoned on the side. The shadowy figure of Guadalupe sat inside doing nothing. With the late afternoon heat and the sun, Gonzalo knew which officer had the easier time of it.

Gonzalo's phone rang. 'Soler,' he said.

'Gonzalo, it's Lalo.'

Gonzalo sat up straighter. 'What do you have for me?'

'I pulled Guadalupe's card and did a side-by-side comparison with the prints taken from that abandoned vehicle. It's a match. I told you the computer is never wrong about these things.'

'You're absolutely certain?'

'What did I just say? I checked it myself.'

'Thanks a lot, Lalo. You're a true friend.'

'You owe me a favor now.'

'Consider it owed. I have to go.'

Gonzalo hung up on Telles. His hand strayed to the folder

with the fingerprint report inside, sitting in the empty passenger seat of his car. He debated taking it with him, but finally left it, getting out into the full glare of the day. The sun blazed at a precise angle to blind as Gonzalo approached the intersection on foot. He waited until Fregoso paused oncoming traffic before he left the sidewalk.

'*Señor, señor*! Get out of the street!' Fregoso called to him.

'I'm a police officer,' Gonzalo said and he held up his identification.

Fregoso was distracted and two overloaded trucks almost collided with each other. The man blew hard on his whistle and gestured sharply to the drivers. The snarl cleared.

Gonzalo came up to the truck and Guadalupe. 'You're disrupting traffic,' Guadalupe told Gonzalo.

'Do you have a couple of minutes?' Gonzalo asked.

'Can it wait?'

'Not really. I'm working on a case where time is of the essence.'

Guadalupe regarded him. They were not so far apart in age, but the uniformed officer looked older, his hair heavily streaked with gray. He got out of the truck. 'What brings an inspector out to see me today?' he asked.

Gonzalo produced pictures of Patricia Sigala and Marina Cobos. 'Have you seen these two girls before?'

Guadalupe examined the photos. Gonzalo watched his face, but there was no moment of recognition. 'I've never seen them,' Guadalupe said. 'Why?'

'Last Friday night you were patrolling the neighborhood near the Town & Country? You know the place?'

'Sure, I know it. We patrol by there all the time. Get a lot of calls, too. Drunken patrons and fights. That kind of thing.'

'You were on patrol all that night,' Gonzalo said. 'I spoke to your duty sergeant. I wonder if you saw a white car with Texas plates.'

'Should I have?'

'It was found abandoned in your area. The driver was this girl. This girl was the passenger. The driver was American.'

'Was she? I definitely would have remembered that.'

Gonzalo looked at Guadalupe's face, but still he saw nothing. The man stared back at him with a blank expression, waiting for Gonzalo to say more, not willing to fill the space with needless words of his own. Suddenly Gonzalo regretted not bringing out the fingerprint report. *These belong to you,* he would say. *How do you explain that?*

'Did something happen to those girls?' Guadalupe asked.

'We don't know,' Gonzalo replied. 'They are missing.'

'Missing? That's no good.'

'No. The parents are worried and the American consulate is involved. I'm under a lot of pressure to get results.'

There was a sudden blare of horns and the screech of rubber. Gonzalo looked and saw a car and a truck nearly nose to nose, directed against each other by Fregoso. The young officer ran over to them and waved them off, shouting and blowing his whistle.

'I hope you find them,' Guadalupe said, 'but I think my partner needs some help.'

'Of course. But before you go: are you *sure* you've never seen either of these girls? They are nineteen and seventeen. They were in a car with Texas plates. That has to be unusual for that time of night in that area.'

Gonzalo held up the pictures again, but Guadalupe barely glanced at them. 'I'm sure of it,' he said. 'Now if you don't mind?'

'We're done,' Gonzalo said.

Guadalupe went, blowing his own whistle and bringing all traffic to a halt. Fregoso struggled to get the opposing vehicles out of each other's way. Gonzalo stood and watched them work, waving and signaling, while he held the pictures of Patricia and Marina in his hands.

When it was safe, he crossed the street and walked the distance to his car. Behind the wheel he saw the intersection smooth itself out, the to-ing and fro-ing of cars and trucks under the guidance of Guadalupe. Fregoso did nothing but stand there.

Gonzalo turned the key in the ignition and edged out. He waited until his lane was waved through and raised a hand to both policemen as he passed. They did not return the gesture.

He saw them for a while in his rear-view mirror and then they were swallowed up by traffic.

FOURTEEN

EVERY MORNING JACK PAUSED BY Marina's bedroom and listened for her breathing, but she was never there. The days were counting down toward the school year and Jack insisted that Lidia go out and see friends even if she would rather linger at home. There was no sense in the two of them living the lives of recluses.

She was gone that evening, staying out for dinner. Jack left the house and made his way to the bridge into Nuevo Laredo. The thought occurred to him to call Lidia and tell her he would be gone a while, but he knew she would only want to come along and for this trip he wanted to go alone.

He found the police station as he had left it: strangely quiet and virtually deserted. Jack remembered reading something about a shortage of police in Nuevo Laredo because of threats of violence, and he supposed this had something to do with it. For a city under siege, it was almost sleepy here. But that was the problem: it was too easy to forget what was happening, and forgetting was what brought him to this.

Gonzalo was not at his desk when Jack arrived, but a uniformed officer promised he would not be gone long. 'He's on a call,' the policeman explained. 'But it's not serious.'

'No one died?' Jack asked.

'No, no one,' the policeman said quickly. 'It is nothing.'

It was over an hour before Gonzalo entered by the front

door, his face decorated with sweat. He spotted Jack before Jack could even stand up and approached with a look of caution. 'Sr Searle?' he said. 'What are you doing here?'

'I came to ask how things were going,' Jack said, and he sounded lame to himself. 'You know… just to see.'

'Come with me and sit down.'

They went back to the familiar desk and chairs and Jack saw Gonzalo put aside a green folder with care, as if it were fragile. The man took off his jacket. His pits were deeply stained with perspiration. His gun was exposed. 'I understand you're busy,' Jack said.

'It's no problem. But you could have called. There's no need for you to trouble yourself with the crossing.'

'I wanted to come.'

'You are always welcome, of course. Can I get you anything, Sr Searle?'

'I'm fine. And you can call me Jack. There's no need to call me *señor*.'

'All right. Then you must call me Gonzalo.'

'Gonzalo.'

'Yes. Jack, I'm afraid there's not much I can tell you today that I haven't told your brother-in-law already. I have some promising leads, but they are still developing. You may have come all this way for nothing.'

Jack breathed. A moment before he'd felt something clutching at him, threatening to squeeze his chest, and he'd shaken it off. From time to time in the night he'd felt it, too, waking him from unpleasant dreams and sitting on his heart in the darkness. Sometimes there was the threat of tears, but he had not cried yet and he would not. This much he'd promised himself.

'You do understand, don't you, Jack?'

'I understand. You told me before: police work is slow.'

'Very slow. I wish that were not the case.'

'It's just… I feel like I ought to be doing *something*. It's not right for me to sit around waiting for a call.'

He felt a surge of something like anger that he knew would lead to no good. His hands closed tightly in his lap, and then opened again slowly.

Finally Gonzalo spoke. 'Jack, have you had something to eat? I skipped lunch and I could use some food.'

'I could eat,' Jack said.

Gonzalo rose from his desk and put his jacket back on. 'Then let's go to a place I know.'

Jack allowed himself to be led away and out the front of the station onto the street, where an eddy of dry, hot wind picked up grit from the roadway and blew it in his face. 'I'll drive,' he said.

They went to Jack's truck. Gonzalo was not a small man, but he seemed so climbing into the big cab. He sighed when the air conditioning came on. 'You saved my life,' he said, and turned the vents toward himself.

Gonzalo gave directions as Jack drove. They passed a Burger King and a McDonald's built right next to each other, indistinguishable from the franchises on the Texas side of the border except for the promotional signage in the windows, which was all in Spanish. The closer to the river one went, the more alike the two cities seemed until they were abruptly divided by 300 feet of concrete-reinforced riverbed and a tall metal fence filled with rust.

'You said you have leads,' Jack said after a while. 'What kind of leads?'

'I can't really talk about such things,' Gonzalo said. 'Nothing specific, anyway.'

'Who would I tell?'

'This is true.'

'Then you can talk about it,' Jack said. 'I'll keep your secrets.'

Gonzalo was quiet for a few minutes except to point out a turn that brought them down a broad street littered on both sides by shops and restaurants and all the normal, ordinary things that a city should have. There was no violence here, nor the promise of violence, and there were not even any police or army vehicles anywhere to be seen. Jack did not understand Nuevo Laredo, and maybe he never had.

'I've interviewed a number of witnesses,' Gonzalo said. 'All of them tell me the same things: that your stepdaughter and her cousin were drinking, that they came to the concert with friends but left alone. I've found not one person to dispute that timeline.'

'But?'

'It's here. Pull in here.'

Jack turned off into the parking lot of a small restaurant called La Pequeña Cocina, the Little Kitchen. A few other cars were already there and the truck bulled up between them like their big brother, casting a long shadow in the early evening light. He killed the engine and they got out. The day was still hot, though it had mellowed somewhat from earlier.

Inside the restaurant there were oscillating fans on tall stands in the corners of a big dining area. Someone had attached tinsel to the fans so they streamed out like cartoon waves of cool. The whole place smelled richly of chilies and cooking meat.

Gonzalo led them to a booth. The laminated menus were pinned against the wall by bottles of hot sauce. They each took one. Though he was not really hungry, the smells of the place stirred something in Jack's stomach and it growled.

'Their *pescado a la veracruzana* is excellent,' Gonzalo said. 'I have it every time I come here. But don't let me decide for you.'

A little old woman emerged from the back and brought them glasses of iced water with slices of lemon in them. Gonzalo greeted her warmly and the old woman leaned in so he could kiss her on both cheeks. Jack merely smiled and nodded his head.

In the end Jack ordered *albóndigas* soup, which came with tortillas for sopping up the broth. Gonzalo had his fish in a cast-iron vessel, the rich odor of tomatoes spilling up from it.

'You were going to tell me more about what's happening,' Jack said.

'I hoped you would forget about that,' Gonzalo said. 'The food was supposed to be a distraction.'

'It worked. I'm full.'

Gonzalo drained his glass. 'Then I suppose I will tell you,' he said.

'What is it?'

'The problem I'm having with your stepdaughter's case is that no one saw her after she left the concert. Or if someone did, they have not come forward. And why would they? People in this city have learned how to mind their own business.'

'Has somebody said something?'

'No,' Gonzalo said.

Jack wanted to pound the table. 'What kind of a secret is that?'

'It is possible that there was someone who saw your stepdaughter on the night who has not come forward. Someone we can identify through evidence taken from the car. I can't tell you who, but what I can say is that I've spoken with this person and I have my concerns. The things they told me and the things I know do not match.'

'Well, then, what comes next?' Jack asked. He was leaning forward now and the table creaked.

'Now I do police work. I told you when all this began that some of us take our jobs very seriously. When there's something that doesn't fit, we investigate until it does.'

'This person did something to Marina, didn't he?' Jack asked, and he felt breathless again, as if there was not enough air in their booth for both of them.

'It's too early for us to know such things.'

'When *will* you know?'

'Soon, Jack. Very soon.'

FIFTEEN

LIDIA WAS WAITING FOR HIM WHEN HE CAME home. 'Where have you been?' she asked.

'I had some people to meet,' Jack said simply. He did not want to share the details of his visit with Gonzalo, not now, and he knew she would get it from him if he wasn't careful.

'I was worried. You should tell me next time,' Lidia said, and Jack became aware of the way she was looking at him, the intensity in her face and the way she held her body. She thought he was lost and it frightened her. He never should have gone without warning her first, even if it was to tell some lie.

'Come here,' Jack said, and he put his arms out for her. She came to him and he held her closely. Lidia wrapped herself around his waist and squeezed as tightly as she could, her face in his chest, but she did not cry. Jack was proud of her for that. 'I was just gone a little while. I promise I won't do it again.'

When they parted, Lidia seemed tired, as if the waiting had depleted her and now she was left with nothing. 'What are you going to do now?' she asked.

'I'm going to hop in the shower. Maybe we can watch some TV?'

'Sure.'

Lidia went to the family room and Jack headed for his bedroom. He closed the door and stripped down and walked to the bathroom to shower. On his skin was the blowing dust of Nuevo Laredo and the stickiness of the ever-present sweat. It was good to get under the spray.

He had not gotten from Gonzalo what he wanted, but it had to be enough. Gonzalo counseled patience and he was patient. It was only that his patience did not last forever. He wanted to wrap his hands around this thing and squeeze it until Marina popped out. The police in Nuevo Laredo would never allow him to do that.

The shower suddenly sputtered and then a deluge of uncontrolled spray blasted Jack in the face. There was the ringing sound of metal hitting the floor of the stall. Jack fumbled blindly for the knob to cut the water. The flow snapped off sharply and Jack stood dripping, blinking water from his eyes.

He examined the showerhead. The plastic face was cracked wide open. It had probably been wearing away for some time like a ticking bomb. Jack pounded the wall of the stall and cursed.

Tomorrow he would go to the store and buy a new head. He toweled off roughly and in the bedroom he put on fresh jeans and a white undershirt that had a hole in one sleeve.

They watched a television show about funny videos off the internet and then some sitcoms Jack didn't follow, but Lidia seemed to know. She even laughed once or twice and Jack was glad.

After a long time, she said, 'Jack.'

'Yeah?'

'How long will it be before they stop looking for her?'

'Not for a long time. They just got started.'

'But they have so many other things to do over there. I read online today that there's a shooting every day. Do you know how many soldiers and police they have there?'

'No, I don't.'

'It's a lot. They say it's not as bad as some places, but the cartels are killing cops. The police won't pay attention to Marina forever.'

'The guy on the case is a good man, and he's not going to let this go. And I won't, either.'

'How do you know you can trust him? I read that the local police over there are always taking bribes from the cartels. Nobody can trust anybody.'

'I trust him,' Jack said. 'That's all I can tell you. He's trustworthy. Maybe there are others over there who take money on the side from the drug dealers or whatever, but he's one of the good guys.'

Lidia was welling up now. 'I miss her,' she said, and her voice was thick.

'I miss her, too. We all miss her: Uncle Bernardo and Aunt Reina, the kids. But we're gonna make it through this to the other side. As long as you stick it out, I'll stick it out, but I need you to keep it together. For Marina.'

Lidia covered her mouth and nodded. The tears were going away now, tamped down fiercely, not allowed to take over. 'Okay,' she managed to say.

'Why don't we just call it a night? Some sleep always helps.'

'All right.'

SIXTEEN

GONZALO HAD A DAY OFF, SO HE SLEPT late. There was a replay of a *fútbol* match from months ago on the television and he watched it with one eye on the clock. When it was time he would be ready.

Afternoon crept in, the day hot against the windows of Gonzalo's apartment, and then cooling into the evening hours. He dressed and put on his weapon. Again he checked the clock. Almost there.

He got out of the apartment and on the road. The station house out of which Eliseo Guadalupe and Darío Fregoso worked was much smaller than Gonzalo's, more like a frontier outpost at the edge of a bad part of the city, a place where gangs were deeply rooted among the poor who were fortunate enough to work and the even poorer who somehow managed to cling on. Only a few vehicles operated out of this station despite the relatively large size of their patrol area. Army and Federal Police helped fill some of the gap, but a person could go a long time without a sign of the authorities.

Getting Guadalupe's schedule had been easy. Gonzalo called the station and represented himself as a commander from another area gathering information for a report to the *federales*. The duty sergeant gave Gonzalo all of the information he asked for, including the names and schedules of officers he didn't care about at all. Guadalupe would never hear a thing about it.

He almost missed Guadalupe when he emerged from the station house because he had already changed into civilian clothes. It was Fregoso who stood out more because he was so slender and wiry, like a bendable toy. The two men walked together to the small lot that adjoined the station and got into the same car with Guadalupe behind the wheel.

They navigated through evening traffic. Gonzalo was sure to keep at least four cars between them.

Finally they reached a squat apartment building and Guadalupe sidled up to the curb. Gonzalo consulted his notebook. Fregoso got out of the car. This was his place.

If he could have, Gonzalo would have followed them both, but it was Guadalupe who interested him. Guadalupe was the senior one, and senior officers always took the lead. Fregoso was a follower; Gonzalo could see it in the way he moved. Yes, Guadalupe was the one to watch.

Fregoso waved from the sidewalk as Guadalupe pulled away and he was already through the front door of the building by the time Gonzalo passed. They were headed north now, trending to the west. Gonzalo had Guadalupe's address and this was not the way. He went on, careful in his distance, as they crossed El Centro.

The shadows were long and the streetlights were on before Gonzalo saw where Guadalupe was going. He saw the painted wall of cinder blocks and the sides of the road already crowded with cars. Visible over the upper lip of the nearest wall was a strip of flashing neon. La Zona. Somewhere inside its walls, Iris Contreras was working on her back. There was no time to think of that now.

Guadalupe parked half a kilometer from the entrance to La Zona and Gonzalo had to be quick to find a spot for himself before Guadalupe was down the street and out of sight. He jogged to catch up and found Guadalupe at an intersection waiting to cross. The man looked both ways, but not back.

They crossed Monterrey Street at almost the same time, half a block from each other. Guadalupe reached the open gate first and left-handed inside, forcing Gonzalo to run again.

Music blared from open doors and multicolored lights blinked and beckoned. Gonzalo dismissed them all and focused on Guadalupe as the man picked his way down a dirt and gravel street called Lucrecia Borgia toward the western-most reaches of La Zona. Guadalupe did not slow to look into open doorways where scantily clad women beckoned and he shrugged off the attentions of talkers looking to lure in a new customer. One man reached out and grabbed Gonzalo by the elbow, directing him toward the entrance to a strip joint and brothel called La Cosa. Gonzalo disengaged himself and located Guadalupe again, still moving.

They went farther and Guadalupe vanished. For one moment he was there and then the street where he had been was empty. Gonzalo hurried forward, looking in open doors. He nearly missed Guadalupe, swathed in the dim interior of a club's bar area. Gonzalo saw him only for a second, and then he was gone again.

The club was called El Pájaro and it boasted a brilliant neon sign of a colorful bird, its animated wings flapping. Behind a clear plastic sheet were small posters and photographs of women in go-go dancer costumes, all faded from the sun. There was something about them that Gonzalo could not place.

A thickset man guarded the door. He wore a leatherette fanny pack that looked strangely awkward under the shelf of his expanding belly. When Gonzalo tried to pass him, the man put out an arm. 'One hundred pesos,' he said.

'Just to get in?' Gonzalo asked.

'I don't make the rules.'

Gonzalo gave the man a two-hundred-peso note and waited while he unzipped the fanny pack and brought out a wad of bills. He carefully peeled off two fifty-peso notes and gave them to Gonzalo. 'Thank you,' Gonzalo said.

'Have fun.'

The inside of El Pájaro was barely lit, but there was enough glow from the purple and green lights to see people moving around. It was impossible to make out faces until Gonzalo was right atop them. He searched the darkness for Guadalupe, hoping to spot a familiar silhouette, but the man was gone.

There was little open space in the place, with many small tables scattered around the floor. Gonzalo made out what looked like the square of a stage with a vertical pole mounted in the center of it, but like everything else it was shrouded in gloom. He bumped a waitress carrying a tray of empty glasses. 'Excuse me,' he said.

'It's all right,' the waitress said. Her voice was pitched low.

Gonzalo skirted tables and people until he was close to one wall. There were booths here. He felt his way, one to the next, hoping he would not stumble across Guadalupe, and then the place was suddenly alight.

Intense bulbs came alive around the stage. Illumination cast off the glittery tinsel backdrop and washed back across the audience, who Gonzalo could see clearly now. The place was only half full of men and women, but they turned their attention forward and in the blaze Gonzalo saw the women were not women at all, but men dressed as ladies.

Everyone knew there were *travestido* bars and brothels in La Zona, but Gonzalo had never visited one. He caught sight of a waitress who looked almost exactly like a woman, maybe the one he'd glimpsed before, but upon a closer look it was clear she was a man, as well. Gonzalo was frozen in place, feeling suddenly and keenly exposed.

Loud dance music abruptly surged from speakers all around the bar area. From beside the stage a transvestite man emerged wearing a go-go dancer's outfit like the ones pictured outside, and began a routine before the assembled crowd. If Gonzalo had not known differently, he would have thought this was another woman, too.

The booth beside him was empty and Gonzalo sat down quickly. His eyes were drawn to the spectacle on the stage even as the music hammered him, but he turned away and scanned the audience instead.

A waitress appeared at his booth without warning. 'Something to drink?' she asked.

'Um, water,' Gonzalo managed to say.

'Something *real* to drink?'

He paused, thinking this man dressed as a woman could see right through him to the badge and the gun beneath his jacket. That she would know everything he was here to do and would shout out his secret. 'A beer,' he said.

'What kind?'

'Any kind.'

The waitress looked annoyed, but she left him and that was all Gonzalo wanted. He realized he was perspiring even though it was cool inside the place. On the stage the dancer was rubbing fake breasts—or were they fake breasts?—on the shiny brass pole. The scene was unsettling, unreal, and once more Gonzalo had difficulty looking away.

He searched along the perimeter of the big room, frustrated by heads turned from him and toward the stage. Guadalupe could be there and Gonzalo might not see him. He looked anyway.

The waitress returned at the same time Gonzalo spotted Guadalupe. The sweating beer went down on a napkin and the waitress leaned in to tell him the price. Gonzalo thrust one of the fifty-peso notes at her and waved away change. He was looking at Guadalupe, ensconced in a corner booth directly adjacent to the stage. Guadalupe was not alone.

Gonzalo did not recognize the second man. He had slicked hair and when he gestured broadly with his beer Gonzalo could see the man had a bright gold watch. The man was talking to Guadalupe over the music, but it was far too loud for Gonzalo to hear anything. When the man with the gold watch turned his head, Gonzalo could see he had a large mole on his cheek.

They stayed together through the dancer's song and when the brightest lights shut down, replaced by a series of rapidly flashing red and yellow bulbs that made the stage area throb, the man with the gold watch waved the dancer over. The dancer, Gonzalo did not know whether to say she or he, came to them and kissed the man with the gold watch on the mouth. Guadalupe got up so the dancer could sit between them.

From their new angle in the booth, Gonzalo could see the man with the gold watch more clearly. He wore a Ralph Lauren shirt with the word LONDON printed across the chest, accompanied by the horse-and-rider seal. The police had a name for shirts like that one: '*Narco* Polo.'

He went on watching them even when the stage brightened again and a new dancer came on. The three spoke animatedly and ordered drink after drink. Gonzalo's beer remained untouched. He wished for a camera to take the man with the gold watch's photo, but there would be no way to get away with that in here, even with the distractions of the light and the music.

A shadow fell over him and then he was crowded into his

booth by a new body. Gonzalo flinched as a man dressed in a wig and skirt and tight top pressed against him. He smelled alcohol when the man spoke. 'Hello. I'm Celia.'

'Hello,' Gonzalo said. 'Look, I'm—'

'You're nervous,' Celia said, and put a hand on his arm. 'I could tell you haven't been here before. You don't need to be afraid. I saw you sitting here alone and thought you could use some company.'

At Guadalupe's table the man with the gold watch was getting up and saying his goodbyes. Gonzalo tried to slip his arm free of Celia's grasp. 'I'm not staying,' he said. 'I'm sorry, but you'll have to talk to someone else.'

'Would you rather go somewhere quiet? There are rooms in back.'

'*No!* I mean, no thank you. You are very nice, but I have to go.'

Celia's grip tightened on his arm. 'Listen, I have to make some money tonight. Are you sure you don't want something?'

The man with the gold watch was making his way across the room toward the exit. Gonzalo fished out his wallet and offered Celia the other fifty-peso note. 'Here's something,' he said. 'Now I have to leave.'

'Fifty pesos? What the hell am I supposed to do with fifty pesos?' Celia exclaimed, and heads turned Gonzalo's way. 'It's a thousand pesos to spend time with me!'

'I don't *have* a thousand pesos! Please, just let me go. I won't come back.'

Gonzalo wrenched his arm free and scooted out of the booth. The man with the gold watch was almost gone.

'You go to hell!' Celia shouted at him. 'You *chingadores* are all alike! Go back to your wife, you coward!'

He did not spare a look back toward Guadalupe in case

the man should see his face and everything would be ruined. Instead he bumbled between tables as Celia yelled after him, making it to the door and freedom before anyone could step in front of him. He bumped the thickset man at the entrance and ignored the man's sound of protest. On the street he looked left and right for the man with the gold watch and saw him going south on Circunvalación Casanova toward Lucrecia Borgia.

The man did not slow or stop all the way back to the entrance to La Zona. At the gates he turned right and walked a hundred meters to a parked Mercedes where a second man was waiting. Gonzalo was trapped between La Zona and the Mercedes, his own car parked well away on the far side. He moved as close to the wall as he could, hoping not to attract attention.

The two men spoke briefly and got into the Mercedes. The headlights went on and the car pulled away from the curb. They passed Gonzalo headed north and he scrambled for his notebook to scratch out their license-plate number. He took off at a run, crossing the road heedless of an oncoming car, and made the distance quickly.

His lungs were burning by the time he was behind his own wheel and his car protested the sudden acceleration and sharp turns that put Gonzalo on the Mercedes' path. La Zona whipped past on his left, but Gonzalo was searching ahead, hoping the man had been slowed by something and was still close enough to catch.

He traveled a kilometer and then another before he slowed. There was no sign of the Mercedes anywhere and the traffic was light enough that they would have free rein on the road. Gonzalo realized he'd been gripping the wheel too tightly and he forced his fingers to relax, his knuckles coloring from white.

'*¡Mierda! ¡Mierda! ¡Mierda!*' Gonzalo cursed out loud and

thumped the dashboard with his hand. 'Who are you?'

For the next hour he traversed the city north of La Zona in slowly widening circles, but he did not spot the Mercedes, the man with the gold watch or the driver. Gonzalo did not expect a miracle, but sometimes a policeman was lucky. Tonight he was not.

He thought briefly about going back to La Zona and picking up Guadalupe's trail again, but by now the man would have finished his business in El Pájaro and gone on home. Certainly Gonzalo could not show his face in the club again without running afoul of Celia. The man at the door would probably throw him out without questions.

Finally he turned toward home and let the slow strobe of passing streetlights lull him into a state of quietude. When he pulled into the lot of his apartment building and parked the car he sat a while behind the wheel just listening to the engine tick as the metal cooled. No Guadalupe. No man with the gold watch.

Gonzalo opened his notebook and looked at the number he'd written down. Tomorrow he would run it through the computer and get a name. Maybe it would not be the name of the man with the gold watch, but it would be something more than he had now. And even if it all had nothing to do with the missing American girl and her cousin he would know something for sure: Eliseo Guadalupe was friendly with *narcos* and he could not be trusted.

SEVENTEEN

GONZALO SAW THE ARMY TRUCKS AND Humvees collected on the street in front of the station when he drove past, and when he approached the entrance to the building on foot he saw the soldiers with their weapons at rest, milling around or simply standing sentry while smoking cigarettes. The soldiers regarded him with something like open contempt as he drew closer, only parting when he was nearly upon them, and lining the route to the door like a gauntlet.

Inside there were still more soldiers. Filing cabinets stood open and there were uniformed men in every office, some searching and some waiting. He passed the empty counter at the fore of the station and saw a soldier sorting through the papers on his desk. 'Hey!' he said. 'What the hell are you doing?'

The soldier stopped rummaging around and turned his attention to Gonzalo. The man's face had a coolness Gonzalo did not like. 'I am checking your outstanding cases,' he said.

'That has nothing to do with the army! Back away from there!'

The soldier did not move. 'You are relieved of duty.'

'The hell I am! Who's in charge here?'

A nod directed Gonzalo to the duty sergeant's office. An armed man guarded the door while another man sat at the desk among Sergeant Ahumada's paperwork. The guard moved to block Gonzalo's way, but the second man spoke first: 'Let him in.'

'Who the hell are you?' Gonzalo demanded. 'What's going on?'

'I am Captain Ernesto Alvares,' the man said. He stood up from the desk and Gonzalo saw he was not tall, but broadly built through the shoulders like a much bigger man. His uniform was pressed and his gold captain's tri-bars polished. Instead of a crew cut, he styled his hair perfectly short and parted sharply on the left. He had a mustache. 'All of these men are under my command.'

'Why are they in my station?' Gonzalo asked.

'The Municipal Police are hereby suspended,' Alvares said. 'The army has assumed all local law enforcement functions in Nuevo Laredo, as well as twenty-one other municipalities in Tamaulipas. Police personnel are to receive professional training and recertification under a process overseen by the military and the State Police.'

Gonzalo felt his mouth drop open and he consciously closed it. 'But...' he said. 'But *why*?'

'What is your name?' Alvares asked.

'Gonzalo Soler. Inspector.'

'Inspector Soler, you know as well as I do that the Municipal Police is rife with corruption and unprofessional behavior. Don't deny it. Police are taking money from the cartels, turning a blind eye to their activities while the military take the brunt of the violence.'

'That's not true,' Gonzalo said. 'Some police may be on the take, but that's no reason to suspend the entire force! And we've taken our losses, too! How many of us have been killed in the last few years? We're fighting beside you!'

Alvares held up a hand. 'This isn't a time for argument, Inspector Soler. May I call you Gonzalo?'

'You can call me Inspector Soler, thank you very much,' Gonzalo said.

'Very well. I won't stand here and bicker with you about who carries more water in this city. The decision has been made that the police force is enjoined from all duties until further notice.'

'What about *pay*?'

'Pay is also suspended.'

'How the hell am I supposed to pay my bills?'

'That's not my *concern*, Inspector Soler,' Alvares said firmly. 'As of this moment I am more interested in making this transition a swift and easy one.'

'And the first step is to take over the station house like an occupying army?'

'You should calm yourself before you say something you might regret, Inspector.'

Gonzalo stopped himself from sneering. 'What will you do? Suspend me? You've already told me my job is forfeit.'

'For the time being only. The process of professionalization and recertification will begin shortly and the best officers will be returned to duty as quickly as possible. Do you consider yourself among the best officers?'

'What kind of a question is that?'

'A simple one. I don't know you, Inspector. We've only just met.'

Gonzalo pointed out the door toward his desk. 'I have cases. I have *pending cases*. How is some soldier going to handle my workload? This isn't shooting up a plaza full of *narcos*, this is real police work.'

Alvares' eyes were flinty. 'I think you underestimate the quality of our men. We are a special unit of two hundred and fifty men trained specifically in security matters. General Santos, our commanding officer, is a respected figure and takes his new role seriously.'

'How are two hundred and fifty men going to police this city effectively?'

'It will be done.'

'Like hell it will! This is an insult and I will make my voice heard!'

'Would you like me to take your complaint now, or would you prefer to wait until you're called before a board of review?'

'Is that some kind of joke?'

Gonzalo turned to leave, but Alvares brought him up with a word: 'Stop!'

'What do you want?'

'Your weapon. You'll have to turn it in.'

'I'm a police officer!'

'You are effectively a civilian until such time as you have been reinstated, and like any civilian you are not authorized to carry a firearm. You can leave it with me. I'll make sure it is well taken care of.'

Gonzalo looked at Alvares and the officer looked back. Neither turned away and in the end it was Gonzalo who unclipped his holster from inside his waistband and put his weapon on the desk. 'Do you want my badge, as well?'

'No, you can keep that.' Alvares put his hand on the pistol and slid it over to his side of the desk. 'I'm sure you have a second weapon that no one knows about that you can use instead of this one. If so, I would advise you not to leave it somewhere it can be discovered easily because as part of the recertification process your home will be searched.'

'You people are unbelievable,' Gonzalo said.

'We're doing a job, Inspector. Just like you do.'

'Not anymore. Now I'm just an unemployed civilian with

the army breathing down his neck. Do you even understand what you're doing here? You want to get rid of the bad cops so you punish *all* the cops? It's insane.'

'If you have suggestions about how we can better address widespread corruption, there are people you may speak to,' Alvares said. 'But I am not one of those people.'

'No, of course not.'

Alvares picked up Gonzalo's weapon and held it in his hand as if weighing it. Again he was blank as a stone. 'Is there anything else, Inspector Soler? I have a great deal of work to do and the more time we spend talking the longer it will be before my men can take up their duties.'

'I'm finished,' Gonzalo said.

'It was a pleasure meeting you, Inspector. I look forward to working with you in the future.'

Gonzalo left without saying anything in reply. He went to his desk, where the soldier was back at his task of sorting through the files he found there. The man stopped when he saw Gonzalo approaching. Gonzalo pointed. 'This is where the pending cases are kept. These over here are closed cases that have not had their final reports written. Don't confuse the two or you'll be wasting your time. If you want to be sure, just look for the sticky yellow tag; I put one on every case file and remove it when it's closed.'

'Thank you,' the soldier said.

'Have you ever worked as an investigator before?'

'No.'

Gonzalo shook his head. 'Just keep things organized and take lots of notes. Good note-taking can mean the difference between closing a case or not. Don't let your files get messy and be sure everything is together at the end of your shift. You want to be able to get right back to work the next time and every minute you spend spinning your wheels is a minute someone is getting away with a crime.'

The soldier began to sort out the files according to closure. To Gonzalo he looked comical in his uniform, with his slung automatic weapon, doing the work of a plainclothes inspector. The whole thing was farcical. He didn't see a single familiar face. All around there were soldiers and no cops.

'Let me give you my telephone number,' Gonzalo said. He took up a pad of sticky notes and scrawled his name and number on the top page, then fastened the note to the desk. 'If you have questions or you just want advice, you can reach me anytime. It's not like I'll have anything else to do.'

'It won't be long,' the soldier said.

'What do you mean?'

'I mean you won't be suspended for very long. The good policemen will be back at work before you know it, and you obviously give a damn. It's the ones who just walk away that will never come back. I've seen some of those already today.'

Gonzalo wanted to ask the soldier which ones, but the question stalled on his tongue. Instead he asked, 'What's your name?'

'Gervasio.'

'Gervasio what?'

'Gervasio Chaidez.'

'My name is Gonzalo Soler,' Gonzalo said, and he offered the soldier his hand. 'And I mean what I say: if you have any questions at all, you can call me day or night. There are people who depend on you now. I can't help them, but you can.'

The soldier was solemn. 'I just wanted to be in the army,' he said.

'Well, you're one of us now. Get used to it.'

PART THREE

PARTNERS

ONE

JACK HAD A HEADACHE AND LAY DOWN on the bed for a while to make it go away. He slipped away into a dreamless sleep and when he woke he was surprised so much time had passed. There was the half-distant buzz of the television playing in the front room, the sound carrying down the hall through the open bedroom door, and outside the cicadas were making their song.

His phone vibrated on the bed stand and began ringing. It was not Marina's tone. Jack did not recognize the number. He answered. 'Hello?'

'Is this the Searle residence?' asked a man in halting English.

'Yes. Who's this?'

'Is this Jack Searle?'

'Yes, it is,' Jack said. 'Who's calling?'

The speaker shifted into Spanish. 'This is Gonzalo Soler calling. I wasn't sure I had the right number.'

Jack held the phone more tightly. 'Is there something new?'

'Yes and no. I have no new information about your step-daughter. But something has come up and I wanted you to hear it from me first.'

'What's going on?'

'It has been decided that the local police in our city are to be temporarily relieved of our duties. This is true for everyone, from the patrol units to the inspectors. I was not excluded.'

Jack searched for words. Finally he said, 'What?'

'I know this must be difficult for you, but I'm afraid I no longer have any control over your case.'

'How is that possible? Can they even do that?'

Gonzalo sighed and his tone was bitter. 'Apparently there are people who feel the army can do a better job of protecting the city than the Municipal Police. I turned over my caseload to a member of the security team responsible for our area.'

'I have to talk to somebody,' Jack said. 'This isn't right.'

'I agree, but I am only one man and not a very influential person. I registered my complaint. I wasn't listened to.'

'They'll listen to me,' Jack said. 'I went to the consulate. They said they could put pressure on the police to get things done. That hasn't changed.'

'You may find the military is less interested in politics than my superiors were,' Gonzalo said. 'They are very good at rooting out *narcos* and killing them, but this kind of thing… it is not what they do.'

'Where are you?'

'I am at home. I've been informed that's where I should stay until I'm called.'

'Can you meet me at the station?'

'I don't think that would do any good, Jack.'

Jack kept himself from shouting down the line. 'Can you meet me at the station or not?'

'My hands are tied. They have no use for me. If you feel you should make yourself heard then you should go, but I'm not going to be a help to you. My part is done.'

'I thought you cared about this case.'

'I do. I care very much, but they've taken my gun and my

authority. I am just another citizen now. They may not allow me back into the ranks again.'

Jack rose from the bed and paced the room. 'I'm coming down there and somebody's going to listen to me. And if you're not going to help me then you just go on hiding out.'

'Jack, you don't understand. I told them they were making a mistake, but these people do not listen. It's the same all over the state: the army is taking over from the police.'

'How does that make any goddamned sense?' Jack exclaimed, and for the first time he raised his voice.

Gonzalo was quiet. 'Things are very strange in Mexico, my friend.'

'Will you come down to the station with me?' Jack asked.

'That would do more harm than good, I think.'

'So you won't.'

'It's better if you go yourself. Bring your brother-in-law. Show them a united front. I don't suggest that you use my name. All police are under suspicion now. Better to make them think you are acting of your own accord. Ask for a captain named Alvares. He's the one in charge.'

Jack stopped his pacing. 'They really can do this to us, can't they?'

'I think you'll find there's very little the army can't do anymore.'

'I have to go,' Jack said.

'*Buena suerte*, Jack. I hope you find your stepdaughter.'

'I will,' said Jack, and he ended the call.

He gathered up his steel-toed work boots and put them on. When he looked he found Lidia in front of the television, but with her phone in her hands, steadily texting. She heard him coming. 'Who was that?' she asked.

'Get your stuff. We're going across the bridge.'

Lidia put her phone down. 'What's happening?'

'Nothing you need to know about right now. Just get your purse and meet me at the truck.'

'Is something going on with Marina?'

'Yes. No. Look, just do what I tell you to do, all right? For once just do it.'

'Okay, I'm going.'

She went away and left Jack to turn off the television. It went black on an image of some talk-show host hawking someone's book. He went out by the front door and stood in the sun on the little concrete walk, feeling strange, as if everything had suddenly fallen out of focus. He got in the truck and turned the key and was careful not to rev the engine though he desperately wanted to.

Lidia appeared at the front door with her bag over her shoulder and hurried to him. Before she had even put on her seatbelt, Jack was backing out of the driveway into the street. Once he was on the road he pressed the accelerator and the truck's big engine rumbled. He was driving too fast and he knew it. 'Jack—' Lidia said.

'Somebody's going to find your sister,' Jack told her. 'Somebody's going to do that.'

TWO

HE HAD BERNARDO WITH HIM WHEN HE returned to the station house. The army vehicles that had been clustered around the front of the building when Gonzalo arrived for his shift had now been arranged in a double roadblock, forming a wall of steel between the station and the rest of the street. Jack was forced to park half a block away and walk.

Men with rifles stood up on the sidewalk or stared down from the back of pick-up trucks. Their eyes were hidden behind sunglasses and some of them wore black balaclavas despite the desperate heat. One swiveled a mounted machine gun toward Jack and Bernardo as they approached. The motion was casual and the man behind the weapon was unreadable.

Jack held up his passport when he came close. Bernardo brandished his identification card. 'I'm an American citizen,' Jack told them. 'This is my *cuñado*. He is Mexican. We have to get through.'

One soldier broke away from the others and approached. He held his carbine across his chest, the muzzle angling downward, cradled. Jack was glad he was not masked, but the soldier's expression was as flat as a mannequin's. He held out a hand for Jack's passport. 'Give it to me,' he said.

The soldier leafed through the passport. He compared the photograph to Jack once and then again before handing the little blue book back and extending his hand for Bernardo's ID. This, too, he checked twice.

'The police are investigating a case for us,' Jack explained. 'Our girls are missing. We want to talk to someone in charge.'

'Come back another day,' the soldier said. He held up Bernardo's ID between two fingers as if he were about to flick it away. 'Things are busy here. We can talk to you tomorrow.'

Jack pressed. 'I don't think you understand. Our girls have been missing for a while now. Every day counts. We can't wait until tomorrow.'

'I said for you to go now,' the soldier returned, and he shifted the gun in front of his body. He did not point it at Jack, but he could tell the soldier wanted to. If he could see the soldier's eyes, he would know for sure. 'This is a secure area.'

'Listen—'

'Get out of here!' the soldier barked.

Bernardo shrank back and looked as if he were about to turn away. Jack caught him by the shoulder and held him to his spot. 'I want to talk to Captain Alvares,' Jack said. 'He's the one in charge, right? Let me talk to Alvares.'

'Captain Alvares isn't available.'

'You haven't even goddamned asked!'

This time the soldier nearly did raise his weapon and Jack felt a shrinking sensation in his stomach. He did not step away. 'If you don't clear the street I'll arrest you,' the soldier said.

'Arrest me, then,' Jack said. 'Then you have to take me inside.'

The soldier paused, and then called to another soldier, stepping away to confer with him. Jack heard them murmuring, but none of the words. His hands were shaking. He made them into fists.

When the soldier returned, his comrade jogged off toward the entrance of the building. 'You will wait here,' the soldier said.

'I'm not going anywhere.'

A long minute passed and then another. Jack looked at Bernardo and he saw his brother-in-law had paled. He licked his lips over and over again, his gaze roaming over the assembled soldiers and their weapons.

Finally the other soldier emerged. Again he conferred with the first soldier, and then both of them approached Jack. 'Well?' Jack said.

'You may pass. Corporal Govea will take you to Captain Alvares.'

'*Gracias*,' Jack said.

The soldier did not reply.

Corporal Govea signaled for Jack and Bernardo to follow and they trailed him past the cordon of vehicles to the inner circle where no vehicles could go. It occurred to Jack that they were hardened against an attack and he wondered how likely it was that they would be hit right then, directly in front of the station house. A Nuevo Laredo police chief had been shot to death his first day on the job. The cartels were not afraid to fight.

They were led into the building to an office Jack hadn't visited before. Behind the desk was a man who must have been Alvares. He noticed no one wore their names on their uniforms. Like those who wore masks, the rest chose to be anonymous at least that much.

Alvares stood up as they entered. He put out his hand. 'Captain Ernesto Alvares,' he said. 'What are your names, please?'

'Jack Searle. This is Bernardo Sigala.'

'You are an American, Sr Searle?'

'That's right.'

'Are you involved with the police?'

'What? No, I'm just a contractor.'

'And you, Sr Sigala?'

Bernardo shook his head. 'No, no.'

'Then who gave you my name?' Alvares asked.

Jack dodged the question. 'We have a case the police have been working on. Missing persons. My stepdaughter and her cousin vanished over a week ago. I was told you were in charge now. The army, that is.'

'You'll have to forgive me, but this is my unit's first day,' Alvares said. 'We haven't had time to examine ongoing cases.'

'I can tell you what we know, but it's not much,' Jack said.

Alvares made an open-handed gesture. 'Go on.'

Jack told the story from the beginning and Alvares listened. When Jack reached the part where Marina's car was found in the impound, Alvares raised his eyebrows, but said nothing. The tale petered out with the last dregs of information Gonzalo had shared and Jack's account came to a halting stop.

'Who was the inspector working on this case?'

Jack hesitated. 'Gonzalo Soler.'

Alvares nodded briefly. 'I know of Inspector Soler. He seems... very passionate. Is he the one who sent you to me?'

'I came on my own,' Jack said.

'Of course. And you have every reason to be concerned. If it was my daughter, I would feel the same.'

'Then you can help,' Jack said.

'It will take time,' Alvares said, and he steepled his fingers in front of him. 'Our unit is tasked with keeping the peace in the absence of a regular police force and we have been forced to hit the ground running. I can assign someone to this case, but it would not be right away.'

'How long?' Jack asked.

'No more than a week.'

'This can't *wait* a week.'

'Believe me, I wish I could work more quickly, but I can only do so much.'

'Then what about letting Inspector Soler help out? He knows the case already.'

'I'm afraid that is impossible. All members of the Municipal Police are subject to retraining and extensive background checks before they will be allowed to resume work. You must understand, the corruption situation in Tamaulipas is out of control. This municipality is not the only one affected.'

Bernardo spoke for the first time. 'Please, Captain. Something must be done.'

'And something will be done. As soon as I can organize my men.'

'Inspector Soler was helping us,' Bernardo said. 'He is a good policeman.'

Alvares considered them both before putting both hands flat on the blotter in front of him. 'That remains to be seen. Did Inspector Soler ever solicit you for money?'

'No, never,' Jack said.

'Did he suggest that you work through some outside channel to speed the investigation? Did he have a partner who was not a policeman?'

'No. He's clean. He flat-out refused to take any cash from me when I offered it to him,' Jack said.

Again Alvares' eyebrows went up. 'You offered him a bribe?'

Jack stopped. He was aware of Bernardo frozen next to him. 'I didn't know how things operated down here,' Jack said carefully. 'I thought it would help.'

'But you offered a police inspector money.'

'I did. I'm not proud of it.'

Alvares' face turned to stone. 'You'll find that sort of thing is not tolerated by the army.'

'Listen, I'm not in the habit of bribing cops.'

'Just Mexican ones.'

'It wasn't like that!'

'Don't raise your voice to *me*, Sr Searle.'

Jack looked down at his hands. His face was flushed. 'I'm sorry,' he said.

'If you had offered me money I could have had you arrested,' Alvares said. 'Inspector Soler did you a favor by not doing the same. Corruption is killing us, *señor*.'

'I didn't mean it,' Jack said.

'I'd like to believe you.'

'I just want to find our girls,' Jack said. 'That's all.'

Alvares was quiet for a long moment and then his expression softened. 'I want to help you, Sr Searle. If you think I don't care, then you are mistaken. I do care.'

'Then you'll put someone on the case right away?' Bernardo asked.

'I will do what I can, but I make you no promises.'

'Thank you,' Jack said.

'Don't thank me yet, Sr Searle. We are a long way from that. I am not a policeman like Inspector Soler, but I know a difficult case when I hear one. With work and with luck, we will bring your daughters home to you. But you must be patient.'

'That's what he said.'

'What's that?'

'That's what he said. Inspector Soler. What do we do now?' Jack asked Alvares.

'I would like you to file another form with us,' Alvares said. 'It will be something you have done before, but it will make it official that we are handling the case. Then we will consult Inspector Soler's notes and proceed from there. Once I have a man available, that is.'

'If you need us to do something, we're ready to help,' Jack said. 'We're tired of sitting around waiting. We want to do our part.'

Alvares shook his head. 'No, that won't be necessary. This is a military affair now and civilians will only complicate matters. What's more, you are an American citizen. How would it look if something happened to you on my watch? I can't allow that.'

'I don't mind taking risks,' Jack said. 'I do it every time I cross the bridge.'

'No,' Alvares said. 'Inspector Soler was absolutely right to keep you at home with your families. It's not safe to police the streets of this city even with an army at your disposal. You would only be hurt.'

With that, Alvares stood up and Jack and Bernardo stood up, too. The little man shook both of their hands firmly and for the first time he offered them a smile. 'My men are very good at their jobs. At first we have to find our bearings, but once we have done so the city will be safer than ever. It's our promise to you.'

Jack hesitated at the door. 'We were counting on Inspector Soler to get this done and now he's gone. What happens if you go, too?'

'We won't,' Alvares replied. 'Until Nuevo Laredo is free of the *narcos*, we're not going anywhere. Now, please, see the man at the front of the building. He will ensure you have the proper forms.'

Jack left the office reluctantly. A soldier escorted them to the tall wooden counter just inside the entrance where a uniformed policeman usually sat, only now there was a man in camouflaged battle dress, a ballistic vest bulking out his chest and back and making him seem huge. His automatic rifle lay on the counter where it could easily be reached.

Everything was changed.

THREE

BERNARDO SAID NOTHING AS THEY DROVE away from the police station, but Jack could sense from him a great disquiet. Bernardo drummed his thumb against his leg in quick time and after a while his knee began to bob. There was no music.

'What are you thinking?' Jack asked him at last.

'It's all gone wrong. Did you see their weapons? Their trucks? Alvares can say whatever he wants, but they are here to fight *narcos*, not to help the fathers of missing daughters.'

Jack wanted to disagree, but he could not. He had seen the weapons and the armor of the soldiers and though there were many men moving about inside the police station, he saw no one he could point to and say they looked like policemen. Not like Gonzalo. Gonzalo was a real cop, and now he had been pushed aside.

'Alvares is right about one thing: the police in this city are a joke,' Bernardo said. 'They don't stand up to the *narcos* or fight the battles. When you need one they are never there, and when they do come, they always have their hand out.'

Jack drove a little farther. They were stopped at a light that stayed red a long time. 'I want to find out what Gonzalo knows,' he told Bernardo. 'Everything he knows, not just what he told me. He was holding back the last time we talked.'

Bernardo looked at Jack and once again Jack saw the

bleakness in the man's eyes, as if he had put away his hopes right from the start and there was nothing left but world-weariness. 'And if he tells you, what will you do? You are not a policeman, Jack. This isn't a movie. This is Mexico. People die when they say the wrong things, make the wrong moves. You're an Anglo. Everyone will notice you, and if you step outside of the lines you will be punished for it.'

'What do you want me to do, then? Just sit on my ass?' Jack asked sharply.

Bernardo's gaze fell. 'I don't know.'

The light changed. They moved on. At the intersection up ahead, an army truck crossed, briefly holding up traffic. Men were clustered in the bed of the truck, holding onto the raised metal frame, weapons ready.

'I try to believe,' Bernardo said after a long silence.

'Don't start thinking that way,' Jack said.

'I didn't tell you what I was thinking,' Bernardo replied.

'You said enough. I know where that train goes and I'm not hopping on. And you need to get off, too. You have a family at home that's counting on you to stay strong. You start doubting, they'll start doubting, and then where will you be? It's no help to anybody.'

'Then you're sure?' Bernardo asked.

'I'm sure,' Jack said, and he set his teeth against one another. He gripped the steering wheel firmly. 'I'm sure.'

'I won't think about it anymore,' Bernardo said.

They returned to Bernardo's home ahead of the night and Jack came in. Bernardo took Reina aside and spoke to her quietly. Jack could not hear, but he saw the ripple of emotions on Reina's face as Bernardo told the story. He wondered whether he was so easy to read, and whether Alvares had seen such a look of despair on his face when he'd told them Gonzalo was gone and the rest of the police with him.

Reina's expression was stolid when he came to the kitchen. She set Jack to washing rice and soaking beans ahead of the evening meal. Once Lidia came to Jack to find out what had happened, but Jack turned her away. There would be time to discuss such things later.

Bernardo used the computer in Patricia's room and when he came out again he had a printout in his hand. 'Here,' he said to Jack. "This is where Inspector Soler lives.'

There were directions to a part of town Jack didn't know and a little map to go with them. It wouldn't take too long to get there. 'I should go now.'

'Won't you stay for dinner?' Reina asked. 'There's enough for everyone.'

'You'll have to save me a plate,' Jack said. 'I need to see this man right away.'

'But if he is no longer a policeman, what good can he do for you?' Reina asked.

'I won't know until I talk to him. You'll watch Lidia for me?'

'Of course. Will you be back tonight?'

'I shouldn't be gone long at all,' Jack said.

Bernardo touched Jack's arm. 'Be careful, Jack. It will be dark soon.'

'I'm not afraid of the dark.'

FOUR

THE STREETLIGHTS WERE COMING ON here and there by the time Jack reached the address. It had been a while since he'd seen a patrol and as the neighborhood broke down around him Jack felt more and more exposed. He was reminded of what Bernardo had said, and suddenly a big white truck with a big white man behind the wheel seemed very much out of place.

Gonzalo's building was a crumbling dump, indifferently painted. The concrete and metal stairs creaked under his feet. The whole place seemed vaguely unstable, as if long neglect had eaten away at the basic structure of the building and only good intentions were keeping it together. Compared to this, Bernardo's home was a paradise.

Television light flickered against the blinds of the apartment window, but Jack heard no sound. He knocked firmly.

He was aware of unseen movement and then he heard several locks open. The door opened slightly, a chain spanning the gap. Gonzalo peered out at him. 'What are you doing here?'

'I came to talk,' Jack said.

The door closed and there was the click of the chain being unfastened. Gonzalo opened the door wide. Jack saw he was in shorts and a T-shirt. He held a small revolver. 'Come inside,' Gonzalo said.

Jack's impression of the apartment was that it was small and slightly untidy, but it did not reflect the squalor of the grounds or the decay of the building itself. A long crack snaked along one wall from the lower corner to the ceiling, but for the most part it looked no better or worse than any place Jack had kept in the years he was alone.

The television was on, the volume low. Gonzalo shut it off. 'I wasn't expecting guests,' he said. 'I don't have anything to offer you.'

'I'm fine.'

'Please sit down. Move something if you have to.'

Jack cleared some magazines from a chair and settled into it. The arms of the chair were worn and had been patched with cloth that didn't match the upholstery, but the cushions supported him and the chair did not collapse. The couch was likewise worn and both pieces of furniture had the look of something scavenged or bought second- or third-hand. It occurred to Jack that he did not know how much police officers made in Mexico. It could not be much.

Gonzalo sat on the couch. The revolver was somewhere out of sight. 'How did you find me?' he asked.

'The internet,' Jack replied.

'The internet,' Gonzalo repeated. 'You can find anything there.'

'I came because I went and talked to the army like you told me to. I saw Alvares.'

'And what did the captain have to say?'

'He told me he would get right on it once things settled down.'

'Did you believe him?'

'Would you?' Jack asked.

'No. I would not.'

'Now you know why I'm here.'

Gonzalo pulled from his bottle and then held it low, between his knees. He carried a new weight that Jack hadn't seen on him before. Jack saw it mostly in the dark of his eyes, or maybe it was the dimming light that the room's lone lamp weakly pushed away. 'I told you before: I'm of no use to you anymore. I'm not a policeman.'

'I can't do this on my own,' Jack said.

'Is that what you think I'm telling you to do? You can't look for your stepdaughter by yourself, Jack.'

'That's what I'm saying. I can't. I need you.'

'You don't need me. You need Alvares' men.'

'Alvares' men don't give a shit about this case and you know it. You said it yourself.'

Gonzalo shifted on the couch uncomfortably. 'Anything I do now could jeopardize my return to the police force. We are all under suspicion now. If they saw me conspiring with an American behind their backs, it could be all over for me. I need that job.'

'I'll pay you,' Jack said.

'Jack—'

'No, hear me out. I'll pay you out of my own pocket to look into this. You'll be a private investigator. However much you want. A hundred dollars a day. Two hundred dollars a day. I'm not rich, but I can bankroll you for a while. And if you don't find out anything you can still keep the money.'

'Do you think I need money so badly?'

'Don't you? How much do they pay you?'

'As of now they pay me nothing. I am at the mercy of my savings.'

'Then let me help you. I hire guys all the time. Payment for services rendered.'

'You've given this a lot of thought.'

'Some. Enough to know it's the right thing to do.'

'How can you be sure I won't simply take your money and do nothing?'

Jack leaned forward. 'I don't, but you wouldn't do that, would you?'

Gonzalo considered. 'You don't know me, Jack. You may think you do, but you don't.'

'I know you well enough to know you wouldn't take the *mordida* when I offered it. You've got character. That's what I need.'

'You understand that if I agree to do this, I can stop at any time. The army might intervene or I might think it's too dangerous to go on. You have to be prepared for that. Are you?'

'Yes. You know something about Marina and Patricia, don't you?'

'I've seen some things that I don't understand yet.'

'Like what?'

'Now is not the time. We'll meet in a couple of days and I'll tell you what I know.'

'Why not meet tomorrow?'

'Because I need time to decide if I really want to do this. You don't know what you're asking, Jack.'

'I think I do.'

'That's where you and I disagree.'

FIVE

IT WAS WELL AFTER NINE BY THE TIME Jack and Lidia returned home. Jack paused in the front room and turned on the lights. 'I want to talk to you for a little bit,' he told her. 'Why don't you sit down?'

They sat on the couch. Lidia bundled into her end with her arms closed around her chest. 'What is it?' she asked.

'I know you want to know more about what's going on and I'm ready to tell you.'

'You haven't told me *anything*, Jack. I'm not a little kid like Bernardino and Leandra. I can handle it!'

'I know, I know. I just thought as long as I kept a lid on things that meant they were under control. But they're not. Not really.'

Lidia did not blink. 'What's happening?'

'First thing's first: in a couple of days we're headed over the border for a while. You'll stay with your cousins and I'm going to take a room at a hotel somewhere. I don't know how long we're going to be there.'

'But school's starting soon.'

'We'll cross that bridge when we come to it. The thing is, the police aren't gonna be looking for Marina anymore, so it's up to us to pick up where they left off.'

'What do you mean the police aren't going to keep looking? You *said* they would keep looking!'

'I was wrong!' Jack exclaimed. 'The whole goddamned police force got thrown off the job and now they have a bunch of soldiers running around! They say they're gonna look into it, but I know they're not and I can't take it anymore! So I hired a guy.'

'What guy?'

'He's a cop. Or he used to be. He knows the case already and he's willing to help.'

'But why do you have to be there?'

'Because I'm going to go out with him. We'll be working together. Partners. He knows the city better than I do and I've got the drive. Together we have to come up with something.'

Lidia was quiet a while. 'Could you get hurt?' she asked finally.

'I don't want you to worry about that. Okay? We're gonna be safe and we're gonna do this right. The way it should have been done from the beginning. I never should have let them do this without me.'

'You're not a detective, Jack.'

'I know, but… I owe it to Marina to do everything I can and I wasn't doing that before. Now I am. Me and this man, we're going to make it right.'

'I should do something, too,' Lidia said.

'No. I've got enough to worry about without you getting yourself in trouble.'

'So you can go out and play cop and I have to sit at home with the kids?'

'Yes, because you *are* a kid.'

'I'm thirteen!'

'You're a kid!'

'What am I supposed to do if something happens to you, Jack?'

'I already told you, nothing's going to happen to me.'

'But what if something does? People get shot in Nuevo Laredo all the time. Who's going to take care of me then, Jack?'

Jack moved closer to Lidia and held out his arms. For a moment she resisted, but then she allowed herself to be hugged, her arms wrapped inside Jack's. He could feel her heart beating quickly, birdlike. 'I'm going to take care of you,' he said. 'No matter what happens, I'll be here to take care of you. I promised your mother and I haven't broken that promise yet, have I?'

'No.'

'I made a mistake letting Marina go. But I'm going to find her and I'm going to bring her back home and we're going to be a family again.'

'And Patricia?'

'And Patricia. It's gonna work out for everybody. You'll see.'

Lidia pulled away from him, but it was gentle and she allowed Jack to take her hand and squeeze it. 'There's nothing good about this,' she said.

'I know.'

'When Marina gets back, we're never going over the bridge again.'

'If that's what you want, then that's what we'll do.'

'It's what I want. I hate that place.'

'Don't hate the city,' Jack said. 'There are good people there. Your aunt and uncle. Your cousins. Lots of people like them. It's just that there are a lot of scumbags running around that have to be dealt with, that's all.'

'I don't care. I'll go back this time, but I'm not doing it again.'

'Okay,' Jack said.

Lidia got up from the couch and her hand slipped from

his. 'I'm going to go pack a bag,' she said. 'Then I'm going to sleep.'

'All right. I'll see you in the morning.'

'Goodnight, Jack.'

'Goodnight. I love you.'

She vanished from the room and Jack sat a while on the couch alone. When he got up, he turned off the lamp and walked the dark house to his bedroom. For the first time in a long time, he closed the door.

Jack put on the bedside lamp and opened the top drawer of his chest of drawers. He found the gun wrapped up in an old, torn T-shirt, along with an extra magazine. It was matte black except for the burnished wooden grips, a 9mm Browning Hi-Power that was thirty years old. Jack kept it loaded.

He spread the old T-shirt on the bed and sat down with the gun. He ejected the clip and cleared the chamber before working the action once or twice. It still worked smoothly. Jack could not remember the last time he'd fired it.

From the closet he brought out a green duffel bag with his last name and first initial printed on it. He stuffed it with clothes: jeans and shirts and underwear. The Hi-Power and its spare clip nestled in the center of everything where it would not immediately be found. He wondered whether drug-sniffing dogs looked for guns, too.

The duffel bag went by the bedroom door. Jack stripped and put on pajama bottoms and got into bed. He shut off the light and in the darkness he thought of Nuevo Laredo and the streets that beckoned with shadows of their own. He thought of the onrushing night that came upon him when Marina disappeared, and how the dawn seemed as though it might never come.

SIX

'LOOK AT THESE,' BERNARDO SAID. 'I HAD them printed yesterday.'

The flyers were full color and featured the digital pictures of Marina and Patricia under red block letters that read DESAPARECIDAS. Text described the girls and followed this with a short account of where they were last seen. At the very bottom was Bernardo's phone number and email address.

'How many do you have?' Jack asked.

'Two hundred. I'm going to put them all over that neighborhood. You won't be able to avoid them.'

'They're good,' Jack said. 'Real good. Somebody will call.'

Bernardo nodded energetically and took the flyer back. He looked at it with real fire in his eyes and his expression was uplifted, no longer dismal. Reina looked on from the entrance of the kitchen, a dishcloth twisted between her hands. Jack saw hope.

'I should have done this from the beginning,' Bernardo said. 'I was too upset to think, but now I know what I have to do.'

'Don't be too hard on yourself,' Jack said.

'Someone might have come forward if I had just put these up sooner,' Bernardo continued.

'Or maybe not. Anyway, it's done now.'

Little Bernardo strode into the room with a stack of the flyers in his hand. '*I'm* going to help!' he declared.

'You are?' Jack asked, and he caught a glimpse of Lidia watching darkly. 'Don't you think you should wait at home?'

'No. I'm going to help.'

'I guess I can't argue with that,' Jack said. Lidia left the room. Jack knew he would hear from her later.

It was still early. Jack and Lidia had come across the bridge before the morning rush and they came to a house awash in breakfast smells. Reina fed everyone without sitting down to take any food for herself and now she lingered at the fringe of their conversation. Jack did not know how she kept her peace. Maybe she saved it all for Bernardo when they were alone. But now she was a rock.

'Where is the policeman?' Bernardo asked Jack.

'He'll be here soon. I gave him directions.'

'Let's sit outside and wait. Bernardino, don't make a mess out of those flyers. We will go out soon.'

'Yes, *Papá.*'

There was still something of the cool night lingering in the enclosed courtyard, but the rising sun was already warming the air. Bernardo sat by the barbecue grill and picked up the length of twisted iron he used to stir the coals. He poked at the ashes. 'Is he really coming?' he asked.

'He said he was. I don't expect he'll break his word.'

'He wants his money.'

'I don't think that's the only reason,' Jack said.

After that they let the silence grow between them until they heard the sound of a car on the other side of the streetward wall. It idled for a moment and then cut off. A door opened and closed.

Gonzalo appeared at the gate and rapped the metal with his key. '*¿Hola?*' he called.

Bernardo hastened to unlock the gate and Gonzalo came

in. He was dressed as he had been the first day Jack met him: in slacks and a jacket, but with no tie for his shirt. If he was carrying a gun it wasn't immediately obvious. Jack was very aware of the Browning Hi-Power tucked in the back of his pants beneath the tail of his blue work shirt.

'Good morning, good morning,' Gonzalo greeted them. 'I hope I'm not late.'

'No, you're fine,' Jack said. He shook Gonzalo's hand.

'Today is our first day,' Gonzalo said. 'A fresh start.'

'I've made flyers,' Bernardo said. 'To spread around and show Patricia's face to people. Would you like to see one?'

'Of course.'

Bernardo retreated into the house and left Jack and Gonzalo alone. They stood opposite each other under the roof of the car park as the sunlight angled in. 'I'm glad you came,' Jack said.

'It was not a guarantee,' Gonzalo replied. 'I thought twice. I thought three times.'

'But now you're here.'

'Yes.'

Bernardo returned with the flyer. Gonzalo looked it over and pronounced it good, and then they all passed inside to sit in the living room. Gonzalo took a chair near the corner, while Jack and Bernardo sat facing the darkened television. Reina and the children were nowhere to be seen.

'I do not have access to my file on this case,' Gonzalo began, 'but that doesn't mean we start with nothing. I know what we have learned thus far and what we must do next. I've asked you before, Jack, and now I'm asking you again not to come with me while I work.'

'I'm going,' Jack said.

Gonzalo nodded slowly. 'I won't argue. But you must promise to follow my lead at all times and when I speak to stay silent. There are people we must speak to who will be hard enough to convince without an American pressuring them for information.'

'I will.'

'We also have a problem: everyone in the city knows the police have been suspended. I won't be able to use my badge or even the threat of arrest. I'm just a man asking questions. We have no protections.'

The gun was at his back, hard and compact. Jack nodded. 'I understand.'

'Bernardo, you will post the flyers today?'

'Yes. Everywhere. *Everywhere*. Do you think someone will call?' Bernardo asked.

'Anything is possible,' Gonzalo said.

'When do we get started?' Jack asked.

'We get started now. Jack, we'll go together in my car. Bernardo, be careful today. Let us hope luck is on our side. We need all the help we can get.'

SEVEN

THERE WAS THE LOW HUM OF MEN working outside the office where Ernesto Alvares sat and it made him feel as if things were functioning as they should: smoothly and with the highest degree of professionalism. When a citizen came into this station, he should be faced with an operation every bit as good as the one it had replaced. Or better. That was the goal.

The desk he used was stacked high with file folders, some green and some blue. They were arranged alphabetically by the last names of the men Alvares' team had relieved, but he had taken one out of order and spread it on the clean blotter for closer examination. The name on the folder was SOLER, GONZALO.

Gonzalo Soler's file photo had clearly been taken much earlier in his career, because the man no longer had the baby face of a young officer. He was forty-five and that younger face had been replaced with one lined with seriousness and encroaching age. In the younger Gonzalo's expression there was a forthrightness that none of the policemen Alvares had seen or interviewed possessed. The reality of their work had drilled it out of them, perhaps permanently.

Alvares admitted to curiosity. Of all the officers discharged on the day of his arrival, Gonzalo was the only one who'd dared to stand in front of Alvares and deliver a full-throated rebuke. The others had accepted the decision mutely, or with a few mumbled words. They packed away their things and left without any resistance at all. Some even seemed glad to go. A part of Alvares did not blame them. He came from Mexico City and did not like these dirty little border towns, made even worse by the *narcos* that fought to hold them. But this was where the war was, and a soldier did not have a choice. At least these policemen had an out.

Gonzalo's entry into the police force was not dramatic: he took the exam and was admitted to the academy. He was not the most excellent student in his class, but neither was he the worst. His first assignment was patrol duty with a training officer whose reports were positive. Before very long Gonzalo was on his own.

Police could be on their own then. Those early years in Gonzalo's career were before the cartels began their open hostilities, and when Nuevo Laredo was a town built on the back of international trade and tourism. Now the thousands and thousands of trucks headed north were all potential vehicles for drug smuggling and the tourists were all gone. The United States guarded the Laredo port of entry as if it were under siege. Perhaps they were right to do so.

Alvares noted a yellow sheet in Gonzalo's file. It referenced another file related to a disciplinary action, but there were no details. He paged through the next few pieces of paper looking for something related, finding nothing. On a pad of notepaper he wrote down the case file and resolved to ask for it when he had a spare moment. There was more to read here.

Gonzalo became an inspector and was partnered for a time with another young investigator named Amando Armas. The name was familiar. Alvares looked through the duty roster and found Armas there. He wrote Armas' name beneath his other note. Perhaps Armas' file was already in the piles, but if not, he would find it.

By the time he came to the end of Gonzalo's career on paper, Alvares was surprised that Gonzalo's story was so ordinary. At no point in his time with the Municipal Police had Gonzalo received a citation or some recognition of effort beyond the call of duty. Alvares had expected more, expected *something*, but Gonzalo was undistinguished in virtually every way. A man with that much passion must be extraordinary, Alvares thought, but he was wrong.

He tore the page from the notepad and left the office. He found Gervasio Chaidez near the fax machine trying haplessly to load too many sheets into the feeder. Chaidez looked around embarrassedly when Alvares touched him on the shoulder. 'You,' he said, 'you're handling the cases for Inspector Soler?'

'Who?'

'Gonzalo Soler.'

'Oh, yes. I have everything arranged just like he said.'

'What do you mean?'

Chaidez's face fell. 'Nothing, sir. What do you need?'

'I want you to find this file. You might have to send out for it, but I want it just as soon as you get it.'

'Yes, sir.'

Alvares paused. 'What was Soler working on when he left?'

'A few things.'

'Make me a list of all his pending cases and have it on my desk before you leave tonight, okay.'

'Yes, sir.'

'Have you seen Lieutenant Casiano?'

'He went out with the patrols, sir. He won't be back until the end of the shift. Do you want me to get in touch with him, too?'

'No, it's all right. I'll speak with him then. Now get to work. I want that stuff as quickly as possible.'

Chaidez rushed off and Alvares lingered by the fax machine. He took up the pile of documents Chaidez had left behind and fed them into the device one page at a time. When he was done he took the paperwork to the desk where Gonzalo Soler used to work and laid them there.

'I'm not finished with you, Inspector,' Alvares said to no one. 'I'll figure you out.'

EIGHT

GONZALO DROVE WITH THE WINDOWS down and Jack sweated freely as they cruised the block, looking for something Gonzalo had not shared, but which was important enough for them to circle the same streets again and again.

Finally Jack asked, 'What are we doing?'

'We were being followed,' Gonzalo said.

Jack looked behind them reflexively, but he saw nothing except another car and a truck laden with a pile of broken furniture tied down with rope. 'Followed?' he said.

Gonzalo nodded. The reflection from the rear-view mirror painted a band of silver across his face. 'For a little while. After I doubled back a few times they got tired of trailing us. Probably thugs looking to make an easy score. We get carjackings through here all the time. Sometimes there's violence.'

'Shit,' Jack said.

They reached a familiar intersection, but this time Gonzalo did not turn and they continued on. After a few minutes he slowed the car and slotted it in along a broken curb in front of a string of dusty shops, half of which were shuttered and empty. Gonzalo didn't bother to put up the windows. The car would bake in the sun anyway, but at least it wouldn't turn into a furnace. He tossed a towel over the steering wheel. 'There's a bar up here,' Gonzalo said. 'We'll go and have a beer and if the right person is there, we'll talk.'

They passed along the shabby storefronts and past the open doors of a laundromat. A couple of dried-up-looking women lurked in the partially lit *lavandería* and as Jack walked by they watched him with hard eyes. He tried to ignore them.

The bar was fronted with black-painted wood and had the words *bebidas*, *vino* and *cerveza* stenciled by the door. If the place had a name, it wasn't printed anywhere Jack could see.

Inside there was the smell of stale beer and cigarettes. The bar had a pool table and a darkened jukebox and a scattering of tables to go with a pair of booths. It was practically deserted, with just the bartender and two other customers in sight. A big yellow-neon Corona sign crested the bartender's head like a halo.

'Hey, *hombre*,' Gonzalo said to the bartender. '*¿Qué pasa?*'

'Not much,' the bartender said. He looked past Gonzalo to Jack and Jack could almost see his face closing up. Suddenly he wished he wasn't here and had let Gonzalo go alone.

'A beer for me and my friend,' Gonzalo said.

'The cooler's broken. It's gonna be warm.'

'Warm beer is okay with me. Come on, Jack, sit down.'

Jack took a stool beside Gonzalo at the bar while the bartender filled pint glasses. The man put the fresh beers in front of them and there was no pleasant wetness on the glass, no rings on the bar. When Jack sipped, it was like drinking blood.

'I'm looking for Aarón,' Gonzalo said.

'You see everyone who's here,' the bartender replied.

'Don't bullshit me,' Gonzalo said. 'Where is he?'

'Who is this one?' the bartender asked, and he jerked a thumb at Jack.

'A friend. Now do you know where Aarón is, or not?'

The bartender pushed back from the bar and regarded both of them for a long moment, and then he said, 'He's in back.'

'Let me pay you,' Gonzalo said, and he reached for his wallet.

'No need. Nobody should have to pay for warm beer.'

Gonzalo left his stool. He waved Jack on. 'Follow me,' he said.

Jack let Gonzalo lead him to a short hallway in the back of the bar where the restrooms were and then to another door marked *Sólo los Empleados Autorizados*—employees only. The door was not locked and they entered a surprisingly large room lined on every side with metal shelves of beer and wine in bottles. A row of kegs lined up along one wall.

Three men sat playing cards at a folding table using metal kegs for seats. They were all painfully thin and one of them had scrawny arms scrawled with tattoos. All three looked around when Gonzalo entered. One of them took off his hat and placed it over his cards and the small scattering of bills and coins in front of him.

The man with the tattoos smiled and Jack saw he had no front teeth. 'Gonzalo!' he called out. 'Come to play a hand?'

Jack expected Gonzalo to show his ID or something to establish himself, but he merely approached the table and stood over the men. 'No games today, Aarón. I wanted to talk to you.'

'I'm kind of busy right now.'

'It'll only take a minute.'

Aarón looked at Gonzalo and then looked at Jack and then to Gonzalo again. He put down his cards. 'I'll be right back,' he told the other men. 'Don't play without me.'

'Let's talk outside,' Gonzalo said.

A battered metal door opened out into an alley behind the building. Deep ruts marked where vehicles passed through and there was a gray dumpster covered in looping graffiti that obscured the name of the garbage company. Lots of cardboard boxes marked with the names of beer brands and logos for hard liquor were heaped up in the dumpster, as if it had been a long time since anyone had come to empty it. Drained kegs were scattered around like tombstones, some tied together with red string. At least it was shaded here and the sun was not so terrible.

'I'm sorry I interrupted you,' Gonzalo told Aarón.

'I'm going to make a killing off those two,' Aarón said. 'I'm just letting them win a little first.'

'Eliseo Guadalupe,' Gonzalo said.

'Guadalupe?' Aarón shifted his weight from foot to foot. Up close Jack could see that his tattoos were not professional.

'You know him?'

Aarón eyed Jack now. 'I don't think I should say with him around.'

'What difference does it make? He's just somebody.'

'Somebody,' Aarón repeated.

'Yeah. Now do you know Guadalupe or not?'

A smile. A wide, toothless smile that did not reach Aarón's eyes. 'Of course I know him. He patrols through here a lot. Stops for a drink sometimes, him and his partner. Once in a while he sits in on a game.'

The uneasy way Aarón kept moving his body side to side on the balls of his feet made Jack nervous. He was sweating, but not from the heat, and the sour taste of the warm beer was in his mouth. The man did not seem dangerous, but looked as if he were about to break into flight at any moment and they would have to chase him down the long, cratered alleyway.

'I need to know about him. Where he goes. Who he sees,' Gonzalo said.

Aarón shook his head. 'I'm not the person to ask.'

'Who is?'

'Ramiro.'

'Ramiro *who*?'

'Ramiro Veloz.'

Jack could not keep quiet. 'Do you know him?' he asked Gonzalo.

'I've heard his name,' Gonzalo replied, and his voice was flat. 'We've never met.'

'Ramiro's your man,' Aarón said. 'I don't know nothing.'

'Where is this guy?' Jack asked.

Aarón's eyes flicked to Gonzalo. 'I don't want to talk to him.'

'Where is he?' Gonzalo pressed.

'Goyo's. He's there every night.'

'You're sure about that?' Gonzalo asked.

'Why would I lie to you? You can't do nothing to me anyway. The army cut your balls off.'

'I'm not going to be a civilian forever,' Gonzalo said.

'We'll see.'

Aarón went back to his game and Gonzalo escorted Jack out the front door of the bar onto the bright, crumbling street. Gonzalo found a spot in the shade. 'That was good,' he told Jack.

'It was?'

'Yes, very good. Aarón is nobody, a small-timer, but he knows people. This place is right in the heart of Guadalupe's patrol area. He was bound to stop here sooner or later. I would be more surprised if he did not.'

'Who is Guadalupe?' Jack asked.

Jack could see Gonzalo hesitate and for a moment Jack thought he wouldn't answer, but then he said, 'I think he may be the last person to have seen your stepdaughter.'

'What? Why didn't you tell me this?'

'Because I couldn't be sure! There were three sets of prints taken from your stepdaughter's car. One set belonged to Patricia Sigala. The other was likely Marina's. The third set was Eliseo Guadalupe's. I had it checked twice.'

Jack's heart was thumping. 'What does this mean?'

'It means that sometime on the night your stepdaughter disappeared, Eliseo Guadalupe had contact with her vehicle. But he claims he never saw her or the car. Why would he lie unless it was to cover up something else? All I can say for certain is that we have to learn more about Guadalupe. He's the key. I know it.'

'Why don't we just go to Guadalupe now and get the truth from him?'

'Little steps, Jack. First we need evidence, and then we can confront him with it. This is how a policeman works. If we move too quickly, we lose everything. Are you going to be all right?'

'I'm fine,' Jack said.

'We don't have to go out until tonight. I can do this alone.'

'No, I want to.'

'We'll find her. I promise you we'll find her. Just give me time to work.'

Jack nodded. 'Okay,' he said.

NINE

THEY WERE IN THE CAR TOGETHER when traffic began to slow. Brake lights flashed in the road before them and then they were stopped completely. Gonzalo craned his neck out the window to look ahead.

'What is it?' Jack asked.

'Roadblock,' Gonzalo said.

'Can we go around?'

Gonzalo glanced in the rear-view mirror. Cars were already beginning to stack up behind him, clogging the one-way street all the way back to the corner. 'No,' he said simply.

The line crept up slowly and Gonzalo's engine idled unevenly during the long periods of stillness, threatening to stall. He had almost 200,000 miles on the car and it was expensive to service frequently. What he could do he did for himself and the rest waited until he had scraped together enough savings to pay the bill. Gonzalo touched the dashboard gently as if to reassure the car that its suffering was not unnoticed.

Jack shifted uncomfortably in his seat and Gonzalo saw he was sweating. 'I'm sorry I have no air conditioning for you, Jack,' Gonzalo said.

'I'm fine. What do they do at these roadblocks, anyway?'

'Check papers and vehicles, look for suspicious persons.'

'They search all the vehicles?'

Gonzalo looked over at Jack. The man was sweating harder now. 'No, not unless they have good reason. What's the matter with you?'

The words were slow in coming. Gonzalo could see Jack struggle with them and Jack's face grew redder and redder. 'I've got to tell you something,' he said finally.

'What?'

'I'm carrying a gun.'

'Get out,' Gonzalo said.

'Wait, listen, I—'

'Get out of the car *now* before someone sees you,' Gonzalo said sharply. 'Walk back the way we came. Go until you can find somewhere to sit down and stay there until I can come back around. Call me.'

'I'm sorry, I thought—'

'No, no more talking. Get out of the car.'

Jack paused as if he wanted to say something more, but then he unfastened his seatbelt and bailed out of the car onto the street. He slammed the door and headed for the sidewalk, turning away from the roadblock and not looking back. Gonzalo watched until he was completely out of sight.

'*Jesús Cristo,*' Gonzalo breathed. His heart was beating fast. He brought out his phone and laid it on the seat where Jack had sat. Already he was wondering whether someone had made a note of Jack fleeing and whether they would say anything to the men at the roadblock. He was sweating now himself.

It was fifteen minutes before his phone rang, and by then he had only gone a short distance. He could see the corner of a parked army truck now, half up on the sidewalk. 'I'm in a *taquería* about two blocks down,' Jack told him.

'You should have told me before this, Jack.'

'What good would it have done?'

'It would have given me a chance to convince you not to bring it. For God's sake, Jack, do you know what could happen to you if the army found your gun? You would get years, Jack. *Years.*'

'I needed some insurance.'

Gonzalo shook his head though Jack could not see him. The line of cars crept up a little. 'What good do you think your gun is going to do against all the guns of Los Zetas?'

'What do you mean, Los Zetas?'

'Who do you think we were going to be talking with? The Zetas and the Golfos *own* this city. They touch everything, control everyone. Aarón, Ramiro Veloz… they are the lowest rung in the Zetas ladder.'

'And these people will *talk* to you?'

'They talk to me because they know I can't hurt them,' Gonzalo said. He was close enough now to see the soldiers with their weapons pull someone from their car for a search. If that had been Jack, it all would have gone to pieces. 'Even if I had a badge, they are small fish. Everyone lets the small fish swim.'

'To catch bigger fish,' Jack said.

'You understand now. I believe Guadalupe knows much more than he admits,' Gonzalo said. He did not press on to describe the *narco* with the gold watch he'd seen in La Zona. Jack did not need to know such things yet. They would only frighten him.

Only two cars were ahead of Gonzalo now and as he watched the first was waved through with just a glance. The driver in front of him handed his ID card out the window to the soldier in charge. 'I have to go.'

'I'll be waiting.'

Gonzalo put his phone away in his pocket. Now he eased up

to the roadblock formed by two trucks parked nose-in across the street, providing only a small passage for traffic. '*Hola*,' he said to the soldiers.

'Identification.'

Gonzalo presented his badge and his ID. 'I'm one of the good guys,' he said.

The soldier looked at the picture on the ID and compared it to Gonzalo's face. 'Are you so sure about that? The last time I looked, we were doing your job for you.'

'Only temporarily.'

'From your lips to God's ear,' the soldier said, and he handed back Gonzalo's things. 'Do you have anything in the car?'

'Nothing except myself.'

'All right, move on.'

'*Gracias. Buena suerte*,' Gonzalo said, but the soldier was already looking to the next car. The other soldiers with him stared down from the backs of the trucks, their weapons ready. At a signal they would tear a vehicle apart. Gonzalo was glad to get out from under their gaze.

He drove to the end of the block and turned twice to head back the way he'd come. It took a few minutes to find the little *taquería*, tucked in as it was between a shuttered storefront and a dress shop. Gonzalo idled at the curb until Jack came out.

'I'm sorry,' Jack said when he got in.

'There's no need to talk about it. You're renting a room? I'll take you there and you can leave the gun.'

'How will we protect ourselves?' Jack asked.

'The same way everyone else does,' Gonzalo replied. 'With a prayer.'

TEN

BERNARDO PARKED HIS CAR AT THE dance hall where the concert was held and took his flyers with him. Little Bernardo went with him, carrying still more of the flyers, though Bernardo held the staple gun. At the first telephone pole they reached, they put up a flyer on both sides, coming and going. Every ten or fifteen meters there was another pole. They would walk the line papering each one.

They had been working for the better part of two hours before Bernardo realized he wasn't sure where they were any longer. A turn here and there to a new street had led them inexorably away from the dance hall into a section of the city that was completely unfamiliar. He could navigate by the sun and eventually work his way back, but for now he was lost, and every time a strange car passed on the street he tensed a little, not knowing who was behind the wheel.

'We should start heading back,' Bernardo told his son.

'But we have lots more to put up!' Little Bernardo protested. 'A few more blocks, *Papá*, please.'

'Wouldn't you like something to drink? We can go somewhere and get ices.'

'When we're done.'

'All right,' Bernardo said, and he tousled the boy's hair. 'You are more dedicated than I am.'

'It's the only way we'll find Patricia.'

Bernardo looked up the block at the poles still left bare. 'Yes,' he said. 'I think so.'

The neighborhood they were in had given way from commercial to residential. Little houses were planted on small lots with scrub grass around their front walks, and there were apartment blocks here and there, as well. A bodega allowed them to put up several flyers in their windows and even lent them the tape. A liquor store chased them off, but there was a telephone pole less than a meter from their door and they put the papers up anyway.

He almost missed the woman in the glare of a passing car's windshield, but then she came closer to them and raised a hand in greeting. Bernardo stopped and let her come on, seeing her gray hair and thick middle, the colorful splash of her blouse and her clean, white pants. She must have been in her seventies and she walked carefully, as if she was afraid of falling.

'*Hola*,' the woman said to them when she was close.

'*Hola*,' Bernardo returned.

'You are putting up those things?'

'Yes, I am,' Bernardo said, and he held out one for the woman to take. 'My daughter is missing from around here. Have you seen her?'

The woman studied the flyer carefully. Bernardo saw her lips moving slightly as she read the text. Finally she shook her head and offered it back to him. 'No,' she said. 'They are not familiar to me.'

'Thank you anyway,' Bernardo said.

'This is your son?' the woman asked.

'Yes. Say hello, Bernardino.'

'*Hola*.'

'Very handsome. And your daughter is pretty. Which one is she?'

'This one here. Are you sure you haven't seen her?'

'I'm sure. I would have remembered.'

Bernardo tried not to show his disappointment. He began to turn away, but he saw in the woman's face that she had more to say and he paused. 'Is there something else?' he asked.

'Only that I wonder if it's such a good idea to leave those everywhere,' the woman said.

'My daughter was last seen not far from here,' Bernardo told the woman. 'I have to do everything I can to help find her.'

'It's just that you don't know who might see them.'

'What do you mean?'

The woman fretted, biting her lip for a long moment before she spoke again. 'You know the types. You know. *Pandillas. Narcos.* They are in our neighborhood, too. They're everywhere.'

'I can't be afraid of that,' Bernardo said.

'Don't be mistaken,' the woman said, 'I want you to find your daughter. It's only that we have learned not to call attention to ourselves here. They notice. They do things.'

Bernardo saw Little Bernardo watching him and he straightened up. 'I don't have any problems with them unless they are the ones behind my daughter's disappearance. And if they are… the army will deal with them. I won't have to.'

'The army!' the woman exclaimed. 'Do they know about this?'

'They are looking even now,' Bernardo said. 'Everyone is looking for my daughter and my niece. There is nowhere they won't go to find them. These papers are only part of it.'

He knew even as he said it that he was boasting, but there was something about the woman that he did not like. She irked him. He wanted her to know this was not a joke, though she was not laughing.

'I hope they find her,' the woman said simply.

'They will.'

'Good luck to you, then.'

The woman turned away and walked off the way she'd come. Bernardo and his son watched her leave until Little Bernardo tugged at his father's shirt. '*Papá*,' he said.

'What is it, son?'

'She's not the only one. Lots of people will see these.'

'I know. She's just scared. Lots of people are scared, but we must be brave.'

'Shall we put up more?'

'Yes, more,' Bernardo said, and they went to the next pole with the last of the flyers in their hands.

ELEVEN

THE HOTEL ROOM WAS NOT LARGE AND was not meant for company. Jack sat on the edge of the bed while Gonzalo commandeered the only chair. While Gonzalo watched, Jack brought out the Browning Hi-Power and put it under the pillow after unloading it. Gonzalo nodded his satisfaction.

Street sounds were barely audible from three stories down. The thrum of passing engines and the occasional honk touched the window at the front of the room. A weird, low buzzing carried through the room and it took a while before Jack realized it was the hum of the electric clock beside the bed. It was too quiet, but they did not talk.

Gonzalo seemed unperturbed by the stillness, but Jack found it infuriating. He had brought nothing to read, not even a magazine, because he had not foreseen long hours of downtime. In his mind he would be searching, always searching, with Gonzalo alongside him to smooth the way. The wait was forever and the hands on that electric clock moved glacially slowly.

When he could stand no more quiet, Jack said, 'I've got to get out of here.'

'There's nowhere to go. Better if we stay here until we have to move. Wandering the streets without a plan is no good. Waiting is part of police work,' Gonzalo said.

'Is there some rule against talking to your partner while you wait?'

Gonzalo had been looking off toward the window, but now he turned his eyes on Jack. He seemed strangely calm, or perhaps it was just because Jack felt so agitated. 'No,' he said. 'There isn't.'

'Well, then, talk to me.'

'I should tell you that you were a damned fool to bring that gun into the country,' Gonzalo said. 'If I were still on active duty I would be obliged to bring you in.'

'Guess it's lucky you're not.'

A strange look of melancholy crossed Gonzalo's face and he stared away again toward the framed rectangle of sunlight at the front of the room. He nodded slowly. 'I suppose it is lucky,' he said at last.

Jack turned on the bed so he could look at Gonzalo more directly. There was only a scant few feet between them. 'Why won't they have you back? I told them you wouldn't take money from me. If it's corruption they're worried about then you aren't part of the problem.'

'Everyone is under suspicion now,' Gonzalo said without looking at him.

'But I told them—'

'*Everyone*, Jack. I am no exception.'

A long quiet grew between them until Jack could clearly hear the buzz of the electric clock again. He cursed out loud. 'You're a good cop,' he said.

'And you know this how?'

'I told you: because you wouldn't take my money. Because you gave a damn. Because you're helping me now.'

Gonzalo smiled a thin smile with no humor. 'There are a dozen policemen who would gladly take my place for the wages you're offering me. That doesn't mean they truly care.'

'Well, *do* you?'

They matched gazes again. 'Yes.'

'How did you get here?' Jack asked. 'What do they have on you?'

'I'd rather not say.'

'Hey, you're already hip-deep in it with me because of the gun. You might as well come all the way in.'

Gonzalo was quiet a while and then he took a deep breath. He said, 'When I was a patrol officer I shared a beat with an older policeman. His name was Leopoldo and he'd been on the force for many years. He was senior enough that he could have worked at a desk, but he stayed in a car on patrol.'

'Why?'

'Because the money was better,' Gonzalo said.

'The money? You mean the bribe money.'

Gonzalo nodded. 'The *mordida*. He collected it everywhere, from everyone. There was no one he wouldn't put his hand out to. And the Golfos owned him, though back then it was not so terrible a thing as it is now. They paid him and he protected their interests.'

'How?'

'There are many ways a policeman can make himself useful to the *narcos*. But Leopoldo was not so young anymore that he could do it all alone. There was money to spare and he offered it to brother officers who could help him.'

Jack watched Gonzalo carefully. He could see the story being pulled out of him word by word and his voice sounded labored, as if it took effort to speak. Gonzalo looked at his lap, at his open hands. 'He gave you money?' Jack asked.

'Yes.'

'And you took it?'

'I did.'

'Why?'

'Because it was easy to do. Easier than arguing the point. I took the *narco* money and when Leopoldo asked me to do a favor for his friends, I obliged. For a year I did this.'

Jack let Gonzalo speak.

'It was a good year,' Gonzalo said. 'I had plenty of money for everything I wanted and the things they asked were simple enough to do. In those days there was no war between the Golfos and the Zetas. The Zetas were a part of the Golfos and there was peace. A kind of peace. The police had only to let them do their business and the angel of death would pass by.

'Then Leopoldo told me there was going to be a shooting. He knew the day and the time. We were told to stay away when the call came in, to let it happen. And on that day and hour we heard on our radios that an officer was shot. He radioed for assistance, but no one went to him because we had all agreed what was to be done. He died waiting.'

Now Gonzalo stopped talking and after a while Jack realized he was not going to say anything more. Gonzalo went on staring at his hands.

'What happened?' Jack asked.

Gonzalo stirred like someone nudged out of a nap. He rubbed his palms on the legs of his pants. 'What happened? The investigators went to work and we were all brought in, one by one, to tell our stories. Where we were. Why we were so late. Everyone knew, of course, but no one would tell the truth.'

Jack sat upright with a thought. 'You did,' he said.

'Yes.'

'What did they do to you?'

'They disciplined me like all the rest and then they went after Leopoldo. It was not hard to find something to charge him with. And when he went on trial I was asked to testify against him in a closed courtroom with my identity concealed.'

'You did that?'

'I did.'

'Jesus. What happened to Leopoldo?'

'He went to prison and I went back to my patrol car. And when the chance came for me to become an inspector, I was helped along by friends in high places.'

'Does anyone know?'

Gonzalo shook his head. 'I don't think so. Leopoldo had to suspect me, but he was stabbed to death three months after he went inside. I don't know if he ever said anything.'

Jack searched for words. 'No wonder you wouldn't take my money,' he managed.

'Never,' Gonzalo said, and his jawline firmed. 'Never another centavo. What you're paying me now is for my work, not my silence.'

'All I ever ask for is an honest day's work for an honest day's pay,' Jack said.

'Yes,' Gonzalo said.

'I don't know if I have your balls,' Jack said.

'You are in Mexico with an illegal gun, asking questions of *narcos* in a city filled with killers,' Gonzalo said. 'Your bravery is not in question.'

'I just want to find my girl.'

'And we will,' Gonzalo said. 'We will.'

TWELVE

NIGHT CAME AND GONZALO DROVE them to the place called Goyo's. Jack recognized landmarks here and there and estimated that they were not more than a few minutes from Bernardo's house. He hadn't spoken to Bernardo all day and he wondered how it had gone with the flyers and if anyone had called. If not, it was only a matter of time. The city wasn't blind.

There was a large dirt parking lot around the place and the edges of the flat-roofed building were decorated with unblinking Christmas lights. A few cars and trucks were scattered around in front, empty of anyone. Gonzalo parked carefully on the side.

'What kind of place is this?' Jack asked when they had gotten out. There was still residual heat rising off the earth and the air had not yet cooled, but it was a relief from the unrelenting day. 'Another bar?'

'It's like that. You buy drinks, but there are also girls,' Gonzalo said.

'So it's a whorehouse.'

'No, you buy drinks for the girls and they dance with you. And if you want to touch them, that's okay, too.'

Jack frowned. 'Everybody's selling somebody,' he said.

'What was that?'

'Nothing. Let's go.'

He heard the music playing before they even opened the door: the bright sounds of brass and the bass thump of *norteño* music and the singing voices of two men in tandem professing love for the same woman. They passed through the entrance into the half-lit bar, smelling fresh cigarette smoke from the slowly forming cloud clinging to the ceiling. Lazily turning ceiling fan paddles stirred the air around, forming swirls of gray in the light.

Jack saw the girls first, arranged along the bar in a row for selection. They wore shorts and had bare arms and it was hard to tell if they were young or old from a distance. The bar had a dance floor and on it a man and a woman swayed, the man's hands clutching at the woman.

There were other men scattered among the tables and there were women with them, too. All were sitting close and at the nearest table he saw the couple's hands were in each other's laps, steadily moving in physical rhythm.

Gonzalo led Jack to the bar. No stools here. A drinker could put up a foot on the rail, but there was nowhere to sit except at the tables. Out of the corner of his eye, Jack saw the girls arranging themselves to be more visible. It was a quiet shuffling that seemed unconscious, but had the calculation of long practice.

'*Hola, señor,*' Gonzalo said to the man at the bar. 'Two beers for me and my friend.'

The bartender looked at them both. 'You got to buy drinks for the girls, too.'

'Not right now. Just for us.'

'I don't make the rules.'

'How about we just pay double for the beers?' Jack asked.

'It's drinks for the girls or nothing.'

Gonzalo put up his hand. '*Está bien.* We'll buy for the girls.'

The bartender waved the girls over and immediately women surrounded them. Jack held his breath. A few were older, but most were very young and they looked at him with dark eyes that were tired and wanting at the same time. They made smiles that didn't reach those eyes and one touched Jack on the chest lightly with her fingers and said, 'Hello, baby', in English.

'I'll take that one', Gonzalo said, and waved a finger at one of the crowd.

The rest coalesced around Jack, pushing in, but the face of the girl who spoke English held him. She was slender, with fine features that were marred by too much makeup. Her hair was long and fell to her shoulders in straight waves. She could not be older than eighteen.

'Jack?' Gonzalo asked.

'This one', Jack forced out, and the girl stepped up next to him so that he could smell her perfume and feel her hip touching his.

'Beer', the girl ordered from the bartender.

The woman Gonzalo chose was plain and going soft, but he ignored her completely except to give her the drink he paid for. Jack could not stop looking at his girl, even when the beers came. His throat was too tight to swallow.

'What's your name?' the girl asked him.

'Jack', he said huskily.

'That's a nice name. Like Jack Daniel. I am Ercilia.'

Gonzalo was saying something to the bartender, but Jack didn't hear. The bartender pointed then and Gonzalo passed him a hundred-peso bill. 'I'll be back', he told Jack, and he and the woman slipped away.

'Do you like me, Jack?' Ercilia asked.

'I don't know you.'

'Would you like to dance?'

'Maybe later.'

Jack drank desperately from his beer, gulping heavily. It was cheap stuff and bitter, but it was something to keep him from looking at the girl. He felt her fingers on his arm and he nearly recoiled. Even without turning his head toward her he could sense her nearness and then she bumped him with her hip again.

'You speak good Spanish,' Ercilia said.

'Thanks.'

'But you're American, aren't you?'

'Yeah.'

'We don't see many Americans in here. Just locals. It's nice for a change.'

He searched around for Gonzalo and saw him sitting at a table with another man and his rental girl. He and the man were deep in conversation, their heads bowed, and the women looked away, indifferent. Jack wanted to be there with them.

Ercilia touched him and despite himself he looked at her. She stood with her back to the bar and held her shoulders back so that he could see her small breasts. 'Are you sure you don't want to dance?' she asked. 'It's all right if you don't know how. We can go slow.'

'I just want to drink my beer,' Jack said, and then he asked, 'How old are you?'

The girl's brow furrowed. 'What kind of a question is that?'

'I'm just curious,' Jack said quickly.

'I'm nineteen, if you want to know.' Ercilia took a drink from her beer and watched Jack from over the brim of the mug. 'Are you here to try and save me?'

'What? No. No, I was only asking.'

'Then put your hands on me.'

'That's okay,' Jack said.

Ercilia put down her beer, and her voice turned low. 'Put your hands on me. What, are you shy?'

'I'm not shy. I came here with a friend to see somebody, that's all.'

The girl leaned in close. 'They say you can only touch, but for five hundred pesos you can do whatever you want. There's a place we can go. All you have to do is ask.'

She put her hand on him again, touching him in the crotch, and Jack jumped. He reached for his wallet and fumbled out a twenty-dollar bill. He thrust it at her and mumbled something like 'No, thanks,' before heading for the door. The clean air from outside rushed in when he flung the door wide and then he was out in it, the music fading and the girl left behind.

His breaths came shallow and fast. Jack steadied himself against a wall. Specks of hyperventilation passed his vision and died away. He went to Gonzalo's car and tried the passenger door. It was still unlocked.

He was still in the car when Gonzalo came out again. 'Jack, what happened?' Gonzalo asked.

'Nothing,' Jack said.

'One minute you are there and the next you are gone.'

'I said it was nothing.'

Gonzalo watched him. 'You shouldn't have come with me,' he said finally.

'I wanted to come. I'm fine.'

A new car pulled up beside them and a pair of men got out, conversing loudly. Gonzalo waited until they had gone before he said, 'Was it the girls?'

'No.'

'Was it?'

Jack hesitated before nodding. 'Marina's that age. She's no

older than that girl.'

'Jack, you have to realize… this is what they do.'

'She offered to let me screw her! A kid!'

'It's worse in La Zona,' Gonzalo said. 'Places like these are nothing. You want a young girl, you can find one there, and you don't have to buy her a drink before you do what you want to do to her.'

Jack wiped his mouth with the back of a shaking hand. 'I didn't think it'd be *right there*. I'm not stupid, I know what goes on, but… she's just a kid.'

'I should do the rest of this alone tonight,' Gonzalo said.

'No, I'm sticking it out till the end.'

'You want to go back in there again? Because that is what you'll have to do. Ramiro isn't here yet and he won't be until after midnight.'

'I'll wait out here.'

'No, you won't. I'm taking you back to your hotel. You'll sleep and I'll see you in the morning.'

Jack opened his mouth to protest, but he said nothing. When Gonzalo started the car, Jack did not try to stop him and on the drive back they didn't talk at all.

THIRTEEN

THE HOTEL ROOM WAS LIKE A CELL. Jack was reluctant to mount the steps to his floor and slower still to pass through the door and lock it behind him. Waiting there earlier in the day had been excruciating, but at least then he was with someone. Now he was alone with his thoughts and that was no good.

His phone was on the bed stand and he used it to call Bernardo despite the hour. Bernardo answered right away, as if he had been waiting by the phone for just that moment. 'What have you learned?' he asked.

'Not much,' Jack confessed.

'All the flyers have been put up,' Bernardo told him. 'There is nowhere in that neighborhood where you can't see Patricia's face.'

'That's good. That's real good.'

'I have been hoping someone would call,' Bernardo said, and Jack heard the disappointment there. 'So far... no one.'

'Someone will call,' Jack said.

'I know it. Reina lit a candle at the church and she said she felt God's presence. He will guide someone to us.'

Jack said nothing to that. God had put many obstacles in his way. It was not like Him to take them back. Finally he said, 'How's Lidia?'

'She is asleep. The kids kept her busy.'

'That's good. She needs something to take her mind off this.'

'It would be better for her to be at home with her friends,' Bernardo said. 'We have nothing to offer but four walls. On the other side, she can pretend that things aren't changed. For a little while.'

'We'll go home when this is done,' Jack said. 'She'll survive. She's strong, like her mother. Like Marina. She can make do without her friends for a little while.'

'You know she's welcome as long as it takes,' Bernardo said. 'I only thought it would be easier on her.'

'There's nothing easy about this. I'm not going to pretend that there is.'

'Are you going to be all right, Jack?'

'I'm fine. Don't worry about me. Listen, I should clear the line so you can take a call if you have to. Just tell me if you hear anything.'

'I will, Jack. You will be the first to know.'

'Goodnight, Bernardo.'

'Goodnight.'

Jack put the phone aside and pulled back the sheets on the bed and slipped in between them. He snuffed the lamp so that the only light in the room came from the street, ghostly and orange. The electric clock's buzzing rose in his ear again and he rode it away into a strange and unrestful sleep where he was lost on a lonely road with no one to help him on his way.

FOURTEEN

THE RENT-GIRL'S NAME WAS MÓNICA and Gonzalo fed her enough beer that he was sure she could not stand up. He felt guilty doing it, but every now and then a thickset man in a black T-shirt patrolled the tables and commanded the patrons to buy another drink or get out. His own beer remained untouched, mostly flat by now, but there were many bottles on the table from Mónica's drinking.

She seemed happy enough not to dance for her drinks and talked to Gonzalo instead. He learned about her childhood in Chiapas and how she came north with her father when she was only fourteen. She had five brothers and sisters, all older. Most were back in Chiapas, barely getting by, while she was the earner. She sent money from her earnings home every week. They could not survive without her.

Iris Contreras had sent no money home, though perhaps the thought might have occurred to her. Likely her father would not have accepted such generosity, earned as it was and tainted because of it. Gonzalo had heard a variation on this tale a hundred times and only the details changed. Sometimes the woman telling the tale ended up dead, by the hand of a customer or the bite of a needle or the cruel attentions of a *chulo*. What was Iris doing tonight?

He thought all of this and let Mónica talk, though by now

her stories bounced off him. It was enough that she was taking up time and she did not show any interest in him at all. He wouldn't have told her anything even if she had asked.

Whenever someone entered the place, Gonzalo looked to his contact, a man named Luis. He did not know what Ramiro Veloz looked like and every time Luis shook his head at the newcomers. The night crawled on toward midnight, the bar filling up steadily. By now there were half a dozen men on the dance floor with their girls, feeling them up as they swayed out of time to the music.

It was half past twelve when a pair of newcomers passed through the door. Both wore Polo shirts, one red and the other blue. Gonzalo shot a glance toward Luis. The man nodded.

Mónica was in the middle of telling the story of how her first boyfriend left her when Gonzalo got up from the table. She stopped woozily and tried to rise, but her legs did not cooperate and she felt back into her seat. 'Just a minute,' she slurred. 'I'm coming.'

'Stay where you are,' Gonzalo said. 'We're all done.'

'But we haven't danced!'

'We can dance another time.'

She caught at Gonzalo's sleeve and whined, 'Don't leave me.'

Gonzalo extricated himself gently and laid a five-hundred-peso note on the table. She focused on it with difficulty. 'That should cover us for the rest of the night,' Gonzalo said. 'Tell your boss, okay?'

The bill was swept up in her hands. Mónica looked at Gonzalo with glassy eyes. '*Gracias*,' she said. 'You are a good man.'

'Take care of yourself,' Gonzalo said.

It took a few moments to locate the men in the crowd that now held the bar. Gonzalo spotted them getting beers from the bartender, who by now was assisted by another man to handle the overflow. The choice of girls was dwindling, too, and the remains flocked to them to flirt and preen.

Gonzalo reached the men as they settled arms around their ladies. He did not know who was who, so he addressed them both. 'Ramiro Veloz?'

The man in the blue Polo shirt narrowed his eyes. He was slender, with lank hair and a carefully maintained beard of stubble. Up close Gonzalo could see that his shirt was not a real Ralph Lauren, but a knockoff. His pants were frayed at the cuffs and he wore simple tennis shoes. 'Who are you?' the man asked.

'My name is Soler. Aarón told me where to find you.'

Ramiro smiled and Gonzalo saw he had a gold tooth. He punched his companion in the shoulder. 'He's a cop,' he said. 'I guess no one told him there are no cops anymore.'

'I just want to talk. Five minutes.'

'I'm here to drink with the ladies.'

'I'm only asking for five minutes.'

The man's smile melted into a frown and he drank from his mug. The girl under his arm looked bored even as she touched his chest in an intimate way. Gonzalo wondered whether she, too, had a long story to tell.

'How about it?' Gonzalo asked.

'All right, five minutes.'

'Let's go outside.'

Ramiro whispered something in his girl's ear and then slipped free of her. His companion's face was written with suspicion, but he did not try to stop Ramiro when he turned toward the door. Gonzalo followed him out.

It was a clear night outside and there was a half-moon. The city lights burned the rest of the sky and there were no stars to see. They stopped just by the Christmas trees and Ramiro brought out a pack of cigarettes. He offered one to Gonzalo. Gonzalo waved them away.

Ramiro made a production out of putting a cigarette between his lips and firing it up with a stainless-steel lighter. He exhaled a cloud of smoke. 'What do the police want with me?' he asked.

'Eliseo Guadalupe,' Gonzalo said. 'Aarón says you know him?'

'I've heard the name. Another cop.'

'The other night he stopped a car. Two girls. What happened to them?'

'What makes you think I know anything about that?'

'I'm just asking,' Gonzalo said.

'As far as I know, Guadalupe doesn't do nothing but take his piece and look the other way. I don't know nothing about girls. What girls are these?'

'Who *would* know?'

Ramiro picked a speck of tobacco from his tongue and flicked it away. 'You don't want to go down that road.'

'I know Guadalupe's in with the *narcos*,' Gonzalo said. 'Who tells him what to do?'

'What's this worth to me?'

'You want money?' Gonzalo asked.

'Of course I want money! How much do you have?'

Gonzalo brought out his wallet. 'I don't have much.'

'Give me it all.'

'First tell me what I want to know.'

'*¡Dame el dinero!*' Ramiro barked. He thrust out his hand.

Gonzalo took a sheaf of bills from his wallet and put them on Ramiro's palm. In the back of his mind he calculated the loss and it pained him. 'That's all I have,' Gonzalo said.

The man counted quickly. 'This is shit. Cops never have any money.'

'Tell me who runs Guadalupe. Please.'

Ramiro cast a sour eye on Gonzalo. 'Can you get me more money?'

'I don't have a *job*,' Gonzalo said. 'How can I get you more money?'

'What you're asking me for is a dangerous thing.'

'And you don't think I can be dangerous?'

'What do you mean?'

Gonzalo fixed him with a stare. 'One day the police will be back in business. They can make things easy, or they can make things difficult. And accidents happen when arrests are made.'

Ramiro looked at Gonzalo carefully now. 'You cops are all corrupt.'

'That's what they say.'

'But you aren't everywhere. Not even the army is everywhere.'

'My friend, if you don't tell me what I want to know, I will make it my business to be wherever you are all the time. You won't be able to shave without seeing me in the mirror behind you.'

'I think you would.'

'Then tell me.'

'All right, I'll tell you, but you did not hear it from me. My name should never be mentioned.'

'I promise.'

'Okay.'

'Who tells Guadalupe what to do?' Gonzalo asked.

'Águila.'

'Who is Águila?'

'He runs the cops over there.'

'Is he a Zeta? A Golfo?'

'What do you think?'

'A Zeta,' Gonzalo said. 'What does he look like?'

'I don't know. My height, a little heavier. He got a mole on his cheek.'

A little sensation thrilled up Gonzalo's spine. The man with the gold watch. 'Where can I find him?'

Ramiro held up Gonzalo's money. 'You didn't pay me enough for that. Ask Guadalupe.'

'I'm asking *you*,' Gonzalo said.

'Well, I ain't talking no more.'

The man turned to go and Gonzalo grabbed his arm. 'Listen—' he said.

'Get your hand off me, *coño*,' Ramiro said, and his voice was like a razor.

Gonzalo released his grip. 'Does Águila know about the girls?'

'Ask Guadalupe.'

Ramiro turned his back on Gonzalo and went into the bar. A burst of music, chatter and smoke passed through the open door and then it closed again. Gonzalo let his arms fall slack at his sides. 'Ask Guadalupe,' he said to himself. 'Ask fucking Guadalupe.'

He went to his car and drove away.

FIFTEEN

GONZALO WOKE LATE WITH GUADALUPE on his mind and through his morning shower and breakfast he turned the issue of the man over and over. It occurred to him to call Jack, but he was not sure of what he would say. By the time he was dressed and ready to leave, he still had no idea.

He opened the front door just as they were preparing to knock: two armed soldiers in uniform, their eyes hidden behind sunglasses. The first one introduced himself: 'I am Lieutenant Casiano,' he said. 'You are to come with us.'

'What have I done?' Gonzalo asked.

'Everything will be explained.'

Gonzalo held back in the doorway, suddenly tempted to shut the door in Lieutenant Casiano's face, but knowing that would lead to no good. His gaze drifted to the other soldier and he saw the man held nylon zip cuffs in a gloved hand. He felt weak in the knees. 'Can you tell me what this is about?'

'Please, Inspector, come quietly.'

'I have to get some things.'

'You won't need anything.'

'I need to make a phone call.'

'You'll have time to make calls later,' Lieutenant Casiano said, his face blank. 'And if you would give me your phone…?'

'Why do you want my phone?'

The second soldier took a step forward, but Lieutenant Casiano stopped him with a hand. He slipped off his sunglasses and Gonzalo saw where long hours in the sun had traced a line around his eyes and across the bridge of his nose in paler skin. 'Captain Alvares requests that you come to the station to answer some questions. There's no need for this to be ugly. Now… your phone, please.'

Gonzalo fished his phone out of his pocket and handed it over. Lieutenant Casiano passed it to the other soldier, who put it away.

They led Gonzalo down to the small lot beside the building where three army trucks stood idling. In all there were nearly ten soldiers, most standing sentry in the open beds of their trucks. The third vehicle was an SUV and it was pleasantly cool inside.

Lieutenant Casiano rode in the back seat with Gonzalo. With the SUV in the lead, the little convoy turned out onto the street and headed toward El Centro. A radio tuned to a military band squawked in the front of the truck as units called out to each other across the airwaves like singing birds.

'Am I the only one being picked up?' Gonzalo asked after they had driven a little while.

'I'm afraid I can't tell you that, Inspector,' Lieutenant Casiano said.

'Can you tell me anything at all?'

'As I said, all will be explained.'

Gonzalo sat quietly as two blocks passed, and then he said, 'I've been working privately since my suspension. If that's what this is about, I can assure you that I have done nothing illegal.'

'I really don't know anything,' Lieutenant Casiano replied. 'Relax and enjoy the ride.'

When finally they turned onto the street that led to the station house, Gonzalo forced himself to take deep breaths. His palms were sweating and they soaked through the material of his pant legs despite the chill from the air conditioning. A trickle of nervous perspiration escaped his armpit and trailed down his side beneath his shirt.

Sandbags and concrete dividers had replaced vehicles in the blockade around the station entrance, but the ways in and out were still covered by guards. The convoy slipped past the last defenses and cruised to a halt before the building. Lieutenant Casiano got out, reflexively scanning the rooftops with his hand on his weapon, and then signaled Gonzalo to disembark.

Inside he was bustled past the front counter, past his empty desk and to the back stairs. They climbed to the second floor and down a familiar hall with a door at the end. When they got there, Lieutenant Casiano held the door open for him and let Gonzalo pass through.

The interrogation room was small, barely large enough for a scuffed and worn wooden table and three plastic chairs. It was empty. Gonzalo did not know what he had expected.

'Captain Alvares will be with you shortly,' Lieutenant Casiano said, and he closed the door.

Gonzalo looked up. The unblinking eye of a security camera pointed directly down from a high corner. The video feed was in a nearby room and everything could be recorded on tape. If he had been the interrogator, Gonzalo would have taken a seat that put his back to the lens, but now he sat so that his face was visible.

It was close in the little room. Gonzalo sweated freely now and his mouth was dry. There was no clock in here and no windows. Foam attached to the walls deadened the sounds from the rest of the building. The walls leaned in.

He did not know how much time had passed before Alvares opened the door. The captain carried a pair of folders under his arm and he looked very fresh in his short-sleeved uniform. 'Good morning,' he told Gonzalo. He sat at the opposite end of the table. His back would be to the camera.

'Why am I here?' Gonzalo asked.

Alvares put the folders down on the table and squared them neatly before answering. 'All police personnel are subject to interview as part of the review process,' he said. 'We'll call this your first session.'

'You didn't have to send armed men to bring me in.'

'I wanted to impress upon you how seriously we take this.'

'Is this because I lost my temper with you? If so, I apologize. I was upset and I spoke too hastily.'

Alvares leveled his gaze on Gonzalo. 'This is not about that.'

'Oh.' Gonzalo could think of nothing else to add.

The first folder was opened. 'I have been through your records,' Alvares said. 'I found it interesting. Especially the part about Leopoldo Sisneros.'

Gonzalo stiffened. 'That's not supposed to be in my regular file.'

'It wasn't. We had to go searching.'

'Then you know everything,' Gonzalo said.

'I do.'

They looked at each other for a long time, though Gonzalo did not know for how long. 'What are you going to do with me?' Gonzalo asked.

'What should be done with you?'

'I'm no longer the policeman I was back then. I committed to change and I meant it.'

Alvares nodded. 'I believe you.'

'I don't understand.'

'I said I believe you. I don't think you take money anymore. I don't think you are in the pocket of *narcos*. I think you are an honest policeman and my evaluation will reflect that.'

'Then why—?'

'I'm getting to that. I said I have been reviewing your records, and that includes the cases you were working at the time of your suspension. There is one in particular I would like to discuss with you. If I may.'

Gonzalo said nothing.

Alvares closed the first folder and set it aside. He opened the second. 'I assigned one of my men, Gervasio Chaidez, to your caseload. He is not doing a very good job continuing where you left off, I'm sorry to say. You were right when you said we are better at fighting *narcos* than we are doing police work. This particular case has to do with two missing girls, one of them an American. I think you're familiar with the one.'

'Yes.'

'I should think so, since you've been spotted in the city with the father of the American girl.'

'I can explain,' Gonzalo said.

'Save it for after. I said we were not expert policemen, but we do have our resources. We also have your notes. What do you know about Eliseo Guadalupe?'

Gonzalo's mouth worked. 'He's a fellow officer,' he managed to say. 'He works the area where the girls were last seen.'

'And his prints were found on the girls' car,' Alvares finished.

'Yes.'

'What do you think happened?'

'I don't know what happened,' Gonzalo said.

'But you have suspicions.'

'Nothing I can prove.'

'And if you were given the opportunity to prove them?'

'What are you saying?'

Alvares flipped the folder shut and then he thrust it across the table. 'Take it,' he said.

Gonzalo obeyed. He fidgeted with the folder, felt its lightness. The emptiness of little evidence and fewer leads. He thought of Jack.

'I have been over Eliseo Guadalupe's file, as well. He does not have your record for honesty. Three times he's been charged with corruption and three times he's managed to escape punishment. That is three times too many.'

'What do you want me to do?' Gonzalo asked.

'I want you to interrogate Guadalupe. Here. In this very room.'

'About the missing girls?'

'About them. About taking bribes. Anything he's suspected of.'

'Why would you allow this?'

Alvares folded his hands together on the table and leaned in toward Gonzalo. 'I am here to clean this city up, and policemen like Guadalupe are part of the problem. If he's not guilty of this, he's guilty of something. You're a cop, *be* a cop. Do this for me.'

'What do you want in return?'

'That's something we can discuss later.'

'When would this happen?'

'Is tomorrow soon enough?' Alvares asked.

Gonzalo put the folder down. His hands were shaking, but not from fear. He swallowed. 'I'm just an inspector, not an inquisitor,' he said. 'I can't guarantee anything.'

Alvares smiled. 'Just do your best. I'm sure that will be good enough.'

SIXTEEN

CALLING GONZALO DID NO GOOD BECAUSE Gonzalo did not answer. The phone would ring a long time before finally turning over to voicemail, and though Jack left several messages, none were returned.

Leaving the hotel was out of the question. Jack wanted to be there when Gonzalo arrived, but the hours kept ticking away and Gonzalo did not come. A pair of old men, guests at the hotel, wandered down to the lobby and took up positions near the television, not talking to each other, but watching the screen intently. Jack had seen them before. They would be here all day.

It was nearly noon when he called Bernardo. 'Have you heard from Gonzalo?' Jack asked.

'No. I've heard from no one,' Bernardo said, and he sounded tired. Jack imagined him up all night, waiting for his phone to ring with the tip that would end all of this. His brother-in-law's voice was desolate.

'He won't answer his phone. He's not showing up.'

'Maybe something came up.'

'He's gone out alone,' Jack said. 'He went out and left me here, goddamn it.'

'Even if that were true, he would have called you,' Bernardo said.

'No, he's keeping things from me,' Jack said, and in that

moment he was convinced. Gonzalo had been quick to take him away from Goyo's, to go back on his own. He'd disarmed Jack and now he was pushing him aside.

'He'll come,' Bernardo said.

Light reflected off chrome in the street and Jack saw Gonzalo's car pull up to the curb. Jack felt his heart surge. 'He's here,' he said.

'Jack, listen—'

'I've got to go.' Jack closed the phone and went out to Gonzalo. He was ready to shout before he got there, the frustration of hours bubbling up. 'Where the hell have you been?'

Gonzalo did not flinch. 'Get in,' he said.

Jack lowered himself into the car and slammed the door hard. 'I've been trying to *call* you,' he said.

Gonzalo pulled away from the curb. 'Some important things have happened and I need you to listen carefully.'

'Don't ever leave me hanging like that,' Jack said. 'Ever.'

'No promises, Jack. Things are moving very quickly now and there may not be time to brief you every step of the way.'

'What's going on?'

'I have access to Guadalupe. *Official* access.'

'How?'

Gonzalo waved the question away. 'It's difficult to explain. What matters is that I will be face to face with Guadalupe tomorrow and I can demand answers. This is a major breakthrough. You should be very pleased.'

Jack watched the streets slip by. He wasn't sure which way Gonzalo was going. 'I'd be happier if I knew what he had to do with all of this.'

'That is what I intend to find out,' Gonzalo said. 'Where he was on the night in question. What he was doing. Why he lied to me about seeing the girls.'

'Do you think he did something to them?' Jack asked.

'I don't have those answers, Jack. But we'll know soon enough. I have the cooperation of the army and Captain Alvares. He'll talk.'

'What makes you so sure?'

'He's caught,' Gonzalo said. 'It would be one thing if I could not link him to your stepdaughter's car, but I can. I can prove he was there with the girls that night.'

'He'll just deny it.'

'Let him deny it. I still have the evidence. And I've learned other things, as well.'

'Like what?'

'I'd rather not say. For your own protection, Jack. If you said the wrong thing to the wrong person, bad things could happen and I don't wish that on you.'

'Tell me,' Jack said.

'It has to do with the Zetas, but I am still piecing it together.'

'They're involved?'

'I don't know and I'm not sure I would tell you even if I did.'

'Where are we going?'

'I'm taking you to your brother-in-law's house,' Gonzalo said. 'I want you to take your other girl and leave the city as soon as you can.'

Jack shook his head sharply. 'I'm not going anywhere.'

'Please, Jack, it's safer if you let me continue this on my own.'

'I *knew* you were trying to cut me loose!' Jack exclaimed. 'I knew it!'

'It's not like that. The situation… the situation is more complicated than one crooked policeman. You know what the city is like now; you know it's not safe for you to continue being seen with me. Even the army knows we've been together asking questions.'

'*You're* in the middle of it.'

'That's the risk I take as a police officer.'

'Then this is the risk I'm taking.'

Gonzalo gave Jack a sidelong look. 'You're a very stubborn man, Jack Searle.'

'I just want my girl back at home,' Jack said. 'That's all I want.'

'That's what I want, too,' Gonzalo replied. 'You may have your doubts, but from the beginning I've been on your side.'

'Then don't try to send me away,' Jack said.

Gonzalo sighed and his shoulders slumped. 'At least stay with your brother-in-law today. Be close to your family. Tomorrow we move forward.'

SEVENTEEN

JACK HAD BEEN RIGHT AND BERNARDO had not slept the whole night. When he ended the phone call with Jack, he felt a wave of tiredness wash over him that made his eyelids flutter. The chair he was in seemed suddenly very comfortable, and though he wanted to rise, he found his body did not wish to cooperate. It took real effort to stand.

The children were playing in their rooms and Reina had gone away to her work. Bernardo appreciated having Lidia there to keep the little ones busy because he was good for nothing else but waiting for the telephone to ring. He wandered to the kitchen and got *limonada* from the refrigerator, and then he settled into a chair by the large, empty table to drink and think. A sudden burst of happy giggles carried to him from Leandra's part of the house and for a moment Bernardo almost smiled.

He held the phone in his hand as he had all night. Even in bed he kept it clutched in his fist lest he miss the call, though he was attuned to every sound. Now it vibrated once and followed with a jolly tune that shattered the stillness. Bernardo checked the number, did not recognize it, and put the phone to his ear. '*Bueno*,' he said.

Silence on the other end, but the line was open. Bernardo thought he caught the hint of breathing, but it was too faint. The quiet went on for so long that he was certain the caller would hang up, but then he heard a throat clear and a man's voice kept low. 'You are the one who put up the flyers? About the missing girls?'

'I am. They are my daughter and niece.'

Another long pause and this time Bernardo could hear the caller's breath. 'Is there a reward for information?'

'I am not a rich man,' Bernardo said, 'but if the information is good, I may be able to pay something for it. Do you know anything?'

'*Sí.*'

'What do you know?'

This time the caller fell silent for so long that Bernardo had to check to see whether the line was still open. Finally, the man said, 'I saw it.'

All the tiredness rushed out of Bernardo and his body was flushed with sudden electricity that made him tingle. He sat upright in the chair. His hand on the phone trembled. 'What did you see?' he asked.

'Two girls in a white car. It was late and they were driving around like they were lost. Too slow, you know? They were stopped.'

Bernardo was slow to ask the next question, afraid that it would scare the caller away and he would learn no more. 'Who stopped them?'

'I don't know if I should say. If someone found out what I told you… it would go badly for me.'

'Please,' Bernardo said, 'I only want to know. My daughter has been missing for weeks. Her mother wants to know. Her brother and sister. Anything you can tell me. Anything at all.'

'Maybe I should wait until you can give me a reward.'

'Whatever you want,' Bernardo said.

Bernardo thought he heard a car honk its horn in the

background of the call. He imagined the man on the street, huddled in a doorway where no one could see. Maybe he was there, where it happened. Maybe he could see the spot right now.

'Are you still there?' Bernardo asked.

'I'm still here,' the caller said.

'Will you tell me what you know?'

'You have to understand,' the caller said, 'I had nothing to do with it. I was on the street when it happened. I was drunk, but that doesn't mean I didn't see it.'

'What did you see?' Bernardo asked again.

'There were two of them. Two cops. They stopped the girls with their lights.'

Bernardo realized he was holding his breath. He let go. 'Policemen,' he said.

'Yes. They didn't see me, but I saw them. I *know* them. They come through this neighborhood all the time. When they stopped the girls, I hid and watched.'

'What are their names?' Bernardo asked. 'Do you know their names?'

'No, I don't. I know their faces. And I know they belong to Los Zetas. Lots of police do, but these two for certain.'

At the mention of the Zetas, Bernardo felt a pang of fear and his grip on the phone loosened. A faintness passed through him. He had to force himself to breathe again. 'What did they do?'

'They stopped the car. They made the girls get out. They searched them.'

'And then?'

'They took them.'

'What do you mean, they took them?' Bernardo asked.

'They put handcuffs on them and put them in the back of

their car. The girls were shouting at them, but they didn't listen. They put them in the car and took them away.'

'To where?'

'I don't know where!' the caller suddenly erupted. 'Isn't it enough that I told you the rest? They left me behind! I didn't see anything else!'

Bernardo licked his lips and found them dry. 'This information is good. I will pay for it. As much as I can afford. You can tell us what the policemen looked like.'

'I'm not telling you anything else.'

'Don't you want money? I said I'll give you money.'

'I've changed my mind. I told you, these men belong to the Zetas. I was stupid to even call you.'

'No, no!' Bernardo said. 'It's good that you called! Please, is there anything more? Did you get the number of the police car? Which way were they headed when they drove away?'

The caller made an angry noise. 'There is no more! And if you were smart, you would forget about finding those girls! No good can come of this. They're gone.'

'Please—' Bernardo said, but the line clicked and he was speaking to a dead phone. The trembling overtook him again and he held the phone between both hands to keep from dropping it. His mind was awhirl.

He heard the jangle of the bells at the front gate.

EIGHTEEN

GONZALO LISTENED TO BERNARDO'S STORY with an expression of concentration on his face, as if every word counted. Jack supposed it did. He saw that Bernardo was visibly shaken and he wondered whether he looked the same way. His stomach was a knot.

When Bernardo was finished, Gonzalo asked him questions about the caller. What he sounded like, where he might have been calling from, anything that might lead them to the man, but there was nothing to be had. There was only the phone number he had called from, and when Bernardo tried the line it simply rang and rang.

'I can run the number through the system tomorrow,' Gonzalo said. 'If it belongs to someone we can track down, then we will have a witness.'

'Those cops,' Jack said, 'they were Guadalupe and his partner. You have evidence. It had to be them.'

Gonzalo nodded slowly. 'I believe so, yes.'

'How can we find out for sure?'

'If we can locate this witness and persuade him to talk to Alvares and his men, then we will have something,' Gonzalo said.

'There's got to be some way we can use this now.'

'There is. Guadalupe does not know that the witness is anonymous. I can confront him with the information that he was seen on the night in the company of the girls. I can prove he was there from his fingerprints. I can use his disciplinary record against him. He is corrupt, and if he is the type to run scared, then he may tell me the whole story.'

'What about Los Zetas?' Jack asked.

Bernardo held shaky fingers to his lips. He took them away and said, 'The caller said the policemen belonged to the Zetas.'

Gonzalo's face darkened. 'That is another matter altogether.'

'What do you mean?'

'I mean that it is one thing to get a crooked policeman to confess to taking bribes but something else entirely to accuse him of cooperation with the cartels.'

'But you think it's true,' Jack said. 'You told me—'

'I have learned some things that can't yet be proved, but they concern me. That is why I've asked you to leave, Jack. Perhaps you didn't understand before, but now you realize what we're up against in this city. The cartels offer two options to the policemen they wish to buy: *plata o plomo*.'

'Silver or lead?'

'Police who do not take the money are given the gun,' Gonzalo said. 'Even good cops can break under that kind of pressure.'

'Guadalupe is not a good cop,' Jack said.

'No. He's an opportunist. And we must hope he's also a coward, because he must fear Alvares and his men more than he fears the Zetas. That part is not so easy. The Zetas can reach anywhere.'

'I don't understand why he would take them,' Bernardo suddenly burst out. His fingers twitched erratically, but he was still holding onto his phone so tightly that his knuckles shone white. 'Why would he take them in his car in the middle of the night?'

Gonzalo spoke in soothing tones. 'That is not something that should worry you now, Sr Sigala. The important thing is that he did not harm them. They were under arrest, but they were alive when the witness saw them. Concentrate on that.'

'They weren't hurting anyone!'

Jack reached out and put his hand on Bernardo's shoulder. He felt the muscles knotted underneath the skin, the invisible tremors that coursed through Bernardo's body and showed in his face and hands. If he could have, he would have put his arms around Bernardo, but he sensed that Bernardo would only pull away. 'It's going to be all right,' Jack said, and it sounded lame even to him.

'Promise me you will get the truth from him, Inspector Soler,' Bernardo said. 'Make him admit where he took our girls. It's not too late. They could still be unharmed.'

'I promise you I will do everything I can to find out what happened that night,' Gonzalo said.

Bernardo nodded shakily. 'All right.'

'Jack, may I speak to you alone?' Gonzalo asked.

'Sure. Let's go outside.'

Gonzalo left by the front door and Jack met him in the little courtyard by the cold, ashy grill. His mouth was a flat line and his eyes were dark.

'What is it?' Jack asked.

'I've deliberately kept things from your brother-in-law because I don't want him to fall apart,' Gonzalo said. 'You can see already what a mess he is just hearing the name of Los Zetas.'

'What do you want me to do?'

'Try to help him through this and let me be the one to tell

him anything new that we learn. I know he is your brother-in-law, but it would be better for me to withhold information as needed.'

'I don't like keeping him in the dark.'

'It's in his best interest, Jack. Bernardo has a family and he must be strong for them. He can't do that if he's in a blind panic.'

Jack considered. 'I'll do it, but no more trying to freeze me out. I have more invested in this than you do and I want to be involved. Don't try to send me back over the bridge.'

'It may not be my choice to make. If Alvares decides you are interfering with an ongoing investigation, he may have you expelled. He has the power to do that.'

'I'd go to my government and file a complaint,' Jack said.

'And in the meantime things will go on just as Alvares wants them. It could be weeks or months before you gathered enough cover to come back. The army owns this city now. Between them and the Federal Police, you wouldn't be able to make a move without being picked up.'

'Don't they understand that I'm just trying to help?' Jack asked.

'You're a civilian. Not a policeman. Not a soldier. In their eyes, you are at best an impediment to a clean investigation, at worst an outright liability. And if they knew you brought a gun into the country you would have crossed the line to criminal, suitable only to be squashed. So far you've been treated with kid gloves. Don't give them any excuse to take them off.'

NINETEEN

ON THE MORNING OF THE NEXT DAY, Gonzalo took special care to present himself properly. He brought out an iron and pressed his shirt and pants. A new tie came out for the occasion and he wore his best jacket. He made sure to be freshly shaved and his only regret was that he had not taken the opportunity to get a haircut. When he looked in the mirror, he was the image of a police inspector. He still missed his gun.

Alvares had given him a timetable and he drove to the station house early to prepare. Gonzalo was pleased to note that the soldier, Gervasio Chaidez, had followed his instructions about organizing the case files and he did not have to search for the right folders for long. After that he ensconced himself in the interrogation room alone, poring over the scanty information he had, adding notes in the margins and a whole page of additional observations gathered since.

The sound-absorbing foam kept him from hearing the approaching footsteps of Guadalupe and his escort, but somehow Gonzalo sensed they were on their way. He glanced up at the eye of the video camera and half-waved to whomever was watching. Keys rattled in the lock and the door swung wide.

Guadalupe was in civilian clothes. His shirt was rumpled and looked as though it had been rescued from a laundry pile.

He wore no tie and had on battered sneakers. When he saw Gonzalo there was an instant of surprise that hardened into visible distaste.

The soldiers with Guadalupe had not cuffed him. They crowded him through the door and shut it firmly behind him. Gonzalo did not rise to shake Guadalupe's hand, nor did he greet him. They simply looked at each other for a long minute marked by total silence.

Gonzalo spoke first. 'Sit down,' he said.

'What are you doing here?' Guadalupe asked.

'Sit down. Please.'

Guadalupe was slow to comply, but eventually he did sit opposite Gonzalo at the undersized table. His gaze roamed over the notes and papers laid out in front of Gonzalo. Gonzalo hoped for some sign of nerves, but there was none.

'Am I under arrest?' asked Guadalupe.

'Not as far as I'm aware,' Gonzalo said. 'What did they tell you when you were brought in?'

'That I had to answer questions related to reinstatement. I expected an interview for a background check, not this. Aren't you sidelined like all the rest of us?'

'I've been given special permission to speak with you,' Gonzalo replied.

'Did you cut some kind of deal?'

'No deals. I'm assisting with an investigation.'

'What investigation?'

Gonzalo brought out the pictures of Marina Cobos and Patricia Sigala. He laid them side by side on the table facing Guadalupe and let the man look over them before answering. 'These girls are missing,' Gonzalo said. 'I asked you about them before.'

'And I told you I've never seen them.'

'Is that the answer you want to stick with?' Gonzalo asked.

'It's the truth.'

He left the pictures where they were and paged through the file until he reached the fingerprint results. A black-and-white printout showed Guadalupe's prints from his file and the prints taken from the car, the points of similarity marked with circles so they could not be missed. 'Before we continue,' Gonzalo said, 'I should warn you that what you say today could affect your position in the police force.'

'What is that supposed to mean?'

'It means you could be terminated permanently.'

'I've got nothing to hide.'

'Then you won't mind explaining how your thumb and forefinger prints managed to make their way onto the vehicle those girls were driving on the night of their disappearance.'

Gonzalo thought he caught the flicker of something then, but it was gone in an eye blink, supplanted by the same smoldering dislike. Guadalupe pushed back from the table, but the back of his chair hit the wall and he was forced to scoot forward again. The interrogation room was meant to be intimate. There was no avoiding it.

'Can you explain your prints being there?' Gonzalo asked.

'How do I know that's even true?'

'I have the report here if you want to see it. Would you like to?'

'No, I don't need to see it.'

'Then you admit to having contact with these two girls.'

'I'm not admitting anything!' Guadalupe shot back. 'If you say my fingerprints are there, then I can't argue with you. Maybe sometime I pulled the car over. Maybe it was that night, maybe it was some other night.'

'You told me before that you hadn't seen the vehicle I

described. A white Galant. Texas plates.'

'I pull over a lot of cars with Texas plates,' Guadalupe said. 'Those people come over here and drive like they own the road. They don't have diplomatic immunity. We pull them over, they get tickets the same as anyone else.'

'And sometimes they pay to avoid the tickets altogether,' Gonzalo said.

'Are you accusing me of something?'

'I only note that in your personnel report you were accused on three separate occasions of taking bribes.'

'And none of them stuck,' Guadalupe returned. 'How about you? Have you ever been accused of taking the *mordida*?'

Gonzalo looked down before Guadalupe could see something he did not want to reveal. Instead he riffled the pages of the case file as if looking for something in particular, though his next question was already prepared. 'Is it possible that on the night in question you stopped the girls for some infraction and tried to get money from them?'

'How stupid would I be to answer that?' Guadalupe asked.

'Then let me put it another way. Is it possible you pulled the car over and it simply slipped your mind when asked about it later? For whatever reason.'

Guadalupe was slow to speak. 'I guess it's possible,' he said carefully.

'Then the fingerprints on the car can be explained. You made a routine traffic stop in the middle of the night. Maybe you put your hand on the door when you talked to the driver.'

'Maybe,' Guadalupe said.

'So it would stand to reason that if you did pull the girls over, you would have written them a ticket?'

Guadalupe said nothing.

'You would have a copy of any citation you wrote that night, wouldn't you?' Gonzalo asked. 'Something you could show me?'

'What are you playing at?' Guadalupe asked.

'I'm simply asking the question.'

'All right, let's say I pulled them over,' Guadalupe said. 'Let's say I gave the driver a talking to. That doesn't mean I wrote her a ticket. I could have let them off with a warning.'

'Did you?'

'I'm not admitting I stopped them at all.'

Gonzalo slammed his open palm down on the table hard enough to make Guadalupe flinch. 'Let's cut the bullshit! If you pulled that car over, I want to know that you did it. *Now.*'

They matched gazes and for a long moment Gonzalo thought Guadalupe would not speak at all, then the man glanced away. 'Okay, I pulled them over,' he said. 'What about it? I didn't do anything to them.'

Gonzalo let his breath go. He'd been holding it and his heart beat heavily. With a finger he nudged the pictures of the girls closer to Guadalupe. 'I knew you stopped their car all along,' he said. 'Do you want to know how?'

'How?' Guadalupe asked.

'I have a witness who saw it happen.'

'What witness? There was nobody around.'

'A witness identified you and your partner,' Gonzalo said. It was half a lie, but Guadalupe would not know. 'They said you pulled them over and had them step out of the vehicle.'

'That didn't happen.'

'And then you put the cuffs on them.'

'That's a lie!' Guadalupe shouted.

'And then you made them get in the back of your patrol unit,' Gonzalo said with a raised voice. 'They saw the entire thing from start to finish, so if you're going to keep denying it you're doing yourself no good.'

'I made no arrests that night,' Guadalupe said.

'My witness says otherwise.'

'Your witness is full of shit! Check the records! Have you checked them? I didn't arrest anyone.'

'What would your partner say if I asked him?'

'The same! I admit to pulling them over, but it was only to give them a talking to. They were driving too slowly and they were weaving. I could smell the alcohol on the driver's breath as soon as she put down the window.'

'If she was drunk, why *wouldn't* you arrest her?'

'I didn't think it was that bad. And she was young and pretty and maybe I didn't want to see her get into that kind of trouble.'

'That was very thoughtful of you.'

'You go to hell! I'm not going to answer these kinds of questions.'

Guadalupe made to get up from his chair and Gonzalo froze him with his voice: 'Don't you move! You'll go when I say it's time to go and no sooner!'

The man fell back into his seat and a bitter smile played on his lips. 'You're tough now, are you, Inspector? Tougher than me?'

'I don't have to prove myself to you,' Gonzalo said. 'You're a liar and I don't believe you for a second when you say you don't take money. What I want to know is this: did they refuse to pay up, or was it your intention all along to arrest them?'

'I told you: I didn't arrest anyone. If there's someone who says differently, they're the ones who lie.' With that, Guadalupe crossed his arms across his chest and fixed a stony look on Gonzalo.

Gonzalo let him stare. He carefully set back the pages in the case file and then closed the cover. He folded his hands atop the marbled green paper. 'Tell me about Águila.'

Guadalupe's mouth drooped open before he could snap it shut again. His arms tightened around his chest and he shifted uncomfortably in his chair. 'I don't know anyone called Águila.'

'Haven't you figured out by now that I don't ask questions I don't already know the answers to?' Gonzalo asked. 'You can try and string me along as much as you want, but in the end I'll get the answers I'm looking for. I have nowhere else to be and nothing else to do. I'm suspended, remember? So let me refresh your memory: you and Águila at El Pájaro in La Zona. Together. *I was there.*'

Gonzalo saw the flicker of Guadalupe's eyes, felt the sudden aura of vulnerability that surged out of the man, across the desk and filling the room. Guadalupe fidgeted still more, his hands tucked into his armpits. He looked left and right, but there was only the tiny space and the two of them, the camera glaring down.

'I'm not going to say any more,' Guadalupe said finally.

'Just tell me how far into Águila's pocket you are.'

'Let me out of here.'

'It's not too late to make a deal,' Gonzalo pressed. 'Tell me everything you know and you could still save yourself.'

Guadalupe unwound his limbs and waved his hands in front of himself as if trying to conjure Gonzalo away. 'No, no, no! I won't say anything more.'

'Is it Águila you're protecting?'

When Guadalupe looked at Gonzalo again, his eyes shone. The bravado was gone and now there was only fear. He spoke and his voice was tremulous. 'You don't know what you're asking. Now let me out.'

'Eliseo—' Gonzalo began, using Guadalupe's name for the first time.

'*Let me out!*'

Gonzalo looked at Guadalupe for a long time, but the man was inured to his gaze, his attention turned inward. His arms were wrapped around his body once more and there was the sense that he would burst out of his chair and attack the door if it did not open. Gonzalo sighed. He turned to the camera. 'Let him out,' he said. 'We're finished here.'

TWENTY

'WHO IS THIS ÁGUILA?' ALVARES asked.

'I can only tell you what I've learned, and that is very little,' Gonzalo said.

'He's a *narco*,' Alvares said flatly.

'Yes. A Zeta. I don't know how far up and no one is saying. On the night I saw him, I managed to get the number from his license plate, but the plates were stolen from another vehicle. It was a dead end.'

They sat in Alvares' office. From outside the open door came the muted bustle of activity and the sound of an upraised voice complaining about a vandalized storefront. When the Municipal Police were still in charge, a complaint like that would have been looked into. Gonzalo did not think the army would pay it much mind at all.

'We'll tear Guadalupe's life apart,' Alvares said. 'Everything from his phone records to his financials. Nothing will be off the table. What we cannot do ourselves, we'll pass on to our federal colleagues. It doesn't matter that he won't talk. By the time we're finished, he won't have to.'

Gonzalo nodded, though his mind was elsewhere, lingering in the small interrogation room where Guadalupe had said so much while admitting so little. His thoughts flitted to the man with the gold watch, Águila, and his Ralph Lauren shirt and dark Mercedes, the garish lights and sudden shadows of El Pájaro. He remembered the moment he first suspected Guadalupe of lying and he regretted how little distance he had come since then.

'Inspector Soler?'

'What? I'm sorry, can you repeat that?'

'I said I wanted to thank you for your assistance. You're a credit to the Municipal Police. When the time comes, you can expect to receive my highest recommendation for readmittance to the force.'

'Thank you, Captain.'

'What will you tell your American friend?'

'I will tell him the truth,' Gonzalo said. 'As much as he would like to continue the investigation into his stepdaughter's disappearance, the matter is best left in the hands of the army and the Federal Police.'

'That sounds wise. We're dealing with dangers a civilian has no business involving himself with. He should go home and wait.'

'I've been telling him that all along. Maybe now he'll listen.'

'And what will you do?'

Gonzalo attempted a smile. 'I will try to make my savings last as long as possible. The review process is going to take some time even with your recommendation and I would like to be able to keep eating.'

'I'm sorry you were caught up in this,' Alvares said. 'It's policemen like Guadalupe that we're trying to root out, not cops like you. If it were up to me, things would be done very differently. It's chaos out there.'

Gonzalo rose from his chair. 'I should go. Thank you for the opportunity, Captain Alvares.'

Alvares got up and offered Gonzalo his hand. 'We'll be in touch with you the moment anything changes in regard to this case. You can tell the parents yourself what is happening.'

'I'm sure they will appreciate that,' Gonzalo said. 'Thank you again, Captain.'

Alvares stopped to scribble something on a sticky note and passed it to Gonzalo. 'Take this: it's my personal number. If you need anything at all, feel free to call me.'

'I will. Goodbye.'

Gonzalo waited until he was outside the building before he dialed Jack's number. Jack answered immediately. 'What's happening?' he asked.

'I did not get the confession I was hoping for,' Gonzalo said, 'but I learned enough. Guadalupe was there and he did take your stepdaughter in his patrol unit. He's too afraid of incriminating himself to admit more.'

'Then what do we do?'

'It's doubtful that Guadalupe will do anything to endanger himself more than he already has. That leaves us one option: Fregoso.'

'Fregoso. The partner?'

'Yes. So far he's managed to avoid any attention, so he may be useful to us. Guadalupe will also try to get in touch with him to get their stories straight. If this panics Fregoso as much as I think it will, he might do something stupid.'

'Like what?'

Gonzalo reached his car. The inside was roasting, so he stood with the door open as he talked. 'I know the name of a Zeta I believe Guadalupe knows well: Águila.'

'Who is he?'

'That is one of the things I do not know, Jack. But when I asked Guadalupe about Águila, he didn't respond well. Fregoso is in this with Guadalupe at least part of the way. I believe that if either of them is to reach out to Águila for help or protection, it will be the partner no one's watching. Fregoso will lead us right to him.'

TWENTY-ONE

THE NEXT DAY JACK CAME TO THE PLACE Gonzalo described and found Gonzalo's car parked against the uneven curb of a sleepy street. It was early and only a few places were open, so there was room enough for Jack to slide in behind Gonzalo and stop. He brought a Thermos of coffee and a bag of churros with him and got into Gonzalo's car.

'*Buenos días*,' Gonzalo said, and Jack saw that he was unshaven and bleary. He stretched in the small car, his shoulder making popping noises.

'Did you sleep in your car last night?' Jack asked.

'I did not sleep at all,' Gonzalo answered. He produced a Styrofoam cup and Jack poured a measure of coffee into it. Jack put the churros between them. He liked to dip them in his coffee.

'You should have told me you needed someone to cover for you,' Jack said.

'Then we would both be tired. It's all right.'

'Which one is Fregoso's place?'

'There,' Gonzalo said, and he pointed to a turquoise-colored apartment building that sat sidelong to the street, its narrow face toward traffic. A second-floor doorway was just visible from this angle and part of a window.

'Has he been out?'

'Not since he came home last night.'

'What's he doing in there?'

'Probably sleeping. He was out very late.'

'Did he meet with Guadalupe?'

'No.'

They ate and drank and when Gonzalo emptied his cup, Jack poured more for him. The smell of cinnamon and coffee was strong in the car. A few other vehicles lazily plied the street, but for the most part it was quiet, without a sign of distress. Jack thought this was the way it ought to be. No *narcos*. No soldiers. No guns.

'What makes you think Guadalupe will come now if he hasn't already?' Jack asked.

'He'll be too afraid to use his phone. People could be listening in. He'll want to meet Fregoso face to face. I thought for sure they would meet at some bar, but Fregoso kept to himself all night. Perhaps Guadalupe didn't want to take a chance that someone followed him from the station.'

'Someone like you,' Jack said.

'Exactly. Though this work isn't what the army is here for. They have no patience for the waiting game. Seeing me may have given Guadalupe some pause. He doesn't know who is working with the army now. It could be me, it could be anybody.'

'Will Alvares bring in more people?'

'I don't know. It's doubtful. He made a special case for you and me. It's not likely he will do the same for anyone else.'

The churros were all gone. Jack crumpled up the bag and tucked the paper ball under his leg. The Thermos was almost empty, too. He finished the last of it.

Morning sun spilled over the edges of buildings and cascaded into the street, turning asphalt into molten gold.

The more pleasant cool of night bled away and Jack felt the prickling of sweat beneath his shirt.

The hands on Jack's watch turned around and around. Though he shifted time and again in the uncomfortable seat, Gonzalo sat motionless, watching Fregoso's apartment with an air of total attention. Jack did not want to interrupt him to speak.

Fregoso did not come out. Guadalupe did not appear. Eventually Jack's stomach growled for lunch.

'Maybe he's not coming,' Jack said.

'He'll come.'

'He could have just called. If he's not as afraid to use the phone as you think, he could have touched base with Fregoso already and we're sitting here for nothing.'

For the first time in hours, Gonzalo turned his gaze away from Fregoso's apartment. He looked at Jack. 'Is that what you think? That we're wasting our time?'

'The thought crossed my mind. What exactly have we gotten so far? A confession that's not a confession, a witness who won't come forward and the name of a narco who might not even exist.'

'He exists,' Gonzalo said.

'We ought to lean on Fregoso. Get him to tell us what he knows.'

'I'm not a vigilante, Jack. Are you?'

Jack's face turned into a scowl. 'I don't know what I am. Along for the ride, I guess.'

'I'm doing what I can.'

'It just feels like every day we get farther away.'

Gonzalo nodded. 'I can understand that. But you must believe that we will find Marina. And Patricia, too.'

'Why are you even doing this, anyway?' Jack said. 'Staying

up all night in your car, sticking your neck out... what's in it for you?'

'You *are* paying me, Jack.'

'But you were on this before I started paying you. Right from the beginning. You've got a whole city full of drug dealers and murderers and God knows what and you chose to spend your time looking for Marina.'

Gonzalo looked away and scratched the back of his neck thoughtfully. 'It is difficult to put into words you would understand. You are not a policeman. You're not even a Mexican.'

'Try me.'

Jack waited until it seemed as though Gonzalo would not speak, but then he said, 'It's because I am not proud of what we've become in this city. Everyone tends to his little patch, but no one looks out for anyone else. As a policeman it's supposed to be different; we are meant to care for others before ourselves. But we do not. We are like Guadalupe and Fregoso. That's why Alvares and his men are here now: because we failed.'

A lengthy silence passed between them. Gonzalo resumed his vigil and Jack shifted so that his sweaty back peeled free of the vinyl upholstery of the little car's seat.

'You haven't failed me yet,' Jack said.

'Thank you for saying so. I know it's been difficult for you.'

'Just so long as we keep moving forward.'

'That much I can promise. We will always move forward.'

'What will you do if you see Guadalupe and Fregoso together?' Jack asked to change the subject.

'I will go on watching Fregoso for another twenty-four hours to track his movements. If he leads me to Águila, then I'll have my connection. If he does not, I will go back to Alvares to ask for permission to interrogate him.'

'That's it?'

'What else would you have me do?'

'What about moving forward?'

'That is moving forward, Jack.'

Jack closed his mouth on the words he was about to say. His eyes strayed toward the apartment. The door was open and Fregoso was out. Gonzalo sat up sharply. 'He's on the move.'

Fregoso closed the door behind himself and locked it, then moved out of sight. Jack gripped the edge of the open window. 'Where's he going?'

'There's a small place for parking cars next to the building,' Gonzalo said. 'He drives a gold Camry.'

It was a long minute before Jack saw the gold Camry nose out from beside the building and into the street. It turned toward them and came on quickly, picking up speed. Gonzalo started his car.

Jack wanted to duck down when Fregoso came close, but the man did not even glance in their direction as he passed. Gonzalo goosed the accelerator and his car lurched around in a clumsy U-turn in the middle of the street. 'We'll have to come back for your truck,' Gonzalo said.

Fregoso drove well above the limit and ducked around slower-moving cars without signaling. Gonzalo raced to keep up with him, nearly lost the Camry at a red light and then made up some of the distance. After another handful of blocks they saw Fregoso turn into the parking lot of a *taquería* with all of its tables arranged outside on a covered porch. Gonzalo stopped where he could, so close that Jack was certain Fregoso would see them if he turned his head the wrong way.

'There is Guadalupe,' Gonzalo said.

Guadalupe sat at one of the tables and he waved Fregoso closer. They sat down together and Jack saw them sharing food out of a paper-lined plastic basket as they talked. He wanted to be close to them, to hear what they were saying. He wished for some kind of high-tech listening device like the cops used on television. At least he could be close enough to read their lips.

'What is he telling him?' Jack asked.

'I'm sure he is telling him everything. What we know. What we don't know.'

'Now Fregoso will be watching his back.'

'That's part of the price we must pay to play this game.'

The two policemen conferred a while longer and then said their goodbyes. Jack watched Guadalupe throw away his trash before heading to his car. He itched to follow. 'I should have driven myself.'

'You would be too conspicuous,' Gonzalo said.

'What if you have it backward? What if Guadalupe goes to Águila and not Fregoso?'

'We're committed to this now, Jack. Look: Fregoso is going.'

Fregoso drove away from the restaurant and Gonzalo followed. This time Fregoso did not speed, but his driving took on an elusive quality. He made extra turns and more than once he passed stop signs without pausing. Jack's forehead was sweating. He saw Gonzalo's knuckles were white on the wheel and he was biting his lip.

Eventually Jack recognized the street and he realized they were coming at Fregoso's apartment from the opposite direction. Fregoso abruptly turned into the narrow drive that led to the parking area. Gonzalo cruised past. Jack heard a held breath hiss out of him.

Gonzalo steered them back into a spot where they could watch the apartment once more. Within a minute they saw Fregoso at his doorstep. He glanced around once and then vanished inside.

'What now? We wait again?' Jack asked.

'As I said,' Gonzalo replied. 'We must see what he does next.'

'Meanwhile Guadalupe's running around with no one keeping an eye on him.'

'*He* doesn't know that,' Gonzalo said. 'It will be Fregoso, Jack. Fregoso is a night owl, so it's likely he won't move until sundown. When he does, we will be here.'

'I don't think I can take another six or seven hours cooped up in this car,' Jack said.

'If you want, I can call you when he makes his move. You don't have to be here. Spend time with your stepdaughter. This must be very difficult for her.'

Jack thought of Lidia and pushed away a dark feeling of self-reproach. All of this time he had been away from her, forcing her to stay with Bernardo and his family, telling her nothing. He did not know why he had done that, because Lidia was smart and strong and if anyone could handle it then it would be her. But she was only thirteen and he could not bring himself to lay that burden on her. 'She'll be all right,' he told Gonzalo.

'Even so, you shouldn't be spending all your time with me. It's no good for you, Jack. I told you why I'm doing this, but it's different.'

'It's different for me, too,' Jack said. 'Marina got into this because of me, because of what I let her do. I'm not going to treat this like some job I can subcontract out. I want to do the heavy lifting.'

'Then you have a decision to make,' Gonzalo said.

Jack looked out through the sun-frosted windshield toward Fregoso's apartment. He felt as though he'd been staring at it forever. He would recognize it anywhere. 'I'll go,' he said. 'But I'm coming back tonight. You haven't slept in twenty-four hours. You need someone with you.'

'I appreciate it, Jack.'

'I'm just doing what I got to do.'

TWENTY-TWO

EVEN WHEN ALL OF THEM WERE TOGETHER, there was room enough at Bernardo and Reina's kitchen table, but now there were two ugly spaces that no one filled. Bernardo tried not to look at them when Little Bernardo set out the flatware and made places for his sister and his cousin though they were not there. He thought that if he stared too long at the empty chairs, he would cry again and that was something he wanted to avoid at any cost.

Reina had made *birria* and she took charge of ladling the heavy, spicy goat stew into each of their bowls before her own. Then it was time for grace, when the family joined hands and the vacant chairs were even more obvious because they threatened to break the chain. Bernardo had no words. He left it up to his wife to say the blessing.

A covered plate of corn tortillas was passed around. Bernardo took one and dipped it in the *birria*. 'What are we celebrating?' he asked, and the flatness of his voice surprised him.

'It's always a good time to celebrate life,' Reina said, and the look on her face silenced any reply.

Bernardo turned to Jack. 'When will you go out tonight?' he asked.

'Soon.'

'I wish I could go with you,' Bernardo said.

'It's better if you are here.'

Lidia had been quiet for days, barely speaking to anyone. She spent time with the children, especially Leandra, but she was scarcely present when they took meals. Now she looked up from her *birria* and looked at Jack a long time before she said, 'Do you think this is going to lead anywhere?'

Jack ducked his eyes from Lidia and concentrated on his bowl. 'We have to hope so. There isn't anything else.'

'Is this guy just taking your money?'

'No. No, he's doing everything he can.'

'Eat your food, Lidia,' Bernardo said. 'Don't let it get cold.'

The meal proceeded without comment from anyone, with just the clink of spoons in bowls to accompany their taciturn eating. Bernardo found himself wishing Jack would go away quickly so he could return to his beer without self-consciousness. 'That was great,' Jack said finally, and he pushed away from the table. 'I've got to go.'

Bernardo felt a rush of relief. 'I'll walk you out.'

Jack paused at Lidia's side to kiss her on her head and hug her, but then he was out of the kitchen and to the front door with Bernardo just behind. They went out into the night and stopped at the gate for their own goodbye. 'I'll be back tomorrow sometime,' Jack said.

'Lidia will be here.'

'I can't leave her here much longer. School starts soon. We'll both have to go back to Laredo.'

'And the policeman?'

Jack looked down. 'I guess he'll have to go on without me.'

Bernardo put his hand on Jack's shoulder. 'Be careful tonight, Jack.'

'I will be.'

Bernardo set the latch after Jack passed through the gate and went back inside reluctantly. He sat on the couch and twisted the cap off a beer, grateful for the smell and taste that followed.

'*Papá?*'

He started a bit and looked and saw Little Bernardo standing in the shadows by the couch, the light from the television flickering over him.

'What is it, Bernardino?'

'Is tonight the night Tío Jack finds Patricia?'

'You've never called him *tío* before.'

'He is Marina and Lidia's father.'

'Their stepfather.'

'It's the same.'

For reasons he could not express, Bernardo suddenly felt a terrible sadness and he gathered up Little Bernardo in his arms and held him closely. 'You are a very smart boy,' Bernardo said. 'For some it is the same.'

'So will he find her?'

'I hope so. I hope so very much.'

'Goodnight, *Papá.*'

'Goodnight.'

A tear gathered in the corner of Bernardo's eye and he wiped it away. His next gulp of beer did not taste so fresh or clean and his face soured. There was some stupid thing on the television and he changed the channel angrily.

He knew Reina was finished in the kitchen when she appeared quietly beside him. She stood without speaking for a while, though Bernardo felt her holding it back. Finally she said, 'I'm going to bed.'

'I will be there soon.'

'How much will you drink?'

'Are you keeping track of it now?'

'You don't go out. You don't help Jack. You just sit in front of the TV and drink.'

'I'm waiting!' Bernardo said sharply.

'We are all waiting,' Reina said.

'What do you want me to do?'

Reina paused. He heard her sigh. 'Nothing. Don't do anything.'

She slipped away. Bernardo felt the urge to shout something after her, but he kept his silence. Better to open another bottle and concentrate on the artless, pointless images on the screen. He was glad when she was gone.

At some point after midnight he drifted and twice he jerked out of sleep to sit upright. His empty bottles were arranged on the floor by his feet, but he did not count them. He frowned because he could not avoid bed any longer. Even when she slept, Reina judged him.

The bell on the gate jangled once and was silent. Bernardo checked the time. It was almost two o'clock in the morning.

He rose from the couch and went to the front door. 'Jack?' he said out loud.

His fingers were clumsy undoing the locks, but he managed to get them open. Bernardo cracked the door to peer outside. He saw them.

There were four in the little courtyard in front of the house, figures turned black by the shadows thrown from the street-light beyond the wall. Bernardo did not look to see whether they were armed because he knew immediately that they were. He knew everything in a moment and then he slammed the door shut with his body.

Someone crashed against the door on the other side. Bernardo fumbled with the locks, catching the first one and hurrying to the next. He felt short of breath, but he forced himself to fill his lungs and shout, 'Reina! Reina!'

Lights came on deeper in the house and Reina came out in her nightdress. Bernardo fastened the door's chain before another heavy blow fell against it. The children emerged blinking with sleep before the danger came to them in perfect clarity and their eyes were wide open, their faces drawn.

'Bernardo, what's happening?' Reina called to him.

'Get the children out! Out through the back. Hurry up!'

'What will you do?'

'I will keep them here!'

Leandra started crying and Reina gathered her to her side. Little Bernardo seemed frozen, his mouth hanging open, and he did not react when Lidia took his hand. '*Papá!*' he shouted.

'Go! Get out!'

The blows were falling faster and harder on the door and it jumped in its frame with every impact. Bernardo could do nothing but place his body in the way. He knew that if he backed away, the door would come crashing open and then there would be no escape for any of them.

One by one the children vanished through the kitchen with Reina just behind. She paused long enough to look back at Bernardo. Bernardo nodded to her. 'I'll be all right,' he said. His voice had a terrible calm he did not feel.

Reina slipped away. They would all leave by the back door, which opened directly into an alley where neighbors left their trash for the sanitation trucks. They would be safe, so long as the men at the front had not sent more around to the back.

An especially strong crash against the door cracked the frame where the deadbolts were set. Bernardo sweated all over, his hands slick as he pushed back. How long before they broke a window and stormed in that way? He could not keep them out then and he could not fight.

At least two men pounded on the door, an irregular rhythm

of kicks that Bernardo could feel even through the wood. He leaned so hard against the door that his bare feet slipped on the floor. A little longer. Reina and the children would be at the end of the alley by now. If they kept running, no one could catch them. They would find a house that would take them in. They would be all right.

He had never wished for an army patrol to pass his house before, but he wished for one now. They came in their trucks and Humvees and shone spotlights on the faces of the houses, or in windows. If they came now, they could not help but see what was happening. Bernardo would be saved.

'*Papá?*'

Bernardo had been squeezing his eyes shut with exertion. He opened them. Little Bernardo stood an arm's length away, still dressed in his short pajamas with a picture of Spider Man on the shirt. His eyes were dark and he trembled.

'What the hell are you doing here?' Bernardo demanded. 'I told you to go with your mother! Go on! Quickly!'

'I will help you,' Little Bernardo said, and he laid his little body against the door under Bernardo's arm. 'We'll stop them together.'

Bernardo's eyes stung from sweat. 'You have to go, *hijo,*' he said. 'This is no good.'

'I'll stay!'

'Please go!'

The bolts in the door gave way all at once and Bernardo was thrown back from the door. He tripped over his own feet and fell sprawling with Little Bernardo beside him. Men boiled into the open doorway, their faces covered with black masks like those the police and soldiers often wore. The men had guns.

Bernardo closed his arms around his son as the men converged. 'No, leave the boy alone! Leave him alone!'

Little Bernardo was wrenched away from him and someone hit him hard on the side of the head with something solid and metal. The room swam. He was dragged up onto his knees, strong hands on his shoulders. Little Bernardo was forced to kneel as well, and Bernardo saw his own terror reflected in the face of his son.

He was bleeding from his scalp. He was grabbed by the hair and a paper was thrust into his face. He saw the bold letters: DESAPARECIDO.

'Is this yours?' asked one of the masked men.

Bernardo nodded slackly. The flyer was thrown down in front of him.

'You're stupid and you don't know what you're doing,' the masked man said. He brandished a pistol. 'This is what happens when people are stupid.'

The pistol barely touched Little Bernardo's head before it fired. Bernardino's skull absorbed the blast and snapped over as if his neck had broken. One of his eyes was instantly shot through with red and the other rolled up white. The man holding him let him crumple.

Bernardo made a sound he had never made before, one that was not a word or a scream, but some anguished wail that welled up out of him and seemed to push back the ring of men, if only for a moment. He was blinded by his tears, which felt scalding hot and burned his skin. When the masked man turned the gun on him, there was no room for fear. Little Bernardo was gone.

PART FOUR

UNCHAINED

ONE

HE HEARD THE KNOCKING ON THE DOOR unconsciously, smothered by sleep, until finally he surfaced into wakefulness and realized where he was. Jack threw the thin sheet off him and got up. At the door he asked, '¿Quién es?'

'Sr Jack Searle? My name is Lieutenant Patricio Casiano. I am under the command of Captain Alvares.'

Jack did not open the door. 'What do you want?'

'Captain Alvares wishes to see you urgently. It can't wait.'

'Give me a minute.'

His jeans were draped over the back of the room's only chair. Jack pulled them on and found a clean T-shirt to wear beneath yesterday's work shirt.

When he opened the door he saw a short man and a second soldier. The shorter man extended his hand without smiling. 'Sr Searle,' he said.

'What's this about?'

'Something terrible has happened. Captain Alvares must see you immediately.'

'Did something happen to Gonzalo?'

'No, señor. It is your family.'

Jack's knees went weak. He caught the frame of the door and kept himself from swaying. 'My stepdaughter?'

Casiano's face was stone. 'Your stepdaughter is Lidia Cobos?'

'Yes. Is she all right?'

'She's fine, Sr Searle. But there was an attack last night and she was in great danger. I did not want to be the one to tell you this, but Bernardo Sigala is dead. I understand he was your brother-in-law?'

'What about… what about the rest of Bernardo's family?'

'Sr Sigala's son was also killed.'

'Oh, my God.'

'Please, Sr Searle. Come with me.'

Jack was barely conscious of locking the hotel room door behind himself, or of being led down the stairs to the street. Put in the passenger seat of a pick-up truck manned by two men with automatic rifles, he was shuttled through the city, but he saw nothing and heard nothing along the way. When they reached the police station, it was like an awful dream he was having with his eyes open.

Lieutenant Casiano brought Jack to the office where Captain Alvares was. Alvares' aspect was funereal and without being prompted he rose from his desk and came to Jack to clasp him by both arms. 'Sr Searle,' he said. 'You have my deepest sympathy.'

'How did it happen?' Jack said, and his voice seemed far away.

'Sit down. I will tell you everything we know.'

'I think I'll stand if that's okay.'

'I understand.' Alvares went back to his seat. He had a set of photographs on the desktop in front of him. Jack did not look at them closely because he saw man-shapes and the brilliant red of blood. He did not want to see Bernardo dead. He did not want to see Bernardino dead.

'Where is Lidia?' Jack asked.

'She is upstairs. We have a place for officers to sleep between shifts. She and her relations are being made as comfortable as we can make them.'

'I'd like to see her.'

'Very soon.'

Jack could not find the strength to argue.

'Last night in the early morning hours, some men attacked your brother-in-law's house,' Alvares said. 'Sr Sigala was quick enough and strong enough to hold them off until his family could escape. For some reason his son broke away from his mother and returned. When the men gained entry to the house... they were killed.'

'Was it painful?' Jack asked. He felt like a voyeur as soon as the words left his mouth.

'They were shot in the head at close range. I doubt they felt anything at all. But your brother-in-law, he was mutilated after his death. The intruders took his head. We don't know where.'

'Jesus Christ.'

'I'm sorry that I must tell you these things,' Alvares said. 'I wish I did not have to.'

'Did they do anything to the boy?'

'No. He was left alone.'

'I think I'll sit now,' Jack said, and he fell into a chair. His body felt weighted.

'We found with their bodies a copy of a flyer your brother-in-law had been distributing in the area where his daughter went missing. You were aware of these flyers?'

'Yes. He put up a couple hundred of them.'

'As of this moment we think that's why he was targeted.'

'Who would target him?'

'There could be many culprits, but in this city the most likely ones are found among the Zetas. You are familiar with Los Zetas?'

Jack nodded his head mutely.

'The Zetas will strike at anyone who catches their attention,' Alvares continued. 'If the flyers were put up in an area they control, they might wish to send a message.'

'It's because of our girls,' Jack forced out.

'What do you mean?'

'That cop, Guadalupe, and his partner are in with the Zetas. They know we're on to them. This was them trying to shut us up.'

Alvares carefully gathered up the photos and put them inside a folder. If he had meant to show them to Jack, the moment had passed, and Jack was grateful. 'We don't know that for certain,' Alvares said.

'What else could it be?'

'People die in Mexico for all sorts of reasons. We cannot make assumptions.'

'They killed Bernardo to make us back off!' Jack said with sudden energy. 'It's the only thing that makes sense! For God's sake, don't you people *see*? You're as bad as Gonzalo!'

'I don't understand what you mean,' Alvares said.

'I thought you people were fighting a *war* here! This is the enemy we're talking about. They killed Bernardo and his boy and they would have killed them all if they had half a chance. I have one girl missing and my other stepdaughter could be dead right now!'

'Sr Searle, please calm down.'

'What am I supposed to do, just sit and wait for you to come to your senses? Who else has to die before someone *does* something?'

'We are doing—'

'You're not doing anything except twiddling your thumbs while the bad guys get away with murder! Where is Lidia? I want to see my family!'

Alvares signaled and Lieutenant Casiano appeared at the office door. 'Please take Sr Searle to see his family,' he said. 'And Sr Searle?'

Jack rose and stopped at the door. 'What?'

'After you've had time to meet with your stepdaughter and the rest of your family, you will be returned to your hotel. Once you are there, you will pack your things and then you will be escorted to the border with your stepdaughter. It is too dangerous for either of you to remain here any longer.'

Something like anger and sickness roiled in Jack's stomach. He wanted to shout, but instead he said, "That'll make it easier for you. For us to be gone.'

'It's about your safety, Sr Searle, and nothing else.'

'You keep telling yourself that.'

Lieutenant Casiano led Jack away. Jack did not look back.

TWO

THE ARMY TRUCK THAT FOLLOWED THEM from the police station to the hotel continued to trail them all the way to the bridge. They stayed on Jack's rear bumper until he was in the thick of traffic headed toward the port of entry and then they made an awkward turn across the lanes and back away to the city. Even though he could not see them anymore, he was sure they were watching.

Lidia sat in the passenger seat without talking. She wrung her hands, first left over right and then the opposite, but she had said little since the station. When Jack dialed Gonzalo's number on his cell phone she did not even chastise him for making a call from behind the wheel. He almost wished she would.

Gonzalo sounded subdued when he answered. 'I heard the news,' he told Jack, and that was good, because Jack did not want to go through all of it now. Not with Lidia sitting there.

'I'm not giving up,' Jack said. 'We have a contract.'

'It's more complicated than that now, Jack,' Gonzalo said. 'There have been murders. The army will have pressure on them to clear the case. There's no room for us anymore.'

'I'm asking you to stay on Guadalupe and Fregoso, not investigate… not investigate Bernardo's death.'

'I can't be sure how much more of this they will tolerate.'

'Then find out! I'm paying you, aren't I?'

'I've kept an eye on Fregoso.'

'And?'

'So far nothing.'

Jack glanced at Lidia. He did not want to yell in front of her. He closed his hand over the phone tightly, so that the plastic squeaked. 'You told me they were our best bet,' he said evenly. 'You told me that if we watched them, we'd come up with an answer. That's what you told me.'

'I'm sorry, Jack. I thought it was the right way to go. Maybe I was wrong.'

'So what now? You want out? The army sure wants out.'

Gonzalo paused a long time. 'It may be best.'

'Doesn't anybody care what happened?' Jack demanded, his voice rising. Lidia looked at him. 'Isn't there *somebody* who'll do what it takes to find out the truth?'

'Jack, there's no one who cares more about this than me. I've done everything you asked and more.'

'Just not enough.'

'There's nothing I can do,' Gonzalo said.

'Fine,' Jack said. 'You sit the rest of this out. You've got your job to worry about. Meanwhile I'll be sitting at home for the rest of my life wondering what happened to Marina and no one will give a good goddamn because they're too busy covering their own asses!'

'Jack, it's not like that.'

'You sure could have fooled me.'

Jack ended the call and tossed the phone into a cup-holder between the seats.

'So it's over?' Lidia said abruptly.

He did not want to answer, but she turned toward him then and even though he did not look at her, he could feel her eyes on him. His teeth ground. 'Nobody's going to help us anymore,' he said.

'We'll never know what happened.'

Not a question. Jack had no answer.

'You did your best, Jack.'

'I didn't do a goddamned thing. I let everybody else do the work. I just sat there and played along and hoped that if I followed all the rules there'd be a reward at the end. I'd get a gold star.'

Lidia put her hand on his leg. It felt like a feather and she was so small. She was thirteen, but she was still a child. His child. 'Let's just let it be over,' she said.

'I thought I was going to be a hero,' Jack said.

'It's okay, Jack. You don't have to be. Not anymore.'

THREE

HE LET DAYS PASS WITHOUT TRYING to hold onto them. He got up in the morning, he made meals for Lidia, and he went to bed. In the in-between times his hours were fuzzy, unformed, and he did nothing. A scheduled job was coming up and he had done nothing to prepare.

Lidia was like a ghost, coming and going, spending time with friends before school started again. Jack made sure she left a phone number for every friend she met and that he knew wherever she was going. If she objected to this, Lidia made no indication. She was always home in time for the dinners they ate without conversation.

Some days he found himself sitting on the edge of the bed with the Browning Hi-Power in his hands, just looking at it. He did not have the urge to put it to his skull, but there was something else lurking that he could not quite give shape or a name to. Somehow he knew it was coming.

When he could finally think clearly enough, he went to Home Depot to buy the first round of supplies he'd need for the new job. He overspent and loaded his truck with expensive things he would not have bought otherwise.

At the grocery store he traveled the aisles without a plan, simply putting things that caught his eye into his cart, until the basket was completely full. He bagged the groceries himself instead of waiting for the teenaged kid at the register to do it and he hauled everything home. The cupboards were full, the refrigerator completely stocked.

He went to Marina's room and sat at her desk. Sitting on her bed seemed wrong and he didn't want to muss the covers. On her computer he found her email program open and he browsed through the messages that had come in since she vanished. If he hoped to find something there he was disappointed. Everyone was worried for her. He knew that already.

Sleep. Wake. Another day.

It did not surprise him that he did not hear from Gonzalo or Alvares. He was invisible on the other side of the border and they had lives of their own to live. One Sunday he called Reina and she told him that they were only going to the house to get things they needed and the rest of the time they were living at her sister's home. The police could not say the *sicarios* would not return. Better to leave the place darkened and empty. Maybe they would never go home again.

On the night he had the dream, Jack ate another mute dinner with Lidia and went to bed early. He did not remember falling asleep, but abruptly the bed and the darkness were gone and he was driving on a dirt road. He could not recall how he got there.

'You're almost there,' Gonzalo told him. They were together in the truck where before Jack had been alone. 'Just keep going.'

'There's a roadblock,' Jack said.

'They won't stop you.'

A wall of hundred-foot-high army trucks blocked the way and the soldiers who stood sentry by them were giants. Jack put his foot down and charged for the center of them and they melted away like an optical illusion.

They found a house with a wall around it, but it was not a house at all but a village in the middle of the city, its gates locked tight. Jack was out of the truck at a thought and he had his gun. He put his foot to the gates and they slammed wide. The villagers scattered.

From door to door he went, looking into the little spaces like rooms in a dollhouse, where people cowered because he was a giant now, too. And there was light, a glowing light as if from a hundred candles, ahead of him, and in that light was the shape of a woman.

'Marina,' Jack said.

'She's here,' Gonzalo whispered in his ear.

She was hidden behind layered curtains that fell between them in waves, the light showing through them to make Marina's silhouette. Jack grabbed the curtains and rent them with his hands, stepping through the ragged holes he made until he was surrounded by ruined cloth that bellied from a steady breeze.

He had his hands on Marina then, drawing her out of the heart of the light. He could feel the firmness of real flesh, the heat of skin. Her face was hidden, still trapped, and he pulled and pulled until suddenly she came free and he could carry her away, saying, 'I'm here now. I'm here now.'

And then he woke. The first light of morning touched the window of his bedroom. His hands were filled with bedsheets and he was awash in sweat.

The images were slow to fade, though he took a long shower to wash them out of his mind. He toweled off and dressed himself and from the drawer in the bed stand he fetched the Browning Hi-Power. He held it a long time, until the sun was strong at his back.

He felt as though he were replaying a scene in his head when he brought out his duffel bag and stuffed it with clothes. From an empty peanut can in a cabinet in the kitchen he brought out $1,000 in cash. Half he took for himself and the other half he put on the table. He wrote a note—*Lidia, I'm sorry*—and weighted it down under a glass with the money.

It occurred to him to unload the truck, but he did not want to be delayed. Lidia might wake and then it would all be ruined. He turned over the truck's engine on the quiet street and backed out of the driveway. When he drove away from the house, he did not look back.

FOUR

THE BRIDGE ON THE AMERICAN SIDE WAS practically deserted. At the checkpoint he showed his passport and explained that he was bringing building supplies to some Mexican friends. The officer nosed through the bed of the truck briefly before waving him through. The Mexican officials asked no questions at all.

It took him a while to orient himself in the city because he was traveling an unfamiliar route. Whenever he crossed paths with a police patrol he tensed behind the wheel, but the Federal Police were not interested in his truck and they passed without stopping. He got lost twice, but eventually found the street he was looking for.

He parked in almost the same spot as Gonzalo had on the day they watched Fregoso's apartment for all those hours. From the back of the truck he retrieved a handful of black plastic zip ties and stuffed them into his pocket. When he looked, there was no one paying him any attention and the street was barely stirring.

Up close the turquoise building was even rattier than it appeared at a distance. There were heavy cracks in the plaster façade and the metal of the steps was rusty. Jack moved into the cool shadow of the building and took the steps up lightly. He paused at the window to Fregoso's apartment.

The blinds were closed, but they were pulled to one side

and Jack could see the crowded, dirty front room. Fregoso was not on the couch or visible anywhere else. This was good.

Kicking down the door was easier than he expected it to be. He drove his foot into it once and then again and a whole section of the frame splintered off into the apartment and the door was flung wide. Jack brought out the pistol from underneath his shirt and stormed into the front room.

It was hot inside and there were only two doors leading off from the combined front room and eat-in kitchen. Through one door was the bathroom. From the other Jack heard the sound of a man startled from sleep.

He bulled into the bedroom and was on Fregoso before the man could find the baseball bat leaning in the corner near the head of the bed. Jack hit him hard across the face with the Browning three times until he was sure he'd broken the man's nose, then he dragged him out of the room by the back of his neck.

'¿*Qué carajo?*' Fregoso managed to say. He was naked except for underpants and Jack threw him down hard onto his hands and knees. He grabbed a zip tie and fastened it around Fregoso's wrist. He stomped on the man's back and drove him flat onto the floor. Another zip tie went around his other wrist. A third fastened the loops together.

Jack was breathing hard and bright sparks flashed in his vision. He consciously took deeper breaths then and brought out the pistol again. 'You shut the fuck up unless I ask you a question,' he commanded. He put the Browning behind Fregoso's ear. 'Do you understand me?'

'*Sí, sí, lo entiendo,*' Fregoso said. 'Please don't kill me. I'm a cop! Don't kill me!'

'Get up!'

Fregoso allowed himself to be hauled to his feet. Jack

shoved him hard toward the bathroom and Fregoso stumbled, crashing into the toilet and slamming his head against the wall. Blood already flowed from his nose, but now a cut opened over his eye and ran freely.

Jack snapped on the light. The bathroom had a small tub with a rubber plug for the drain. He put the plug in and started the water.

Fregoso flopped around until he was seated on the toilet. He was bleeding into one of his eyes and it made him squint. His face was heavy with perspiration. Jack was sweating, too.

'If you want money, I don't have much, but you can have it,' Fregoso said.

'I said shut the fuck up,' Jack said, and he kicked Fregoso in the bare chest. His work boot left a deep welt.

'Please, *señor*, I'm nobody. You don't have to kill me.'

'Open your mouth one more time and I'll put a bullet in it.'

Fregoso was quiet. Now there was just the sound of both men panting and the noisy jumble of the tub filling. Steam rose heavily and fogged the tiny shaving mirror attached to the wall.

When the tub was nearly full, Jack turned off the flow. He pointed the gun at Fregoso. 'Get on your knees,' he commanded. 'Right here. Get down on your knees.'

'Don't shoot me,' Fregoso said.

'*Get on your goddamned knees!*'

Fregoso obeyed. He knelt by the tub as if praying to the water, his hands fixed behind his back. It was clear he did not want to look at Jack, but his eyes kept straying toward him before flickering away just as quickly.

Jack put the gun away. 'I'm going to ask you questions,' he said. 'And you're gonna answer them.'

'Anything you want.'

'Two girls in a white car with Texas plates. Your partner Guadalupe pulled them over one night. Do you remember that?'

'What? I don't know—'

Jack seized Fregoso by the wrists and the back of his neck and forced him forward over the edge of the tub. Fregoso's head went under the water and his body spasmed, his legs kicking out in the small space, hammering the wall. Jack held him there ten seconds, and then hauled him out again. Fregoso struggled for breath.

'Two girls. A white car. You pulled them over,' Jack said.

'I don't remember!'

This time Jack held Fregoso under for nearly half a minute, until his struggles became so frenzied he nearly lost hold of him. When he brought Fregoso up, the man's face was scalded. He choked and spat water.

'I'm going to ask you again,' Jack said, 'and this time I don't care if you fucking drown. *Two girls. A white car.*'

'*Please!*'

FIVE

GONZALO HAD JUST FINISHED BREAKFAST when the call came in. He saw the number. 'Hello, Jack,' he answered.

'I think you and I should meet.'

Jack's voice was completely flat, emotionless. Gonzalo felt a tremor of something hearing it. He thought he could hear Jack breathing. 'I don't think I can come to Laredo right now,' Gonzalo said.

'You don't have to. I'm in the city.'

'Jack, what are you doing? You know you're not supposed to be here. Captain Alvares said—'

'Alvares can go fuck himself. I'm here.'

Now Jack was quiet and Gonzalo could hear him breathing: a steady in and out as blank as Jack's voice. Gonzalo licked his lips. '*Where* are you, Jack?'

'I'm in Fregoso's apartment.'

Gonzalo felt a stab of panic and fear that passed completely through him. He was riveted to his chair, the phone at his ear, unable to move. 'What are you doing there?'

'Your goddamned job.'

Gonzalo steadied himself before he spoke again. 'Jack,' he said carefully, 'is Fregoso still alive?'

'He's alive,' Jack said.

Gonzalo felt a flood of relief. 'I'll come to see you,' he said.

'Don't do anything until I get there.'

'I'll try not to.'

Gonzalo closed the line and put one hand over the other to stop it from shaking. He sat a moment simply breathing and then headed for the bedroom to dress. He hurried into his clothes, took his pistol from its hiding place and holstered it at his ankle.

Driving to Fregoso's apartment seemed to take days. Every light was against him and traffic slowed whenever it was most inconvenient. Gonzalo sat hunched over the wheel, tension coiled in his back. Whenever another car moved into his path, he cursed out loud.

He spotted Jack's truck on Fregoso's street and immediately he hoped that no patrol had passed this way. A Texas plate would be noticed this far into the city. Whatever lay at the other end of this journey, Gonzalo knew it was not something for the police or the army to see.

Parking around the corner, Gonzalo waited a few moments before getting out to scan the street for watchful eyes. He saw only a woman pulling a grocery cart and a lone car headed in the opposite direction. By the time he was onto the sidewalk, both of them were gone.

The door to Fregoso's apartment was pushed closed, but the damage was evident to anyone who cared to look. There was a loaded silence behind it. Gonzalo brought out his revolver from its ankle holster before he eased the door open.

Jack sat in the middle of the disorderly room on a straight-backed metal chair. His hands rested in his lap and Gonzalo saw the gun, the same gun he had told Jack not to carry. It was impossible to see whether the safety was off.

'Are you going to shoot me?' Jack asked.

'I could ask you the same question,' Gonzalo said.

'You forget: I know where you live. If I wanted you to be dead, you'd be dead.'

Gonzalo lowered his weapon. 'Where is Fregoso?'

Jack jerked a thumb over his shoulder. 'In the bedroom.'

He slipped past Jack and into the bedroom. Fregoso was facedown on the bed, his feet bound with torn sheets and his wrists zip-tied together so tightly that his hands were discolored. At first he thought Fregoso was unconscious, but the man turned his head and Gonzalo saw the blood and the fear. Fregoso's mouth was stuffed with a sock.

Gonzalo returned to Jack. 'What are you going to do with him?' he asked.

'I'm gonna leave him here until someone finds him.'

'That could be a long time.'

'Oh, well.'

Gonzalo's hands were trembling again. He found another of the straight backed chairs by the little table in the kitchen and brought it to sit by Jack. He lowered himself into it. Jack did not look at him. 'What did you do to him?' Gonzalo asked.

'I did what I should have done from the start.'

'He's bleeding.'

'Good.'

'What are you *doing*, Jack? Do you realize what can happen to you if someone finds out you've done this? Life in our prisons is no place for a man like you. Who else knows you're here?'

'Nobody.'

'*Mierda*,' Gonzalo said. 'And now you've brought me into it.'

'He told me everything he knows,' Jack said. 'Don't you want to hear it?'

Gonzalo hesitated. 'Go ahead,' he said.

'It's just like we knew already: Guadalupe pulled the girls over that night and arrested them. Maybe it didn't go in the logbooks, but he took them back to the lock-up. Fregoso helped him do it.'

'Why? Why did Guadalupe do it?'

'Fregoso says Guadalupe was looking for a girl to pull over. A pretty one. He seemed real excited about it. When he got two, he was thrilled.'

'What happened to them then?'

Jack frowned for the first time. 'He doesn't know. Guadalupe told him to quit his shift early and said he'd take off the rest.'

'What rest?'

'I said he doesn't know,' Jack said sharply. 'And if he did know, he would have told me.'

'You have to get out of here,' Gonzalo said. 'Out of Mexico.'

'I'm not afraid of the police.'

'The police are the least of your worries. Once Fregoso gets the chance, he's going to tell Guadalupe everything that's happened and then Guadalupe's friends will be after *you*. What you're doing isn't just criminal, Jack, it's suicidal. Look what they did to Sr Sigala and his son.'

Jack glared at Gonzalo. 'Don't bring them into this.'

'They'll kill you, Jack. They'll kill you and there will be no one to look after the child you have left. Is that what you want?'

'I want Guadalupe's address. It's up to you if you stick around to see what happens.'

'This is *insane*!'

Jack erupted out of his seat, upsetting the chair. It fell on its back, legs up like a dead creature. 'This whole goddamned country is insane! All your stakeouts and interrogations and I got the same information in half the time! It's no wonder you can't keep a police force together when you can't even get corrupt cops for doing what they've done! They took Marina and Patricia to one of your own police stations! Don't you get it?'

'I can't just let you torture Guadalupe,' Gonzalo returned. 'Maybe some other policeman could, but not me. I won't tell you where to find him.'

'You tell me what I want to know,' Jack said, and his voice was flat again.

A tremor passed through Gonzalo. 'Will you beat the information out of me next?'

'I will if I have to.'

'You've lost your mind.'

'I want to find my girl!'

'We *both* want to! Don't you think I would give anything for you to have your stepdaughter back? Have you listened to nothing I've said?'

Jack raised his pistol and pointed it at Gonzalo's face. A single quiver became a torrent of shakiness that crawled up Gonzalo's back and into his limbs. His hand felt weak on his weapon when he stood and leveled it at Jack.

'You're going to tell me where Guadalupe is,' Jack said.

'You're going to leave Mexico and let the authorities handle this.'

'Goddamn it, Gonzalo, I'll kill you.'

'I believe you,' Gonzalo said, and the barrel of his pistol wavered.

Gonzalo saw Jack's finger move on the trigger and for a moment everything stopped. He pictured the bullet exploding from the barrel of the gun, the impact against flesh, the pain. He did not breathe.

Jack lowered his gun. 'I'm not going to do it.'

It took all Gonzalo's strength to keep hold of his weapon when he dropped his hand to his side. He took a shuddery breath that did not revitalize him. 'Will you go, Jack?'

'No. I'll find him on my own.'

Jack put his pistol away and took a step toward the door. Gonzalo held up a hand that Jack could easily have knocked away, but it brought him up short and Gonzalo felt breathless all over again. 'You can't,' he forced out.

'There's too much blood in this for me to stop now,' Jack said.

'If I don't bring you to him, you'll die trying to find him.'

'The city's not that big.'

'It is for you.'

'So you'll help me?'

'I don't know if I can.'

'It's the only way to do this,' Jack said.

Gonzalo put a foot up on his chair and holstered his weapon. He was aware of the sound of a passing heavy truck, the engine grinding, on the street below. In the bedroom, Fregoso had to be listening.

'You'll take me there?' Jack asked.

Another breath. It came easier now and the room seemed to steady. 'I'll take you there,' he said.

Jack nodded. 'Now we have to deal with Fregoso.'

'How?'

'Do you think he can get loose of those ties?'

'I don't know. Maybe, given time.'

'We'll leave him. Once we're done with Guadalupe we can call the army and they can cut him free.'

'And what if he tells them everything, Jack?'

'He doesn't know me. I'm just some white guy from the States.'

'He saw my face, Jack. He knows me. With that information it won't take someone like Alvares long to figure out who it was asking questions about two missing girls. You should never have done this, Jack. The only solution is...' Gonzalo let it trail off.

Jack drew his gun again. Gonzalo felt the blood seeping from his hands at the sight of it and his face went cold. 'I'll make it quick,' Jack said.

Gonzalo could think of nothing else to say. Jack left for the bedroom.

Gonzalo rushed out the door of the apartment and pulled it shut behind him. He gripped the metal railing by the steps until the flesh of his palms burned. Though he was waiting for it, the muted report of the pistol made him flinch. 'What have you done?' Gonzalo whispered to himself. 'What have you done?'

Jack reappeared. 'Did you touch anything in there?' he asked.

'A chair.'

'Wipe it down. They can have my fingerprints if they want them, but you should cover yourself.'

They went back inside together. The atmosphere inside the apartment seemed leaden and Gonzalo was very aware of the total stillness in the bedroom, as if he could sense life before and felt the absence of life acutely now. A part of him wanted to look and see for himself, but he had seen enough bodies already that one more would do him no good.

He used a handkerchief to carefully wipe down the chair he'd used, starting at the top and working all the way down to the floor where his fingers had never touched. Cleaning it seemed very important. When he was finished he swabbed the nervous perspiration from his palms and dragged an arm across his face.

They met on the ground floor near Fregoso's car. No one else was parked there. The building seemed abandoned. Would anyone even notice the broken door, the body within?

'I'll follow you,' Jack said. 'All right?'

Gonzalo nodded numbly. 'All right.'

SIX

Jack trailed Gonzalo for the better part of twenty minutes before he began to think they were headed nowhere at all. Gonzalo made too many turns and at one point seemed to double back on himself. A quick phone call would straighten things out, but then Gonzalo resumed a normal course. He was trying to evade any other followers. Jack did not even know what to watch for. There were many eyes in Nuevo Laredo.

Gonzalo was slowing to park before Jack realized they were there and he passed the lead car before circling around the block to find a spot of his own. Neither man hurried to get out of their vehicle. Pedestrian traffic was heavier here than in Fregoso's neighborhood and there was a lively bodega across the street where customers shopped for fresh fruits and vegetables in wooden stands out front. Jack could not hide here.

He waited until Gonzalo stepped out of his car and walked toward a plain-sided building with only one entrance on the street. Jack slipped out of the truck and came up slowly, watching carefully for any eye that might turn his way. They met at the door.

A tarnished metal plate was set into the wall beside a locked set of glass doors, one beyond the other. Little strips of white had names scribbled on them in faded ink and most of them were illegible. There was a mesh panel, badly dented, that covered a speaker. 'Which one is Guadalupe?' Jack asked.

'This one, but he will never open the door for us. Let's hope there is someone else home.'

Gonzalo pushed each button in turn, careful to avoid only Guadalupe's. Most did not answer, but finally a woman's voice rattled out of the speaker. '*¿Quién es?*'

'We have a package for—' Gonzalo examined the crabbed handwriting beside the button. 'Sra Saravia. Is this she?'

'Who is it from?'

'There is no name, I'm sorry. The address is from Sonora.'

'Sonora? I don't... you had better come up so I can see.'

'*Gracias, señora.*'

The door made an ugly buzzing sound and Jack heard the bolts pop. They went in together. The second door was unlocked and opened into a lobby that was surprisingly cool, light falling from a window on the second-floor landing to reveal rows of brass mailboxes marked with apartment numbers.

'That woman needs to be safer,' Gonzalo said. 'We could be thieves, or worse.'

'We are worse,' Jack said.

'Fourth floor.'

There was no elevator, so they took the central stairs, winding around the open center that let hot air rise to the very top and left the rest comfortable. Somewhere up above a fan rattled, venting the worst to the outside. Jack caught sounds through apartment doors as they climbed. A television. A muted conversation. This place was not deserted like Fregoso's and they would have to be more careful. People like these would call for help if they heard a gunshot.

'Here,' Gonzalo said after they mounted the last stair.

The door was plain and brown and the number was a peeling sticker. There was no doorbell and, better yet, there was no peephole.

'You knock,' Jack said. He saw the nervous speckling of moisture on Gonzalo's lip. 'Get him to crack the door.'

He brought out the Browning and held it low to his side. He leaned against the wall beside the door and he watched Gonzalo carefully.

'*Knock*.'

Gonzalo raised his hand, wavered a moment, and then struck knuckles to metal. The door sounded hollow and cheap. If they had to, they might be able to break it down, but that would give Guadalupe time to find a weapon, call for help, escape.

There was no noise from the other side of the door. Jack gripped the Browning more tightly. It was not possible to prepare for everything, but it occurred to him that the simplest thing might be the most likely: Eliseo Guadalupe might not even be home.

Gonzalo knocked a second time.

Silent seconds ticked over into a minute and Jack was aware that he was grinding his teeth. He opened his mouth to speak when there was the scrape of something against the other side of the door and Guadalupe called out, 'Who's out there?'

'*Hermano, soy yo*,' Gonzalo said in a rough voice that was not his own.

'I don't know you. What do you want?'

'I got a message for you,' Gonzalo said. 'Come on, it's important.'

'I've got a gun I'll stick right up your ass if you fuck with me,' Guadalupe said through the door. 'I'm a cop.'

'Just open up.'

Jack held his breath as the locks clicked. He heard the sliding sound of a chain coming loose and then the door was opening. Guadalupe's fingers appeared. Jack crashed into the door.

His full weight drove Guadalupe backward down a short hall. He crashed into a little table stacked with mail and the table fell to the floor. The man held a gun, a small revolver, in his right hand. Jack grabbed for his wrist and pressed forward with his Browning so that the barrel came up under Guadalupe's ribcage and drove the wind from him.

Both men fell onto the couch in the apartment's front room. Jack's hand covered Guadalupe's gun now, his fingers clamped down over the hammer to keep it from moving back. He drove a knee into Guadalupe's balls again and again until Guadalupe doubled up underneath him, gasping for breath. A lamp fell from a side table.

Jack was vaguely aware of Gonzalo slamming the door to the apartment and coming up beside him. He felt Gonzalo clawing at the revolver, bending back Guadalupe's thumb, yanking the weapon free.

Guadalupe thrashed, but Jack's weight bore him down. Jack butted him in the face, grabbed him by the hair, and pulled his head back so that he could push the Browning into his eye. Just as abruptly as it started, the struggle was over. Guadalupe went limp.

'Do you know me?' Jack asked Guadalupe. 'Do you recognize me?'

But Guadalupe was not looking at Jack. He rolled his uncovered eye toward Gonzalo. 'You son of a bitch,' he said. 'You fucking bastard!'

'Hey,' Jack said, and he slapped Guadalupe in the head. 'Pay attention to me.'

'You fucked with the wrong person, *pendejo*! Go ahead and shoot me! Shoot me now!'

'Not yet.'

Jack eased his body off Guadalupe's and sat back into a chair that matched the couch. Guadalupe's apartment was surprisingly large, tidy except for the shattered lamp on the floor and the scattered mail. The kitchen was separated from the front room by a counter where three barstools were set up. He had art on his walls and shelves full of books. His television was new.

Gonzalo stood over Guadalupe. 'You shouldn't open your door to people you don't know.'

'Go to hell! You're out of your mind if you think you can do this!'

'It's done,' Jack said. The Browning was still pointed at Guadalupe.

'What now, Jack?' Gonzalo asked.

'We tie him up.'

'Did you bring any rope, *cabrón*?' Guadalupe said.

'Anything will do,' Jack said. 'I've still got zip-ties.'

Gonzalo left them to search the kitchen. Jack rose from the chair. 'Turn over on your stomach,' he told Guadalupe.

'You're not going to kill me. You're not going to kill a *cop*.'

'I'm not going to tell you again.'

Guadalupe obeyed and Jack repeated what he had done to Fregoso. The plastic loops went around the wrists and then were cinched together. He did not make them so tight this time, though he did not care if Guadalupe's hands rotted off. When he was finished, he helped Guadalupe back into a seated position on the couch, where the man sat rigidly.

Gonzalo reappeared. 'This is all I could find,' he said, and brandished a roll of blue duct tape.

'Get his legs, then. He's not going anywhere.'

Half the roll mummified Guadalupe's legs together from ankle to knee. The man watched Gonzalo while he worked, his eyes boiling, but he could not keep from looking back to Jack and the gun.

'I've been to see Fregoso,' Jack told Guadalupe. 'He told me everything.'

'Then you don't need anything from me.'

'He told me everything *he* knew. Not everything you know.'

'*Vete a la chingada,*' Guadalupe said.

Jack moved from the chair and brought the pistol around hard against the side of Guadalupe's head. Out of the corner of his eye he saw Gonzalo flinch.

'We know about the girls. How you took them to the lock-up,' Gonzalo cut in. 'You're not doing yourself any good.'

'What do I care what you know? The minute you're out of here I'm going to be on the phone and the two of you are dead! *Dead!* You won't even make it back across the river. You're *dead men!*'

Jack felt a terrible stillness. 'You're the one who's going to die.'

Guadalupe saw something in Jack's face that made him fall silent. He wriggled on the couch, but it was half-hearted. Every movement would make the zip-ties cut more tightly.

'I want to know what you did with my girl,' Jack told Guadalupe. 'After you took her to the lock-up, what happened then? You sent Fregoso home. Why?'

'Fregoso is an idiot,' Guadalupe declared. 'You're an idiot.'

'I'm the one with the gun.'

'*Fuck* your gun!'

Jack snapped up from the chair with the pistol poised to strike again, but he did not. He looked to Gonzalo. 'Turn on the TV. Turn it up. I'll be right back.'

He went to the kitchen. In the third drawer he searched he found steak knives. They were cheap, with stamped plastic handles. He put the Browning away and took a knife, then he went back to Guadalupe.

'What the hell are you going to do with that?' Guadalupe asked.

Jack grabbed Guadalupe by the neck and pushed him over on the couch. Guadalupe's arms stuck out behind him, his wrists bound, his fingers clenched into fists. Jack pried at them with his bare hands, and then used the sharp edge of the steak knife as a lever to break a fist open. A gash in Guadalupe's palm oozed blood.

'Jack, what are you doing?' Gonzalo demanded.

'Turn that TV up!'

It was easier to isolate one finger and hold it steady. Jack put the knife to the second knuckle and sawed into the joint.

At the first bite of the blade, Guadalupe screamed. Jack pressed down on Guadalupe's back, forcing the man's face into the couch cushion. On the television, a daytime talk show blared, the hosts discussing cheaper alternatives to expensive cosmetics. It meant nothing.

The knife was not as sharp as he wanted it to be and the tendon and cartilage were tougher than the most overcooked meat. Jack bent the finger until it broke along the line of the cut and then he attacked the exposed tissue with the serrated blade. Guadalupe was weeping now, but Jack could not hear him over the pounding of his own heart in his ears.

Gonzalo rushed away into another room, the bathroom, to vomit.

It seemed forever before the finger came loose in his hands. The couch cushion was sodden with blood and it flowed steadily out of the ragged stump Jack left behind. He flung the knife away and dragged Guadalupe up by the throat. '*What happened to the girls?*'

Gonzalo was back now and he spoke weakly. 'Jack, for God's sake.'

'Shut up! Tell me now! Tell me *right now*!' A bubble of mucus blew up and burst in Guadalupe's nostril. His face was streaked with tears and the words that came were fragmented and babbling. Jack smacked Guadalupe with his open hand until he bled from the mouth. 'I swear to Christ I'll cut off another one if you don't start talking.'

'I sold them,' Guadalupe said. His lips were swelling and one was broken.

'What?'

'I sold them!'

'Who did you sell them to, you son of a bitch? Where are they?'

'I sold them to Águila,' Guadalupe said, and then he slumped. Jack smelled urine.

'Águila,' Jack said. 'The Zeta? Águila the Zeta?'

'Leave him alone, Jack,' Gonzalo said. 'Don't do this anymore.'

'No! You tell me: what happened? You sold them to Águila. Did he collect them himself?'

Guadalupe shook his head. 'He sent men to get them. They paid me.'

'Where did they go?'

'La Zona.'

Jack took Guadalupe by the face and forced his mouth open, his fingers slippery with blood. He jammed the severed finger between Guadalupe's teeth and then mashed his jaw shut. 'You...' he said. 'You...'

'Jack, he's told you now!'

He searched for the steak knife and found it on a scattering of envelopes. He closed his fist around the handle and turned on Guadalupe. He stabbed Guadalupe in the chest and then again, then more and more as the man struggled against his bonds. Gonzalo's hands were on him, dragging him away, but he kept on stabbing until the knife stuck between ribs and would not move. Only then did he allow Gonzalo to draw him off.

'Jack,' Gonzalo said, 'come back. Come back, Jack. It's over. He's dead.'

Jack tore himself away from Gonzalo and staggered toward the back hallway. He found the bathroom and saw himself in the mirror, his face and chest spattered with blood and his hands crimson. Hot running water cleansed his hands and he splashed more on his face. His eyes were rimmed with red.

Back in the front room he found Gonzalo standing over Guadalupe's body. Gonzalo's expression was bleak and he held his hands out at his sides as if he didn't know what to do with them. There was more blood on the television screen. 'My God, Jack,' Gonzalo said.

'We have to get out of here,' Jack said, and he slurred his words. A feeling of drunkenness came over him and he was unsteady on his feet. It was the last of the adrenaline draining from him.

'You have blood all over you,' Gonzalo said. 'Someone will see.'

'I'll see if he has a jacket.'

Jack went to the bedroom and searched the closet until he found a nylon windbreaker. It was much too small, but it could close across his chest and hide the worst of the stains. When he returned to Gonzalo, he found that Gonzalo had not moved.

'You'll never get past the army or the Federal Police looking like that,' Gonzalo said.

'We'll figure it out,' Jack replied. 'Let's go.'

'We'll leave Guadalupe like this?'

Jack spared one last look at Guadalupe's corpse, the knife still jutting from his torso. He felt nothing. 'He won't care.'

SEVEN

HE GAVE MONEY TO GONZALO TO GO into a little market and buy new clothes for him. Gonzalo returned with a blue work shirt and a package of white undershirts. Jack changed without getting out of the truck and rolled his stained clothes into a ball inside Guadalupe's windbreaker before stuffing all of it under the front seat. 'Let's find somewhere to eat,' Jack told Gonzalo.

They stopped at a storefront restaurant with a cartoon cactus painted on the front window and took a table against the wall. Jack ordered cheese enchiladas and Gonzalo had tamales and rice. Jack found that he was terribly hungry and he tore into his plate. Gonzalo picked at his food.

'Are you thinking about things?' Jack asked Gonzalo after a while.

'Yes.'

'Don't. I'm not going to think one minute about those *cabrones*. They don't deserve anything from you, either.'

Gonzalo cut the end off a tamale with the edge of his fork, stabbed at the piece and twirled it in a pool of sauce without raising it to his lips. He did not look at Jack. 'I'm party to two murders,' he said. 'This morning I was a policeman. Now I am a criminal.'

'Say it a little louder,' Jack said.

'I'm serious, Jack.'

'I know. But you made your decision and now you have to live with it. I am.'

'I've said it before and I'll say it again: it's not too late for you to back out of this. Take your truck and drive across the river and never come back to Mexico again. I'll do what I can to protect you from my end. They can even suspect me of being party to it, but they'll have no proof.'

Jack shoveled refried beans and rice onto a tortilla. 'If Guadalupe and Fregoso were in as deep as you say, there'll be a lot more people to suspect. Maybe they'll pass it off as drug-related.'

'I don't feel so sure.'

'Well, goddamn it, what else do you want from me?' Jack demanded, though he kept his voice low. There were others in the restaurant, but no one turned his way. 'I needed what they could tell me and then I needed to keep them quiet. This was the only way. We would have wasted weeks doing things your way. Months, maybe. Don't you get that Marina and Patricia were *alive* when Guadalupe saw them last? That means they're *waiting* for us. We can't play games anymore.'

Gonzalo took a few desultory bites and then put his fork down. 'I never saw this as a game, Jack. I did what I had to do because that is the way things are supposed to be carried out. We don't live in the Wild West. Mexico has laws. Maybe they aren't well enforced, but we have to at least try, otherwise there would be anarchy.'

Jack bit and chewed instead of snapping back. He was aware of Gonzalo's body, hunkered down guiltily in his seat, rarely raising his eyes to look at Jack. The man was playing with his food again and suddenly Jack wanted to smack the fork out of Gonzalo's hand. He forced a tone of calm into his voice. 'The minute you took my money to work on this case, you stepped out of bounds. This is just more of the same. And besides, your hands are clean. I'm the one who did the two of them and if it comes to it I'll do it again.'

'How many people are you prepared to kill?'

'As many as it takes.'

'Are you prepared to die?'

'I've been ready for that ever since Marina disappeared. You just don't get it, do you? She may not have been my blood, but she was my *daughter*. You don't have any kids, so you don't know what it's like when they're in trouble. You'll do anything, say anything, to get them out of it. My only mistake was waiting so long, and if it turns out that I'm too late, I'll never forgive myself.'

'No one's doubting your love for Marina,' Gonzalo said.

'You're just doubting me.'

Now Gonzalo looked at Jack directly. He gestured with his fork. 'Should I not doubt you? You are a killer, Jack. I am your accomplice. We sit here eating this meal and talking when I could haul you in front of Alvares' men and be congratulated for bringing you in. If I doubt you, then I have a *right* to doubt you. I must be mad!'

'You're not crazy. You're clear, that's all. For the first time, things are happening the way they should.'

Gonzalo shook his head. 'I *am* insane. Totally. Completely. Without question. What have we done?'

Jack's plate was clear. He signaled the waitress, a young woman no older than Marina, for a fresh glass of iced tea. Gonzalo's eyes were on him, on the edge of wildness. 'All right,' Jack said. 'I'm sorry. Turn me in.'

'Don't be stupid. First you would go to prison and then I would follow close behind. I am as guilty as you are. And the worst thing is that I *allowed* it to happen because I could not speak against it when the moment was right.'

'Why didn't you?'

Gonzalo pushed his fingers through his hair and sighed. 'Because I know it's the only way. I knew it from the moment they suspended me. There was no alternative. Thinking anything else was foolish.'

'Then it's done,' Jack said. 'We're in it.'

'We have to discuss what comes next,' Gonzalo said. 'We are in uncharted territory now. Fregoso and Guadalupe were the easy ones. They were weak. From now on we'll have to deal with Los Zetas, and they are harder than you can imagine.'

The new glass came and the old one was taken away. Jack thanked the girl. When she was gone, he said, 'Marina was taken to La Zona. There can't be that many places she could have gone. We'll need to talk to some people.'

'I will talk to them,' Gonzalo said. 'Some things are the same now as they were before: you are too obvious and the first person you question will spread the word about you far and wide.'

'I'm not going to be sidelined again,' Jack said.

'You won't be. I will keep you close, but I will be the leader for this. La Zona is a small place and there are only so many places the girls could have gone. It helps that we know Águila's name. That will make it easier to get to the bottom of things.'

'If people will talk.'

'Yes, if they will talk. And they *will* talk because you are going to give me American dollars to spread around. La Zona is about money, first and foremost. All other considerations fall by the wayside.'

'Who are you going to talk to? Other Zetas?'

'La Zona is neutral territory,' Gonzalo said. 'Everybody takes a little from everybody else. There are plenty of other eyes and ears there besides the Zetas and their associates.'

'Do you know where you're going to start?'

Gonzalo nodded. 'When I first saw Guadalupe and Águila together it was at a club in La Zona. They were well known there. Someone will tell me about Águila.'

'If I find him, I'm gonna kill him,' Jack said.

'Not before he tells us where to find the girls,' Gonzalo said. 'I do not know how far up the chain of command Águila goes. He may be acting on behalf of someone we don't know yet. If he dies too soon, we may never get the answers we seek. Besides, are you so eager to have another man's blood on your hands?'

'This man's,' Jack said.

Gonzalo put his fork down and pushed his plate away. It was barely touched. 'Let us be perfectly clear: I won't be a party to wanton slaughter,' he said. 'If your intention is to kill every Zeta we meet, you will have to find some other partner. My first priority is the girls. Where are they? Are they safe? Everything else is secondary.'

'I'm not out of control,' Jack said.

'You did not see yourself in Guadalupe's apartment.'

'I've said I'm calm.'

'There is no sense getting ahead of ourselves anyway,' Gonzalo said. 'We have not found Águila, nor do we even know where he might be. We'll get those answers in La Zona, I'm certain of it.'

Jack's phone vibrated in his pocket and then began to chirp. He looked at the screen and did not recognize the number. It was a Mexican area code. He opened the line. 'Hello?'

'Sr Searle? This is Captain Alvares.'

His first instinct was to look over his shoulder, through the front window of the restaurant and into the street. He was convinced he would see an army Humvee there. '*Capitán*,' Jack said. 'I didn't expect to hear from you.'

Across the table, Gonzalo stiffened. Jack motioned for silence.

'I wanted to call and ask how you are doing,' Alvares said. 'If you are well and your stepdaughter is well.'

'Have… have you heard something about Marina?' Jack stuttered.

Alvares' voice was somber. 'I'm afraid I have not. But we are still looking into it.'

'Thank you,' Jack said.

'There is no need to thank me. I also wanted to tell you that we were able to recover the last of your brother-in-law's remains. The family has not held the funeral yet?'

'No. No, they haven't. You found the… the head?'

'Yes. It was discovered at a roadside shrine to Santísima Muerte, just outside the city. Identification was not immediate.'

'A shrine?' Jack asked.

'The *narcos* have shrines to Saint Death in many places. They make offerings there for protection and good fortune, burn prayer candles… and sometimes leave trophies. I'm very sorry.'

'You can't help it.'

'Will you return to Nuevo Laredo for the services?'

'Yes, I think so.'

'I'm afraid I will not be able to attend, but I wish to extend my deepest condolences to you and your entire family. There is no good way to lose a loved one, and this is one of the worst.'

'Thank you for calling,' Jack said robotically.

'Until we meet again, Sr Searle. *Adiós*.'

Jack closed his phone and put it on the table beside his empty plate. 'They found Bernardo's head.'

'Does he know you've crossed the bridge?'

'If he does, he didn't say so.'

'Then there's still time. We need to find a place to stay until dark. La Zona comes alive at night.'

'I know a place,' Jack said, and he signaled for the check.

EIGHT

NO ONE HAD BOTHERED TO REPAIR THE shattered front door of Bernardo's home. Jack opened the gate to park his truck in the carport and Gonzalo left his car on the street. Everything was as the police and the army had left it: the collection of empty bottles still stood by the couch, and the floor was thick with bloodstains.

Jack did his best not to look at the blood, but his eyes were drawn to it. There were two clear puddles, one markedly smaller than the other. He had stabbed Guadalupe to death without blinking, but imagining Little Bernardo there made him feel ill and he had to retreat into the kitchen for distance.

The refrigerator still had food inside and Jack and Gonzalo shared Reina's *limonada*. 'When will they have the funeral for your brother-in-law and his boy?' Gonzalo asked.

Jack had to think. 'In a couple of days. They had to wait until the coroner was through with the bodies. I don't know what took them so long. It's not like there was some big mystery to solve.'

'Things move slowly here.'

'Isn't that the goddamned truth.'

They lingered around the bare kitchen table until the sun began to dim through the window above the sink. Though he could not understand why at first, he still took the time to rinse the glasses they used and put them on the drying rack. Reina and Leandra would come back here someday. It should be tidy for them when they did. Jack wondered whether Reina would have to clean the blood of her husband and son from the floor herself.

'We'll take my car,' Gonzalo said.

By the time they reached La Zona it was nearly full dark and all the lights were on. As they drove past the little police station at the entrance, Jack turned his head to watch the army truck stationed there. He saw no soldiers, but a Federal Police truck was parked directly behind the other truck and the barred windows of the station glowed.

Gonzalo took a space directly in front of a place that advertised gambling and women. Trailing along the row of structures toward the west were cribs, the little rooms where prostitutes rented a space and a bed to do their work, the kind Iris Contreras had rented. Many of the prostitutes were already out on the dirt on the lookout, dressed in as little as they could get away with, which in La Zona was very little. Thankfully he did not see Iris among them, though he knew she could not be far.

'El Pájaro,' Gonzalo told Jack. 'It's down at the end of the block. I should warn you: it's a transvestite place.'

'Am I supposed to be dressed up?'

'No, not you,' Gonzalo said.

They proceeded down the street and the prostitutes gave way reluctantly, catching at Jack's arm or standing in his way until it was clear he would not stop. Most were young, but some were not and many were plain. When they turned from Jack and Gonzalo they hailed other men who wandered along the street or cruised the block. Some cars pulled into open spaces and their drivers got out to haggle with the women openly. Jack had never been to this area, Boys' Town, before. He had not imagined it like this. They did not even have paved roads and there was a frontier-town feel to everything he saw.

By the time they reached El Pájaro, Jack was tired of the come-ons and the touches and wanted to lash out at the next woman who came near him, but the cribs were left behind and the worst with them. Now there were just the loud-talking men in the doors of the bars and brothels, acting like human billboards under the orange luminescence of the streetlights.

The music inside El Pájaro was punishing and Jack felt it pulsing out the front door onto the street. A heavyset man in a black T-shirt looked strangely at Gonzalo, as if the man were trying to place a vaguely familiar face, but he gave ground and let them in without protest.

Gonzalo beckoned Jack close so that he could shout directly into his ear. 'I have to move around and talk to some people,' he said. 'Stay at the bar and don't leave. The girls here will try to get you to come away with them. Just tip them and say not right now.'

'How long will this take?' Jack shouted back.

'I don't know. Be patient. I won't leave without you.'

Jack let Gonzalo break away from him and plunge into the space between shadowy tables. The interior of the place was lit up with blasts and flickers of light as the cross-dressing man on the stage performed a routine. There was an open stretch of bar. A man who looked almost exactly like a woman approached him for his order. He asked for beer. When he looked around again, he could not find Gonzalo anywhere.

NINE

HE HAD NOT EXPECTED TO COME HERE again, but he was not nervous or frightened. After Fregoso and Guadalupe, the scene in El Pájaro was more like a real policeman's beat, with people and things he could at least understand. Today he had questioned himself too many times for someplace like this to bother him anymore.

The strobing lights left his eyes dazzled whenever there was darkness, so Gonzalo saw the people in the place only when they were brightly lit by the stage, their faces turned upward. Some were harder to spot as men dressed as girls gave lap dances on couches and in booths. But Gonzalo was not looking for customers, so the search was halved.

In his mind's eye he had a perfect picture of the person he sought. He remembered the go-go dancer outfit, the streaming red hair, and the large breasts. He remembered the performer kissing Águila when Gonzalo knew him only as the man with the gold watch. This person would know things.

Someone stepped into Gonzalo's path. He saw a silhouette and a golden flash of blond hair and then a face revealed in a flash. Another transvestite, but a familiar one. 'I know you,' she said, and Gonzalo knew her, too. A name came floating up, carried on a sudden surge of anxiety mixed with panic.

'Celia,' Gonzalo said.

'Come back again to look and not touch?' Celia asked.

Celia stood with her legs apart so that there was no way around her. Tables hemmed them in on both sides. Celia was dressed like an American cheerleader, though she did not carry pom-poms. 'I'm looking for someone,' Gonzalo said.

'Why not me? I'm not doing anything.'

When he had left Celia before, she'd railed at him and driven him out on a wave of attention. He did not want that tonight. The dancer with the go-go outfit was somewhere and he could not risk being thrown out.

'Well?' Celia demanded.

'Okay,' Gonzalo said.

'Show me your money first.'

Gonzalo reached for his wallet and brought it out. He did not show Celia his badge. Such a thing would do no good and then he would be remembered. He showed Celia a fifty-dollar bill. 'Is that good enough?' he asked.

'You want to go in the back?'

He made another slow turn. The techno music was exhausting, beyond deafening. He did not see the person he was after. 'Yes,' he said.

Celia took his hand and Gonzalo allowed himself to be led toward the stage. Looming out of the shadows was an archway that was practically invisible, shrouded by a curtain and painted jet black. Celia pushed the curtain aside to let them both through.

Off the main floor it was not so overwhelming, though the bass from the speakers reverberated through the floor and walls. They were in a hallway lined with doors, a staircase at the far end. Some of the doors were open and showed tiny spaces with beds small enough to be for children. Celia seemed to pick one at random and stood aside to let Gonzalo in. She closed the door behind them.

The room was like a closet and the bed took up most of the space. It had a headboard and a footboard painted white. The headboard had a design with pink roses on it. Light came from a bare bulb in a socket in the ceiling.

'Fifty dollars US gets you a suck, but if you want to fuck me, it'll be more,' Celia informed him flatly.

'I don't want to fuck you,' Gonzalo said.

'Okay. Give me the money now.'

They were too close in the room and Gonzalo could smell sweat and perfume on Celia. Under real light it looked as though her hair was real, though bleached. She had it pony-tailed, but it was long. It was also easy to tell she was not a woman. The planes of her face were too pronounced and the giveaway was the lump at her throat. Besides that, she had small hands like a woman's and small feet.

'*The money.*'

'Just a minute,' Gonzalo said. He brought out his wallet again and took one of Jack's fifty-dollar bills out. When Celia reached for it, he jerked it out of her grasp. She scowled. 'Just a minute, I said.'

'If you came here to fuck around, I'll get someone to come back here and kick your ass,' Celia said. 'Okay, *imbécil*? Give me that money.'

'I'm not gay,' Gonzalo said.

'Of course you're not. Give it to me!'

'I'm not here for a *mamada.*'

Celia reached for the door. 'That's it, you're fucking with the wrong girl!'

She had the doorknob in her grasp when Gonzalo brought his hand down on hers. He squeezed hard and for a moment they struggled as Celia tried to twist the knob. 'Calm down,' Gonzalo said. 'You can have the money.'

'Let go of me!'

Gonzalo released Celia's hand. He offered the bill. 'Here,' he said. 'Take it.'

Celia snatched the money from Gonzalo's fingers and tucked it into the waistband of the short cheerleader's skirt she wore. Her expression was curdled. 'If you don't want nothing from me then what's the money for? You just want to yank it?'

'I'm looking for someone who works here. Maybe you can tell me who she is,' Gonzalo said.

'Are you police?'

'Would it matter if I was?'

'I guess not. Who do you want?'

Gonzalo described the dancer in the go-go outfit to Celia in as much detail as he could remember. He was not finished when he saw the light rise in her eyes. 'You know her?' he asked.

'Angélica.'

'Is she working here tonight?'

'No.'

Gonzalo bit his lip to keep from cursing out loud. 'When does she work again?'

'I don't know. She hasn't been in for a few days. Sometimes the girls don't come back. They go to work in the cribs or they get out of the business.'

'Was she the type to get out of the business?'

'Angélica? Oh, no. She makes the big money.'

'Sit down,' Gonzalo said.

'If you're not going to get nothing, I should get back to work,' Celia said.

'I'm paying you for your time,' Gonzalo replied. 'You can talk to me for five minutes.'

'Okay.'

Celia sat and Gonzalo leaned against the closed door.

He covered his eyes with his hand and realized there was a headache brewing deep inside his skull. A sigh slipped past his lips. This day would never end.

'Why do you want to know about Angélica?'

Gonzalo uncovered his face and looked down on Celia. 'I want to know about her customers. One customer in particular. You may have seen him. A man about my height, wavy hair, wears a gold watch and Ralph Lauren Polo shirts.'

'Águila,' Celia said.

Gonzalo's heart leaped. 'You know Águila?'

'He comes in here a lot. Spends a lot, too. You don't want nothing to do with him.'

'Why's that?'

'He's a Zeta. Nobody fucks with them. *Nobody.*'

'He doesn't have a piece of this place, does he?' Gonzalo asked.

'No, he just likes to come in. He's fucked every girl here.'

'Don't you think the Zetas would have a problem with him fucking men?'

Celia's expression blackened. 'He's fucking *girls*. Your type don't see it like that, but he does. And there are lots of guys who think the same way. What do you think I am, anyway?'

'I don't know,' Gonzalo said. 'I've never thought about it before.'

'I am *woman, señor.* I'm not something you can step on and then scrape off your shoe.'

'All right, whatever,' Gonzalo said. 'You're a woman, then. I'm sorry. You're all women. But does he have a favorite? This Angélica, does he like her best?'

'Maybe.'

'*No me jodas,*' Gonzalo said. 'Is she his favorite, or what?'

'Okay, she's his favorite. So? I have some *chicos* who come here just for me. It doesn't mean nothing.'

'If I asked you, could you get me Angélica's number? Her address? Some way for me to get ahold of her?'

'We're not supposed to give that kind of thing out. It's not safe.'

Gonzalo went to his wallet again and produced another fifty. 'This is yours if you can put me in touch with her. I don't need a lot. Just a number will do.'

'Give me the money first.'

'After.'

'Give it to me now or I won't do nothing for you.'

Gonzalo gave her the bill. It disappeared with the other. She rose from the bed. He put out his hand. 'Where are you going?'

'You want me to find out for you, or what? I don't know everything all by myself. I have to ask. You wait here.'

'I told you: don't fuck me about,' Gonzalo said.

'I won't. Just stay here. I'll be back.'

Celia slipped out of the room and closed the door behind her. Gonzalo allowed himself to sit on the bed. The mattress was stiff and unyielding and was too short to lie down on fully, but he supposed no one slept there. Outside in the hall he heard laughter in a strange register: not quite man, but not quite woman, either.

He looked at his hands. There was no blood on them and there would not be, but a part of him expected to find them soaked to the wrists. When he closed his eyes he could see Jack sinking the knife into Guadalupe over and over. Gonzalo's thoughts were in a welter at that moment and they were barely comprehensible now. He understood what he was doing, but the why of it was still in flux.

By rights he should have turned Jack in the moment he killed Fregoso with a gunshot to the head. The Gonzalo who made sense of himself was one who would have taken out his phone and called in Alvares. Maybe Jack would have run, but he would not have made it across the bridge before the Federal Police or the army caught up to him. And if he had done that, Eliseo Guadalupe would still be alive.

Gonzalo did not feel sorrow for Guadalupe's death. That was too simple an emotion. A part of him had hated Guadalupe for what he was and hated him still more when he confessed to his crimes, but the part of Gonzalo Soler that upheld the rule of law could not condemn him to death.

There was no tremor in his hands. He did not understand because he was no surer of himself, no less afraid. More than ever he was aware of what it would mean if the collusion between him and Jack was discovered. They would send Jack away for the rest of his life and they would be no kinder to Gonzalo.

A policeman in a Mexican prison would not last for very long.

Now he waited, and as the minutes ticked by he felt the tightness of the walls. In his mind he tried to picture Águila in this place, the little skirt of Celia's cheerleader costume pulled up, her bent over the bed… 'Enough,' he said out loud.

There was a step outside the door and then it opened. Celia returned. She handed Gonzalo a scrap of paper with a string of numbers written on it in ink. 'Here is her number,' she said.

Gonzalo stood up. 'Thank you for your help.'

'What will you do to her?'

'What do you mean?'

'Are you going to kill her?'

'No. Why would you think that?'

'Your face. I saw it in your face.'

Gonzalo shook his head. 'I'm not going to kill her. You don't have to worry about that.'

TEN

JACK SAW GONZALO APPROACHING through the strobe lights and smoke and was relieved. A part of him had thought that if he let Gonzalo out of his sight, even for a minute, the man would flee and Jack would be caught with nowhere to go except across the bridge and away from Nuevo Laredo forever. That was not something he could abide, not after coming this far.

The beers he had drunk had no effect on him. They could not take the adrenaline edge off his perception, where everything was too loud, too bright, too crowded. Whenever one of the cross-dressing men came to him, he did as Gonzalo said and paid them off with dollars before sending them on their way. They seemed happy to get the money for doing nothing and they did not complain.

Gonzalo came close. 'What did you find out?' Jack yelled in his ear.

'Let's go outside,' Gonzalo said.

His hearing was dulled on the street, fuzzed by the loud music and upraised voices. Foot traffic was busier and the little streets of Boys' Town were filling with cars and trucks, trolling slowly for parking spaces or a glimpse at the girls. Gonzalo took Jack's elbow and directed him away from El Pájaro, down the street.

'Tell me,' Jack said.

'I hoped we might find Águila there, but he has not been around,' Gonzalo replied. 'I talked to one of the... girls and she said he has a favorite. Her name is Angélica. I have her number here.'

'What is she going to tell us?'

'If what I was told is true, Águila might have done some talking to this Angélica. Maybe he let slip where his favorite places are. Maybe he even took her to his home. We won't know until we call.'

'Well, what are you waiting for?'

They walked along a line of cantinas that could have been taken from anywhere in the city and set down here. No dirty pictures, no come-on men lying in wait. It suddenly seemed unusually quiet and Jack realized how quickly he'd become accustomed to the commotion of the main streets.

'Call her,' Jack urged Gonzalo.

'I'll do it now,' Gonzalo said. He brought out his phone and dialed the number he'd brought out from the back room of El Pájaro. After a moment he put up a finger. 'It's ringing.'

Jack's phone vibrated in his pocket. He had turned off the ringer before, but had forgotten to silence the phone completely. When he saw the calling number, he felt the blood pool at the base of his spine.

He answered. 'Hello, Lidia,' he said.

She was not crying, but she had been and not long before. Jack heard the hitch in her voice when she spoke, the elevated pitch of a throat held too tightly. 'What are you doing, Jack?' she asked.

'I'm just taking care of some things.'

'I wasn't going to c-call you because I thought maybe you would come home, but you didn't come home. Why are you over there, Jack?'

Jack glanced at Gonzalo. The man was talking, half-turned from Jack, oblivious. Jack took a few steps away. 'I can't let this go.'

'I thought we decided that you would stay with *me*,' Lidia said. 'You can't help Marina, Jack. The police have to do that.'

'I told you, honey, there are no police anymore. And the army isn't going to do a goddamned thing. I can *do* something here.'

Lidia fell quiet and Jack heard her weeping softly. If he listened hard enough, he thought, he could hear her tears falling. He felt a pain in his throat and swallowing did not make it go away.

'Lidia—'

'You're going to *die*, Jack,' Lidia interrupted. 'They're going to find you and they're going to murder you!'

'That won't happen.'

'*How do you know?*'

Jack looked around, but there was no escape. At the end of the block a dark SUV turned the corner slowly, the front windows down. The passenger had his arm resting against the outside of the door, a cigarette between his fingers. It was strange the things you noticed when you wanted desperately to be somewhere else. 'I just know,' he told Lidia. 'I'm not going to let it happen.'

'You won't have a choice! You think Tío Bernardo let it happen to him?'

'I can't argue with you,' Jack said. 'I have somewhere I have to be.'

'Where?'

'I think it's better if I don't tell you anything.'

'Who am I going to tell, Jack? I'm *alone*. There's no one *here*.'

'I'm going to hang up now,' Jack said.

'Please, just come home,' Lidia said, the words rushing out. 'Come home and forget about it. We're all we have left now. It's just you and me. If you don't come home, what will happen to me? What's going to happen to me, Dad?'

Dad. The pain in Jack's throat was sharper, more intense. He did not have tears, but he knew they were coming. His knees trembled. 'I have to go,' he roughed out. 'I'll call you.'

'Don't hang up! Don't hang up on me!'

'Goodbye,' Jack said.

He ended the call. With clumsy thumbs he made it so it would not vibrate any longer. If Lidia called again, he would not know. It was better that way.

'Is there a problem?'

Jack turned to Gonzalo. 'No problem,' he said.

'Good, because—'

'*¡Oye, gilipollas!*'

They looked at the same time and Jack saw the black SUV almost abreast of them. The man with the cigarette half-leaned out the window. He took a drag and the cigarette's coal glowed hot and then he blasted smoke in a cloud around his face.

'Ignore them,' Gonzalo said to Jack. 'Let's go.'

Jack walked with Gonzalo down the strip of cantinas, but the SUV kept pace with them. He could feel the man with the cigarette watching him, and could almost see him out of the corner of his eye. 'What about the girl?' he asked Gonzalo.

'Hey, I'm talking to you two faggots!' shouted the man with the cigarette.

Gonzalo stopped. 'Look, we're only walking here. We don't want trouble.'

'Are you two boyfriends or something?'

Two men emerged from a cantina and, seeing the SUV, doubled back inside. Jack looked at the truck, which had stopped just short of them, very close to the rear bumpers of the parked cars along the street. The man with the cigarette flicked his butt away and it struck sparks off the roof of a car before falling out of sight.

'Like my friend said, we don't want trouble,' Jack said.

The man was so lean-faced that he looked like a leather skull. His eyes were black. 'You look lost, *hombre*.'

'We're just looking around.'

The rear doors of the SUV opened and three men piled out of the vehicle onto the street. Jack braced himself, conscious of the pistol in his waistband, knowing it was there and knowing he could not bring it out. Gonzalo was at his elbow.

'Run,' Gonzalo said quietly.

The three men slipped between an old Malibu and an orange Camry. Jack took a step back.

'Run!' Gonzalo yelled, and then they were dashing down the row of cantinas. The three men were behind them and Jack heard the rush of the SUV's engine as the vehicle surged forward. Across the street prostitutes standing outside their cribs hollered at them as they ran and one laughed.

Later he was not sure how it happened, but they reached a bend in the dirty road where an earthen turnabout cut into a greening stand of hardy summer trees and somehow one of the men got his foot underneath Jack's and Jack fell hard. He skinned both palms on the ground and still landed hard enough to knock the wind from his lungs. In a moment Gonzalo was down, too, and the three men swarmed over them.

Something black and confining passed over his head and for an instant Jack felt as though he couldn't breathe, but it was not a plastic bag. He struggled to take a deep breath, a man's knee on his back. The lean man, the one who smoked the cigarette, called out, 'Hurry up, hurry up!'

Cold metal on his wrists. They cuffed his hands together behind his back and made the bracelets tight. Unseen hands rooted around in his waistband and his pistol was taken from him.

Jack deliberately dragged his feet when they lifted him off the ground. The men were strong and they muscled him toward the black SUV, which he heard idling noisily in the street. Suddenly he was thrust forward, something hard catching him across the shins, and he tumbled onto short, scratchy carpeting over steel. He was in the back of the SUV, on the floor. A moment later Gonzalo was jammed in beside him, Jack's knees against Gonzalo's chest. He could feel Gonzalo breathing quickly, like a rabbit.

Doors slammed. It was cold in the truck, the air conditioner turned up high. The driver stomped the accelerator and Jack rocked against a solid panel. The material of the bag on his head stuck to his lips and he spat drily to break them free.

'Watch for soldiers!' someone said.

The SUV made a sharp turn and then another and its wheels chirped on asphalt. They were outside Boys' Town, on a real road. The big vehicle roared as they picked up speed. Jack did not know whether they were headed north or south.

'Jack.' Gonzalo was not breathing so hard anymore and he whispered.

'Don't talk,' Jack said.

'Are you all right?'

'Hey, you shut up back there!' shouted someone from the seats in front of them. 'You say another fucking thing, I'll dump your body on the side of the road!'

The top of Jack's head was pressed against the flexible material at the back of a seat, but he could feel the coils underneath and they poked him whenever the SUV hit an uneven patch on the road. They made more turns, and though they slowed down Jack still had no idea of their direction or even how far they had come. On television it looked so easy, but he was lost in the picture inside his mind of crowded streets patched with trees, each block blending into the next.

He tried moving his wrists. He was lying on them and the handcuffs cut into his flesh. The movement made his knees dig into Gonzalo's chest and Gonzalo groaned. Jack tensed for another outburst from the men in the SUV, but there were no more corrections forthcoming.

Someone put on the radio and the sounds of Tejano filled the void. A station identifier came on. They were listening to KJBZ out of Laredo. When the next song came on, one of the men began to sing along. Soon others were, and they swelled into the chorus as the SUV drove on.

ELEVEN

TIME AS WELL AS DISTANCE ESCAPED JACK. He only knew that after a long while the SUV slowed down and ground to a stop on a gravel surface. The men in the front of the truck abandoned their seats and Jack heard them talking to each other outside.

The door holding Jack and Gonzalo in place was opened and the pressure between them was released. Gonzalo was able to relieve the weight on his chest and blood returned to Jack's calves. His bent knees had cut off the flow as surely as the handcuffs on his wrists.

Hands were on him and he was dragged out. Jack teetered, but someone held his arm tightly and he didn't fall. He felt sharp stones under his boots, and dirt. It was quiet here and Jack thought maybe they had driven out of the city proper and were somewhere beyond its limits where no Federal Police went and the army did not venture.

'Walk,' said someone very close to him. Jack walked.

Jack tripped on the edge of something, a raised flat that felt like concrete. It was a patio or a walk of some kind. The guiding hand on his arm was unwavering. Ahead of him there came the sound of a door opening, a television playing. Men greeted one another without using names. Jack stumbled again on the threshold.

He was led across carpet to another door that had a bad

squeak. This time the man on his arm said, 'You have to step down here.' Jack felt with his toe where the floor dropped off and he did not lose his footing. Now his steps were hollow and he smelled cement dust. Jack knew the sounds and smells of an incomplete room.

'Sit.'

Jack sat when a chair was nudged against the backs of his knees. Someone unfastened the cuffs and then refastened them, securing him to the chair. This time they were not so tight, but he would never be able to slip them. A clicking and ratcheting came from very close. They were doing the same to Gonzalo.

His heart was beating fast, but the fear was not overwhelming. There had been an edge of panic when they chased him down, when the bag went over his head, but Jack had numbed to it on the drive. A part of him expected the kiss of a gun against his head and sudden blackness, but the longer this went on the more he began to hope that things would not end that way. He let that hope be his beacon.

'Is he here yet?' asked a voice.

'No, not yet.'

'I need something to drink.'

'Come on, then.'

There was the sound of wrinkling plastic and the scuff of feet on bare flooring and Jack felt that they were alone. He waited until he counted off one hundred before he risked saying a word. 'Gonzalo,' he said.

'I am here.'

'Who are they?'

Gonzalo was slow to answer. 'Zetas.'

Now the cold press of alarm coiled up in his stomach and his carefully cultivated hope shattered. A shiver passed through him from head to foot.

'How do you know?' Jack asked.

'I know.'

Jack opened his mouth to reply, but he heard a footstep and he went silent. Again there was the sound of crinkling plastic and the sense of someone near. A man said, 'Are you two talking?'

They stayed silent.

'I know I heard you talking,' the man said. 'And I told you before: if I hear one word out of you, I'll shoot you and dump your fucking body. Did you *forget* what I said? Answer me!'

TWELVE

JACK LACED HIS FINGERS TOGETHER behind his back. If he could hold them tightly enough, he would not shake. His mouth was dry. 'I didn't forget.'

A hammer clicked. Something solid and metal pressed against Jack's temple. This was the moment he had waited for. The next would come quickly and then he would know nothing else. At least he wouldn't be alive for them to torture. 'If you didn't forget, then why are you *talking*?'

'It won't happen again.'

'It had better not, *idiota*. You don't know who you're fucking with.'

The gun went away. Jack had been holding his breath and he let it go now. His bowels felt loose. This was the fear, he knew. The tireless, crawling fear that could not be defeated by wishful thinking.

'I hear you make one more sound, I come in here shooting, *entiendes*?'

This time Jack only nodded. He hoped the man could see.

'Good. Now just sit there and wait. It won't be long.'

He listened to the man walk away. In the other room there was the murmur of a question and the man answered, though Jack could not hear what was said. The television was the clearest thing, ringing out like the tone of a bell. Jack had never thought he would die to the sound of a *Chespirito* rerun.

After what seemed like an eternity the television was switched off and Jack was alert again. The place where they were kept fell deathly silent, as if the TV had been the only thing with a semblance of life and the men watching it had all gone. He heard his heart beating.

The men came into the unfinished room then, their footsteps clear in the quiet. Jack tried counting them, but it was impossible. There could have been a few or many and they would have sounded the same to him. He wondered whether Gonzalo was able to do any better, if he had a trained ear for such things. He wanted to ask out loud, but he kept his mouth shut and his teeth clenched together. His jaw ached.

Someone poked Jack in the ribs with something blunt and hard. 'What is your name?' a voice asked.

'Jack.'

'Are we friends now? What is your *whole* name?'

'Jack Searle.'

'How about you, *cabrón*?'

'I am Gonzalo Soler.'

'Okay,' said the voice.

Jack tried to put an imaginary face to it. Was the man short or tall? Was he fat or skinny? He could not even tell whether the voice was young or old. Why did he think he could do this thing? What had he been thinking when he came across the river?

'Would it surprise you to know that I already knew your names?' the voice asked. 'You can answer.'

'No,' Jack said.

'You shouldn't be surprised. Nuevo Laredo is not a large city. Word gets around. Especially a Mexican cop and an American man working together. You two are like a couple of big, stupid bears putting on a show for the rest of us. Watch the bear ride a bicycle, you know? Watch it do something it was not meant to do. And everybody laughs.'

Someone grabbed the bag on Jack's head and whipped it off. Lights shocked his eyes and they started to water. Instinctively he tried to raise his hands, but they were still locked behind him. A teardrop formed on his cheek.

Across from him, Gonzalo was unblinded. They were seated facing each other and around them was a ring of seven men. All of the men had guns, some in their waistbands and others held casually, as if it was the most natural thing in the world. The room was fairly large, about the size of a garage, and had bare drywall everywhere Jack could see. The floor was plain concrete, but it had been spread with a blue plastic tarp.

Gonzalo's eyes were wide and his hair mussed. He looked panicked and Jack wanted to put a hand on him and bring him down. Now he tried to catch Gonzalo's attention, but he was too busy watching the men.

One of the men took a step forward. He was a bit older than the rest. They seemed mostly to be in their early twenties, but he was in his thirties and had started to form lines on his face. His pistol had mother-of-pearl grips and stood out above a big silver-and-turquoise belt buckle. He wore cowboy boots and a red shirt like a workman might. The rest were shabbier, in T-shirts or knockoff Ralph Lauren tops. 'Welcome,' the man said.

'You're Águila,' Jack said.

A man moved out of the ring and smacked Jack hard on the back of the head. Jack recognized his voice when he said, 'Don't say nothing unless you're answering a question!'

'It's okay,' said the older man. He waved the other back and looked down on Jack without smiling. 'No, I am not Águila.'

Someone came into the room with a handheld camcorder. 'I found it,' he said.

'Hurry up and get started, then. I want their faces first.'

The man with the camcorder stepped in between Jack and Gonzalo and recorded first Gonzalo's face and then Jack's. He stepped back to get a wider shot of the two of them together, close enough that Jack could reach out with his foot and just touch Gonzalo's knee. The little red light on the face of the camcorder glowed. The man held it low so that no one else could be identified.

'What's that for?' Jack asked.

'For my people to review later,' the older man said. 'They want to know if I'm doing a good job. If I ask the right questions. If you give the right answers. Some people are very curious about you.'

'I'm not interesting,' Jack said.

'Oh, but you are. You have no idea.'

'Jack, don't say anything,' Gonzalo said. His eyes were still tinged with wildness.

'Don't listen to your friend. If you talk, things might turn out all right for you. If you don't, then I can make no guarantees. Videos like these go on the internet for everyone to see. If they're bloody enough.'

'Look, if you're just going to kill us, then kill us,' Jack said with nerve he did not have. 'I'm ready.'

'I don't think you are.'

'Jack…' Gonzalo said.

'What do you want to know?' Jack asked the older man.

The man smiled thinly and Jack saw he was missing a tooth. Something like that he could use to identify him later to the police, only there would be no report and the police would never know they had been here. Though Gonzalo was there,

Jack felt very alone.

'What do you want to know?' Jack asked again.

'Let's start again,' the older man said. 'I will tell you my name, except it is not my name. You can call me Guadarrama and I will call you Jack. Your friend the policeman we will call *señor*, because policemen are very important.'

Jack's eyes flicked toward Gonzalo. 'What he's doing is for me, not for the police.'

'I know. But we are very fond of policemen here. Aren't we, *cabrón*?'

All the men laughed. Gonzalo kept his mouth shut, but Jack could see he was shaking despite himself. In that moment Jack was more afraid for Gonzalo than he was for himself, and abruptly he wondered whether the reverse were true. He might never get the chance to ask.

'You want to know things,' Jack said quickly. 'I'll tell you everything.'

'All right,' Guadarrama said. 'Let's begin.'

THIRTEEN

'**Y**OU DON'T KNOW HOW MUCH I KNOW already,' Guadarrama said, 'so if you lie and I catch you, it will go badly for you.'

'I'm not going to lie.'

'Let's start with something simple: you say your friend, Inspector Soler, is not working for the police. He's working for you?'

'Yes, I'm paying him.'

'Paying him to do what?'

'To find my stepdaughter and her cousin.'

Guadarrama reached into his back pocket and produced a square of paper. Slowly he unfolded it and then held it up for Jack to see. 'These girls?' he asked.

Jack looked away from the flyer. 'Yes.'

'How long have they been gone now?'

'A month,' Jack said.

'And the army does nothing for you? The Federal Police do nothing? You have to hire some nobody from the Municipal Police to help you? Every one of them is corrupt down to the last officer. If I told you how many of them my people own, you would be shocked.'

Jack saw Gonzalo hang his head. He tried to catch his eye. 'Gonzalo isn't one of those. He's an honest man.'

'The last honest man in Mexico,' Guadarrama said.

'I trust him,' Jack said. Gonzalo looked up. Jack nodded to him. He tried to smile, but his lips would not obey.

'So what has this great detective uncovered, Jack? Has he told you where the girls are?'

'No. Not yet.'

'That is the way it is with police here. They promise a lot and they deliver a little. It's a good thing they were all put out to pasture. The new ones won't be any better, but the old ones were fucking useless.'

'He found out that you took them,' Jack said sharply.

Guadarrama looked puzzled. 'I?'

'Your people. You Zetas. You took them.'

Now Guadarrama smiled broadly and the gap in his teeth was on full display. He nudged the man next to him and that man smiled and suddenly there were chuckles and smiles all around the bare-walled room.

'You really don't know anything at all, do you?' Guadarrama asked.

Jack saw Gonzalo sit up in his chair. 'You're Golfos,' Gonzalo said.

'Maybe Inspector Soler is not so useless, after all!' Guadarrama declared.

Jack racked his brain trying to think of everything he knew about the Gulf Cartel, but his mind kept turning up blanks. On the news it was always the Zetas who were responsible for terrible things. A shooting. A kidnapping. A case of extortion. The Golfos were no better, but they did not make the headlines.

'You look confused, Jack,' Guadarrama said.

'Águila is a Zeta. He's not even one of yours.'

'No, he is not.'

'So why do you care about my girl? She's got nothing to do with you.'

'You want to kill Águila for taking her.'

'I just want to bring my stepdaughter and her cousin home.'

Guadarrama shook his head. 'Jack, those girls are both dead.'

Jack sagged against the chair and a wall of black rushed up at him from a dark undercurrent in the vaults of his mind. His ears filled with the sound of his rushing blood. The room tilted on its axis and only steadied when he forced it to. Guadarrama was watching him. He did not want his face to betray him.

Marina. Marina.

Jack's mouth felt mushy and words were difficult to form. 'I don't believe you,' he managed. 'You have no proof.'

'I don't have to have proof,' Guadarrama said. 'I know the Zetas better than anyone, and I can tell you that they are not alive. Águila killed them.'

'It's not true.'

'Then tell me, Jack: where are they? Where did they go?'

'I'm going to find out.'

'You're going to get the truth from Águila,' Guadarrama said.

'I will.'

'And how will you get the truth from him if you can't find him? Do you think it's so easy to track down a man like Águila?' Guadarrama bent low to catch Jack's eye. 'Águila will not be found unless he wants to be found. And he does not.'

'What do you know about Águila?' Gonzalo asked.

'What do you want to know? His age? His favorite color?'

'You know where to find him.'

Guadarrama nudged Jack on the shoulder. 'You should listen to your friend. He's turning out to be smarter and smarter.'

Jack looked at Guadarrama. The terrible pressure in his

chest was fading. 'Is it true?'

'Yes, it's true. I don't know where he is this very minute, but I do know where he will be in three days. That's almost as good, don't you think?'

'Tell me,' Jack said.

'Even if I tell you, what makes you think you'll be able to do anything about it?' Guadarrama asked. 'You are our prisoner. All it takes is one word and you're gone forever. No one will ever know you were here.'

'You brought me here because of Águila,' Jack said. 'You wanted me to know.'

'On one condition,' Guadarrama said. 'You must kill him.'

'I have to know the truth from him first.'

'I told you the truth: those girls are gone. All that's left to you is revenge against the man who took them. Is this what you want?'

It hurt less the second time he said it, like a phantom pain reawakened. He paused. 'Yes, it's what I want.'

Guadarrama moved very close to Jack. 'If I tell you what you want to know, then I must know that you will finish the job. Águila dies. No matter what else, he dies. Otherwise we will bring you back here and we will make another film. We will have to use the plastic.'

Jack did not look away. 'Just point me at him.'

FOURTEEN

THEY RODE WITH THE BAGS OVER THEIR heads, but this time in a seat behind the driver. Jack could feel the cool of the air conditioner venting against him, Gonzalo at his side, an unseen man on the other. Guadarrama was not with them. That much he knew for certain, because Guadarrama had said goodbye and *buena suerte* after they were hooded and marched out of the house. Jack knew he would never see Guadarrama again.

On the drive he turned Guadarrama's words over and over again in his mind. The things he had said and the things unspoken. He still felt the heartbreak, but it was tempered by a festering anger. Already that anger had boiled over and consumed Guadalupe and Fregoso. Now he would turn it on Águila, but only if he knew the truth.

The SUV rolled onto gravelly, pitted ground and Jack heard a snatch of music from outside the closed windows. They were back in Boys' Town. 'Get ready,' said one unseen man to another.

Now the truck slowed to a stop and the doors were thrown open. Jack was caught by the arm and hustled out into the evening air. It felt dry and hot after the air conditioning, though in the night the land cooled. Jack was turned around roughly and he felt a key being applied to his cuffs. His hands fell free. The bag was slipped off his head. 'Don't watch us go,' said a voice in his ear.

Jack heard the doors slam and the SUV accelerated away. He waited until the sound of its big engine faded completely before he looked to Gonzalo and dared turn toward the street. They were in the open space where they had first been taken. They were alone.

'Are you all right?' Gonzalo asked.

'I'll be fine,' Jack said, and he rubbed his wrists. They were raw.

'I thought it… I thought it was all over,' Gonzalo said, and he put his hands on his knees and wavered.

Jack put his hand on Gonzalo's back. 'Hey, hey, hey. Don't pass out on me now. We made it. We're alive.'

'You don't know how close we came, Jack.'

'I know,' Jack said. He looked north and then east. Some of the cantinas were closed. He checked his phone and saw that it was nearly four o'clock in the morning. He also saw that he had eight missed calls and a handful of messages. He left those alone.

Down the street, a pair of figures moved slowly through the cast illumination of a lone streetlight, supporting each other. From a distance, Jack and Gonzalo must have looked very much the same.

Gonzalo straightened slowly, though he was unsteady on his feet. 'We have to get out of here,' he said.

'They're not coming back,' Jack said.

'It is not them that I'm worried about. If the Golfos know so much about us, Jack, then the Zetas know, too. The only thing we can know for certain is that they haven't found us yet, but that will change. They could be watching my apartment now. They could be watching the ways to the border.'

'I'm not going to run,' Jack said. 'We know where Águila is

going to be. He's gonna tell me the truth.'

'Do you really believe that, Jack?'

'You don't?'

Gonzalo dropped his gaze. 'I don't know what to believe. The Golfos have no reason to lie. If they say the girls are dead then you have to at least consider the possibility that they are dead.'

'They are *not* dead!' Jack shot back.

'Jack—'

'Guadalupe sold them to Águila. He brought them here. *Right here.* How many places are there to hide in Boys' Town? Marina could be a hundred feet from where I'm standing right now, and she's alone and she's scared, but she knows I'm looking for her. I'm looking for her! And if that son of a bitch won't tell me where he took her then I'll do him worse than I did either of those two scumbags I killed already. Do you hear me?'

Gonzalo was quiet. 'I hear you.'

'We'll stay at Bernardo's house tonight. Tomorrow you can swing by your apartment and see if anyone's put a watch on it. We just have to wait now. Three days.'

'Jack...' Gonzalo said.

'What?'

'Nothing. Let's go.'

They trudged up the unpaved thoroughfare. Many of the cribs were closed up, the prostitutes having finished their working hours. A few places were still open, but soon they would close and Boys' Town would be a dead zone.

Gonzalo's car was where they had left it, though the spaces along the road were bare. Jack rode shotgun and Gonzalo got behind the wheel. It took three tries for the engine to catch, but finally it did and they pulled away from a shuttered strip club and turned up the street.

Jack watched the police station as they went by. At this hour it was as still as it had been at the height of the evening. Maybe it was empty. Maybe that was all policing meant in Mexico: empty buildings, empty uniforms to be filled up with whatever happened along. He felt a spasm of anger toward Guadalupe and Fregoso, but they were gone now and would never wear a badge again. A part of him felt he should be remorseful for that, but he wasn't and that would have to do.

'Let's have a little music,' Jack said.

'My radio is broken,' Gonzalo said.

'Of course it is.'

FIFTEEN

Jack slept in Bernardo's bed and Gonzalo in Patricia's. Jack's sleep was not restful and he was up before noon and in the kitchen scavenging food from the refrigerator and the cupboards for some kind of meal. He felt as though he hadn't eaten in days.

'Coffee?' Jack asked Gonzalo.

'Please.'

'I'm making eggs and they have some bacon left.'

For a while they ate without talking, but finally Gonzalo spoke. 'It would be best if you stayed here, out of sight,' he said. 'The less you are seen in public, the less chance for something to happen.'

'You mean the less chance one of the Zetas will try to kill me.'

'As you say.'

'When do you want to get in touch again?'

'We have three days,' Gonzalo said. 'There is no hurry.'

Gonzalo got up and Jack watched him. 'You're sticking with me on this, aren't you?' Jack asked.

'Of course.'

'It's just that I'm getting the feeling you'd rather call it quits.'

Gonzalo did not look at him. 'After what happened last night, I think you can forgive me. To be taken by *narcos*...'

'We made it out all right.'

'That was good luck, not good planning,' Gonzalo said. 'If it had been Águila's men who took us from the street, we would not be having this conversation. They would have found us hanging from an overpass. If we had all our arms and legs it would be a miracle.'

'The Golfos have our back,' Jack said.

'The Golfos are using you to get something they want for free,' Gonzalo returned. 'If you kill Águila then it's a win for them. If he kills you, they lose nothing and can try again. They did not help you out of the kindness of their hearts. It's a joke to them. A game.'

'It's not a joke to me,' Jack said.

'That's exactly why they find it funny.'

Gonzalo left the kitchen and Jack followed. 'You know, I don't care why they did what they did. I'll be glad to kill Águila. If that makes me a stooge then I guess it makes me a stooge.'

'Goodbye, Jack.'

'Goddamn it, don't you walk out of here like this!' Jack shouted. He still held his plate in his hand and he gestured with it violently, as if he was going to smash it onto the floor. 'The Golfos gave me a *gift* and I'm gonna use it!'

Gonzalo turned on him. 'Fine, Jack! We'll do it, then! We'll go get Águila and we'll find your stepdaughter and everything will be perfect again! Then you get to go back to Texas with everything you want and I have to remain here with the consequences.'

'Are you afraid? Is that what it is?'

'*Of course* I'm afraid! I'm terrified! Were you not there last night? You listened to everything they said, but you heard nothing. You are convinced that everything will turn out exactly as you believe it will, but wishing does not make it so,

Jack. Wishing does not make it so.'

'Then why are you even helping me?' Jack demanded. 'And don't give me any of that bullshit about how Mexicans have to look out for each other! I'm not a Mexican and you're not obliged to me for anything.'

'Because—' Gonzalo cut himself off. His hands moved in front of him as if he were tussling with his own words. 'You don't know what it's like, Jack. You live in Laredo and you read about us in the news, but you don't *know*. I want things to turn out the way you want them to. I want to find your stepdaughter and her cousin and I want there to be peace for one family for once. Instead we get this.' Gonzalo pointed to the floor where the dried blood had pooled and the lonely flyer, sodden through, pasted to the vinyl tiles.

The anger left Jack. He held the plate between his two hands, suddenly ashamed of his fury. His face flushed. 'It's going to happen,' he said quietly. 'We're gonna have a happy ending.'

'It's already too late for that,' Gonzalo said, and his voice was bleak. He turned away.

'Gonzalo, we're going to make this work,' Jack called after him. 'Somehow we'll make it work.'

Gonzalo raised his hand in farewell, but he said nothing and he did not look back. He passed through the broken front door of Bernardo's house. He pulled it shut behind him.

SIXTEEN

A STRIDENT KNOCKING AT HIS APARTMENT door stirred Gonzalo out of sleep instantly. He reached for his gun on the bed stand and felt immediate relief when it came into his hand. He sat up, waiting, and then the knocking came again.

Gonzalo slipped from the bedroom into the front room and to the door. He pressed his eye up against the peephole. Framed in the circle of glass was Lieutenant Casiano.

He hid the gun under the cushions of the couch and called, 'I'm coming!'

When he opened the door he saw that Casiano was alone. The man looked at Gonzalo in his shorts and T-shirt and a little smile tugged at his lips. 'Sleeping in?' he asked.

Gonzalo did not even know the time. 'I don't have anything else to do,' he said.

'Now you do. Captain Alvares would like to see you.'

'What about?'

'May I come in?'

'Of course,' Gonzalo said, and he stepped back to allow Casiano into the apartment. The lieutenant looked very neat in the messiness of the front room and Gonzalo was embarrassed. 'I should get dressed,' he said.

'A good idea.'

Gonzalo retreated to the bedroom and put on his working

clothes, the slacks and the jacket over shirtsleeves. He put on a green tie. In the bathroom he washed his face and dragged wet fingers through his hair to make himself presentable. When he returned to Casiano, he found the lieutenant still standing where he had been before. 'I'm ready,' Gonzalo said.

'Follow me.'

Casiano had come to his door alone, but he was not on his own. Parked on the street level was a Humvee with a mounted gun. Casiano opened the rear door and motioned Gonzalo in. Gonzalo obeyed. Casiano got in the front just ahead of him. The legs of the soldier on the gun came down between the rear seats.

They drove away. The Humvee had an incredibly stiff suspension and every ripple and gouge in the road translated directly through the wheels into Gonzalo's tailbone. The man on the gun swiveled his weapon left and right, crowding Gonzalo when he turned so that he was pressed against the door.

'You didn't say what this was all about,' Gonzalo said to Casiano.

'There have been some new developments. The captain wants you to be aware of them.'

With that, Casiano said no more. The ride was hot and grew no smoother until finally they were in El Centro and the police station came into view. Beyond the barricades the Humvee's brakes grated and the big vehicle slowed to a stop.

Casiano was out of his seat and holding the door for Gonzalo before Gonzalo could even touch the handle, as if this were a limousine and Casiano his driver. Gonzalo felt guilty for asking questions at all.

He found Captain Alvares where he always did, though his desk was not so clean anymore and the paperwork had seemed to accumulate into a solid wall that threatened to overtake the small working space the man had left. Alvares rose to shake his hand and offered him a seat. 'It's good to see you,' he said.

'I'm not sure why I'm here,' Gonzalo said.

'It's good news,' Alvares replied. 'You will be happy to know that I have expedited your processing. You're at the top of the list for testing and retraining. Also, I have been authorized to offer you a small stipend. It is not a replacement for a full salary, but it is at least something.'

Gonzalo sat with his hands in his lap. 'Why me? What did I do?'

'You impressed me. I passed that on to my superiors.'

'I did very little. Only what you allowed me to do.'

'There is also this,' Alvares said, and he handed a thin folder over the wall. 'Look.'

Gonzalo opened the folder. When he looked inside he nearly dropped it. A sheaf of photographs spilled out onto the floor. He hurried to gather them up, but the first image was seared into his brain: Guadalupe, bound with duct tape around the legs, arms secured behind his back, his torso a mass of blood out of which the handle of a knife protruded.

There were other pictures. Fregoso in his bed with a gunshot wound over his brow, the pillow beneath his head sodden. Gonzalo closed the folder. 'Guadalupe and Fregoso,' he said thickly.

'Yes. Killed. Their bodies were reported yesterday. Guadalupe was partially mutilated.'

'Any suspects?' Gonzalo asked.

'*Narcos*, of course. This man Águila you were talking about. He must have found out that you had been questioning Guadalupe and disposed of him. The same for his partner. You were right to suspect them of corruption. Now they are no longer this city's problem.'

Gonzalo swallowed. 'I'm not sure I can take credit for something the *narcos* did.'

'You smoked them out.'

'But I didn't find the girls.'

'Yes, there is that,' Alvares said, and his face fell. 'Now we'll never know.'

Gonzalo handed the folder back to Alvares. The captain put it away.

'Thank you for your confidence in me, *Capitán*,' Gonzalo said. 'I hope I won't disappoint you.'

'If you play your cards right, you'll be the first Municipal Police officer returned to duty. That will make all the difference in your future career. And you'll have my personal recommendation.'

'I don't know what to say.'

'Tell me that when you're back to work you'll help me find this Águila. We have two murders to pin on him and two disappearances. And who's to say what else he has done?'

'I'll be happy to go after him,' Gonzalo said.

'It's good to be on the right side of the law,' Alvares said. 'Guadalupe and Fregoso learned what it's like to be on the wrong one.'

Gonzalo dried his palms on his pants legs. 'Yes, sir,' he said. 'They did.'

SEVENTEEN

THE PHONE RANG. IT WAS GONZALO. 'I was wondering when you were going to call,' Jack said.

'Where are you, Jack?'

'In the same place. I'm losing my mind here.'

'You mustn't be seen out in the city,' Gonzalo said. 'Don't leave.'

'Where are *you*?'

'I am at home. I just returned from a meeting with Captain Alvares.'

'Alvares? What did he want?'

'To tell me Guadalupe and Fregoso are dead.'

Jack breathed. Then he said, 'What did you tell him?'

'I told him nothing. As far as Alvares is concerned, Águila is responsible for their deaths.'

'Then that's good,' Jack said.

'Only until Águila is found dead. How will that be explained away?'

Jack was in Bernardo's bedroom and he stood looking out the dirty window at the alley. As he watched, a rat scurried from the dented trashcans of a neighbor and vanished out of sight. At night the cats went hunting and he heard them calling to one another and fighting. The alley was the same as the city. 'By the time anyone figures out what's happened, Marina and I will be across the bridge.'

'And when they come to ask Patricia Sigala how she came to return home? What will she tell them? That some helpful *narcos* killed the man who took her before carrying out a rescue? You have to think, Jack.'

'Don't tell me I can't do this. If you don't want to go the rest of the way, then I'll understand. I can do it alone,' Jack said.

'No, you can't.'

'Then are you in?'

'I could walk away, Jack. I could. They're dangling my job in front of me. All I have to do is reach out and take it. Then I can go back to the way things were. Before all of this.'

'You know the way things were was shit.'

'Yes.'

'I have to know, Gonzalo. I have to know you're in this. I can't make plans if you're halfway out the door. I need a *partner*.'

Gonzalo sighed deeply and for a moment Jack thought the call was ended. 'If I don't come with you, you'll die,' Gonzalo said. 'I can't let that happen.'

Jack felt relief he hadn't expected. For the first time he felt as though he could take a real breath and his lips were not dry. 'I told you: we're going to make this work.'

'There is one other thing, Jack.'

'What?'

'What if we do not find what we are looking for?'

Jack felt a muscle in his cheek twitch. 'You mean what if they're dead,' he said.

'Yes.'

'They aren't dead. This all means something. They're alive.'

'All right. I believe you. Tomorrow we'll meet,' Gonzalo said. 'We'll see Águila together.'

'Thank you, Gonzalo.'

'*De nada*. Rest now. We'll talk again in the morning.'

'Goodbye.'

He held the quiet phone in his hand and for a long time he stood in the square of light from the window without moving or thinking or hearing anything but the sound of his own breathing. Jack was elsewhere, on a city street in front of a cantina with no name.

When the daydream passed and he was back again, he sat on the edge of the bed and dialed a number from memory. It rang and rang and finally it went to voicemail. Silently Jack was relieved. 'Lidia,' he said, 'it's me. I wanted to talk to you one more time, but I guess you're not answering your phone. That's okay because I have a lot to say and I don't think we're gonna get anywhere if we just go around and around.

'I need you to listen to me. I know I've been real bad about explaining why I'm here and what I'm doing, but you have to trust me when I say it's the only way. And it's not about me being a hero like I said before. It's about me being a father. And I don't care what anyone else says, I am your father and I'm Marina's father, too. Fathers have to do things sometimes.

'Tomorrow I'm gonna talk to a man who's gonna tell me where Marina and Patricia are. He's gonna tell me whether he wants to or not. But I'm not gonna lie to you and say it won't be dangerous, because it is.

'If I don't… if I don't make it back, I want you to know that I love you. I have a will and you and Marina are entitled to everything I have, including the house. I got a life insurance policy after your mother died. That's all yours, too. I don't know how the state's going to handle things if you don't have any mother or father, but I do know that you'll be taken care of. You're a smart girl and you'll make it through all right.'

Jack paused then and he took a few deep breaths to quash

the tears that threatened to rise up and take him over. He would not cry. When he hung up it would be different, but he wouldn't have Lidia hear him cry.

'I have to go now. I wish I could see you again, but you're safer where you are. Just promise me that you'll look after yourself no matter what happens and don't forget that I love you like you were my own. You and Marina both. Never forget. Goodbye.'

He ended the call and put his face in his hands and cried then. His body shuddered with aching sobs and for a wild moment he thought of leaving this place and driving away, away, over the bridge and back to the home he shared with Marina and Lidia, but that thought did not last long. He drowned it in tears, and when he surfaced again he was empty of everything but the belief that he would not cross the river again until he had Marina with him.

'I'm sorry, honey,' he said to the deserted bedroom. 'God knows I'm sorry.'

EIGHTEEN

GONZALO HAD PASSED THE CHURCH many times, but he had never gone inside. He had been raised Catholic and so he had a fear of God in the great spaces inside God's houses, but when he was grown he found the fear did not call him to worship anymore, but drove him away instead. The last church he had entered had been the little one his mother had attended in the years after his father died, and then only to see her away to the graveyard herself. He hadn't known any of the people who introduced themselves to him, and the priest who said the mass seemed interested only in doing what needed to be done as quickly as possible.

On the morning of the day, Gonzalo dressed as if he were having an audience with the commander of the police force. Everything was pressed and clean and still held the heat of the iron when he put it on. He put his badge and identification in his inside pocket where it belonged. He put on the ankle holster that held his gun.

He bought breakfast at a little restaurant near his apartment even though he wasn't at all hungry. The tip he left behind was generous. His plan was to drive straight to Bernardo Sigala's house to meet Jack, but he had passed the church and before he had time to think about it he had circled around and found a place to park near by.

No doubt there were bigger and more impressive churches

to be found. The city had its own cathedral, its central pillar a tower of stained glass surmounted by a great white cross. It must have been very majestic in there. By contrast this church had the feel of something old, with the dingy elegance of a thing left neglected for a long time, but never quite abandoned. Gold paint had been allowed to dull. Here and there he spotted cobwebs someone had missed.

There was a place for supplicants to light votive candles and say a prayer and Gonzalo gravitated there, but when he was kneeling and the long match was lit he could think of no words to speak inwardly or outwardly. He buried the burning head of the match in a little trough of sand.

'Welcome.'

Gonzalo turned from the candles and saw a slender young man in black watching him. A touch of white at the throat told Gonzalo this was a priest, but the man looked barely old enough to shave.

'If I'm interrupting, I'm sorry,' the priest said. 'It's only that we don't get too many people in here at this time of the morning.'

'I was just going,' Gonzalo said, and he stood to leave.

'Please don't,' the priest said. 'I mean, feel free to go if you like, but as long as I'm here and you're here, why don't we talk a little?'

Gonzalo glanced at the exit, then back to the priest. 'All right,' he said.

'Come and have a seat.'

They sat down together at a pew. The priest held a small, leather-bound Bible that looked well loved. He rested it on his knee. 'I'm Father Salamón,' he said.

'No offense, Father, but how old are you?'

Father Salamón laughed. 'I'm not the senior man here, if that's what you're thinking. Father Anselmo is probably more of what you're looking for: gray-haired, full of wrinkles. But he's also not as much fun.'

'I should tell you: I'm not religious.'

'I don't presume to judge.'

Gonzalo put his hands together, fingertip to fingertip, and molded them with each other as if he had his troubles caught in a net to be closed up within them. 'I will ask you this,' he said.

'Yes?'

'Is it always possible to find forgiveness, even if one does a terrible thing?'

Father Salamón looked serious. 'You are not the first person in your position to ask me that question.'

'What position?'

'I shouldn't say. We are in the house of God and accusations have no place there.'

Gonzalo sat up straight. 'You think I am a *narco*?'

'Are you not?'

Now it was Gonzalo's turn to laugh. He reached inside his jacket and brought out his identification. 'I'm a police officer,' he said. 'An inspector.'

Father Salamón flushed. 'I'm sorry. When you asked me… I assumed.'

'You don't need to apologize.'

'I feel awful.'

'I know sometimes the people of this city don't make a distinction between the *narcos* and the police. And they have every right to that. We have not done much to earn their respect.'

'Then I must ask: if you are a policeman, what terrible thing could you possibly have done?'

The laughter passed from Gonzalo and he looked down

again. 'That's not so easy to answer.'

'I'm here to listen.'

'I have been party to acts that are not in keeping with my commitments. Some of these things I have had to live with for a long time.'

'What is your name?' Father Salamón asked.

'Gonzalo.'

'Gonzalo, did you come here looking for absolution?'

'I don't know what I'm doing here.'

'Has it been some time since you last confessed?'

'A lifetime ago.'

'Would you like to now?'

Gonzalo met Father Salamón's searching look. 'No.'

'Then what can I do for you? It doesn't feel right letting you carry your burden alone. My job is very important to me.'

'If I tell you something, will you keep it between us?' Gonzalo asked.

'There are some who say that what we discuss right now is subject to the Seal of the Confessional even if we do not perform the rite.'

'And that means you can't tell anyone? No matter what?'

Father Salamón nodded slowly, but Gonzalo could see the doubt in his eyes.

'A few days ago I stood by while two men were murdered. And today a third man will die. I will not do anything. I will even help.'

'Who were these men you saw killed?'

'Bad ones.'

'And what they did deserved death?'

'I don't know,' Gonzalo said. 'But I do know that no one will mourn them.'

'And this third man. Does *he* deserve death?'

'If what we have been told is true… yes.'

Father Salamón sat back in the pew with the Bible held between his hands, his thumbs rubbing insistently at the worn leather. Gonzalo saw a muscle in his jaw working. 'They don't teach you how to answer these kinds of questions in seminary,' he said at last.

'I should go.'

'No, please give me a chance.'

Gonzalo looked at his watch. 'I have time.'

'You're a policeman,' Father Salamón said with hesitation. 'I don't have to tell you that Mexico is full of evil men who do abominable things. You say the men you saw die were that kind. That this third man is also that kind.'

'Yes,' Gonzalo said.

'I know parishioners who have lost family members in this city and elsewhere,' Father Salamón said. 'They are good people who only want to live their lives, worship God and be at peace. But I cannot give them peace. No matter how many communions I give, no matter how many homilies, I must stand by while the police and the army and the *narcos* do battle in the streets. I am powerless. Though God gives me strength, it is not the kind of strength that can stop a single bullet.'

'I'm sorry.'

Father Salamón waved the comment away. 'What I'm saying is this: if I had it within my power to put a stop to things, I would. And God forgive me for saying so, but if it meant that some of these evil men had to die to bring that about, I would not lose a minute's sleep.'

'The commandment says "thou shall not kill,"' Gonzalo said.

'Did you know that in the Hebrew it says "thou shall not murder"?' Father Salamón asked.

'What's the difference?'

'Something tells me you know the difference already.'

Gonzalo thought, and then he said, 'You thought I was a *narco*. Would you say the same things to me then?'

'I'm required to extend God's grace to all who pass through those doors, sinner and saint alike. That doesn't mean I have to approve of everything they do. I will make jokes with them and when they ask for absolution I give it, but there is a difference between what God offers and what Man can provide. That is my failing as a priest, and I think it's likely that I'll struggle with it for as long as I wear the collar.'

'You're young,' Gonzalo said.

'You are not so old,' Father Salamón replied.

'I feel old. I feel very old.'

'Then why go through with it? If it pains you so much, is it worth it?'

Gonzalo inclined his head. 'You want to give your parishioners peace? There's a man who will have no peace until this is done. No matter what I think, I have to do this. For him. And maybe for me. I can't explain.'

'I can give you my blessing, but unless you ask to be absolved of your sins, I can't do that for you,' Father Salamón said.

'You'd give your blessing to a killer?' Gonzalo asked.

'It sounds as though you need it more than anyone.'

'Then I'll take it.'

'Kneel here.'

Gonzalo lowered himself to the bare wooden kneeler and Father Salamón stood over him. The priest placed a hand on Gonzalo's head and he invoked the Father, the Son and the Holy Spirit. He pleaded for God's mercy. He asked for God's grace. Gonzalo kept his eyes tightly closed, though he did not pray. In the dark parts of his mind he was reminded of his mother, of endless masses, of women with their hair covered and many sad, drawn faces.

'You're welcome to stay,' Father Salamón said when it was done. 'A church is not just a place of worship, but a sanctuary from the evils of the world. You can let this dark cloud go past.'

'I told you, I can't do that.'

Father Salamón shrugged and attempted to smile, but his face wouldn't obey. 'I had to try.'

Gonzalo rose from the kneeler. He brushed at his jacket and the folds fell out smoothly. 'I appreciate everything you've said,' he told Father Salamón. 'I'm sorry it was a waste of your time.'

Father Salamón followed him to the doors in the narthex. 'It wasn't a waste. Don't go away thinking that.'

'Goodbye, Father,' Gonzalo said.

'Goodbye, Gonzalo. Come back when you can.'

'I may do that,' Gonzalo said, and he went out into the sun.

On the front steps of the church he stopped and brought out his phone. A yellow Post-it note was stuck to the back. He dialed the number there. There were three rings at the other end and someone answered whom Gonzalo didn't recognize.

'My name is Inspector Gonzalo Soler. I'd like to speak with Captain Alvares, please,' Gonzalo said.

'Captain Alvares is not available.'

'When will he be back?'

'I can't give out that information.'

Gonzalo cursed under his breath. 'All right,' he said, 'listen to me, then. Write this down. It's *important*. Be sure Alvares sees it right away.'

'What's your message?'

Gonzalo told him.

NINETEEN

JACK COULD NOT BE CONVINCED TO RIDE with Gonzalo to the cantina. 'I need to be able to move when we find out where Marina is,' he told Gonzalo. 'We can't get across the border in your car.'

He could see Gonzalo in his rear-view mirror, keeping close as they passed through the city. This time Jack knew where he was going and a block away he found a place to park and waited until Gonzalo had settled in, too, before stepping out of the truck. They would walk the rest of the way.

It was not terribly hot, but Jack was sweating as though it was. He knew it was nervous sweat and he knew that when it came down to it he would get it done. Maybe it would be clean, like Fregoso, or maybe it would be dirty, like Guadalupe, but he would get it done.

Gonzalo was dressed as if he were headed to a formal review. Even if Jack did not already know, he would have spotted Gonzalo as a cop at first glance. There was nothing to be done about it now. An American and a cop. Neither of them belonged.

Jack saw Gonzalo watching him, and he spoke before Gonzalo could: 'Don't tell me we can walk away. We can't.'

They walked side by side along the sidewalk toward the cantina. The entire block looked shabby and the few cars parked here and there were old and rusty and full of dents. No tourist ever walked this street.

'Do you see?' Gonzalo asked.

'See what?'

'Across the street. A man in a car, watching.'

Jack looked and saw the man sitting behind the wheel of a slightly newer vehicle, the windows down. His eyes were on them. Jack averted his gaze.

A man leaned against the wall outside the door. He looked at them and his expression curdled, but he did not move to block them.

Jack went through the door first.

The windows were barred, but they were big enough to let in sunlight and the open space of the cantina was brightly illuminated. Tables were scattered around and in the back there were booths that sat in a line perpendicular to the front doors, so it was possible to sit in them and not be seen by anyone coming in.

Three of the tables were occupied, two by groups of men playing dominoes and drinking beer. The third table was bare, the two men seated there simply watching Jack and Gonzalo as they entered. Their eyes were lidded and somehow they managed to convey distaste without moving at all.

Gonzalo stepped up beside Jack. 'He's not here,' he said quietly.

'The booths,' Jack said.

'I'll be at the bar.'

The cantina's bar was not large, but it was stocked with so many bottles that it seemed to bristle with glass. Jack was aware of Gonzalo moving away on his left hand as he walked past the two men and their empty table. He could barely feel his own feet, but he felt the weight of the men's stares keenly.

There were four booths, each separated from the next by a lattice of brown-painted wood. Jack's breath quickened as he came to the first. He looked and it was empty. To the next. Empty. Suddenly he was aware of a burgeoning panic that somehow Guadarrama had gotten it all wrong and Águila was *not* here. Or he had been and gone.

The third booth was empty. At the end of the row there were batwing doors leading to restrooms and an open doorway through which came the clatter of cookware and the smell of meat. A short man in a cook's cap poked his head out briefly, saw Jack and then retreated.

He came to the fourth booth.

Gonzalo had not told Jack what Águila looked like except for one thing: the mole on his cheek and his gold watch. The man sitting in the booth had both and in front of him was a plate of enchiladas, half eaten, and a tall glass of beer. He wore a Ralph Lauren Polo shirt in deep blue.

Jack froze. His first urge was to grab the man and haul him out of the booth by the front of his shirt. The next urge was more violent still. He clenched his fingers.

Águila took a long time to look up, and when he did Jack saw a handsome face marred only by the mole. The man smiled and had straight, white teeth. 'Who are you supposed to be?' he asked.

The words wouldn't come. Jack pushed them out. 'I want to talk to you.'

'Sit. Talk.'

Jack slid into the booth across from Águila, face to face over a plate of food and a sweating glass. The butt of the Browning Hi-Power in his waistband pushed hard against the wooden back of the seat. Jack could feel it against his flesh.

'You are from the States?' Águila asked.

Jack nodded mutely.

'What does a man from the States want with me?'

'You're Águila,' Jack said.

Águila took a drink from his beer. 'Yes, I am. And what is *your* name?'

'Jack.'

'*Mucho gusto*, Jack.' The man's eyes were a deep, woody brown and he did not blink when he looked at Jack. He cut a bite of enchilada with his fork and ate it, still watching.

'I've been looking for you,' Jack managed to say at last.

'You found me.'

'I have questions.'

Águila gestured with his fork. 'Questions are bad for business. You're here for business, aren't you?'

'Yeah, I've got business.'

'I have people who do things like this for me,' Águila said. 'You really should be talking to them.'

'I didn't want to talk to your people.'

'Okay, so you don't want to talk to them. I can respect that. A *gringo* coming across the bridge to do a deal... that takes *cojones*. Like coming in here when I have my lunch. *Cojones*.'

Jack cleared his throat. 'I wanted to talk to you about something that happened a month ago.'

'That's a long time for me to remember things, Jack.'

'You bought a couple of girls.'

Águila had raised his glass to drink, but now he stopped. The brown eyes went black. He put the glass down firmly. 'Let me tell you something, Jack: I don't put up with a lot of bullshit. I don't know what you heard on the other side, but I don't. If you want to talk to me about *mota* or *chinaloa*, we talk. You want *metanfetaminas*? We talk. But I'm not talking to some *gabacho* about girls.'

'You bought them off a cop named Guadalupe,' Jack said. His voice trembled, but he was not afraid. 'Two girls. Remember them?'

'You get the fuck out of here,' Águila said. 'You leave right now and maybe I don't take those big, swinging *cojones* and cut them off.'

Jack grabbed the edge of the table and ripped it away from the wall. Plate and glass shattered on the floor and the table flipped onto its back. He snatched up a fistful of Águila's shirt and dragged him from the booth. '*You tell me!*'

At the front of the cantina, the two men at their empty table leaped up. They yanked guns out from beneath their shirts. A game of dominoes was scattered as the players went for cover and the bartender vanished behind his forest of glass.

'Don't move!' Gonzalo shouted. He had his pistol out and leveled at the gunmen. His aim did not waver.

Jack closed his arm around Águila's neck and used his free hand to draw his gun. He put the Browning against Águila's head and put the man between himself and the gunmen. 'You back off!' he told them. 'Put your guns down!'

'You're being stupid,' Águila said quietly. 'You're being very stupid.'

'Shut up! The two of you put your guns on the ground!'

The gunmen looked at Gonzalo and then Jack and then they laid their pistols on the floor. They held their hands high.

Jack shoved Águila back into the empty space where the booth's table had been and Águila collided heavily with the wall. He turned toward Jack and Jack pointed the Browning at his face. 'I have questions and you're going answer them,' he said.

A trickle of blood slipped from Águila's hairline. He swiped at it. 'You think you're so smart? You think you're so tough?

You're a dead man, Jack.'

'I don't give a shit,' Jack said.

'What do you want?'

'I want the two girls you bought. You had them in Boys' Town. I want to know where they are now.'

Águila's expression changed. 'Are you serious? This is about some cheap *coño*? You're out of your mind, *man*.'

Jack cocked the Browning. 'You call my daughter cheap pussy again and I'll shoot you in the fucking knee. Where are they?'

'*Vete a la mierda*.'

The bullet went through Águila's leg, but it missed the knee. Águila went down as if he'd had his foot swept from underneath him. Blood spattered the white-painted wall in drooling specks.

'*Where are they?*'

'Jack!' Gonzalo shouted.

If he had not looked, he would not have seen the man from outside pass through the open door, or the gun in his hand. He would not have seen the gunshot or the way it crashed into Gonzalo's side. He would not have seen Gonzalo fall.

The man was silhouetted against the light and Jack fired, striking twice. The man spilled backward out of the doorway, his gun discharging into the ceiling.

The two gunmen kicked over their table and went for their weapons. Jack heard gunfire and realized Gonzalo was shooting from the floor. Blood soaked his jacket and he scrambled with his feet to make the end of the short bar before the gunmen had their pistols again and opened fire. Their bullets stripped wood from the face of the bar.

'Are you all right?' Jack asked Gonzalo.

Gonzalo nodded, but did not speak.

Jack leaned out far enough to take two shots at the men huddled behind their table. The bullets went low and blasted into the plastic surface, spraying splinters from underneath. The men returned fire and Jack ducked back.

He put his hand in a puddle of blood. Gonzalo's wound was bleeding freely and his face was drawn with pain. His grip on his gun was loose, the weapon resting on his leg. 'Can you walk?' Jack asked. 'We'll try for the door.'

'I'm better… here,' Gonzalo managed.

More gunfire smacked into the bar and showers of colored glass fell down on Jack's head. He poked out again and caught one of the men in the open. The Browning opened up two expanding holes in the man's chest and he flopped over as if all the bones had been yanked from his body.

A new figure exploded into the doorway from outside. The watcher from the car. He held a submachine gun in his fists. Jack took a shot that missed and the watcher returned a burst of fire.

'*¡Yo me voy de aquí!*' the bartender cried from his hiding place, and he broke from behind the bar for the rear of the cantina. He was cut down in mid-stride by the watcher and his automatic weapon. He collapsed onto his face.

Águila chose that moment to head for the kitchen door. He moved more slowly than the bartender, forced to lean heavily on his good leg. Jack took that from him with two shots to the back of the knee. Águila crumpled.

Gonzalo sagged against Jack. His eyelids fluttered. Jack shook him. 'Gonzalo! Wake up! Stay awake!' Gonzalo did not respond.

'Take him!' shouted the watcher from his place by the door.

Jack took a breath. He let it go slowly, as slow as time. He rose from behind the bar at the same time the last gunman exposed himself from behind the overturned table. For an instant they were face to face, gun against gun, but Jack pulled the trigger first and ruined the man's face with a wild shot that went high.

The watcher shot Jack with his submachine gun. The bullets struck him low, beneath the ribcage, and the impact drove the air from his lungs. He stumbled but did not fall, aware of the slugs passing through his body, bursting out of his back, and the pain, the nerve-searing pain that impaled him.

He fired as he staggered and the first two shots went wide. The watcher stepped forward, triggering his weapon again. A new explosion of glass sent fragments flying into Jack's face. Jack kept on shooting until his bullets found their target and then the watcher and his submachine gun were falling to the floor in silence.

Jack collapsed onto his backside, one leg twisted beneath him. He tasted blood in his mouth. The empty Browning was out of his hand, lying amid a shower of glass and wood fragments. It was impossible to catch his breath because breathing itself was painful. His lungs burned as if he had run a dozen miles.

Gonzalo sat against the bar, his head hanging. Jack pulled himself across the floor to him, the movement pulling things inside him that were not meant to be pulled. His wounds felt like hot metal. He was bleeding everywhere.

'Gonzalo,' Jack said. When he touched Gonzalo on the shoulder, Gonzalo slumped over completely. His eyes were closed. Jack put his hand on Gonzalo's neck and felt a pulse, however faint. He patted Gonzalo's cheek. 'Gonzalo.'

First Jack saw only the whites of Gonzalo's eyes, but then they rolled into focus, the lids barely parted. Gonzalo whispered something. Jack's ears were stunned from the ferocious noise of the guns. He put his head closer.

'Help is coming,' Gonzalo said.

Movement made Jack bring his head up and he saw the domino-playing men emerging from their hiding places amid the overturned tables. They put their hands up and moved sidelong toward the door, watching Jack the whole time. He raised an empty hand to them, as if to say *go*, and then dropped it.

'Jack.'

'What is it?'

'There's too many of them, Jack.'

'It's done. It's all done, okay. Listen, you rest,' Jack said. 'Just rest here.'

He took Gonzalo's pistol and using the bar as a lever he managed to make it to his feet, though the floor was dangerously unstable.

Águila was gone from the main room. Blood trailed into the kitchen. Jack found him halfway to the rear door of the cantina, clawing at the plain concrete floor with fingernails that had splintered and bled. His legs were almost useless, though they moved when he urged himself forward.

Jack knelt beside the man and seized him by the shoulder. Águila rolled over without resistance. He was pale around the eyes and lips from blood loss, but his expression was hard. Jack put the gun in Águila's face. 'I want to know where my daughter is,' he said, and blood slipped over his tongue.

'Who are you?' Águila asked.

'What did you do with the *girls*?' Jack shouted, and specks of red sprayed from his mouth to dot Águila's face.

'Why do you want some fucking girls?'

Jack's face wrinkled and his eyes were suddenly hot with tears. He pushed the barrel of Gonzalo's gun against Águila's cheek and thumbed back the hammer. 'Just tell me what happened to them.'

Now the hardness fragmented and Jack saw the fear underneath. Águila saw the red face of death in Jack, streaked in blood. He felt the steel of the gun. 'I don't remember any girls,' Águila said. 'I don't remember them. Please don't kill me.'

'The girls,' Jack murmured. It was harder to speak clearly. 'Please don't kill me.'

Jack's vision darkened. As he bled, his heart beat faster and faster and the edges of the world blackened. The gun was firm in his grip, his finger on the trigger. Squeezing was easy. *Marina.*

Águila spasmed once and then he was still. A crimson halo of blood painted the kitchen floor. The hole in his face was strangely small, but starred with black. His eyes were open, but they saw nothing.

Jack cried even when he could no longer sit up, his wounds forcing him flat until he could only see the cliffs of the rising cooktop and counters and the grease-spotted ceiling. He coughed up red and it painted his face, mingling with tears. He knew he was breathing blood.

He did not know how long he lay there, but he was aware of a dark spot in his memory that came and passed. Maybe his eyes had been closed. He was not sure.

'Lidia,' he said.

There were places to get a grip on the unlit stove. Jack climbed them until he could get his feet underneath himself. Gonzalo's gun was lost somewhere. It didn't matter. He made it to the kitchen door, then through the door into the main room and across the main room to the bar. Gonzalo was there, though if he was alive or dead, Jack couldn't tell. Instead he moved, now from the bar to the front door, past the bodies of the dead. Through the door into the bright street. He was trailing blood in spots and splatters.

Jack lurched across the street and down the block. Each step forward was a lifetime's effort. His arms flopped at his sides. When he saw the truck it seemed alive with white, as gleaming as the surface of the sun and just as blinding. He smeared red on the panel and door. It took all his power to step up into the cab, to lean back into the seat with his hands on the wheel.

Keys. They were slippery in his grasp. The blast of the air conditioning when he turned over the engine was breathtaking.

He drove lying on the wheel, aware that he was weaving, that signs were passed unheeded. Horns blasted at him and once he clipped another car but kept on, taking no notice of the shouting he left behind. He knew he was headed north, but the details were lost to him, just a buzz in the back of his mind that told him when to turn and when to drive.

The Federal Police vehicle fell in behind him when the bridge was in sight. It flashed its lights and put on the siren. Jack pressed the accelerator and the truck surged forward.

A man's voice crackled over a speaker, telling him to stop. Jack went faster. His lap felt full of hot liquid and blood drooled over his lower lip as he drove. Four lanes with booths appeared ahead. A few men in colored smocks stood in the street selling newspapers. A large sign read FELIZ VIAJE.

Jack did not thread the needle. He crashed into a lane and tore off a chunk of concrete, glass and metal from one of the booths, strewing the mess behind him. The side mirror was ripped from the truck. In the other mirrors, the flashing red and blue lights surged closer.

The footbridge was on his right, the path across the river ahead. The traffic grew thick ahead, red brake lights in a forest aglitter. Jack jammed his foot to the floor and aimed for the gap between a small car and a looming tractor-trailer.

The truck speared between them, then wrenched to a halt. Unencumbered by a seatbelt, Jack slammed into the steering wheel. The airbag deployed in his face.

He opened the door against the side of another car and fell out amidst angry shouting that he could not understand. Words meant nothing to him anymore. There was only the pain and the bone-deep weariness that threatened to pull him to the ground forever.

A woman stepped in his way, but she saw the blood and jumped back to let him pass. Jack heard the skirling of more sirens behind him. He looked ahead through the gathered shadows that pressed on him and put one foot ahead of the other.

Panicked faces appeared in windows as he passed them, frightened by the noise and the vision of a man dressed in his own blood. More voices followed him, authoritative shouts with the hint of a threat in them. Jack did not look back. One foot ahead of the other.

His balance fled him again and he bumped side to side, leaving streaks of deep crimson on glass and metal. Soon there would be no more; there could be no more. He would be empty and then everything would stop. Jack put out a hand and left a perfect handprint on the closed window of a yellow minivan. One foot ahead of the other.

Jack saw the flags. They were mounted on the bridge side by side, Mexican and American. The middle of the span, suspended over the Rio Grande, where one divided against the other. He coughed and something tore inside. His knees gave way and he fell to the ground to crawl, crawl, and crawl until the flags were nearly overhead.

Footsteps rushed up behind him. The flags barely fluttered

in the breathless afternoon. The concrete surface of the bridge was hot on his hands, but he did not feel that pain. The other pain, the grinding agony of things wrenched apart and left to bleed and bleed, swallowed it.

He stretched his hand out, but there was no more left. He collapsed onto his side. The flags were behind him. They had passed over him on their own somehow because he could not have pulled himself that distance.

Looking up from the ground, Jack saw for the first time the men in black with their weapons. They stood gathered at the invisible line beneath the flags with their weapons, watching Jack with angry eyes as dark as their uniforms. Jack wanted to call out to them, but he did not have energy enough to do anything except pant like a dying dog under the sun.

More shadows. The sun moved in the time he blinked his eyes. New men swirled around him, wearing blue. He watched their lips move. One knelt over him and waved his hand in front of Jack's eyes. The cords of his neck stood out when he shouted to someone Jack did not see.

He was weightless in his pain. He did not know where he was, but he knew that it was good. Jack closed his eyes and the blackness enveloped him. A vision of Marina appeared through the dark. She stood over him and kissed him on the forehead. He felt her hand in his hand. They would go home to Lidia together.

TWENTY

CAPTAIN ERNESTO ALVARES PARKED HIS car in front of the unassuming little house in Laredo and killed the engine. It was not an official vehicle, but one he had borrowed from one of his soldiers, who had local family. He did not wear his uniform.

There was no outward sign of life. The blinds in the front windows were closed, but there was a white car in the driveway. Alvares got out of his vehicle and felt the dying heat of the day. The worst of summer was over. The children were back in school. He had been caught behind a bus for most of the way.

He crossed the grass to the walk and then to the door. He rang once and knocked, as well. One of the blinds stirred. Someone was peeking out.

A young girl answered the door. Alvares had never seen her before, but he saw the resemblance to the picture of Marina Cobos in the files. This was the sister. She looked serious and guarded and when he introduced himself she seemed hesitant to speak. Finally she said, 'What do you want?'

'To see Sr Searle. If I may.'

'Come in.'

Jack Searle's house was small, but welcoming. Alvares did not imagine Searle had decorated it himself, but perhaps he would be surprised. The girl left him in the front room where the TV was turned low and said Searle would be there soon.

Alvares heard the man before he saw him. Jack Searle walked with the assistance of a metal cane that made a distinct rapping sound on the house's vinyl flooring. Alvares was surprised to see he was able to walk at all. They had told him how badly he was hurt on the bridge, how much blood he had left in his truck. Alvares did not know whether he could have found the strength to do what Searle did. Not much time had passed. Searle was a hardy man. The younger sister stood close behind him. 'Dad?' she asked.

'It's okay,' Searle said. 'Watch some TV.'

Alvares nodded to her as kindly as he could. She averted her gaze.

'Captain Alvares,' Searle said.

'Sr Searle.'

'I guess you might as well call me Jack.'

'I will. Is there somewhere we can talk?'

'Sure.'

Jack led Alvares to the kitchen, where a table awaited, neatly set with a vertical roll of paper towels and a metal flatware holder bristling with forks, knives and spoons. Alvares sat in the chair Jack pulled out for him. He saw pain flash on Jack's face when he sat down.

'It is good to see you,' Alvares said.

'I'm sorry I can't say the same,' Jack replied.

'I am not offended.'

'Good. What are you doing here?'

'You would not come to me, so I came to you.'

'And now you're in my house.'

'I thought you might like to know that Gonzalo Soler's funeral was very lovely. It was well attended and he was given honors. I wish you could have been there. You were the last one to see him, after all.'

'I don't think I'll be coming back to Mexico again.'

Alvares nodded. 'You will also be happy to know that there will be no extradition hearing for you. The matter has been deemed *narco*-related and you are no longer part of the inquiry. You *could* return to Mexico if you wanted. You could even claim what's left of your truck.'

'That's good. I guess.'

'What did you tell your people when they asked you what happened?' Alvares asked.

'I told them I was ambushed by thugs. They shot up my truck and they got me. I barely made it out.'

'And they believed this?'

'No one knew better at the time.'

'And now no one will know.'

They sat quietly for a while, each looking at the table and not each other. Alvares was dimly aware of the television noises from the other room. Somehow they made the house seem emptier. Alvares did not know how Jack could stand it.

'I'm sorry that I did not come quickly enough,' Alvares said to break the silence. 'Gonzalo's message reached me too late.'

'You just would have stopped us.'

'Yes, I would have.'

'Then I'm glad you were late.'

'I could have spared you this,' Alvares said, and he indicated the cane.

'Small price to pay. It cost Gonzalo more.'

'Which is what I wanted to ask you: did you find what you were looking for? Did Gonzalo die for something meaningful?'

Jack's face fell. 'I don't know how to answer that.'

'We were never your enemy, Jack. We fought for you always.'

'That wasn't enough.'

'And now so many people are dead. Gonzalo Soler was a good policeman.'

'He was a good *man*.'

'Do you regret drawing him into your game?'

Jack looked at Alvares sharply. 'It wasn't a game.'

'Just so. But Gonzalo was trapped in it as surely as you. Was there ever a chance he could escape?'

'Not once we got started. We had to see it through.'

'The case of your stepdaughter's disappearance remains open. We are still looking into it, though without Gonzalo's help I'm afraid my people will not make much progress. We are soldiers. The people who sent us don't seem to understand that.'

'So you'll keep searching?'

Alvares caught Jack's eye and for a moment he saw a sorrow so deep that a man could drown in it just by looking. 'May I see her room?'

'Why?'

'I only ask as a favor.'

'Okay.'

Jack rose from the table with difficulty and led the way, his cane tapping with each step. They came to a closed door and Jack opened it. He stood aside so Alvares could see the neat bed, the perfectly arranged desk, the bright walls and the little touches of a young woman.

'He didn't remember her,' Jack said. 'He didn't care so much that he couldn't even remember her. He didn't even know her name.'

Alvares put his hand on Jack's shoulder and Jack did not pull away. They stood like that for a long moment and then Alvares grasped the knob and gently closed the door.

AFTERWORD

MISSING IS FICTION, BUT IS INSPIRED by true events. The violence in Nuevo Laredo is real. The disappearances are real. The drug cartels are real.

All across Mexico, people are dying. It does not matter how old or how young they are, or whether they are honest people or criminals. Since 2006, more than 60,000 people have died. In 2009 (the last year we have figures for) 1,200 children under the age of seventeen were killed by drug violence. Many were the victims of stray bullets, but a heartbreaking number were specifically targeted for execution. A particularly horrible case involved an entire family butchered by *narcos*, including a twenty-two-month-old baby girl, shot to death. In another, a police commander was riddled with bullets while carrying her five-year-old daughter. Neither survived.

As if this were not bad enough, tens of thousands are missing. Human trafficking, particularly for sexual exploitation, is thriving in Mexico, and kidnapping drives this trade. Kidnapping purely for ransom is also a booming industry. The kidnappers do not seem to care whether their victims are Mexicans or not, with more than forty Americans vanishing in the Nuevo Laredo region since 2004.

Sadly, I did not even invent the circumstances of the Municipal Police in Nuevo Laredo. In June of 2011, the entire

Municipal Police force was dismissed pending 'professional-ization and certification.' As of this writing, they still have not returned to work and Nuevo Laredo is a madhouse of crime. The mayor of Nuevo Laredo has begged for the Municipal Police to be restored, despite their corruption, just to reestablish some semblance of order.

Mexico is a country in deep crisis. There is no end in sight.

Sam Hawken

As always I would like to thank my wife, Mariann, for her invaluable contribution to my work. Without her input, I wouldn't be able to write a word.